THE DARK
FAITH

THE DARK HARVEST TRILOGY

The Dark Faith
The Scarlet Bishop
The Threefold Cord

THE DARK FAITH

JEREMIAH W. MONTGOMERY

P&R PUBLISHING

P.O. BOX 817 • PHILLIPSBURG • NEW JERSEY 08865-0817

© 2012 by Jeremiah W. Montgomery

All rights reserved. No part of this book may be reproduced, stored in a retrieval system, or transmitted in any form or by any means—electronic, mechanical, photocopy, recording, or otherwise—except for brief quotations for the purpose of review or comment, without the prior permission of the publisher, P&R Publishing Company, P.O. Box 817, Phillipsburg, New Jersey 08865–0817.

ISBN: 978-1-59638-187-2 (pbk)
ISBN: 978-1-59638-544-3 (ePub)
ISBN: 978-1-59638-313-5 (Mobi)

Printed in the United States of America

Library of Congress Control Number: 2012943095

To Gavin, Logan, Ewan, & Aidan:

But especially to Logan,
who prayed for Daddy's book

CONTENTS

PART I

THE DARK MADNESS

PROLOGUE

The little girl picked her way as quickly as she dared up the path toward the hill fort. The sky overhead was the color of dark slate and brimmed with thick clouds. It had not rained in this part of Dyfann for over a week, yet the track winding up the slope was slick. The mud squelched between her toes as she climbed. The air about her was cool and tense, and carried a metallic taste.

"Death is a natural part of life," her father always told her, "We needn't fear it any more than we fear birth. One feeds into the other, and the other back into the first."

Like most little girls, this one wanted to believe her father. And so she did, in nearly everything. Until today, she had never questioned what he said about the naturalness of death. Yet as she left her escort behind, she found her faith . . . unsettled. Try as she might, she could not long bear the sight of the hill now that she ascended it alone. Too many lifeless gazes lined her path.

Some of the faces were smooth and young. Others, old and grizzled. All of them were vacant. Some of the bodies wore nothing but battle-paint. Others wore the tunics of Mersex. All were but empty husks, some with deep gouges across their chests, others with middles slashed open and their bowels spilled out. Still others had lost arm or leg or head to the hacking blows of the enemy. All of them lay strewn like broken twigs. She remembered when the hillside had been green and lovely. Now everywhere she looked it was red and ugly. Blood smeared the dirty faces of the dead. Blood puddled between the heaps and ran downhill in ruddy rivulets. Blood had turned the dirt track to the hill fort into a foul mud.

The little girl always wanted to believe her father, but she did not understand. How could such a horrid thing be natural?

The wall of the hill fort had been burned in several places during the battle. She saw the charred beams and cracked timbers as she approached the gate. Though the gate itself remained intact and stood open, one could hardly say the same for the man who stood beside it. In his right hand he held an axe, his grip relaxed now that the battle was over. Yet where his left arm should have been, nothing remained but a short, wrapped stump above the elbow. Seeing her approach, the man smiled and stooped down.

"And who might we have here?" He did his best to sound grave.

Now that she saw him up close, the little girl smiled. "You know who I am, Firin!" She was only too happy for the *deaclaid*'s smile: it turned her mind from all those masks of death.

Sacred law forbade priests to carry a weapon or fight in battle. According to the Old Faith of Dyfann, offerings of blood could only be poured by hands that had shed none. This rule was inviolable: those who broke it were forever after barred from the Holy Groves. And so arose the office of *deaclaid*, Dyfanni for "right hand." If a priest had to go near battle, he would take a *deaclaid*, a chosen warrior, with him to act as his protector. To receive this title was an honor reserved only for the most proven warriors.

"Yes, lass, I know you. Not a face as pretty as yours in all of Dyfann!" Firin stood and beckoned with his good arm. "Your da's inside. Go on in and brighten his day. He could use it."

The little girl paused, looking up at the bandaged stump. "You are injured, Firin."

"A bit."

"Does it hurt?"

"A bit," repeated the man with a slight grimace.

"Was the battle bad?"

"Not as bad for us as for the Mersians."

"Did my brother—"

"No more questions, lass. They're all waiting for you inside. Off you go!" His tone was still gentle, but his gesture was now insistent.

Leaving Firin behind, the little girl pushed on past the gate toward the hall. Like the outer fortifications, the timber-built hall showed signs of the recent battle. At several places along its long roof, charred holes marked spots where Mersian torches had landed on the thatch. Yet today, the little girl saw smoke rising at one point only: through a man-made hole at the midpoint of the roof's ridge.

The interior of the hall was dim, for the fire in the central pit was undersized and underfed. Yet even in the meager light the girl saw the crowd of men standing around the hearth. Each wore a long white robe wrapped in a green cloak, the attire reserved by her people for priests. It was only after she perceived the large number of them present—at least a dozen—that the little girl realized what she was witnessing.

It was an extremely rare thing for the Circle of the Holy Groves to meet in full. It had not happened in the girl's life-time. Even her brother—who was much older than she—had gone with their father only once to a meeting of the whole sacred council. Thus the little girl kept her steps soft as she approached the circle. Her silence stemmed not from fear of

13

discovery: having been summoned, she could draw near to the circle without fear of death. Rather, she stepped lightly out of reverence. Though she was too young to have seen much of the wider world, as a daughter of a priestly family she understood the significance of what was transpiring. For the full council to meet at all, something important had to happen. But for the full council to meet outside the *Mutha-dannach*—the Mother Glen—whatever happened must have been just short of cataclysmic. Whatever it was, the assembled men were too engaged in their discussion to see the girl come up behind them.

"How long do you plan to keep us in suspense, son of Comnadh?" asked one voice.

The little girl did not know the speaker, but Comnadh was her father, the priest of Banr Cluidan. Thus "son of Comnadh" could refer to only one person . . .

The girl caught sight of her brother through a space between two priests. All of her careful reserve in approaching the group melted away the moment she realized he had returned. "Somnadh!"

The conversation jerked to a halt as fourteen surprised faces turned in her direction. Slipping between the men into the circle, the little girl looked across the round hearth. There, standing apart from the others near the fire's brink, were her brother and father.

"Urien!" Somnadh's face lit up.

Beside him, her father's face lifted in a broad smile. A bit of gloom seemed to lift from his features as he kneeled. "Come to me, my daughter!"

For years to come, Urien would look back on this moment with fondness. Here was everything she cared about. Neither Comnadh nor Somnadh possessed an imposing physical presence. Both had long, brown hair and, because of their office, both wore it tied with a golden cord behind the nape of the neck. Likewise their facial features were more knobby than commanding, their dark eyes more pensive than piercing. In short, but for their priestly garments, neither father nor son would have garnered more than a single look among a crowd of Dyfanni. Yet none of this mattered. To one who had grown up deprived of a mother, father and brother were everything. Urien stepped around the hearth and buried her face in her father's waiting embrace.

"Father." She sighed, tears of joy escaping down her cheeks.

After a long moment, the silence was broken by one of the other priests.

"It is good to see such affections, Comnadh"—the grandfatherly voice came from somewhere behind Urien—"especially in days as bleak as these. The tenderness of our daughters is the strength of our people. Yet your son has summoned us with a promise of great tidings, and we have come at great risk and through many dangers to hear them. It has been generations since we have met beyond the shade of the Mother—and never by the call of an apprentice. Were Somnadh not the son of Comnadh, I would not have consented to this gathering. But even a great name can be lost, and our time grows short. If there are tidings, we will hear them now."

"Stand beside me now, my dear." Comnadh released his daughter and rose to his feet.

"Your words are truth, Seanguth." Her father used the formal language required when addressing the Eldest of the Circle. He stepped back into the ranks of the ring, pulling Urien with him. "My son will speak."

Somnadh, who now stood alone in the center of the circle near the brim of the hearth-pit, turned in place. He looked each of the assembled priests in the eye before stopping with his face toward the Eldest. He bowed, "Though I am but an apprentice, I beg leave to address the Circle."

"You have it." Seanguth, the Eldest, was a short, wizened old man. His face was grave, but not unkind.

"Thank you, Eldest." Urien's brother bowed again, then began his formal declamation. "Fathers of the Circle, I bring you great and marvelous tidings. Two moons past, I stood among the throngs in the square of Toberstan as word of our raid on Hoccaster reached the ears of the king of Mersex. As this Circle hoped, the raid proved successful. The Aesusian council dissolved before an agreement could be reached."

"*These* are the great tidings?"

Urien frowned at the scoffing priest who stood two places to the right of Seanguth. But he went on.

"Did we need to assemble for this? There are plenty of slain across our land—and outside these walls—who could testify as much!"

"Agreed," said another, this time several places to the left of the Eldest, "And it was not 'this Circle' that sent the clans on such an ill-begotten raid." He jabbed a finger across the fire. "It was the poor counsel of a few!"

"Poor counsel!" The accused, a grim-faced priest standing to the left hand of Urien's father, all but spat the words "The Aesusians of the north are far more dangerous than the Mersians. Had we not broken up this council with our raid, they would all soon be at our throats!"

"They are at our throats *because* of this raid!"

"*Peace!*" Seanguth's command boomed through the hall.

Instantly the disputants fell silent.

Urien had jumped at the Eldest's exclamation. Who knew such a small man could make such a great sound? When she looked up she saw irritation in the furrows of his wrinkled brow.

"What is past is past. The apprentice misspoke. I am sure that the son of Comnadh did not call us here to speak in our ears what our eyes can see." The warning in his tone was obvious: Urien's brother *better* have something more to say.

"The words of the Eldest are truth." Somnadh nodded and touched one hand to his forehead. "Forgive me, Fathers: my words were poorly chosen. I was sent to observe the Aesusian council in Toberstan as soon as my father heard that it was to convene—before the raid on Hoccaster. I assumed that the raid had been the will of the whole Circle; I see now that it was otherwise. I withdraw the words." Somnadh pinched the air with his hand, and then touched his fingers to his mouth.

Seanguth and several of the other priests nodded acknowledgement of the gesture. Then Somnadh resumed in a brighter tone.

"Yet I do have great and marvelous tidings, Fathers! As our law requires for priests who go beyond the mountains, upon my return I went to the *Muthadannach* to offer some of my own blood."

"That is not strictly required in all cases, boy," corrected Seanguth. "But you do well to show such zeal."

Somnadh's tone was deferential. "Thank you, Eldest. After Mother tasted and knew that I had not shed blood beyond her sight, I prayed beneath her boughs. It was then that it happened: I received a vision."

The announcement was greeted with silence.

"Tell them what you saw, son."

From beside him, Urien looked up at her father. There she saw the urgency in his voice matched by an unsettled expression on his features. In front of them, Somnadh never turned his face from the Eldest. But he nodded before continuing.

"In my vision I saw one of Mother's limbs descending toward me. Held in her leaves was her Seed. She planted this Seed in the ground before me, and immediately it sprang up. But there was something strange about this sapling. It was white like the Mother, yet its form was strange. When it grew, I saw that it was shaped like an Aesusian cross!"

17

"What!" murmured several voices around the Circle.

"Yes!" Somnadh nodded. "I myself was at first repelled! I could not fathom what it meant. But then I heard Mother's voice. She said, 'I am the Mother. This is my Seed.' Then I understood. After this, another of Mother's limbs descended. Like the first, this one also held her Seed. 'This is my Daughter,' she said, handing the Seed to me. Then she showed me where I should plant it. It is a place far from here—beyond the mountains, beyond even Mersex—a place where our people dwelt long ago."

For a long moment the only sound was the crackle of the fire, which by now burned quite low in the hearth. Finally, Seanguth broke the silence.

"Oh son of Comnadh"—he spoke slowly, as though choosing each word with great care—"these are great tidings indeed—quite marvelous to be borne by one so young." His tone grew grim. "If you do not speak truth, you will pour out *all* of your blood before Mother as payment for sacrilege. If you *do* speak truth"—here he paused, surveying each face around the Circle before resettling on Somnadh—"you must show proof."

Urien held her breath. She sensed that her brother was in great danger. What was going to happen?

"My words are truth." Somnadh reached into his cloak. Withdrawing his hand, he stretched it forth so that all could see. Cradled in his open palm was an object the size of a walnut. At its appearance, the fire in the hearth seemed to flare up.

The light of the flames reflected across a pure white surface.

Urien was not the only person standing around the circle to gasp. In the next instant, everyone but Somnadh had fallen to his knees.

"The Holy Seed." Seanguth's voice quivered. "The first in thirteen generations!" He looked up at Somnadh, eyes wide. "You have been chosen by the Mother, son of Comnadh."

"Yes, Eldest." Somnadh gestured toward Urien. "Now you see why I asked the Circle to wait for my sister to arrive."

Seanguth nodded. "'The Hand of the Seed must provide a Heart for the Queen.' Thus it is spoken in the ancient law."

"I have no virgin daughter of my own," said Somnadh, "only a sister."

"W-what does it mean, brother?" Visions of the slain on the hill below the hall rose unbidden before Urien's eyes. "Am I—am I going to die?"

"Oh no, dear Urien!" Somnadh turned to face her. "Far from it, my sister!"

Comnadh leaned down and gave his daughter a hug. "It means that you must go away with your brother, dear one. You, too, are the Mother's chosen."

It is a rule worth remembering as long as one lives: reality is far more frightening than fantasy. A second is like unto it: unwary travelers through a silent wood seldom come to the end of their way unscathed.

A healthy forest is full of noises. Birds cry, squirrels rustle, and deer tiptoe. Bears plod in their peculiar, preoccupied manner. These are the normal sounds. Yet absolute silence—of this one must take heed. Stillness in the woods is often a sign of something unnatural. Too many old stories speak of forests as the halls of fairy kings . . .

Too few mention them as the haunts of inhuman predators.

And yet, Morumus paid these things little heed this day. He knew well the wooded paths surrounding Lorudin Abbey. He had grown quite familiar with the length and breadth of them since coming to the country of Caeldora. He knew the contours of this forest, and he knew its character. He knew the tilts and turnings of its tracks, and he knew which trails were safe for men to tread. For years he had padded these ancient footways, sometimes in company but usually alone. It was not that company lacked for the asking. Rather, most days he simply preferred the solitude. For Morumus found few circumstances quite as ideally suited for prayer and contemplation as a walk in the woods.

Such was the manner in which Morumus walked through the woods this day: reflective, silent, transported. With eyes as brown as bark, and hair and habit to match, he knew one might imagine him not a man, but rather a spirit of the wood. But Morumus was not prone to such light musings.

Life was almost as serious as death. How could it be otherwise, when the latter so often intruded upon the former without warning? What's more, how could it be otherwise when there were those who celebrated death by destroying life with impunity? Morumus had sworn to a faith that promised life beyond the grave while still regarding death as an enemy. But there existed in the world another faith, a faith that reveled in death. He knew this from bitter experience, for he had witnessed it firsthand. Morumus trusted Aesus alone . . .

But he had seen the Dark Faith.

And that had made Morumus a monk.

He possessed faith from childhood, for his father had raised him to trust and love and obey the Lord. Yet prior to his deadly encounter, Morumus took his faith for granted. But in that single helpless hour, when the Dark Faith destroyed nearly everything he held dear, all began to change.

Depravity was a cruel teacher, yet it taught him to cleave to the Light.

Morumus had spent the years since that hour preparing to return the affront. The power of the Dark Faith seemed somehow linked to its language. Thus he had studied languages and their roots, in the hope of uncovering the Dark Speech. Alongside of this he had studied Holy Writ to learn the True Faith. Someday he would return and spread the truth to those corners of his homeland that harbored and nurtured the Dark Faith. He would destroy the Dark Faith by exposing its lie and preaching the truth.

For years, this had been enough for Morumus. Until yesterday.

Yesterday, Abbot Grahem asked him a question: "You have been here for ten years now, Morumus, and you have learned much. But to what end do you intend to apply your learning? How will you use it?"

Although asked with a good will—for Abbot Grahem was a very gracious superior—the conversation had unsettled Morumus. For one thing, he realized then that he had not kept count of the time. Had he really been in Caeldora for ten years? And then there was the abbot's question itself . . .

A question Morumus could not answer.

Though he had learned much of Holy Writ in ten years, Morumus had not uncovered even a trace of the Dark Speech. He had applied himself diligently; he had learned every language he could. He could speak and write both the language of Caeldora and the language of the Church. He had explored the connections between these languages. Yet for all this he was no closer to his goal today than he had been when he arrived in Lorudin. Abbot Grahem's question had struck deeper than the older man could have imagined. For the first time, Morumus wondered . . .

What if he could *never* find a key to the Dark Speech? Could he still achieve his goal?

And so Morumus trod the forest trails this day, to pray and think over this question. The Rule allotted afternoons for quiet meditation, and he had left the abbey shortly after the conclusion of midday prayers. For hours he had walked, his body meandering while his spirit mulled. The sun was well past its peak before he realized it. When he did, Morumus stopped walking. He would have to turn back soon.

Then he saw it.

The strange color.

Summer had arrived in Caeldora, and all was green with new life. Off to his left, a stream wound through a wide hollow

23

where thick moss covered most of the space between the trees. But something was not right. A pale shape lay unmoving near the brink of the water.

"What is that?" He stepped off the path to investigate.

A sense of dread stirred within him as he approached. By the time he closed half the distance, the hairs on the back of his neck stood on end. He did not understand this apprehension at first, but then he noticed the utter stillness surrounding him—

A thick hush had descended upon the wood like a shroud.

No birds chirped, no chipmunks chattered, no leaves rustled in the wind. The air was still. The only sound was the swift splashing of the water in the stream. Yet even that seemed muted.

It was not until he closed to within a dozen paces that Morumus recognized the shape. A lamb, or at least part of a lamb. But something dark covered the head and neck. At first it looked like a mass of fur or hair shed by whatever predator had made the kill. Yet as he neared the carcass, Morumus began to doubt his guess. The hair was too long and too fine to be animal shedding—it looked almost . . .

Human.

But it seemed attached to the head of the lamb, which made no sense at all. Unable to abide this incongruity or the suspense, Morumus closed the remaining distance and stooped down for a better look.

"*What*—?" He lurched back, losing his balance. Struggling back to his feet, Morumus took several steps away from the carcass.

"How—?" His voice trailed off to a numb whisper. "God have mercy."

The hair looked human because it *was* human. It appeared attached because it *was* attached—but not to the head of a lamb. The carcass was a monstrosity: a lamb's body with a human head and neck. And the face was that of a young girl.

A wave of nausea washed over him. His stomach heaved, and he tasted bile.

The girl had raven-black hair and blue eyes. The eyes were clear and lovely—the sort that would have gladdened hearts. But now the light had departed from those blue depths, and they stared unseeing from a face frozen by death. The girl's hair lay in a haphazard splash upon the ground, and the skin of her face was very, very pale. Morumus could see no color in it at all. He wondered at this, until he saw the deep gash in her neck. Then he knew. This creature—girl or lamb or devilish combination—had been bled empty.

Exsanguination?

Morumus was no stranger to death, not even the unlawful and violent sort. Yet nothing in his experience compared with the grotesque scene spread out before him. It was not just the appearance of the creature that bothered him—though to be sure, this disturbed him plenty—it was the method. Exsanguination was a butcher's technique: a sharp blow to the head followed by a sharp knife to the throat. The blow spared the animal. The bleeding preserved the meat. But who would do this to a child?

Morumus's stomach heaved again, and again came up dry.

Wait!

As the first moment of horror passed, Morumus's mind reverted to its habit of close observation. In so doing, he realized something: whoever had killed this girl had taken the blood, but left the body intact. The discovery did not explain anything, but it did rule out the most obvious—and most revolting—possibility. Whoever had murdered this creature had not been after food. But then why? And for that matter, who?

The next moment a chorus of inhuman cries echoed behind him. Morumus jumped and spun on his heels.

Halfway back to the path, in a wide space where there had been nothing but moss only minutes before, there now stood a white tree. The tree was not tall compared to the surrounding oaks and elms, yet there was a certain regality to its bearing that defied its diminutive stature. Its leaves were the color of blood and looked like thin hands in scarlet gloves. Its well-proportioned trunk and slender limbs might have appeared graceful—had they not drooped with the weight of the crows.

At least a dozen large birds perched among the branches of the tree. From head to tail their feathers were so black that they seemed to absorb the daylight. Though it hardly seemed possible, the birds' eyes were even darker, making them look like empty sockets. These eyes fixed upon Morumus. They bore an unsettling intelligence. But what really made his skin crawl in those obsidian gleams was their unwholesome intensity.

The birds' harsh cries subsided, and for a minute the forest fell back into uncomfortable stillness. Then the tree's leaves began to stir. At first the movement was slight, and Morumus thought it was but a breeze. But as the stirring increased to a steady rustling, he noticed that it affected none of the surrounding trees. Then the noise grew louder and stronger, and Morumus no longer mistook it for a wind.

It was a voice. Somehow, the tree was speaking.

The language was difficult to pick out, for it consisted of a stream of hissing gasps. Each hiss was distinct in pitch, yet each overtook its predecessor so that there were no pauses. As a result, all of the words—for that is what the hisses were—tumbled together in quick succession. The sound was cruel and discordant.

Morumus's blood ran cold. Though he did not understand any of the words, he recognized the language.

The Dark Speech.

The crows resumed calling. The voice of the tree rose in response to their caws, and one by one the crows began dropping to the ground. Upon landing, each bird hopped out from beneath the branches and began to tremble. As it shook, its feathers shook out—almost as if the creature were molting on the spot. But the birds were not molting. They were transforming.

In fits and spurts they grew, becoming with each moment both more human and more horrible. Spindly legs grew long. Long wings shortened to arms. Short, straight spines extended into broad backs hunched over at the middle. Gleaming coats of feathers became long black cloaks. Beady eyes and sharp beaks receded into the shadowy recesses of raised cowls. As these features reconfigured, the piercing caws become painful cries. When the transfigurations finished, the figures were human.

"*Dree.*" Adepts of the Dark Faith. Morumus spoke the word like a curse, standing transfixed, unable to move or look away.

One by one, each of the black-cloaked *Dree* turned its empty gaze toward him. Unaccustomed to the use of the human tongue, the best they could manage at first were awkward noises that sounded like short, raspy coughs. It could scarcely pass for speech, but it must have been adequate.

When the *Dree* next acted, it was in concert. A dozen hands reached into dark cloaks and emerged clutching long knives. A moment later the white tree hissed its malevolent command, and they sprung to the attack. Even in human form, the movements of the *Dree* were distinctly avian. Rather than full strides, they moved in combinations of quick steps and short hops.

Morumus regained his mobility, and in the next moment he was fleeing. He turned and ran as fast he could, holding up the hem of his robe with both hands. He did not bother to look over his shoulder. He would have known the fiends were after him even if he had not heard their angry cries. And he knew what would happen if they overtook him—he knew all too well!

Faster! Move faster!

Cresting a slight rise in the forest terrain, Morumus saw a bend in the stream about a hundred paces ahead of him. The water there appeared shallow, and from shore to shore a handful of rocks peeked wet heads about the waterline. Should he cross the stream? In some of the old stories, dark creatures feared to pursue quarry across running water. Would that be true of the *Dree?*

Fixing his eyes on the goal, Morumus increased his pace. But in that very moment his toe tangled in an unseen root and he tumbled headlong. He hit the ground hard, the breath rushing from his lungs. Gasping for air and choking on a mouthful of dirt, he pushed himself to his knees. Sputtering, he regained his feet and tried to continue running.

"Aagh!" He stumbled back to his knees. "No! No!" His voice strained with fear, frustration, and pain. His ankle—the one that had caught in the root—had twisted.

Behind him, the hissing speech of his pursuers grew louder. Ignoring the searing protests from his foot, he forced himself upright. As he did, he glanced back over his shoulder.

He felt a faint pang of hope as he noticed that there seemed to be fewer of the *Dree* behind him now. Yet this hope dampened as he realized that those which remained were closing the distance to him at an alarming rate. Despite their bird-like run—or perhaps because of it—the *Dree* moved much faster than one would expect from men wearing long cloaks in a wood. Like raptors swooping in for the kill, they seemed to glide above the ground.

"Must not be taken!" He groaned through the burning agony of his ankle. The memory of the murdered girl mingled with the terror of his childhood memories, spurring him to resume his hobbled flight. Grunting with each dragging step, he turned his head back toward the stream.

Instead of seeing water, Morumus found himself face to face with one of the *Dree.*

The realization of his doom struck him like a sledge. He had not eluded any of his pursuers. They had outflanked him. His stomach lurched with a sharp, piercing pain.

Gasping, Morumus looked down. Several inches of a grey, stone blade had vanished through the fabric of his robe. As he watched, the *Dree* plunged the remainder of the knife into his abdomen, twisting it so as to force the blade up toward the heart. Black specks flitted in his vision, followed by a terrifying cold.

Morumus looked up into the face of his murderer. But his dying gaze only met inky blackness. If the *Dree* had a face, it was lost in the deep shadows of its hood. Morumus wanted to shout defiance, but his lungs would no longer fill. For a long moment, all he could do was glare at the *Dree*. Then the black curtain came down over his eyes to meet the rising wave of cold.

omewhere beyond the darkness, a bell tolled.

It was a dull, heavy tone. Yet, since there is no memory of sound in the forgetful halls of death, the tepid bell offered one timely signal to Morumus:

You are still alive!

Morumus opened his eyes.

Like many who jolt awake, for a moment he could not move. As soon as sleep released the rest of his body, he felt all over his middle at the point where the knife had penetrated. When he found both his robe and the flesh beneath it untorn, he let out a breath he had not realized he was holding. Then he sat up.

"Just a dream."

Morumus was drenched with sweat, but otherwise unharmed. The nightmare had been so vivid that he found it disorienting to be alive and at home. In a mixture of disbelief and relief, he let his gaze travel around the walls of his cell. In this he was aided by the faint outlines of dawn shining around the edges of his shuttered window.

A cell was the personal chamber allotted to each monk at Lorudin Abbey. Less than three paces square, the abbey cells aimed to provide only as much space as was necessary for a monk's night rest and private duties. In one corner of Morumus's cell, a stool sat in front of a small table. On top of the table, a folio volume lay open at the middle. Next to it sat an extinguished, half-burned candle. Besides these provisions for his study, the pallet bed on which Morumus now sat provided him a place for rest. For the last duty, prayer—well, there was the whole of the floor.

The thought of prayer reminded Morumus of the bell that had roused him from his nightmare. Had it been the first or the second bell? If it were the latter, then the cooking fires in the refectory would be burning. Rising with a groan from his pallet—despite the fact that he had only dreamt his frantic flight, he felt quite stiff—Morumus moved to the window and swung open the shutter.

Golden light from the dawning sun washed over his face, and he quaffed a deep draught the crisp air. There really are few things quite like the air of a fresh morning, when the only smells are grass and trees. Morumus filled his lungs several times with the clean sweetness, enjoying its crisp savor. He detected no hint of smoke in the air; no brother had yet lit the morning fires. This meant that the bell that had roused him was but the first: the call to Rising Prayers.

With the memory of the dream still foremost in his mind, Morumus did not feel keen to close his eyes again. Yet he knew that he must, for it is when one feels least inclined to pray that prayer is most needful. And so, leaving the shutter open to the fresh air and growing light, he sank to his knees. But no sooner had he shut his eyes than images of the nightmare began to return like black shades behind his eyelids. Resolving to give them no quarter, he began with that most basic of prayers:

"Our Father God in Everlight—"

The white tree hissed its murderous command.

"May Thy name be hallowed right."

The crows were cawing as they dropped to the forest floor.

"Thy realm appear, Thy will be here—"

The *Dree* were chasing him.

Morumus decided to skip ahead a bit. "Lead us not into trials, but deliver from what's vile—"

He was facing the faceless *Dree*. The point of the blade plunged into him.

Morumus opened his eyes. "This is not going to work."

Rising Prayers were not a hurried affair at Lorudin Abbey. It would be at least another hour until the second bell. As Morumus pondered whether he should wait for a bit and try again, another stream of sweet air gusted in through the open window. He looked up at the bright opening, and a different course of action suggested itself. Why remain in a closed room under dark specters, when he might move in open space under full light? Morumus got to his feet.

He emerged from the dormitory into a burgeoning morning. To the east, the sun had just cleared the line of hills on the horizon. Its long, honey-colored rays shot west, illuminating the landscape and setting the bottoms of the clouds ablaze. The sky was a bracing, brilliant blue above his head. For a considerable time he walked in silence, soaking all of it in—or rather, soaking all of himself in it—while the grounds of the monastery passed beneath his feet. With each step a piece of his nightmare receded, displaced by the peace of this glorious morning. The sky was like an ocean of light, and he was like a child wading in the surf. In that instant, he felt an acute pang of finitude. Amidst all of this, he was so small.

"'What are men, that Thou rememberest them?'"

"Lower than the angels, yet loaded with crowns," a voice answered softly from somewhere nearby. "God help us, lest we take ourselves too seriously."

Morumus started. Turning, he saw the familiar figure of Abbot Grahem just a few paces away, kneeling between two rows of grapevine.

"Good morning, sir. I apologize for my intrusion. I did not mean to disturb your prayers."

The abbot rose to his feet. He was slight of build and slight of height, and his face bore the lines of years caring for his flock. Truth be told, there was little remarkable about his outward appearance. Yet there was a certain fire about his blue eyes. Every monk who had ever stepped foot within Lorudin Abbey knew from experience that, when focused, those eyes bored like twin augers. At this moment, they trained their gaze on Morumus.

"No need to apologize, my son," said the abbot. "There is plenty of space. Did you come outside the walls to pray?"

Morumus hesitated. The Rule of Lorudin Abbey imposed discipline for any brother caught neglecting private duties such as Rising Prayers. If he answered the abbot's question in the affirmative, he would avoid any such penalty. But Morumus knew that sin was always worse than censure, so he told the truth.

"No, sir. I came for a walk to clear my head."

"Clear your head?" An arched eyebrow crowned one of the blue eyes.

"Yes, sir. I did not sleep well last night, and found myself too distracted to pray this morning."

"Did you try?"

"Yes, sir."

"Well then"—the abbot sounded genuinely curious—"tell me about this distraction."

"It was a nightmare, sir." Morumus chose his words with care—"a very vivid nightmare." He did not want to sound ridiculous if he could help it. "There were hooded creatures speaking a language I did not understand, and they pursued me with knives. I fled, but they overtook me and stabbed me. I thought I was dead, until I heard the bell for prayer."

"This was your dream?" There was something queer in Abbot Grahem's expression.

The young monk looked down. "I am sorry, sir." How child-ish he must sound. What sort of monk abandoned prayers over a bad dream? "I confess my fault, and admit my liability to the prescribed—"

Unexpectedly, the abbot began to laugh. "Are you certain you've never been to a Church Council before, my son?"

"Sir?" Morumus looked up, frowning.

"It's just that I do not think I have ever heard a better description of the Court of Saint Cephan in my life!" Abbot Grahem laughed heartily for several moments. "Be at ease, Morumus. You are not going to face any penalties this day."

"Thank you, sir. That is most gracious."

"Not at all. Grim dreams often come on the eve of great events. They are one of the burdens of those who bear the care of important tasks."

"Sir, I do not understand." What important task did he have?

"Not yet." The abbot laid his hand on Morumus's shoulder. "Will you walk with me a bit?"

"Of course, sir."

"After our conversation yesterday," began the abbot as they went, "I realized that I had made a mistake." He looked over at Morumus. "You remember what I asked you?"

The younger monk nodded. "You asked me what I was going to do with what I had learned."

"Yes. It was wrong of me to ask that."

"Sir?"

"It was wrong of me to ask, because to ask might seem to imply choice." The abbot grinned. "And I don't intend to give you a choice, Morumus."

If Morumus had been confused a minute ago, now he was thoroughly perplexed. "Please sir, I do not understand any of this."

"You will recall that the Court of Saint Cephan is to meet within three weeks at Versaden?"

35

"Yes, sir." The Court of Saint Cephan was the highest court of the Church, attended triennially by every bishop and presided over by the primates—the five provincial archbishops. This year it was to meet in the imperial capital.

"You will recall as well that I will be traveling to the Court as an attendant to Bishop Anathadus."

Morumus nodded. "Yes, sir."

"What you did not know, however—because it was but lately determined—is that you will be traveling with me."

The speed with which Morumus turned his head caused him to trip, and he only just managed to avoid a fall. "Sir?" he asked after he had recovered his balance.

Abbot Grahem chuckled. "A bit surprised, are we?"

"You could say that, sir." A *bit* surprised?

"Well, I don't blame you there. I too was surprised when word arrived of who would be attending this year's Court. It seems we are to have a few special guests—among them a delegation of your own countrymen."

"From Lothair?"

"From Lothair, yes, and from Nornindaal. The bishops of both nations are to arrive at the port of Naud within days. With them travel the Abbot of Urras Island."

Morumus's eyes widened. The Abbot of the small island monastery of Urras was his father's brother. "Uncle Nerias is coming to Caeldora?"

"Indeed." The abbot smiled. "Are you pleased?"

"Yes, sir. I haven't seen him since—" Bits of his dream stirred, and Morumus shuddered. He didn't want to think about *that*. "Well, it's been years."

"So much the better." Although Abbot Grahem's words came smooth, for the briefest moment Morumus saw something unreadable pass over the older man's expression. "You should have plenty to talk about. But to see your uncle is not the true reason you will be coming with me, Morumus. There are two others traveling with the bishops."

"Sir?"

"One of these other two is a convert from the barbarian tribes who inhabit the north of your island."

Morumus drew a sharp breath. "A Grendannathi?"

The abbot nodded. "It is with him that you shall be most concerned from this point forward."

"Sir, what do you mean? Is this barbarian dangerous?"

Grahem chuckled. "Not to you or I, son. But I am told his tongue can be brutal. Apparently, his abilities with the language of the Church are in need of some assistance."

"You want me to teach him Vilguran?"

"He already knows some. As to how much, we'll see when they arrive. In whatever he is lacking, I want you to tutor him."

"Yes, sir."

"But that's not all, Morumus." The abbot's tone shifted from amused to ardent. "Once you have remedied his skill with our tongue, you are to learn his own native speech. For the two of you together are to undertake a great work—perhaps the greatest thing to which you will ever set your hand."

A sharp thrill coursed through Morumus. A new language was engaging enough . . . but what was this great work to which the abbot referred?

The abbot must have seen the question in Morumus's eyes, for he answered before the younger monk could ask. "You and he, Morumus, are to translate Holy Writ into Grendannathi. The two of you will bring the Word of God to the barbarians."

"Sir—" Morumus fell silent. What could he say? Just like that, the abbot had answered the question that he himself had put to Morumus the day prior. For at least a minute, the younger monk was speechless. The question had been so vexing to Morumus because he had found himself unable to answer it. But now he saw a new horizon dawning before him—and while it might not be exactly what he had planned, it was not entirely unconnected.

The northern portion of the island of Aeld Gowan was divided into three countries. Morumus's homeland of Lothair lay in the west. East of Lothair was the country of Nornindaal. But north of both of these nations was Grendannath, the territory of the barbarians. Surely it was among the barbarians that the *Dree* and their Dark Faith had found the most shelter.

What if something were to remove that shelter? What if the barbarian tribes were to convert to faith in Aesus?

The Dark Faith would have nowhere to hide.

The thrill running up Morumus's spine grew sharper. Some conversions must have already occurred, for it was a barbarian convert with whom he was to work. And if there were conversions among the barbarians *now*, how much more would there be once Holy Writ could be read and proclaimed in the native speech? Even if the Dark Speech should forever remain a secret, the appearance of a translation of Holy Writ in the barbarian language would strike a mortal blow against the Dark Faith.

Abbot Grahem was offering Morumus the opportunity to forge the blade.

"Thank you, sir," said Morumus finally. "This is a great honor—far more than I could have hoped for. It is far, far more than I deserve."

"Is not our whole faith based on the same principle?" The abbot smiled, and again something unreadable flashed across his face. "But you are welcome, my son. I know of nobody better suited to the task."

"Thank you, sir. So I am to go with you to the Court as a tutor to this barbarian, and then afterwards return with him and them to Lothair or Grendannath?"

"You've got the first part right, but you won't be leaving Caeldora. At least not yet. The translation is to be prepared here, at Lorudin."

No sooner had the abbot finished speaking than the morning's second bell rang out from within the abbey walls. Abbot Grahem turned his head briefly in the direction of the sound, then looked back at Morumus. His face no longer seemed tense, but when he spoke his voice was urgent.

"Come, Morumus. The rest of it can wait, but we must not delay."

"Are we leaving now, sir?"

"Leaving?" For the second time, the abbot eyed him from beneath an arched eyebrow.

"You said—"

"Breakfast, my son. Great events await us. But breakfast waits first."

Lorudin Abbey stood in a small vale at the northern edge of the Tumulan Hills. A half-league to its north ran the River Lor. After a stout breakfast that first morning, Morumus and Abbot Grahem crossed the river's ford and joined the remains of an ancient road. As they progressed, Morumus noticed something peculiar. Whereas the river cut a sinuous curve across the landscape before them, the road shot straight ahead like an arrow—or a spear.

"That's because this is an imperial road," Abbot Grahem answered when he asked.

"The emperor built this?"

"Not our emperor. The old emperors—of the old empire."

Morumus frowned. From his studies at Lorudin he had learned of the ancient Vilguran Imperium, that vast empire which had once ruled the entire known world. Yet he also knew that there was a ruler alive in his own day who was called the "Emperor of the Vilgurans."

"But we still have an emperor today. Is it not the same empire?"

"Not at all," Abbot Grahem answered. "The old empire died more than three centuries ago."

Morumus remembered his studies. "The eastern barbarians swept south and sacked the capital."

Grahem nodded. "The city whose reign had stretched nearly a thousand years—undone in a single day."

"And so the emperor we have today . . ." Morumus paused.

". . . rules a different empire," finished the abbot.

"Using the same title?"

"Yes."

Morumus's frown deepened. "That's confusing."

"That's politics."

"I don't understand."

"You're not supposed to. It's not intended to make sense, son. It's intended to leave an impression. The Church gave him the title—"

"Wait! Did you just say the *Church* made him emperor?"

"No." The abbot shook his head. "I said the Church gave him the *title*. He already had the lances and land. Crowning him emperor was simply one archbishop's misguided attempt to bring him to heel."

"I take it that didn't succeed?"

"Not for us. For his part, however, the emperor is more than happy to have his reign associated with the glory and power of the Old Imperium."

"But why would he want that, if the old empire is gone?"

"Because he wants to rebuild it."

"Ah." Now Morumus understood. "Do you think he will succeed, sir?"

The abbot shrugged. "Perhaps. The emperor is a clever man, and clever men gain empires. The real question is, how long will what he builds endure?" Abbot Grahem gestured toward the country before them. "The river is older than the road, yet the road crumbles while the river endures."

"Sir?"

The abbot gave him a gruff look. "'If God builds not the house, in vain do the builders toil.' Meditate on this, my son, while you take the lead for a bit." He dropped his horse back several paces and fell silent.

The rest of that first day passed without event. Abbot Grahem did not offer further conversation, and Morumus occupied his mind with thoughts of the translation work he would soon undertake. He found his eagerness for the work growing, as well as his curiosity. *What will it be like to work with a Grendannathi?* He had never even met a barbarian before!

On their first night in the open country, Morumus did not drop off immediately. That night the sky was so alive with stars, so stunningly woven with violet bands, that it seemed to him almost sinful to close his eyes. Instead, he lay still in his blankets and gazed upward until sleep subdued him on its own. How long this took he never remembered. Nor did he remember dreaming that night: it was as if his mind, even in sleep, was so overawed by the beauty overhead that it dared not stir. His last waking thought was a bit of Lothairin verse from his childhood:

> All of earth be sacred, for no part more contains;
> The all-glory of God, than shines in every place.

The second night of their trip began much as the first. It had been a more difficult day in the saddle, and so neither man had possessed the motivation to build a fire. Supper had been quick and quiet, and the abbot went to his bed almost as soon as darkness fell. Morumus found his own not long after. Yet again he could not fall asleep immediately, for it was another glorious night. The moon was new, the sky was clear, and the canopy above was full of celestial light. For this reason, despite the draining day, Morumus felt almost invigorated.

How long he lay there is impossible to say for certain. For a time he simply watched the heavens, as he had the previous night. From this he passed into that contented halfway state between sleeping and waking where time is immeasurable.

It was some time after this that a scream pierced the night. Both men sat up with a start.

The scream sounded again. This time it was clearly discernible as the voice of a man—a man in great agony. A third time it came: wordless, intense, and close. By now there was a second sound as well: hoof-beats.

There was just enough starlight for Morumus to mark the dim outline of Abbot Grahem a few yards away. Rather than speak aloud, he waited motionless while the older man edged carefully over to him.

"Bandits, sir?" Morumus spoke a low whisper.

"Probably." Grahem replied in the same barely-audible tone. "How near?"

"Less than half a league."

"On the road?"

"Yes."

"We are too close," whispered the abbot. "Get to the horses before they give us away."

"What about you, sir?"

"That man sounded like he was in trouble. I'm going to try to get closer."

"You will be outnumbered. I should come—"

"No. Stay with the horses and wait for me. But if they fright and the bandits approach, mount and flee."

"Sir—"

"That's an order, son." Grahem kept his voice low, but his tone was insistent. "We have a task to perform. Whatever happens tonight, that duty must be done. Wait for me unless there's trouble, but under no circumstances are you to come looking for me before daybreak. Do you understand?"

Morumus inclined his head. "Yes, sir."

"Good. Go on, then."

Morumus rose to his feet and melted away into the dark. They had selected a campsite that night on the backside of a gentle rise, just south of the Naud Road. The men had placed their bedrolls near the top. They had staked the horses farther downhill near a thin copse of trees, in order to give the thirsty beasts access to a runoff crease. Morumus had almost made it to the trees when the man's scream again filled the night.

Reaching the disquieted beasts, Morumus did what he could to calm them. Had he possessed the forethought, he would have brought down some oats from the provisions. Lacking these, he spoke to them in soft, gentle cadences. He stroked their necks and withers. Thankfully, it seemed to be enough. The horses calmed, the sound of their breathing grew more normal, and Morumus settled in to wait for the abbot's return.

Two hours passed. There were no more sounds, either from the hill above or the road beyond. Nor was there any sign of Abbot Grahem. By this time, the horses had settled themselves down onto the grass to sleep. The sudden rush of energy one gets in such circumstances had long since seeped out of Morumus, and he felt exhausted. When he could keep his feet no longer, he sat down with his back against one of the small trees. He could not allow himself to fall asleep, yet at the same time he had to rest. Morning was still several hours away, and though he did not like it, his superior had commanded him to wait.

He yawned. Perhaps if he closed his eyes for just a few moments . . .

Morumus woke to find the hillside awash in grey pre-dawn light. For a brief moment, he did not remember where he was. Then recollection returned, followed by a surge of sickening guilt. He had slept all night! Morumus jumped to his feet, looking all around. Both horses were still at their stakes, grazing in the grass. Yet there was no sign of Abbot Grahem.

Fearing the worst, Morumus left the horses and rushed up the hill. Reaching the campsite near its crest, he found the bedrolls just where they had left them the previous night. Continuing briskly to the top of the rise, he peered down the far side toward the road. For several tense moments, he saw nothing—for the land between hill and road was still heavily draped with night shadows.

Then he spotted it. There, about half the distance between the road and where he stood, a figure moved amid the shadows. It was vaguely man-shaped, but there was something wrong about it—something awry where the head and shoulders should be. Ducking to the ground, he waited—and watched.

Whatever-it-was was moving directly toward his position, though it did not seem to be in a hurry to get there. For the next quarter of an hour, the mysterious form lumbered nearer while the dawn grew gradually brighter. It was not until the sun peeked over the eastern horizon that the shape reached the base of the rise. As the sunrays struck it, Morumus realized it was no nefarious creature that approached him, but rather a man carrying a bundle over his shoulder. The man looked up, and Morumus recognized him at once.

He jumped to his feet. "Abbot Grahem!"

The abbot looked up. "Morumus, ready the horses!"

There was an urgency in the abbot's voice that brooked neither delay nor dissent. As quickly as Morumus had rushed up the rise to look for the abbot, he now dashed back down to retrieve the horses. Reaching the stakes, he freed the mares and led them back up to the campsite, where he saddled each as hastily as he could manage. Once the beasts were ready, he rolled and packed the blankets behind their seats. He had just finished this when Abbot Grahem crested the rise a dozen paces away.

"Are we ready to go?"

"Yes, sir. What hap—?"

"Not now, son. We must move quickly. Here"—he grunted, shifting the large cloth bundle from his shoulder to the back of the nearest horse—"help me fasten this."

Morumus complied without comment, yet he was troubled. Abbot Grahem was the sort of man who never seemed too bothered by anything. No matter what happened, even when everybody else was upset, he remained unruffled—like an impassive cliff overlooking a frothy sea. But on this particular morning he was visibly perturbed. This unsettled Morumus.

If the cliff collapsed into the surf, what was left to keep back the ocean?

Once they had secured the bundle, the men climbed into their saddles. "Follow me." Abbot Grahem spoke over his shoulder as he turned his horse west. "We ride quickly and quietly." His eyes flickered back for a moment toward the rise and the road beyond. "I do not believe we are in any immediate danger. But the sooner we are gone from this place, the better."

And so off they rode, away from the dawn and into what turned out to be a dim, dour morning. The pale light of pre-dawn seemed trapped that day, for it never fully lifted—nor lost its greyness. Thick clouds overtook the sunrise from the east, and by midmorning the men rode under a solidly leaden sky through relentless, heavy rain. For a while they kept away from the road, availing themselves of whatever cover the country provided. They circled out around stands of trees. They stayed on the southern slopes of the gentle hills. Yet by midday, the ground was too soft for them to continue in this cautious course. Though reluctant to do so, Abbot Grahem returned to the main road.

By the time they stopped that night, the rain had abated somewhat. But it did not cease. Likewise, the sun never properly set. Robbed of its glory by the day's grimness, it could manage no grand descent. Instead, it simply sulked to its rest that evening. As dusk settled, Morumus and the abbot took shelter in a stand of hardwoods. Here they found refuge beneath a large oak. If the ground was not exactly dry, it was at least an improvement over what they had endured throughout the day—and the thick boughs overhead kept most of the rain at bay. The respite was most welcome, and allowed them to eat their evening meal in relative comfort.

Morumus turned from securing the horses. "Should I gather wood for a fire, sir? No doubt most of it is soaked, but if we cut away the bark we might find kindling."

"We have little choice but to try." Abbot Grahem removed his traveling cloak and draped it over one of the low-hanging branches nearby. The wood bowed under the weight of the sodden wool. "If we do not dry out, we will catch our deaths this night. Gather what you can, Morumus. I'll strip the bark and see about getting it lit."

About a half hour later, the men and their cloaks huddled around a meager fire. The wood that Morumus had collected hissed defiantly at first, but in the end it burned. The overhead branch upon which the abbot had hung his cloak had finally snapped, so they had constructed makeshift drying racks from long sticks found among the trees. Hung over these, their travel-gear gave off steam as it dried. Beyond the trees, the rain continued its cold, despotic drizzle. Yet beneath the boughs of the oak, the monks grew dry and warm.

A few hours later, with the immediate needs of fire and food met, Morumus decided to venture the question that had been on his mind all that day. Abbot Grahem gave a long sigh before answering.

"There is little to tell." His gaze seemed lost in the flames of the fire as he spoke. "As we suspected, the screams we heard last night were the cries of a man under attack. By the time I reached him, however, it was already too late."

"You found the body?"

"Not quite a body, but near enough. When I found the man, he yet lived. He'd been stabbed numerous times. I could tell by the amount of blood that there was no hope of survival. He knew it, too."

"He spoke to you, sir?"

"Yes. When he realized I was not another attacker, he asked me if I was an Aesusian. When I told him I was, he asked me to pray with him."

"At least there is some hope, then."

"Yes." Grahem nodded. "There was surely faith in his prayer."

For a short while, neither man said anything. Finally, Morumus broke the silence. "I wonder if he had a family. Is there anything we could do?"

"We will do what we can, Morumus. The bundle we are carrying contains the man's belongings. When we arrive in Naud, you will take them to see if you can locate any kin. The man's last words were confused, but he spoke of a child. I promised him that I would help."

"Yes, sir. Is there anything of value?"

"Oh yes." The abbot's face darkened despite the firelight. "There is his purse—his *full* purse."

Morumus started. Had he heard the abbot correctly?

"Yes, that is what I said. The murderers did not take his purse."

"Was it hidden?"

"No. It was strapped to the front of his belt."

"Sir"—Morumus frowned at this disturbing news—"what kind of highwaymen kill a man and leave his purse?"

"Not the kind we want to meet."

"Did you get a look at the attackers, sir?"

"Not a good one. It was too dark. I only saw them from behind at a distance as they rode away. But there were several."

Morumus shook his head. "Several bandits kill one man and leave his purse? Something is rotten here, sir."

"Agreed—"

Morumus sensed a shadow beneath the surface of the abbot's words.

"—but it is beyond us now. We will help the man's family if we can, but then we will focus on the task before us. His murderers we must leave to God's justice . . ." Still gazing into the depths of the fire, Abbot Grahem closed his eyes. His voice trailed off to a nearly inaudible whisper. "And to the *erebanur* whence they came."

Morumus was not sure whether the abbot intended him to hear that last bit, so he did not remark on it. But the word filled him with foreboding. He had heard it spoken aloud only once before—years ago, when he was a boy. To hear it again now, not a week since his nightmare? Morumus shivered. Whether it was from the cold of the night or the darkness of the memory, he could not tell.

Erebanur was an ancient Vilguran word, but not one commonly used. Morumus had read numerous old texts in his years at Lorudin, and had come across the word less than two dozen times. Roughly translated, it meant "dark madness." On rare occasions it described nightmares or dire visions. Yet in most of the instances he had found, the ancient Vilgurans used *erebanur* as a sort of religious curse. It was a denunciation they applied to the religious rites of the period prior to their own history—or to those of the barbarians they conquered. The characterization had stuck with Morumus, for the old Vilgurans themselves had worshipped a pantheon of gods—not all of them friendly.

How black, then, must the *erebanur* religions have been, if even the pagan Vilgurans spoke of them as "dark madness"?

Of course Morumus knew something of the answer to this question . . .

But why had the abbot chosen to use the word now?

It would be a long time before he got an answer to this last question, for neither man spoke again that night. Yet Morumus did not drop immediately off to sleep. For a long while he lay awake, feeling a chill that had nothing to do with the damp weather.

Something sinister was afoot in Caeldora.

rien did not hear the rain that night. The dim passage through which she descended was buried far too deep. With every downward step her tears increased, and she did not try to contain them. A few dripped from her chin into the empty stone pitcher that she carried. Most of them, however, fell onto the stairs beneath her feet to form a melancholy wake.

Usually Urien loved the summers in Caeldora. Warm breezes blew over the tops of the surrounding hills, carrying fresh whispers of the world beyond the vale. Bright flowers blossomed along the paths, bringing welcome color and light into her otherwise dreary routine. On clear days the sky above her garden was a brilliant blue, and she often spent hours lying on the grass staring up at it. The chunky clouds floating above her seemed so cheerful and free. If she occasionally envied the birds soaring high overhead, wishing she could join them, it was but a small indulgence. Summer was the one season of the year in which she felt her solitude least—the few, precious months in which she could almost imagine that she was not a prisoner.

That is what had made today so difficult. All day long, rain had lacerated the roof and windows, forcing her to remain indoors. Today there had been no pretending that she was free. From dawn to dusk—what little there was of either—she had been held captive by circumstances beyond her control. Heavy rains in summer were always a bitter reminder to Urien: *I will never be free.* Like the sky outside her walls, she had passed the hours in grey weeping.

It had not always felt this way. She remembered how excited she was many years ago, when she learned that she was to go with her brother. Together, they would travel away from the wars of Dyfann—across the ocean! Together, they would restore the Old Faith in a land that had forgotten it. It all sounded so exciting at the time. But she had been very young then—and very naïve. Now she was grown—and grown weary. Now there was no more joy.

There was only duty.

Somnadh had no idea what it was like for her. Her brother came and went as often as he pleased. More often than not, he was gone. But there was no such freedom for Urien. Her duties were unending and unremitting. Morning and evening she had to tend to the Mother, and so morning and evening and always she had to be here: here in this narrow valley; here in this old tower with the ghosts of a forgotten people; here practicing the ghastly rituals of a forgotten faith.

How fitting, for she felt much like a ghost herself.

Her brother did everything he could to make her situation comfortable. Anything she asked, he did his best to provide. He built the keep and planted the garden. He obtained servants to work the fields of the valley, and eunuchs to educate her. Years ago, he even secured a maidservant for her—a girl her own age named Neanna. Neanna had kept Urien company and taught her Caeldoran. But as Neanna grew older, she wanted a husband, and eventually she tried to escape. Two days later the servants found her dead, and Urien was again alone.

She hated being alone.

Urien reached the bottom of the stairs. Before her stood a closed wooden door, its surface lacquered black. Over this an image of the Mother had been painted in white. The effect was unsettling: the black absorbed the lamplight, leaving the Mother suspended in midair. Urien paused before her image, setting down her pitcher and making the ritual genuflection. Then she pushed open the door.

The darkness in the chamber beyond was palpable. The only entrance was the one through which she had passed, and her lamp was the only light. The chamber itself was ancient and cavernous—a deep hollow hewn from the heart of the earth. At its center the floor fell away into a deep cistern.

Urien paused and took a deep breath before approaching. The air was cold, and she shivered. She hated coming here alone.

As she stepped into the gloom, Urien tried to think of better days.

The best times were when Somnadh visited, which happened as often as his duties in the wider world permitted. Her brother's visits were never preannounced, and so were always a delightful surprise to Urien. Usually he would stay for several days, during which time they would take long walks in the garden and orchard and vineyard. They would talk for hours. She would ask him question after question about his travels. He in turn would regale her with news of the wider world, telling her all about the peoples he had met and the places he had visited.

And yet the one thing Urien desired most—to go and see those people and places for herself—was the one thing Somnadh would never permit. When she had asked as a girl, he changed the subject or diverted her attention with some new story. As she grew older and continued to ask, he became angry. Now that she had reached womanhood, she no longer bothered to broach the subject. The question only seemed to drive him away again sooner. Besides, she already knew what his answer would be: just as it was his duty to go abroad spreading the Old Faith, so it was her duty to stay and tend to the Mother.

A slight lip in the floor of the chamber marked the perimeter of the cistern. Two stone pillars stood facing each other across its diameter, and a hole in each pillar supported a round wooden beam. On one side this beam extended through its pillar, and to this end a crank wheel had been attached. From the beam, a stone bucket hung hooked to a thick coil of chain.

Urien approached cautiously. The perimeter lip was not high enough to prevent her falling should she misstep. As she reached the edge of the cistern, the air took on a telltale metallic tang. Urien's breath frosted like fog as she held her lamp over the brink and looked down. Less than three yards below the lip, the liquid surface gleamed dark red.

The Well of Souls.

When Urien had been very young, she had not understood the Well. For many years she drew the Mother's drink from its depths with no thought as to how it was filled. Yet as she grew in both age and awareness, Somnadh explained the matter to her:

"The Mother is the source of all life, and it is to her that all life returns. It is for this reason that the Mother has claim on all life."

The riders who brought the Mother's offerings from beyond the vale were simply her hands and feet—those who exercised the Mother's claims. At the time, Urien accepted her brother's explanation without question.

Yet as the years passed, a number of questions began collecting in Urien's conscience—things of which she was ashamed to speak, yet things she could not seem to shake. Once, she dared *voice* these questions to her brother. The conversation had not gone well at all. She had never seen Somnadh so angry, and after that she never again divulged her disquiet. In times of doubt she reminded herself what her father used to say to Dyfanni who complained about the gods: *"You can either dream about the gods you would like, or serve the ones you have."*

Urien repeated the words to herself as she reached for the crank wheel. Whether she liked it or not, she was as bound to the Mother as she was to her brother. And the sooner she filled her pitcher, the sooner she could leave this dark place.

The Well was the Mother's reservoir. When offerings were plentiful, the excess was stored. When fresh food was unavailable, Urien came to draw . . .

Gripping the handle of the wheel, she lowered the bucket. The chain clanked slightly as it unwound. She heard the bucket breach the surface, and once it was full she drew it back up and lifted it off its hook. The chamber was silent as Urien kneeled beside the brink of the Well and poured the contents of the bucket into her pitcher.

Silence.

It was the silence of the Mother that most hurt Urien. Somnadh said that the Mother had spoken to him once, and Urien believed him. Yet the Mother had *never* spoken to her. Not a word to the lady who had given up everything to serve her. Not a single whisper of affection or encouragement to the one who stood before her, day in and day out. What kind of Mother treated her daughter thus?

Why is the goddess so cruel to those who love her?

Why could she not speak tenderly to Urien as she had spoken to Somnadh—just once?

Her tears growing hotter, Urien looked past her pitcher down into the cistern. *The Well of Souls.* She had never seen it empty. How far down did it go? How many lives had been poured out into its depths? How many more would it swallow?

Urien knew the answer to the last question: *It will never stop.* The Mother's appetite was insatiable. *I will never be free.* Day after day, morning and evening, Mother demanded her offerings. *The Mother must be tended. It will never end. Someday, Somnadh will pour* my *blood into this Well.*

The thought revolted her. But worse yet was the one that followed on its heels: *Or will I pour* his?

It was at that moment that Urien's attention was drawn back from the brink by a wet sensation around her feet. She looked down. In her inattention, she had overfilled the pitcher. A thick puddle of blood spread outward from its base. Some of it had already soaked through the soft soles of her slippers.

"Ugh!" Urien jumped to her feet.

Too late she realized her mistake. The spilled blood had already spread behind her heels. No sooner had Urien regained her feet and taken a step back than she slipped sideways—over the brink of the Well!

The only thing that saved her was that she managed to grab onto the bucket as she tumbled over the edge. The clanking of the chain echoed through the chamber as it unwound, and Urien had only a moment to gasp for breath before both she the bucket plunged beneath the red surface. How deep she sank Urien did not know. She kept her eyes and mouth shut and clutched tightly to the bucket. A few seconds later her descent stopped with a jolt.

The chain had run out of length before she hit bottom. Her feet tread nothing but blood. The Well of Souls was deeper than she could have imagined.

It was . . .

Horrifying.

Urien's lungs burned as she frantically pulled herself up the chain, toward the surface. She climbed and climbed, but did not seem to be getting any closer to the surface. *How far down am I?* Though her eyes were already shut, darkness began gathering at the corners of her vision.

Just when she thought she could climb no farther—at the precise moment when she was sure she would have to exhale though it meant drowning—Urien's hands and face broke the surface.

She sucked air, swallowed blood, and gagged.

Trying again, she pulled herself head and shoulders above the surface. This time she managed to get a clean breath.

It was a much greater struggle to regain the lip of the cistern. Urien's arms and shoulders ached, her eyes burned, and the stench of blood filled her nostrils. Her robe, drenched with blood, seemed to want to pull her back below the surface. But the horror of a second submersion—one from which she knew she would not emerge—impelled Urien up the remaining length of chain and back onto the cold stone.

For what might have been minutes or an hour, Urien lay shaking on the floor of the Well chamber. She was freezing and she wanted to flee, but her limbs would not work. When she had regained her breath, she began to scream.

Nobody heard her cries. Nobody came to her aid.

Urien was utterly alone.

Her screams became uncontrollable sobs.

Far above her, the night sky drizzled its commiseration.

he day after Morumus and Abbot Grahem passed night beneath the oak, the rains ceased. For the rest of the ride to Naud, they neither heard nor saw another soul. They arrived in the port city on the fifth morning after their departure from Lorudin.

Naud sat on the north shore of the Lor estuary, originally settled by the ancient Vilgurans. Here, as elsewhere across Caeldora, most of the imperial construction had vanished. Gone was the wall that once protected the town. Gone, too, was the tight organization the wall provided. In imperial times, all structures would have been tucked along straight streets behind the stone wall. Now the collection of buildings and homes sprawling out from the town center possessed all the discipline of a garden vine.

The one notable reminder of Naud's ancient pedigree was its pier. Constructed of white stone and rising a dozen feet above the waterline, it stuck out into the bay like a long, bony finger. Ships of varying sizes and origins moored along both sides of its length. Naud was by no means as busy as the great ports of northern and southern Caeldora. Yet for all this, it maintained a lively maritime bustle and provided a vital trade link for western Caeldora. It also proved a more discreet docking place for foreign travelers who did not wish news of their presence to outpace their persons. It was for this latter reason that the delegation from northern Aeld Gowan had chosen to land at Naud.

The abbot had barely spoken at breakfast, and led the morning's ride in utter silence. Morumus followed behind, his thoughts drifting, unfocused. But as they came in sight of the open water, as they felt the breeze on their faces, and as they breathed the salt air, they seemed to revive.

For a moment, Morumus closed his eyes and drew in a deep breath of the bracing air.

He straightened in the saddle. Though the isolation and tension of the road did not vanish, it receded. But as he and the abbot reached the outlying fringes of town, the latter drew in his reins and motioned for Morumus to come up beside him.

"I am going to the docks to see if I can locate our people." As he spoke, he turned in his seat and reached into one of his saddlebags. A moment later he withdrew his hand and passed two small, round discs to Morumus. The first was a silver coin. The second was made of wood.

The wooden disc had a most extraordinary appearance. Its grain was an interweaving of light and dark, lines and swirls, and the way these flowed together reminded Morumus of fire. Living flames seemed imprisoned in the wood by some clever art. A smooth oil finish magnified the effect and gave the disc a glowing appearance. On both faces the disc was inscribed with a single word: 'GRAEMVS.'

"What is this?" Morumus recognized the Vilguran form of the abbot's name, but he had never seen anything like the wooden coin.

"That, Morumus, is one of my personal tokens. Every abbot, bishop, and archbishop has them. The exotic wood is called *brer*. We use it to protect against forgery. I want you to give both coins to the family of the deceased man, along with the bundle of his possessions. The silver will buy them passage to Lorudin, and my token will assure them entrance."

"What if they do not wish to go to Lorudin, sir?"

"If they do not wish to go, then bring back the token—but leave the silver."

Morumus nodded. "How shall I find them?"

"Make an inquiry at the garrison. Look serious, show them the token, and tell them you are on official Church business. Mention my name, and ask to speak to the captain. Give him my regards: he and I are old acquaintances. Tell him when we found the man, show him the bundle, and ask for help in finding the family. If anybody can keep track of what happens in Naud, it will be him."

"Yes, sir."

"Stick to the basic facts, Morumus. Multiple attackers cut the man down after dark. We found him in the night, and buried him in the morning. Beyond that we know nothing for certain, so do not speculate."

"There is the matter of the full purse."

"If the captain is still as sharp now as he was when I knew him, he will notice that on his own. Don't mention it yourself."

"Understood, sir."

"Have a care when you find the family, Morumus. This is delicate work. Everybody lives with the expectation of death, yet the sting is sharper when the blow is sudden. Offer to pray with them, but do not try to offer spiritual counsel. The head of their family is gone, and nothing you can say will dull that dagger. Piety always falters in the face of pain. Grief must run its course even in the most faithful. Do you understand?"

Morumus understood the words only too well. He nodded.

"To our work, then. Take as much time as the task requires. When you are finished, make your way to the docks. I will not keep the bishops waiting on the pier, but I will see to it that word finds you there."

With these words, the two men split up to their respective tasks.

Morumus guided his mount through the haphazard outer streets toward the center of town. He had no difficulty finding the garrison, for even from a distance he could see the large flag flapping above the rooftops. The banner's field was rich green, and dominated at its center by a golden sun whose rays blazed in every direction. From the end of the flag end streamed three long, triangular tails. These were colored bright red, and pulsed as the flag rippled and snapped in the ocean breeze.

The new imperial standard rose from within the remains of the ancient imperial citadel. The barracks covered an area roughly equivalent to two of Naud's city blocks, and was surrounded by a high, solid wall. Although the locals had long since scavenged away Naud's city wall, things were different here. Here the stone wall remained stolid, and rose to a height of over twenty spans—about three times Morumus's own height. At the few places where the centuries had inflicted minor damage, Naud's rulers had done their best to make repairs. The result, if not exactly up to ancient Vilguran standards, looked functional.

Upon his arrival at the garrison, Morumus proceeded directly to the main gate. This consisted of a pair of large archways set in the wall between two tall, square towers. The wooden doors within the arches stood wide open at this time of the day, and from within Morumus could hear the busy sounds of drill and horse and steel. More immediately, a pair of soldiers, one standing outside each gate, kept lazy watch over passersby. These men wore belted green tabards—short soldier's coats—emblazoned with the golden sun. From the tip of each man's lance hung a red streamer that matched the tails on the banner overhead. Seeing him approach, the closer of the two made an indistinct noise to his companion, and both men straightened officiously.

Pulling up his reins in front of the guards, Morumus remembered the abbot's instructions. If he was to gain admittance, he would have to look and act the part. At first he did not speak a word. Instead, he fixed the guards with what he hoped was a somber, searching gaze.

"Can we help you, lad?" said the soldier nearest him. Of the pair, this man was obviously in charge. There were bits of grey streaked throughout his dark hair, and around his collar he wore a single red stripe. The tired tone of his voice said he was not impressed with Morumus.

"You may indeed." Morumus made his words crisp, doing his best to sound important. "I am here to see your captain."

The soldier smirked. "You and every other cleric, merchant, and lordling passing through Naud. The captain is the emperor's man, not a public servant. What is your business?"

"It is a matter of official Church business. I will speak of it only with the captain."

"The captain is busy this morning."

"Is that so?" Morumus made a show of studying the soldier. "Do not the emperor's men make time for those who gave him his crown?"

If the soldier had been bemused a moment prior, at the implied challenge in Morumus's voice the grip of the man's lance hand tightened and his eyes narrowed.

"Have a care with that tongue, youngling." Beside the speaker, the other soldier's face hardened and his stance widened.

Morumus was not by nature a bold person. Nor did he possess an intrinsically commanding presence. But what did that have to do with anything? His superior had given him a task. Abbot Grahem was counting on him. Besides this, though the soldier's threat sounded only too real, Morumus knew he still had an advantage to press. Reaching into his robe, he withdrew the abbot's token. Then, with a silent prayer for courage, he put what steel he could muster into his words.

"My care is for the Church's business." He infused his words with ice, opening his palm so that the *brer* token was visible to both men. "I am an envoy of Abbot Grahem of Lorudin, himself a son of Bishop Anathadus of Aevor, *himself* a servant and true son of our Lord Aesus. If your captain is too busy to see me, let it be as you say: I will pass his regrets along to my superiors."

Whether it was a direct answer to prayer, or simply that reckless boldness one feels when he knows he has gone too far already, Morumus felt himself warming to his role. Straightening in his saddle and sharpening the edge of his words, he finished with dread flourish. "I assure you, however, that such regrets will not return to him—or to you—void."

For several tense moments, there was nothing but silence. Both soldiers stared hard at Morumus. They seemed to be weighing him, wondering whether this monk could really be who he claimed. Their eyes seemed uncertain when they looked at his face, yet they grew decidedly less so when they regarded the *brer* disc. Flexing his palm ever so slightly and shifting his arm just so, Morumus made sure they looked at it more than once.

Finally, the older soldier broke the silence. "May I take that to the captain?" He gestured at the token.

Morumus nodded. He extended his hand.

The speaker did not budge, but rather motioned to his companion. Looking very uneasy now, the younger soldier stepped forward, plucked the disc from the monk's palm, and handed it to his sergeant.

"Wait here." With that gruff order, the older man turned and stalked through the gate.

In the still aftermath of the exchange, the boldness that had coursed through Morumus only a few moments prior receded sharply. His heart pounded in his chest, and he felt an odd lurch at the top of his stomach. As the sergeant's absence stretched from moments into minutes, he began to replay the conversation in his head. It made him cringe. Had he really threatened to bring the wrath of the bishop down on the heads of these men? What would Abbot Grahem say if he found out? For that matter, what would the bishop say?

Thankfully, Morumus was spared further introspection by the reappearance of the old soldier. He returned the abbot's token to Morumus, then turned and gestured back toward the gate. "Follow me." His tone now was markedly subdued.

Not long thereafter, Morumus stood waiting by the hearth in the private study of the garrison captain. This was a compact, tidy chamber on the second floor of the inner barracks. The furnishings were sparse and unadorned. There was a simple desk by the front windows, a tall bookcase on the wall, and a wide table near the room's center. The shelf was stuffed neatly with charts and ledgers, and the table had been spread with maps of Naud and the surrounding region. Even the fire on the hearth seemed to have caught the spirit of the room: its flames crackled crisply and looked smart as they burned.

Morumus did not have to wait long. The garrison captain entered through a side door near the desk and crossed to meet him. Seeing the man, Morumus immediately understood the room. The captain did not seem to have a single ounce of extraneous flesh about him. He was not emaciated. Rather, he was a man built for efficiency. Of average height, he wore his head clean-shaven. And although he appeared lean, it was clear from his confident bearing that the captain was a man of ample strength and agility.

"Captain Brann." His tone was as firm as the grip on Morumus's extended hand. Sizing Morumus up with a glance, he released his arm and stepped back. "You come from Lorudin, I am told? What is your name?"

"Morumus. Abbot Grahem sends his greetings. He would have come himself, but he had another urgent errand."

"Grahem is here in Naud?"

"Yes."

"Indeed." The captain nodded. "That is very good. What is your business, Morumus?"

Morumus lifted the bundle from the floor and set it on the edge of the desk. He untied the cords binding it, and spread the contents out for the captain to see. "Three nights ago, we found a man murdered on the road. These are his belongings."

Morumus watched as Captain Brann surveyed the pile. First, there was the blanket, which had served to bundle the rest. Next, there was a long steel knife—nothing ornate, but sturdy and useful. Then there was a silver ring, a thick belt, and a tinderbox. Last of all there was the purse, sitting like a large leather pear amidst the rest. Morumus saw Brann's eyes light upon it.

The captain lifted the purse just enough to hear the clink of coins, then sat it back down. He frowned. "The purse is full?"

Morumus nodded.

"Tell me more."

And so Morumus did. Following the abbot's orders, he restricted his report to the basic facts. He told the captain of the screams in the dark, the multiple attackers, and the grim result. He concluded with Abbot Grahem's promise to convey the dead man's possessions to his family.

"That is where we need help, Captain. We do not even have a name."

"I know the name." Brann's words came out low.

"You do?"

"I do." The captain looked up at Morumus, and there was something in his expression that Morumus could not discern.

When he spoke, his tone was grave. "These things belonged to a man named Josias. He was the woodcutter for this garrison. He had a small holding just outside of town, near the forest. But you won't find anybody there."

"Why is that?"

"His wife died years ago, and about a week ago, his only child went missing in the woods. We searched, but found nothing. No body, no child."

A chill crept up Morumus's spine. The face from his nightmare flashed before his eyes. "A daughter?"

"No, a son." But now Brann regarded him with a frightening intensity. "You knew nothing of this?"

"No."

"And the abbot? This is not his business in Naud?"

"It is not."

"You are sure?"

"I am." The conversation was beginning to feel like a duel. "Why do you ask?"

Brann paused a moment, his gaze returning to the items on the desk. "Josias's son is not the first to go missing. There have been others—*including* some daughters." He looked back up and his voice grew dark. "Now you are here. Grahem has come, just like before. It is like it is all happening again. Truly Morumus, you know nothing of this?"

"Nothing." The first chill had begun to recede once Morumus learned the man's missing child was not a daughter. But hearing this account—and seeing the expression on the captain's face as he relayed it—the chill seeped back into him. "What is going on, sir?"

Brann almost answered. He opened his mouth, but then stopped and shook his head. "No. No, Morumus. If Grahem has not told you, then it is not your business to know. It is not your burden to bear, nor your nightmare to remember. Some things are better left to the dark past."

69

The captain turned away from him toward the windows. "I will take care of these items. Please convey my regards to your abbot."

The meeting was over.

Morumus's voice caught in his throat. Inside he was cold all over. *Nightmare. Dark past.* Captain Brann had not used the word *erebanur*, but he might as well have. What did it all mean?

That night, dark shadows once again fell across Morumus's sleep. Only this time it was not a nightmare
that stalked him, but something worse.

It was a memory.

It was a beautiful, warm evening in Lothair. A gentle breeze
flitted through the glen, and the turf on which young Morumus sat was soft and welcoming. The sunset in the west was
glorious. It had been a long day of riding, but Morumus had
never felt so alive.

One often feels most alive in the face of grim events. News
of the Nornish raiders had reached their holding at midday.
A small village on the eastern march had been burned, its
people murdered, and its goods plundered. The few to escape
the slaughter had marked the raiders as fleeing south, toward
the Deasmor. This natural labyrinth of lochs and glens wound
through a range of low, old mountains, and formed a natural
barrier between the north and south of the island of Aeld
Gowan. It divided Lothair and Nornindaal to the north from
Mersex to the south. It also afforded many hidden passages
for rogues and thieves—and raiders.

Morumus's father, Raudorn Red-Fist, was a thane of the Lothairin king and Warden of the Upper Mathway. The Mathway was the central river in Lothair. From its origins in the Deasmor, it flowed north into the Lothairin low country, past the capital at Dunross, and finally into the sea. As Warden of the Upper Mathway, Raudorn was responsible for protecting the scattered population in the high country near the river's roots and along the eastern border with Nornindaal. In Morumus's lifetime, nobody had dared provoke Raudorn Red-Fist.

Until today.

The report of Nornish raiders had rippled through his hall at Aban-Tur like a thunderclap, for the northern countries of Aeld Gowan had lived in peace with each other for a generation. Like the Mersians of the south, the Norns had first come to Aeld Gowan as invaders from across the sea. Viciously they had cut themselves a kingdom along the vulnerable eastern coast of the great island. Yet unlike the Mersians, the Norns had readily adopted the ways—and in time, the faith—of the people they conquered. Over the centuries, even the languages of the two northern peoples had fused together into a common tongue called *Tuasraeth*—the "north speech." The result of this cultural and spiritual assimilation was a peace held precious on both sides. That either side should risk breaching this peace by raiding was unthinkable.

What, then, was the meaning of this reckless, senseless incursion?

In hopes of finding an answer before the perpetrators escaped beyond reach, Raudorn had summoned his men-at-arms and ridden out at once. With Morumus's older brother away at the king's court in Dunross, he had been permitted to accompany his father. For the first time ever, Morumus had "ridden with the lances." It was for this reason that, despite the high stakes and tense circumstances, he could not help but feel a certain exhilaration as events unfolded. Every clop of a horse hoof, every cry of a bird as they pounded across the moors, every jangle of bit and steel—all of these filled him with the wild, naïve energy of those who have never seen battle.

Despite the pace of their pursuit, the Lothairins had not overtaken the villains that day. The pillaged settlement lay leagues east of Aban-Tur, but it was plain fact that the quickest passage into the Deasmor from any location along the eastern marches was the river route. Thus the Lothairin lances had not begun at the burned village. Rather, they had spent the day storming south along the line of the Mathway, following the river toward its source in the high country. By tracing its route rather than tracking the raiders directly, Raudorn hoped to cut off their escape. By evening, the tactic seemed to have worked: with no trace of the Norns ahead, it appeared that the Lothairin company had reached the hill country first.

The sun had begun its descent when Raudorn finally called the halt. The men stopped for the night in a place where the rising dale widened into a flat, narrow plateau. The tree line was never far from the trail as one ascended a vale, yet here the trees graciously yielded space to grass and scrub. Here too even the river took its ease, spreading out lazily into a deep pool whose upper sides were flanked by large boulders. It would have been difficult to find a camp better suited to the twin needs of rest and watch.

Fatigue and tension sap strength as surely as gaping wounds, and men who have spent a day in the saddle brooding over battle have little left by day's end. Accordingly, supper was a cold affair. There could be no fire in the camp, lest they alert the Nornish raiders, who were somewhere behind them, to their presence. Yet the evening meal was not entirely without cheer. Earlier that afternoon the company had stopped at a small holding in the lower foothills. Raudorn had warned the freeman shepherd to remove his family, and questioned him regarding any movements in the hills. Though the man had not been able to provide them with any useful information, the shepherd had given Raudorn two stone flagons of mead in gratitude for his warning.

"Not enough for a dozen men to dull their wits, my lord; but perhaps sufficient to ease their joints at supper."

It was strangely spiced mead, to be sure—Morumus had never tasted the like—but it seemed to have had its intended effect.

With no fire to tend, most of the men were looking for their beds before the sun found its own. Morumus watched as his father made rounds among them, clasping arms and sharing words of encouragement. After this, he inspected the horse-lines and spoke with the sentries. Finally, his work for evening done, Raudorn returned to the center of camp and sat down beside his son.

"Morumus." Raudorn spoke as though the name alone formed a complete thought. And for both of them, it did. Between parents and children, there is a sort of understanding that requires few words.

Morumus looked up into his father's face. Raudorn's green eyes remained bright, even after a long ride. Because he had spent the day wearing a helm, his red hair was matted flat against the sides of his head. Damp from the heat, it looked darker than normal. Raudorn had earned the name 'Red-Fist' through battle-prowess, yet its effect was magnified by his fiery appearance.

"You do not look tired, Father."

Raudorn grinned. "I am getting there, son. How about you? What did you think of your first pursuit?"

"It is exciting!" Morumus let his eagerness out before catching himself. "That is to say, I know it is a serious affair, Father. Yet I am pleased to be accompanying the men."

Raudorn chuckled. "Well said on all counts, son. Well said."

"Do you think we will catch the Norns tomorrow, Father?"

"I suspect that we will. They must expect that we are pursuing. Yet they will not attempt to return to Nornindaal overland, for they know we would easily overtake them in open country. This way, then—up our river into the high country—is their only hope. But they know that we know this, too, so they will be making all speed in the hopes of beating us to the passage. When they arrive, we will be waiting. We can expect to see them tomorrow—if not sooner."

"Why did they do it? We have had peace with the Norns my entire life."

"My entire life, too, son—*and* that of my father."

"Then why?"

Raudorn's voice fell flat as he stared out into the rising night. "I do not know. The village they sacked held no value as a target. It guarded no important road, protected no vital waters, and possessed no appreciable wealth. It was little more than a small market."

"It makes no sense, Father."

Raudorn looked down at him. "No, it does not. That is why we must not allow these raiders to escape. Our king does not want war with Nornindaal. To the best of my knowledge, neither does their king want war with us. And even if I'm wrong, a serious invading force would not waste the advantage of surprise on a trifling target. That is both sloppy strategy and unforgivable foolishness. Something is rotten here, Morumus. The whole affair has the feel of a deliberate ruse. We shall have to be extraordinarily watchful." As he spoke these last words, Raudorn turned his face back toward the dark.

For several long minutes after that, neither father nor son spoke. By now, the last traces of the sun had melted away in the west, and a growing number of stars began winking to life like celestial fireflies. The dome of sky above them was broad and empty of clouds. In the east, the forelock of a pale, full moon began to peek over the horizon.

Raudorn at last broke the silence. "It will be a clear night. The sentries should have no difficulty spotting the Norns, should they attempt to pass this way under cover of dark."

"Do you think they will?"

"Maybe. We shall see. If they do not approach tonight, we shall lie in wait here tomorrow. A few men up-trail to stymie their advance, and the bulk of our forces concealed in the surrounding woods." Raudorn pointed to the tree line on either side of the dale, then over his shoulder at the river pool. "With men on both sides, we can back them up against the water."

"An ambush."

"Exactly. This is the perfect place for it."

A thought occurred to Morumus, and he gazed, eyes narrowed, at the surrounding trees. "How do we know that they haven't had the same idea, Father?"

Raudorn looked down again at his son, and this time both affection and appraisal were evident in his expression. "That is a shrewd question, Morumus. But do not fear: the scouts made a thorough inspection of the woods before we stopped. They found no traces of men or mounts."

Morumus nodded. "Good."

"Indeed. But your question does remind me of something. When we do meet these Nornish raiders, son—whether it be tonight, tomorrow, or the following day—I want you to stay out of the thick of it."

Morumus smarted. "I know how to use a sword, Father."

"I know, Morumus. Master Lareow has informed me of your good progress. But should anything happen to me, your brother will need your cool head. He is far too impulsive for his own good."

"But Father—"

Raudorn cut him off with a stern gesture. "I am not asking you, Morumus. You will do as I say. Is that clear?"

"Yes, sir."

"Good." Seeing the disappointment on his son's face, Raudorn softened his expression. "Cheer up, son. Life is full enough of battles. You will not fail to see your share of them." He squeezed Morumus's shoulder as he stood. "Come then, let us get some sleep."

And so it was that Morumus and Raudorn at last found their own beds at the center of the camp just as the moon rose clear of the eastern hills. It was a mild, pleasant night. All around them, the sounds of summer—birds, crickets, and the occasional owl—rose and fell in a lulling, nocturnal symphony. Within minutes of rolling into their blankets, both father and son were sleeping.

Despite the long day and the warm blanket, Morumus's sleep that night was fitful. For hours it seemed that he was floating somewhere in between wakefulness and rest. The experience was most disturbing. He was not fully asleep, so he could still sense the things around him. Yet neither was he fully awake, so these things took on phantasmal qualities. Midnight came and went, and still he drifted, unable to settle. Finally, in the wee hours of the morning, he got up.

"Enough," he whispered to himself, rising so as not to disturb his father. Beside him, lying flat on his back and breathing in deep, rhythmic cadence, Raudorn did not appear to be sharing any of his son's discomfiture. Moving away from his father, Morumus made for the river pool behind their camp. Upon waking he had found an unpleasant taste in his mouth, and his throat felt dry.

"Probably that mead." He had tasted ale often enough at his father's board in Aban-Tur. Mead, however, was reserved for feast occasions—which did not occur in a lord's hall nearly as often as some of the old stories made it seem.

Coming to the edge of the pool, he looked out across it. Only near its center could one detect the faint ripple of the river current; the rest of the pool was like a giant mirror, still as glass. On its surface he saw reflected the moon and the stars. The arrangement was so perfect that for a few moments, Morumus imagined that he stood beside a portal in heaven looking down at the night sky from above. The effect was potent, and he began to feel as though he might tip right over into the water.

He shook his head. "The mead again." He really was not used to it!

Morumus walked along the edge of the pool until he came to the rocks along its back flanks. Here he stooped down, cupped his hands, and took a long drink. The water was as cool as one might expect from a mountain pool, and quite refreshing. After repeating this process several times, he sat back against a stout boulder and breathed deeply of the night air. He closed his eyes, and was just about certain that he might drop off to sleep—real sleep this time—when he noticed it.

The night around him had gone silent.

The songs of the night birds stopped just as if they had all dropped dead simultaneously. A moment later, the chirps of the crickets ceased. In less than half a minute, the meadow had gone from the sounds of a night garden to the stillness of a tomb. For the next several minutes, the silence grew, its oppressive emptiness becoming almost palpable.

Morumus's eyes were wide open now, and the hair on his arms and neck stood on end. He turned his head and looked back toward the camp. In the clear moonlight, he could see the huddled forms of his father's men. They all appeared to be sleeping soundly, oblivious to the danger.

Danger . . . was that what it was? The notion rose in Morumus's mind unbidden, yet it came with an irrefutable and terrible certainty. But what was this danger? And whence did it come? His eyes moved from the sleeping men-at-arms to the line of trees flanking the dale.

There he found his answer.

The brightness of the full moon had bathed the high meadow with pale light. Yet several black spots now appeared at the forest's edge. *Black* is perhaps not a strong enough word, for the darkness of these spots was anything but passive. They swallowed the surrounding moonlight. The shapes grew as they fed, swelling from a handful of mere spots to two dozen man-sized forms. As they stepped out from the trees, sound once again returned to the dale. Yet it was not the natural night-music of the summer meadow. Rather, it was a rasping wave of hisses and spits—like you might expect to hear from a coven of serpents singing dark worship.

The unholy music seeped into Morumus's mind, and he feared that very soon it would possess him. He had to warn his father and the others before that happened. He opened his mouth and was drawing a breath to shout, when another voice rang like a clarion across the meadow.

"Enemy! Enemy!" One of the sentries had marked the shadows, and was crying the alarm. "Awake! To arms, my lord! To arms, my brothers! We are attacked!"

Between the river pool and the forest's edge, the Lothairin camp sprung to life. Raudorn's men were experienced soldiers, and experienced soldiers have an uncanny knack for slipping in and out of sleep as opportunity arises or necessity demands. Mere moments after the alarm sounded, they leapt from their blankets with such explosiveness that it seemed they must not have been sleeping at all. Steel flashed in the moonlight as men snatched lances and drew swords.

Yet no sooner had the men risen to battle than the shadows responded. Their hissing music rose on the night air, rearing like an uncoiling viper and swelling with venom. The next moment the sound crested and broke over the camp, catching the men as surely as a wave catches a ship. The soldiers jerked and reeled, then stiffened and stopped. Arms and legs became as unresponsive as stone. The men stood suspended in mid-motion.

"I can't move!" yelled one man, his arm extended halfway to a tripod of lances.

"Neither can I!"

"Nor me!"

Morumus realized that he, too, was unable to move. The dark music gripped him just as it held his father's men, and he could not so much as bend a finger! His heart pounded like a drumbeat reverberating through a vacant yard. His breath blew like rapid gusts through an empty cave. He was alive, but paralyzed from the neck down. All he could do was watch, helpless.

What followed next was horrific.

There was no battle. How could there be, when one side was unable to move? The shadows approached the men slow but sure, a lazy river of malice. Like dark water over green stone they glided across the meadow, drawing long knives that glinted dully in the moonlight. The hissing song was an all-encompassing symphony by now, and to its black timing the shadows glided among Raudorn's men. The murderers were thorough. They took sufficient time about the slaughter to inflict maximum suffering, and Morumus saw every detail. Moreover, he heard every last word or prayer of the men-at-arms. Some died well. Some did not.

Among those who died well was Raudorn himself. Though it must have broken his heart to watch his men murdered, though he himself must have felt terror as the shadows surrounded him, he never surrendered to despair. Rather, he gave all his strength to calling his men to faith in the face of death:

"We die, brothers, but our Redeemer lives! Trust that he will deliver your souls! We shall be with him soon!"

Such was the unflagging conduct of Raudorn Red-Fist, Thane of King Heclaid and Warden of the Upper Mathway, until at last he too succumbed to the butcher's blade.

The shadows never saw Morumus. Tucked fast against the boulder beside the quiet river pool, he remained unmoving and unnoticed—an unwilling witness to the slaughter. Transfixed by the macabre spectacle, he could not look away. When it began, he wanted to shout to his father. Yet knowing the futility, he forced himself to remain silent. By the time it ended, he was in such shock that he could not have spoken had he tried. The shadows did not plunder the camp. They did not bother to hide their handiwork or tidy up the mess. When they finished, they simply melted back into the woods. With them went their hissing song, receding into the darkness like a tide washing out to sea.

As the last notes fell silent, Morumus felt his muscles slacken. He could move again. Yet there was nowhere for him to go. He dared not try to escape down the vale that night. Nor dared he even to stir from his position, lest he attract the shadows' attention. All he could do was sit there beside the water and weep. And so he did, until finally he fell asleep.

7

The night drew back gently as the sun stirred itself in the east. The birds began chirping in the trees, and the river rippled gently in the clear pool. Under normal circumstances, it would have been a beautiful summer dawn in the vale. Instead, it seemed a rather cruel thing to young Morumus when the golden rays of dawn finally broke over the ridge of the Deasmor. Where had daylight been when the shadows moved freely? Why come shouting over the horizon now, when it was too late? Why illuminate what had happened in this place? Why should there ever be daylight again, when his father was dead?

Though Morumus lived and moved, he felt that he had lost his being. His flesh was whole, yet the specter of the shadows' inhumanity had cut him to the heart. Like their cruel blades it had sliced, mercilessly plunging, savagely ripping, and violently tearing at everything that made him feel human. He was unmoored and adrift. Once he had been an energetic boy. Now he was but a pale shade. He did not want to join the dead among which he moved. Yet how could he go on living after what he had witnessed? Life tasted like ashes on his tongue.

The worst of all was his father. At first Morumus would not go near him. Instead he walked among the bodies of the other men, circling the fringes of the fallen in an effort to avoid the center of the camp. Yet he knew that he had to look at least once before exposure swallowed dignity in decay. And so gradually he allowed his circling pattern to constrict, his steps spiraling slowly inward until at last he stood beside the body of his father.

The awful sight filled Morumus with abject misery. He felt as though his legs had been cut from beneath him, and he fell to his knees. His whole head suddenly felt closed up, and he began to sob. These were not light tears of anger or injury. Nor even were they the tears of shock, which often come upon one with the stinging suddenness of a summer storm. Rather, these were deep, manful tears—great heaves welling up from the depths of the soul.

Such was his state when the monk found him. At first Morumus thought the robed figure was the glorified spirit of his father. Blazing red hair grew from the untonsured portion of the monk's head. The same piercing green eyes glistened in a face similar to Raudorn's. The resemblance was striking. Despite Morumus's condition, recognition was not long in coming.

"Uncle . . ."

Raudorn's younger brother, Nerias, crossed the remaining distance in an instant and fell upon the boy with his embrace.

"I am too late." He croaked the words, and Morumus felt his uncle's tears mingle with his own. For several minutes there was silence as they both wept together.

After this, Morumus related—through sobs—what had happened. When he finished, Nerias spoke again.

"I am too late, yet praise God you are safe." Releasing Morumus, he stood and surveyed the vale, his tear-streaked face grim. "We must be gone from here at once. The Norns will

84

pass this way within the hour. Wait here while I get your horse."

Morumus did not argue, nor did he question. He just nodded. It had only been the surprise of Nerias's arrival that had moved his tongue. With that initial surprise now gone, he was once again numb. A few minutes passed. Then he heard the light clinking of horse-kit.

"We cannot bury him, Morumus." Nerias helped the boy into his saddle. "There is neither spade among the gear, nor time to spare. Have a last look, and then follow me." The monk climbed into his own saddle, turned, and moved his mount a few respectful steps away.

Morumus paid his last, silent respects to his father. As he looked upon him in this final frame, he was surprised to find a certain hint of dignity that he had missed hitherto. Not in death itself, for that indeed was still a horror and an enemy. Yet there was a repose in his father's face that suggested something beyond mere death. No light remained in those lifeless eyes, but there were also no lines in the brow or hard cast to the jaw. In fact—could it be?—there seemed almost a faint twinge of a smile at the corner of the mouth.

Morumus remembered then the words with which Raudorn had encouraged his men as they were dying. Though this did not diminish the pain that stuck like a dull knife in his stomach, it did wrap his wound in an absorbent, enfolding hope. He managed a faint smile, and a few final tears streaked farewell down his cheeks. Then he turned his mount away.

His father had died well, and someday Morumus would find him again. In the meantime, why seek the living among the dead?

The next few days were spent moving west through the Deasmor. They did not return down the Mathway dale toward Aban-Tur, which would have made less than a day's journey. Instead, Nerias led the way into the heart of the high country.

The paths they traveled were winding and treacherous, often forcing them to pick their way down steep switchbacks and across rough terrain. Although Morumus did not know how or why, his uncle seemed to have anticipated and prepared for this prolonged bivouac. There were ample provisions in his pack, and he seemed to find just the right place to stop each night. Nerias was no warrior, yet his skill in the wild seemed as good as any scout's.

It was a dour afternoon when they descended the last foothill and left the Deasmor behind. The lowland plain onto which they emerged was dreary and unremarkable, and from the fringe of the high country they traveled northwest until they joined a road. For two days they stuck with this road due north, and Morumus began to think that at last he saw his uncle's intent.

The need to avoid the Norns had forced them to travel evasively for a while, yet here at last they were turning back toward home. They would follow the road all the way to Dunross. They would find the king and report his father's murder. The king would rise in wrath, and the shadowy figures who had slaughtered the men of Aban-Tur would be sought out and destroyed. The Norns, too, would meet the king's steel—both for their unprovoked assault on Lothair, and for the loss incurred in giving them chase. Morumus would be reunited with his brother at the king's court. Together they would see justice rendered.

This being Morumus's expectation, he was astonished when Nerias turned his mount west on the third day. At first Morumus thought the departure might be but temporary. The day before, they had left the road for a few hours in order to avoid a village. Yet today there was no village in sight, and it soon appeared to Morumus that they were not merely bypassing a portion of the road. Nerias intended to abandon it. They were striking out over the open country toward the sea. Distressed at this unexpected change of direction, Morumus spurred his mount to bring him up beside his uncle.

"We are not going to Dunross, Morumus," Nerias answered when asked. "We are going to the coast, from whence we shall sail to Urras."

"But what of my father and his men?" He didn't try to quell the anger rising in his voice. "We *must* inform the king."

"It has been over a week since I found you. When the riders failed to return to Aban-Tur, doubtless those there mustered a search party. These will have found your father by now and sent word to the king."

"But my brother . . ." Morumus did not at all like what he was hearing. "He will need my help. Father always says—well, said—that he is too impulsive."

"That is true—Haedorn is much like your father. Yet he is the king's ward, not yours. The king will advise him. You cannot do more than the king."

"I can fight alongside him!" Morumus's temper was slipping.

Nerias put up one hand and shook his head. "No, Morumus. Unless the Norns agree to pay heavy compensation, both the king and your brother will soon be swept up in war. The best thing you can do to help your brother is to stay out of the thick of it."

At these words, Morumus lost control altogether. "The last person who told me to 'stay out of the thick of it' was Father—and he is dead!" He had stopped his horse and was shouting. "I will not sit by and watch like some helpless woman, Uncle! I will not run away—I will not!"

Nerias drew up on his own reins and turned back. "Son, listen to me—"

This time, Morumus cut him off. "I am not a boy, Uncle Nerias!"

"Then stop acting like a child!" Nerias growled, his face turning as red as his hair.

The violence of his response stopped Morumus short. In addition to looking like his brother, Nerias also resembled Raudorn in temperament. Anger seldom came to the surface. When it did, it was terrifying to behold.

Despite his brave words, Morumus subsided immediately. "I am sorry, Uncle. It's just . . ." But he let the sentence wither. What more could he say?

"It's all right, son." As the heat of the moment passed, Nerias resumed his calm. "He was my brother, you know."

Morumus nodded, and after another minute or so they were riding again—west, toward the sea. The country here was empty. Miles of green turf rolled gently toward the horizon, with no sign of human settlement as far as the eye could see. A sky banked heavy with grey clouds cast the whole landscape in faded hues, and tinged the summer air with a hint of rain. By the end of the day, they would have a storm.

After a few miles passed in silence, Nerias dropped back to ride beside Morumus. "I suppose you should like to know how I came to find you."

"I would. When I first saw you, you said you were 'too late.' And for the whole journey since, you seem to have had every step planned—as though you have known for some time exactly what was going to happen."

"Not exactly what would happen." Nerias sighed. "But enough to prepare."

"What do you mean?"

"I was warned that both you and your father were in danger."

"Warned? How?"

"A *tidusangan*."

Morumus started. "The divine song? But I thought that was only legend."

"*Tidusangan* is not 'divine song,' Morumus. That is a corruption. The word was in our language long before the first missionaries arrived in Aeld Gowan. It means 'time-song.'

It is simply a glimpse of what has happened—or what is to come."

"Oh. But do such things not come from God?"

"Only in the most common sense."

"Are they magic, then?"

"No more than possessing sharp wits or a strong arm. Some people see *tidusanganim*, while others—most—do not. Nothing more. It is a gift, son, but not a spiritual—or magical—endowment. How could it be anything more, when even the pagans saw the dreams?"

"Fine," Morumus said a bit sharply, annoyed at the correction. "Have you seen them before?"

Nerias ignored his nephew's tone. "No, but others of our line have. The gift often runs in the blood."

"What did you see?"

"I stood in the feasting hall of Aban-Tur. There was food on the board, but the hall was empty. I heard the noise of men and horses in the yard, but when I followed them outside I found the yard empty—except for a mouse. Yet this was no ordinary mouse. For one thing, it was red. For another, it could speak. When it saw me, the red mouse whispered something in a human voice—I did not catch the words—and then scampered out through the gate. I followed, trying to catch it. But it was too fast. Away it ran across the turf, away south along the river up-country. It moved by great leaps and seemed to glide over the surface of the ground. Somehow I was able to do likewise, so I followed. The mouse kept turning back and whispering to me, but I could never seem to get close enough to hear. All day I chased it like this, until finally at dusk we reached the dale with the river pool. Here the mouse froze in mid-leap, then crumpled to the ground. After this, I was able to catch up with it. But by the time I reached its side, the mouse was dying. Yet just before it died it spoke to me, and this time I heard it. The voice, Morumus, was that of your father."

89

"What did he say?"

Nerias's voice grew dark. "He said, 'Help us, Nerias. The night has gone mad! The shadows are alive!'" He paused for a moment, and when he began again his voice shook. "And indeed, Morumus, when I looked around in my dream, dusk had turned to night. For a few terrifying seconds, I saw the *Dree*. They circled around me, closing in and surrounding us with their terrible song. Then I woke up."

"*Dree*." Morumus repeated the strange word. It tasted foul in his mouth. "Who are the *Dree*, Uncle?"

Nerias turned his face back toward the horizon. He sighed—an old, weary sigh. "I do not know for certain, Morumus. I call them *Dree* because they are more like serpents than men. The name means 'night-adder.' They are the vestiges of the Dark Faith that once ruled all of the continent of Midgaddan as well as these isles. This was before the first missionaries arrived. The old stories speak of the *Dree* often. Yet none of the stories record what became of them after our people forsook heathenism. For a very long time, even centuries, it seemed they had just disappeared. Like so much else of the *erebanur*—the dark past—they were believed to have vanished when the light of our Lord Aesus dawned over Aeld Gowan. Then, some years ago when I was still in Caeldora, they began reappearing. The Church pursued them, but the trail went cold. I returned home. I did not know they had followed me until now."

Morumus nodded. "And now they are in league with the Norns."

"No." Nerias shook his head. "The *Dree* are in league with nobody but the devil."

"But Uncle, it cannot be mere coincidence that they were waiting to ambush us in the very place we laid in wait for the Nornish raiders."

"It is probably not a coincidence, but the *Dree* profess the Dark Faith. They would never ally themselves with an Aesusian such as the king of Nornindaal. As for the Norns, they were not with the *Dree*. I saw them approaching your position on the morning I found you. That is why we had to hurry."

"It still seems strange that the *Dree* knew right where to wait for us, and that they avoided our scouts. Father told me the woods had been searched thoroughly before we made camp."

"The old stories say that the priests of the Dark Faith practiced many black arts. It is told that they could wrap themselves in shadows. It is said, too, that they possessed ways of peering into distant councils."

"*Tidusanganim?*"

"Perhaps," said Nerias, "As I said, even the pagans see them."

Now that the conversation had turned back to dreams, a question arose in Morumus's mind. "Uncle, how did you know that what you saw in your dream had not happened already?"

"The last thing I saw before the dream ended was the full moon over the vale. But on the night of my dream, the moon was new over our monastery on Urras. Thus I concluded that I had roughly a fortnight to reach you. And so the next morning I packed provisions and drew enough coin to buy a horse, then sailed for the mainland. I knew that I could not save Raudorn—but I had hopes of saving you."

Morumus frowned. "But how did you know I would be with Father? That was the first time I ever rode out with the men."

Nerias looked at him, one eyebrow arched. "Yes, but there was the mouse."

"What about the mouse?"

"Your name, Morumus."

Now it was Morumus's turn to regard Nerias askance. "What do you mean, Uncle?"

"Do you not know the meaning of your own name, son?"

"I do." Did his uncle think him so ill-informed? "Father told me a long time ago. It is Old Lothairin, and means 'one who will stand before the great.'"

"Ah, Raudorn"—Nerias shook his head and smiled—"you never could accept it." Then he turned back to Morumus. "The word can mean that. However, that is not what your mother meant when she gave it to you."

"I don't understand."

"During the winter that your mother was pregnant with you, she fell ill and things looked grim. The midwife told her you would probably die, and that even she might not survive. The sickness was only treatable with regular tonic made of *laedhoth* root. Though it was not a common herb of our country, your mother laid some back every year, just in case one of the households needed treatment. She was always prudent like that—a very capable woman. Yet in the very winter of her affliction there had been a fire in one of your father's cellars, and most of the herbs perished—including the entire quantity of *laedhoth*."

Morumus had never heard any of this. "What happened?"

"Things got worse." Nerias stared off into the distance as they continued riding. Though his eyes looked west, it was obvious that they saw another time and place altogether. "The illness grew acute, and it was whispered among the household that your mother would not survive another fortnight. But she herself never gave up. She did not care overmuch for her own life; it was for your safety that she prayed without ceasing."

"I take it something must have happened?"

"Indeed," nodded Nerias. "Something most peculiar. One afternoon, a mouse appeared by your mother's bedside. Nobody had ever seen it before, but there it was—and in its mouth was a sprig of *laedhoth!*"

"For truth?"

"Yes, for truth. At first, none would believe your mother when she recounted how it came to her. They could not explain it themselves, yet her explanation seemed far too fanciful—a feverish delusion. Or so they thought. But then the next day it happened again. By this point, the household steward suspected thievery. He reckoned that one of the servant girls had stolen the *laedhoth* prior to the fire—perhaps even in the act of causing the fire—and was returning it now in discrete quantities with the hope of saving her mistress. So he hid in your mother's chamber one afternoon, hoping to catch the thief. Instead, he witnessed the mouse for himself."

"Mother recovered because of a mouse?"

"Yes, she made a full recovery. You were born a few months later."

"What happened to the mouse?"

"Nobody knows. The mouse vanished and was never seen again. Your mother believed it was a *heosunu*—an angel which took the form of a mouse."

Morumus's eyes widened. "Do you think she was right?"

Nerias shrugged. "What does it matter? You are alive, are you not?" Here he turned and studied Morumus. "The thing to remember, son, is that you owe your very life to the promises made to faithful prayer. Never forget that. Your mother gave you the name she did so that you *would* remember: 'Morumus' means 'root mouse' in Dyfanni—she used Dyfanni because *laedhoth* grows only in Dyfann."

"I will not forget, Uncle. But why have I never heard this before?"

"Your mother died before you were old enough to learn the story, and after her death your father forbade any mention of it to you."

"Why?"

"He said it was because he did not want his son to grow up with a weak name. Yet in truth, I think it was because that particular memory was too tender for him after your mother's death. The only reason I know the story is because the steward himself told me."

Morumus fell quiet for a minute before continuing. "So that is how you knew I would be with Father."

"That is how I knew."

After hearing such a wonderful story of his mother—of whom he knew so little—Morumus hated to turn back to dark considerations. The tale of his mother was a most pleasant portion of the past. Yet even this could not soothe the fresh wounds of the present.

"Even if they are not allied with the *Dree*, Uncle, the Norns still bear at least partial responsibility for my father's death. It was their raid which provoked our pursuit."

"It is so, Morumus." Nerias sighed. "And you can be sure that this point will not be lost in Dunross. But let us pray that the Norns will agree to pay compensation. It will be costly, but war would be more so."

"It may be our way to ransom murder by silver, but I think I would prefer war."

"So would the *Dree*," said Nerias pointedly. "They will turn any circumstance to their advantage. It makes a most sinister sense that they have seized this opportunity to ignite a border incursion into a full-scale war. Aesusians killing Aesusians is good for the pagans—especially if it means destroying the spiritual unity that Lothair and Nornindaal have held in common for generations. I understand how you feel, son. But there are greater things at stake than revenge."

"But it was awful, Uncle." Morumus forced the words through clenched teeth. "There was this noise—a sort of dark song, rising and falling. Once it began, Father and the men could not move. They just stood there helpless while the *Dree* butchered them—slowly. I could not do anything to help."

"You survived, Morumus. You know the truth, and that may be help enough. What's more, you have witnessed the *Dree* firsthand, and have lived to speak of it. I know of no man living who has achieved as much against them."

"But will knowing the truth avert a war, especially if we are not going to Dunross?"

"Nothing will avert a conflict now except heavy compensation."

"Then what good is it, Uncle?"

"At present, I do not know for certain." Nerias shook his head. "You say you witnessed a connection between this 'song' and the power of the *Dree*. None of the Churchmen who pursued them in the past ever learned as much."

"But what good is that, just to know that the *Dree* practice black magic? Didn't you tell me even the old stories say as much?"

"Magic?" Nerias looked cross. "Stop talking nonsense, boy. Whatever the *Dree*'s power is, it is not supernatural."

Morumus shook his head. "It didn't look natural to me."

"Of course not, for there is a powerful illusion involved. But mark my words, Morumus—at root, their power is counterfeit."

"How can you be so sure, Uncle?"

"Because if their power were real, they would conquer by day—rather than murder by night."

Morumus did not respond. His uncle had a point.

"I don't know how it works, son," Nerias continued. "Nobody does. But I suspect it has something to do with their speech." His uncle gave Morumus a tight smile. "Perhaps that is why you have been spared, Morumus. Perhaps God intends you to finally unmask the trickery of the *Dree*. Yet even if *this* be not the reason, Holy Writ tells us that God foreordains all things for his purposes. You were spared for a purpose, Morumus."

"To run and hide?" Retreat. An odious thought.

Nerias glanced over at him, and there was a glimmer of holy wrath in his green eyes. "To *survive* and wait for God's purpose to be revealed. That is why I cannot take you to Dunross, son. That is also why I cannot keep you with me even in Urras for more than a short time."

Morumus was more than a little bewildered by the last statement. "What do you mean, you cannot keep me in Urras? You are the *Abbot of Urras*, Uncle!"

"It's not that. If the *Dree* have returned to Lothair, then Urras is not safe. There is too much travel between our island and the mainland. Word of your survival would spread. And if the *Dree* learn that you are alive, they will kill you. So they must not learn that you are alive."

"Then where will I go?"

"To the same place I went at your age. You will go to Caeldora, to Lorudin Abbey."

PART II

SAVING BLOOD

The morning after Morumus's interview with Captain Brann, the company set out from Naud. For four days they traveled southeast along the same Vilguran road that had brought Grahem and Morumus from Lorudin. Yet on the day when they reached the mouth of the Lorudin Vale, the company did not turn aside to visit the abbey. They were due at Aevor as soon as possible, and the sun was only half-spent. Thus they pressed on. Three days later, the sun was again directly overhead as they closed the final leagues to their goal.

Seven men now constituted the company, and they had developed the habit of riding in three ranks. Leading the first rank was Abbot Grahem. Flanking him, one on either side, were the two bishops from the north countries of Aeld Gowan. The two northerners did not have much in common, so far as one considered their outward appearance. Bishop Ciolbail was a typical Lothairin, lean and dark. By contrast, Bishop Treowin was a husky Norn who looked as if he might be just as much at home on a longship as in a cathedral. Both men wore their hair cut in the peculiar tonsure of the north. Unlike the halo tonsure worn in Caeldora and the rest of

Midgaddan, the northern bishops had cut their hair in a triangular shape. The point of the triangle lay at the peak of the forehead, and the shaved sides curved back to finish behind the ears. Behind the ears, there was no restriction on the length of hair. Accordingly, Ciolbail wore his cropped close to the scalp, while Treowin's long hair gathered to a braid at the nape of his neck.

At the rear of the company rode Morumus and his uncle Nerias. It had been ten years since Nerias sent Morumus to Caeldora, and after such a period their reunion had been most joyful. Each day they rode together at the rear of the company, never lacking for matters to discuss.

The remaining two members of the company—two princes—rode in the middle rank. The first, Donnach, was the son of a Grendannathi chieftain whose name Morumus could not pronounce. The second prince was named Oethur. He was the son of Ulfered, king of Nornindaal—a name Morumus could only pronounce through tight lips and gritted teeth.

Like many second sons of ruling men, Donnach and Oethur had been removed from their home countries and relegated to the Church. This protected their lives and provided for the orderly succession of their elder brothers. Neither man yet wore the garb or tonsure of a monk, but that would soon change. At Aevor, each would receive the brown robe of Lorudin. After the Court of Saint Cephan, they would return to take up residence at the abbey. In the meantime, Morumus would be tutoring both in Vilguran.

Morumus had been looking forward to meeting Donnach. He felt quite different, however, about Oethur. The man was a Norn. It was because of Nornish raiders that his father was dead. That the Norns had not been *directly* responsible for his father's death mattered very little to Morumus.

As the horses climbed the final ascent to the city gates, he prayed that Oethur would be a quick learner.

The city of Aevor sat on a long hill just north of the River Lor. The hill itself was double-crested, allowing both castle and cathedral to look out over the surrounding country from a high vantage. A single massive wall encircled both summits and most of the hill, concealing most of the city behind a towering grey hedge. The western gates, flanked by round towers, formed the terminus of the Naud Road. With many hours yet before sunset, the wooden gates stood open to travelers.

Being a cathedral city, Aevor fell under the aegis of both imperial and ecclesiastical protection. Accordingly, there was a double contingent of guards at her gates. A little over half of them wore the same gold-on-green tabards, and carried the same red-tasseled spears, as the garrison soldiers in Naud. The rest wore light blue tabards with swords belted at their hips. Both groups snapped to attention at the approach of the delegation, but the cathedral guards looked doubly smart once they saw that the first two men carried bishops' staffs.

"Welcome to Aevor, Your Gracious—err, Graces."

Morumus winced at the lead cathedral guard's broken Vilguran. Even amongst the cathedral guards, few men below the rank of lieutenant spoke the ecclesiastical tongue.

"The peace of God be upon you," said Bishop Treowin in his deep, warm voice. "We are here to see your bishop. He is expecting us." The bishop spoke his Vilguran slowly in an attempt to make things easier for the soldier. But his thick Nornish accent made the results dubious—even to a trained ear.

The guardsman's eyes widened. His jaw twitched, but his lips wouldn't budge.

"Morumus, come up here!" called Bishop Ciolbail over his shoulder. Morumus had half expected this, so was ready and nudged his mount forward to the front of the delegation. When he came level with the bishops, Ciolbail directed him to translate for the struggling soldier.

"Make sense for the poor man out of Treowin's porridge" For all that Ciolbail tried to sound gruff, he couldn't quite conceal his amusement. Beside him, the Nornish bishop muttered a half-hearted protest.

"Their Graces the bishops bid you God's peace," Morumus said to the soldier in smooth Caeldoran. "We have come to see your bishop. He is expecting us."

"Ah!" The man's face lifted in relief at the vernacular. "Yes! Yes, indeed! Bishop Anathadus made it known that a distinguished company would be arriving. You are all most welcome." He bowed low to both bishops in turn, then straightened to direct his words to Morumus. "Please tell my lords that, if they please, I will take them to the bishop now."

Morumus related the man's words to the bishops, who nodded their consent. "Their Graces are pleased. Lead on."

The guardsman bowed again, then turned. "This way, Your Gracious!" he called back over his shoulder in Vilguran as he fairly whisked his way through the gates.

Morumus winced.

"I think he wants us to follow," Treowin said in a dry voice.

"I think you scared him, Your Gracious," Ciolbail responded to the Norn with a wink at Morumus.

"Ah," Morumus exhaled, wiping the water from his face with a soft cloth. "Much better."

He was standing in the room assigned to him in the cathedral cloister. It was a small chamber—smaller than his cell at Lorudin Abbey—but it was more than sufficient. The pallet was soft and promised solid rest. The water in the basin was cool, and he felt refreshed already. After so many days on the road, it was enough to have stopped moving. He had just wrung out the cloth and was moving toward the pallet when there was a knock at his door.

"Abbot Grahem." It was a surprise to see his superior standing alone in the doorway. Since the delegation had arrived in Naud, the abbot had rarely parted company from the bishops. "Is everything well, sir?"

"Will you walk with me, Morumus?" The older man stepped back and gestured toward the large courtyard beyond.

"Certainly, sir." He would rest later.

The cathedral cloister was organized around a large, rectangular courtyard. Surrounding this space was a colonnaded walkway, and it was yet mid-afternoon as Morumus emerged from his chamber. Beyond the shade of the portico, the grassy portions of the yard shone brilliant green under the bright sun. At the center of the courtyard, a small, unadorned fountain shimmered in the light like a tiny pool of diamonds.

"Did you get some rest?" Abbot Grahem folded his hands behind him as they walked.

"Not really—but I'll be fine, sir. I will sleep well tonight."

The abbot nodded. "We have not had much opportunity to speak since Naud."

"No, sir, and I still have your token." He reached into his robe to retrieve the abbot's disc.

"Keep it. I may need you to represent me again before too long. It will be some time before we return home. Already the road seems long, does it not?"

"It has been years since I spent so much time in a saddle."

"It has been long enough for me, too." Grahem smiled. "So, you have met Donnach?"

"Yes, sir."

"Is his Vilguran as bad as reported?"

A twinge of a smile tugged at the corner of Morumus's mouth. "It's a bit rough, sir, but with a bit of help I think he'll be fine."

"And Oethur?"

"We haven't spoken as much." The twinge vanished, and Morumus felt himself grow tense. He prayed that the conversation would shift.

The abbot gave Morumus a sideways look, and there was compassion in his expression. But there was also command. "'There is neither Semric nor Koinos, nor slave nor freeman, nor male and female, for ye all be one in Aesus,'" he quoted. "Is that clear, son?"

Morumus looked away. "Yes, sir."

"Good. I am counting on you, Morumus."

Morumus could only nod.

"Now"—the abbot's tone lightened—"about this translation you and Donnach are to undertake. I am afraid there is a problem."

Morumus started, and he looked back at the abbot. "Sir?"

"If you are going to engage in serious work, you will need better resources than we have at Lorudin."

The younger monk said nothing. Where was this going?

"Bishop Anathadus has an extensive personal library. There are certainly more complete lexicons in his collection than in our own. He has already agreed to lend us whatever resources you may find useful. We are going now so that I may introduce you to him."

Morumus's heart soared. "Thank you, sir!"

"You're welcome. But you must promise me that you won't neglect your tutoring—of either man. I don't ever want to hear Donnach or Oethur refer to a bishop as 'Your Gracious.' Is that understood?" Abbot Grahem kept his voice level and his eyes forward as he said this, yet Morumus was sure that he saw the glimmer of a grin at the corner of the older man's mouth.

"I promise, sir."

By this time, they had reached the bishop's apartments on the second floor of the cathedral residence. As might be expected, these were far more spacious than the cells allotted to regular priests and visitors. Bishop Anathadus had a total of five rooms overlooking the cloister courtyard. One of these provided him with sleeping quarters. A second served for his study. The remaining three housed his library.

Upon first glimpse, Morumus found the bishop somewhat underwhelming. He wore no adornments save the ring of his office, and even his cassock was but plain wool. As to his physical stature, Anathadus was short and thin. His tonsure was sparse and wispy, and appeared rather like a faint halo resting atop his olive-toned scalp.

"Grahem!" boomed Anathadus warmly as the two monks entered his study. He stepped around his desk to meet his old friend. "Lyzigus informed me of your arrival, but I did not expect to see you so soon. Do you not ever rest, man?"

"Plenty of time for that in the grave, Your Grace." Grahem smiled.

"'Eye hath not seen, nor mortal minds mused.' You are as hopeful as ever, old friend." The bishop turned his attention toward Morumus. "And who is this?"

"This is Morumus, Your Grace."

Abbot Grahem took a step sideways as he spoke, and Morumus bowed deeply. "It is an honor to meet you, Your Grace."

"And I am very pleased to meet you at last. You are Nerias's nephew, are you not?"

"I am, Your Grace." How did the bishop know his uncle?

"Even if I hadn't known"—the bishop eyed him—"you have the look of the Old People in you. Yet I detect very little of their accent. Your Vilguran is most clear."

"Thank you, Your Grace."

Anathadus smiled. "And you needn't keep up with the 'Your Grace,' Morumus. 'Sir' will do just as well, and is much less cumbersome. I didn't become suddenly holier when they handed me this ring. Nor am I able to dispense that of which I find myself so much in need. I only point the way. If we must retain the title, let us retain it only in public where such accretions are missed. Is that clear?"

Morumus nodded. "Yes, sir."

The bishop's eyes flickered toward the abbot. "The same goes for you, old friend."

Grahem inclined his head.

"That's settled, then," said the bishop. "Now, to our work." He looked back to Morumus. "I know of this translation you and our new barbarian brother are to undertake. This is a very serious task, Morumus, and you must take great care in it. There is no more important help for true religion than Holy Writ: without its illuminating rays, we are *all* bound over to barbarism and darkness. You must labor diligently to make this translation accurate and clear—lest the light be obscured. Do you understand?"

"I do, sir."

"Good." As he spoke, the bishop moved toward a small door set in the side wall near the windows. Taking a small key from somewhere within his robe, he unlocked the door and pushed it open. "To that end, I give you leave to plunder my library. Tomorrow we must depart for Versaden. But until then, you may have full access. My predecessors have acquired a large collection, and I have done what I can to add to their labors. Anything you find today, simply set aside on the table in the first room. When we return from Versaden, I will send it all back with you to Lorudin. There are some old lexicons that are quite large and unwieldy, but useful. Somewhere in there, too—you will have to dig for it—there is a very old copy of Holy Writ that includes Saint Herido's translation annotations. Unless you know Semric and Koinossa, I expect this will be invaluable."

A thrill surged up Morumus's spine. Saint Herido? The notes of the very man who first translated Holy Writ into Vilguran? Could such a treasure really be hiding just beyond that open door?

Beside him, Abbot Grahem chuckled. "Two languages even *you* haven't learned, Morumus."

Anathadus paused. He looked back at Grahem. "What do you mean?"

"He knows all the rest."

"Really?" Anathadus shifted his eyes to Morumus, and there was new regard in his gaze. "Tell me, Morumus, besides Vilguran, what other languages do you speak?"

Although there was nothing unwholesome in the bishop's expression, Morumus felt suddenly nervous. "Well sir, besides *Tuasraeth*—'Northspeech,' the language of my birth—I also learned Dyfannish and Mersian as a boy. My mother's servants spoke the former, and my father's duties at court required him to speak the latter.

"And of tongues this side of the Channel?"

"Only Vilguran and Caeldoran, sir."

"Only!" The bishop laughed. "Only? Ours is hardly an age of great learning. Even to speak Vilguran well might qualify you for an abbot's cowl—or worse, a bishop's ring!"

Beside Morumus, Abbot Grahem snorted. "Don't frighten him, sir. We want to keep him around for a bit!"

"Ah." The bishop nodded. "Quite right, old friend. Speaking of which"—he gestured toward the open library—"why don't you and I go for a walk and leave our young brother to the books. Where are Ciolbail and Treowin? The four of us have much to discuss."

The two men were almost through the study door when the bishop paused, turning back to address Morumus. "On the table in the first room you will find a complete sketch of the library, with the shelves drawn and marked. I should warn you, though: over the years, the plan has taken a more relative than regulative character. You will have to search a bit. But the sketch should at least put you in the right starting place."

Morumus nodded. "That will be most helpful, sir."

Within a minute, the footsteps of the two elder clerics had faded down the hallway. Morumus wasted no time. The open door before him beckoned.

The bishop's library was pure bookish pleasure. Each of the three rooms was the size of the bishop's study, and each connected to the next by a small open door near the windows. As he perched on the threshold and gazed down this makeshift corridor, there seemed to be no end to the collection. Sturdy rows of overstuffed shelves seemed to continue forever, each of them heaving with stacks of worn volumes. Along the wall at his left hand, sunlight streamed through the glass panes in thin beams, catching bits of dust suspended in their golden illumination. Morumus took a deep breath, and an aroma of dignified mustiness filled his nostrils. He let it out reluctantly. The library would not stir a strong potion in every heart. Yet it did in the soul of Morumus. Here was a refuge of whispering wisdom. Here was a hall of hidden treasures.

A painful thought occurred to him. "One afternoon will not be enough."

Yet less than an afternoon was all that he had. Thus Morumus set to work without any further delay. He found the bishop's chart and held it up to the light. Making sure it was oriented properly, he scanned the crowded diagram, scrutinizing the bishop's finely written, tiny handwriting. After a minute, he found the first thing for which he was looking: a shelf in the second room marked 'Grammar.' He took careful note of its position before setting the map back down on the table.

The large, south-facing windows provided each room with ample light, and so Morumus had no difficulty locating the proper shelf in the second room. Once here, it might still have taken him quite a long time to find the lexicons. There were no markings on the spines of these books, nor were they shelved in nice tidy rows. Instead, what Morumus encountered was a mixed arrangement. Large books lay flat in horizontal stacks. Small books stood on edge, but with their spines facing inward rather than out.

Morumus was helped, however, by the nature of his quest. Vilguran lexicons were by their nature large, and the bishop had remarked that the ones in his collection were especially so. Thus it did not take long for Morumus to identify three large folio volumes piled one atop the other near the middle of the shelf. He pulled these down one at a time, examining each individually. Taken together, the three thick volumes formed a single, seemingly exhaustive lexicon of the Vilguran language. The entries were arranged alphabetically, and for each word there was included not only its definition, but also a list of the various forms in which it occurred. Morumus smiled. Then he carried the three volumes back to the first room and set them on the table.

With the lexicon accounted for, all that remained was to find the Herido translation. Morumus consulted the chart. According to it, the shelf containing copies of Holy Writ was at the back of this first room. He found the place easily enough, but none of the books stood out. So he began pulling and checking each volume.

The bishop's collection contained numerous copies of Holy Writ. Several of these were beautifully illuminated: embellished words opened each chapter, and delicate illustrations adorned the margins. Other volumes were less ornate, yet written in a clear script suitable for reading and studying. Indeed, by the time he reached the end of the shelf, Morumus had handled many well-made editions of Holy Writ. Yet the Herido translation had not been among them.

He sighed. "He did say I'd have to hunt for it."

The hunt proved to be frustrating. Returning to the table, Morumus picked up the shelf map and carried it over to the windows. For several minutes he pored over it. Yet scrutinize as he might, he could not find another shelf marked 'Revelation' in any of the three rooms. It occurred to him then that perhaps Herido's work might be in the same place he had found the lexicon. After all, might not commentary on the words of the original languages be somewhat similar to what one found in a dictionary?

Taking the map with him, Morumus went to check—only to find himself several minutes later standing at the end of the 'Grammar' shelf without his prize. After this he tried several more shelves from the map, widening his search with each attempt. 'History' housed several interesting works, and 'Antiquities' contained numerous books in strange-looking scripts. Yet neither contained the one he sought. Even his most desperate attempt—'Miscellanies'—had proven fruitless.

If Morumus was going to find the work of Herido, it would have to be soon. He was standing in the third room at this point, and the daylight that had poured through the windows when he began was now beginning to diminish. If the chart could not lead him to the right location, he would have to find the book by a normal search. He looked down at the map, counting quickly. According to the sketch, there were six rows of shelves in this room. If he hurried, he might get through them all before the light failed.

Morumus set the map down on the table beside the windows and walked toward the back of the room. While the light lasted, he would begin where it penetrated least. He passed each stack in turn: one, two, three, four, five, and six. Reaching the last shelf, Morumus turned to walk down the back aisle behind it. But no sooner he had turned than he stopped short. Tucked into the back corner, perpendicular to the sixth shelf—was a seventh.

Seeing it, Morumus felt a surge of hope. The map had not led him to Herido's work because the map was incomplete! "This has got to be it!" He hurried toward the seventh shelf.

Reaching it, he noticed almost immediately that one volume looked different from the others. Lying flat by itself on the very top shelf, this book was neither overly large nor significantly thicker that the others. What made it stand out was its binding. Every book Morumus had seen so far in the bishop's library was bound in plain boards or leather. Indeed, never in his life had he seen a book that was *not* bound in one or the other. But when he saw this book, he realized that its spine was neither wood nor skin.

It was bone.

"What is this?" He pulled the volume down. Turning it over in his hands, he was relieved—somewhat—to find that the front and back covers were made of regular leather overboards. "So only the spine is bone," he mused—then realized what he was saying. *Only the spine?*

Feeling more than a little apprehensive, Morumus brought the book out from the back corner to the windows. As he set it down on the table, he noticed for the first time that there was an image stamped into the front cover. The image was not easy to see, for the inlay was neither gold nor silver, but rather a dark bronze leaf that barely stood out against the black leather. Gripping the book by the bottom edge of its covers— he did not especially like touching the bone—Morumus tilted the volume up into the light. An instant later he dropped it, gasping and jumping back from the table as suddenly as if the book had become a serpent.

Of course no actual transformation had occurred. Yet the waning afternoon sunlight had revealed something just as sinister—in its own way something much *worse* than a transformation. For

111

in the instant when the light caught the book's cover, Morumus saw darkness come alive.

There was no mistaking it. The image embossed in bronze on the black leather was the tree from his nightmare—the tree whose crows had turned into *Dree*.

The air around Morumus stirred, ominous. He felt a chill crawl up his back.

"No. No, it cannot be real. It cannot."

"Oh, but it is," said a voice from somewhere close by. "It is all too real."

Morumus nearly jumped out of his robe. There, in the doorway to his left, stood Bishop Anathadus. The old man's dark skin looked pale, and Morumus could not read his expression. Was it fear, or fury? Something in between, or both?

"What are you doing with this, Morumus?" Anathadus stepped into the room and picked up the book. Like Morumus, he held the volume by its cover rather than its spine.

"Your Grace—sir," Morumus fumbled for his words, still reeling from the double-shock. "I found it on the back shelf while looking for the Herido translation. It stood out from the others . . ." His voice trailed off under the bishop's penetrating gaze.

"Why did you react so violently at the image on its front?" The bishop's tone demanded a response. "Have you seen such a tree before? Look at me, Morumus, and answer."

Morumus raised his eyes to meet the bishop's. He knew in that instant that those eyes could not be deceived. "I have seen the tree in a nightmare, sir."

"Nowhere else?"

"Nowhere else."

For several tense moments Bishop Anathadus said nothing, but his eyes blazed with a dangerous intensity. It was the kind of look Morumus had seen on the face of his father as a boy, when he was trying to decide whether one of his sons had lied to him.

"Pray God you remain so fortunate." The bishop stepped past Morumus and walked to the back of the room, where he restored the book to its high shelf. When he returned, his expression had lost some of its previous fire.

"So the tree is real?"

"I have never seen it." The bishop's voice was low. "But I believe that it is."

"Sir," Morumus began as the bishop escorted him out of the library, "please, if you could just tell me what it means?"

But Anathadus held up one hand as they stepped through the last door into his study. "No, Morumus. We will leave such things to the dark corners where they belong—my library and your nightmare. We will not speak of them again. Do you understand?"

Understanding was the furthest thing from Morumus's mind, but he nodded his head and answered in a subdued tone. "Yes, sir."

"Good. Now come, we must focus: supper, prayers, and then sleep."

"Sir, I did not find the Herido work."

"Never mind that. Lyzigus will find it while we are away. We have larger events to which we must attend. Tomorrow we leave for Versaden and the Court of Saint Cephan."

9

"But among all people, he who fears Him and practices righteousness—he is accepted to Him."

"That's not bad, Donnach." Morumus looked up from the page where he had been following along. "But in the last phrase, the Vilguran word is 'acceptable,' not 'accepted.' It describes the man, not an action."

"Okay." Donnach looked back down at the breviary he had borrowed from Nerias. "So if I am hearing you good, this verse should speak: 'But among all people, he who fears Him and practices righteousness—he is *acceptable* to Him'?"

"That's right." Morumus winced inwardly at such expressions as "hearing you good" and "verse should speak," yet he did not want to discourage the Grendannathi.

It was now the third evening since the company of churchmen left Aevor. The addition of Bishop Anathadus and one of his guardsmen had increased their number to nine. They were making good progress; if they kept their current pace, they would reach the imperial capital in another day and a half. Tonight they had stopped at a minor town along the straight Versaden Road, and were staying in a few rooms attached to the parish church. The parish was not large, and so neither were the rooms. Consequently, even the bishops had to share.

Morumus turned to third man rooming with him and Donnach. "It's your turn, Oethur."

"Where?" The Norn held Abbot Grahem's loaned breviary up to the lamplight and squinted at the page.

"Verse thirty-six," Morumus answered—a bit tersely. Hadn't Oethur been following along?

"Okay," said Oethur, "I have it. 'The word which he will send to the sons—'"

"No," Morumus interrupted. "You've done it again, Oethur. Look at the form of the word. It's not 'will send,' it's 'sent.' The verb is not future, it's past. Pay attention to the form."

"I *am* paying attention. The words look similar."

Morumus shook his head. "The forms use different principal parts."

"There is only a letter's distance."

"A letter's *difference*." Morumus grit his teeth. "And that's why you need to pay attention."

Tonight was the third time Morumus had sat down with Donnach and Oethur to tutor them in Vilguran. So far, things were going exactly as they had gone the first two nights. Donnach was an eager student and took correction without protest. Oethur, on the other hand . . . well, tutoring him was as bad as Morumus had imagined it would be. The Norn was no less intelligent than Donnach. Yet he was far less amenable to correction, and far more easily frustrated by his own mistakes.

"Let me try it again." This time it was Oethur who spoke through gritted teeth.

"Go ahead."

"The word he sent—"

"*Which* he sent," Morumus interjected.

"I know it!"

"You didn't say it."

"Ugh!" Oethur slammed shut the breviary. "I do not sight why we have to learn this way. Why can we not practice by mouthing?"

Before Morumus could reply, a new voice intruded—making all three of the younger men jump.

"Mouthing?" it said in a thick accent.

Turning in their seats, Morumus, Donnach, and Oethur saw the door to their room filled by the figures of Abbot Grahem and Bishop Treowin. One of them held a small lamp. In its dim orb, the latter's brows were furrowed.

"Bishop Treowin." Oethur sounded suddenly somber. "I did not know you were there."

"Of course not. We didn't intend you to know. Now tell me, Oethur, what in all lands is 'mouthing'?"

Oethur's face flushed. "Sir, what I meant to say was—"

"I know what you meant to say, boy. Your mistake answers your own question. If you cannot get the words right when they are in front of you, how will you fare any better if they are not? If you do not read well, you will not speak well." "I know." Oethur's Vilguran slipped as he spoke. "I just do not sight why always we must use a book."

"Holy Writ is not just a book," retorted Treowin. "It is *the* Book, Oethur—the very Word of God. This is what makes us different from the Mersians back home and most of the Church on this continent. We don't just carry Holy Writ about as though it were an object of worship. We read it. We pray it. We sing it. It is our very life, the supreme rule of everything we do. We live by it, and by it alone. You will not complain about reading Holy Writ again. Is that clear?"

Oethur dropped his gaze before the bishop's rebuke. His cheeks were bright red, his jaw set, and his lowered eyes smoldered with anger. Yet when he spoke, both his voice and his words were well-guarded. "Yes, sir."

"Good," said Treowin gruffly. "Now that's settled, by all means carry on." He turned in the doorway and disappeared down the hall.

Still holding the lamp in the doorway, Abbot Grahem paused before following the bishop. He looked directly at Morumus. "'Neither Semric nor Koinos.' *Is that clear?*"

"Yes, sir," said Morumus.

"Do not forget it." The abbot turned to follow the bishop.

For several minutes after this, the three monks sat in silence, listening to the receding footsteps of their superiors.

"Well," said Donnach after the last echo had faded. He smiled first at Morumus, then at Oethur. "We shall have to remember to latch the door."

Neither man returned the Grendannathi's smile.

"Are we finished for this night?"

"No, Oethur. We will finish the chapter." Morumus gestured toward Donnach. "It's your turn. Verse thirty-seven."

For the next quarter hour, they plowed on through the text. The passage they were reading contained the sermon of Saint Cephan to the household of Coranelix the Legionary, but none of the three men could truly focus. From the cast of his face, Oethur was still seething from the embarrassment of the bishop's censure. Morumus, too, still felt the sting of Abbot Grahem's rebuke. For his part, Donnach tried to counteract the tension by a sort of forced cheerfulness. Yet with every glance at the other two, his effort grew thinner.

The situation finally boiled over when they reached the last verse of the chapter. It was Oethur's turn. He held the small book up to the light, squinting at the text on the page. Morumus was waiting.

"And he will command them to baptize in the name of Aesus—"

"No, Oethur. You've got the verbs wrong. It's not—"

"Wait! I see it. 'And he will command them to *be baptized* in the name of Aesus–'"

"No. That's still wrong."

Oethur held the book closer. "No, it is right. I can sight that it is right. The word is 'to be baptized.'"

Piqued both at the interruption and the attempted correction, Morumus exhaled sharply. When he spoke, his voice was caustic. "Yes, yes, you've figured that one out at last. Well done. But you are still making the very same mistake with the first verb that you have been making all night. It is *not* 'he will command,' Oethur. It is 'he commanded.' The verb is not future; it's past. Don't presume to correct me unless you actually know what you're talking about."

Oethur lowered the book and stared hard at Morumus. "I was not—correcting—you. I thought you meant the other word."

"Did I *say* I meant the other word?"

"No, but I—"

"Then stop interrupting me and start paying more attention to the verb forms."

Oethur's face, which had been gradually returning to normal color as they worked, once again flushed scarlet. "I *am* trying!" he said through gritted teeth.

"Obviously not enough!"

"Aagh!" Oethur growled, slamming shut the book for the second time and surging to his feet. His nostrils flared, and for several moments his eyes contemplated violence.

Morumus was on his feet before he knew it, his own anger blazing. "Go ahead," he hissed, clenching his fists.

"Brothers, please!" Donnach was on his feet now, looking from one to the other. "This is foolish!"

Oethur's eyes flickered toward Donnach, and he relaxed. He shook his head once, then nodded. "You are in the right, Donnach." His breathing grew less agitated. "This is waste."

Donnach nodded. "Yes. Now please, both of you, sit back down."

"No." Oethur gave a hard shake of his head. "What is waste is sitting here with *him*." He jabbed his finger at Morumus. "You are a rotten tutor." He turned toward the door. "I am leaving." As he stepped away, he switched from Vilguran to Northspeech and muttered just loud enough for Morumus to hear. "Insufferable, sanctimonious *scurn*."

Had Donnach not stepped between them at precisely that moment, Morumus would have leapt at Oethur.

"Stop it, brother." Donnach planted himself in Morumus's way. He held up a finger. "Do not try to go after him, and do not taunt him more. Let him go." The tone of his voice carried an implicit warning, and reminded Morumus that though Donnach was a monk now, he had been born a warrior prince.

"Good riddance." Morumus returned to his seat. He picked up his breviary and found the place. "Shall we finish?" When after several moments there was no reply, he looked up.

Donnach had also returned to his seat, and was looking at Morumus. The reproach in his eyes was evident. "Why, brother?"

"Why what?"

"You know what." Donnach gestured toward the door through which Oethur had vanished. "It has been this manner every night. Why do you treat him thus?"

Morumus snorted. "If he won't listen, he won't learn."

"Forgive me brother, but you are not being true. Oethur listens. He learns. His speech is better than mine. Yet you show him no grace. Why?"

Morumus looked away. He liked Donnach, but he didn't want to have this conversation. "It's complicated."

"I do not know this word, 'complicated,' but I have seen my father speak better to his sworn enemy. Why do you treat Oethur like an opposite?"

"Opposite?"

"Sorry." Donnach paused. "I meant 'opponent.'"

"Oh. Well, like I told you, it's complica—" Morumus looked at Donnach—and stopped. There was no guile in the Grendannathi's expression—only confusion, and perhaps a touch of concern. In the next moment, Morumus made up his mind.

"His people are responsible for the death of my father."

"For truth?" Donnach frowned. "But is there not peace between your peoples?"

"There is."

"Then how?"

"A raiding party crossed the border. It was an unprovoked attack."

"I see." Donnach nodded, grim. "Such things often happen among my own people. But Oethur himself was not involved?"

"No, he was not. But his father is the king. Kings must answer for their subjects."

"But Oethur is *not* the king," Donnach pointed out gently.

"No."

"Among my people, where there are many feuds, the missionaries often quote Holy Writ: 'Fathers shall not be killed on account of sons, neither shall sons be killed on account of fathers.'"

Morumus grunted and looked away.

"And then there is this very passage before us tonight."

"What do you mean?"

"Lord Aesus sent Cephan to a Legionary."

"Yes. So?"

"Were not the Legionaries the ones who executed the Lord? Were they not responsible for his death?" Donnach was looking straight at Morumus now. "And yet, brother, the Lord forgave Coranelix."

Morumus's heart lurched, and he rose to his feet. "I think I'll go for a walk, too."

Donnach was right. Morumus knew it.

He just wasn't ready to admit it.

10

"Stop that false grabber!"

"Stop, thief!"

Oethur and Morumus were running as fast as they could. It was market day, and the town's narrow streets were choked with merchants' stalls and milling crowds. Over the din, the two men shouted at the *top* of their lungs—Oethur in his fumbling Vilguran, and Morumus in Caeldoran.

The thief had a good lead on them. A man clad in a shabby brown coat, he shoved his way through the thick crowds, leaving a sea of bewildered faces in his wake. Morumus and Oethur continued to run and shout after him, but the thief seemed to keep just ahead of them. There were so many people in the market, and so much noise. By the time folks became aware of what was happening, the villain had already pushed through their midst. After he had passed, the crowd would again close ranks and gawk after him—only to have to part again moments later for Morumus and Oethur. The result of all this was that the thief continued to elude his two pursuers, and by an ever-increasing margin.

Yet neither monk was about to give up—not when their supper was at stake. The town in which they were staying, called Dericus, was less than a day's journey distant from Versaden. With the Court of Saint Cephan set to convene in the imperial capital two days hence, all of the inns and taverns of Dericus were full. Yet somehow, Bishop Anathadus's guardsman—a very capable fellow named Nack—had managed to find them rooms. He had even managed to secure a promise from the innkeeper to provide the bishops and abbots with supper. When it came to the non-dignitaries, however, the harried landlord was much less accommodating. He would permit Oethur, Donnach, Morumus, and Nack to sleep in his stable loft. But when it came to board, they were on their own.

I wish Nack were here now! Morumus dodged another bystander as the thief turned out of the main stream of people. Forcing a violent passage between two produce carts, the man dashed down an alley. "This way!" Morumus shouted to Oethur as he veered to follow.

In truth, Nack probably *would* have been with them in the market, had it not been for Morumus and Oethur's fight the previous night. Bishop Treowin and Abbot Grahem had been especially piqued that their personal interventions had gone unheeded. The sentence was merciless: until they learned to get on well, Morumus and Oethur would perform *every* chore and errand for the entire company.

Together.

Consequently, the task of fetching provisions for the four stable-dwellers had fallen that afternoon to Morumus and Oethur rather than to Nack. Rather than the one man who could have made short work of this thief, it was the two ill-equipped monks who had to give inglorious chase through the streets and alleys of Dericus. The sight of them stumbling after the thief made an undignified spectacle. The only way in which a robed monk can run is by pulling the back of his robe forward between his legs and tucking it up into the front of his belt—a fairly awkward arrangement. Morumus was sure that both he and Oethur appeared more than slightly ridiculous. Yet he knew they had brought it upon themselves.

Morumus dashed between the two overturned carts, jumping the heaps of spilled produce. They could not afford to lose this thief. The vendors shouted angrily after him as they leapt aside, and he called apologies back over his shoulder. Entering the long alley, he nearly gagged. The stench of human waste was so strong that he could almost taste it, and he dared not think too intently on the sort of mess through which his feet splashed.

"*Scurn!*" Oethur cursed as he entered the alley behind Morumus.

Ahead, Morumus saw the thief nearing the far end where this alley dumped into a second running perpendicular to it. Keeping his eyes on the man to see whether he would turn left or right, Morumus forced his tiring legs to increase their pace. He had little doubt that losing sight of the thief would mean losing their supper. Dark alleys were for thieves as deep woods were for deer: a natural habitat in which they could easily disappear.

Yet as it turned out, Morumus never got the opportunity to test his thesis. The thief reached the end of the alley running full tilt, but as he tried to turn left he planted his right foot smack into the middle of a puddle of scurn. The foot slipped sideways as he pivoted, and the next instant he lost his footing entirely. The thief hit the ground hard, his breath knocked from his lungs. There was a loud grunt, and for several moments the man did not move.

"Come on!" Morumus shouted over his shoulder, rushing forward. "We have him!" With the thief lying stunned and Morumus running, the gap between them disappeared. Still gasping for air, the man pushed up to his hands and knees. But by this time, Morumus had closed to within a dozen paces. In mere moments he would be on him.

"Careful!" Oethur warned. But it was too late. Just as Morumus reached the thief, the man made as if he were going to stand. Seeing this, Morumus leapt.

"Stop!" he shouted in mid-flight.

But the thief's movement had been a ruse. As Morumus dove, he sprang to action. Instead of leaping forward, he pushed straight up and turned under the tackle. Now Morumus's momentum worked against him. With a single fluid movement, the thief rolled Morumus over his back and flung him away. Before the younger man knew what had happened, he lay sprawled on his back. His vision blurred with bits of black. Through the ringing in his ears, he could hear the thief's coarse laughter and heavy footsteps receding quickly.

Oethur arrived a moment later. "Are you broken, Morumus?"

"I'll be fine," Morumus gasped. "Go after him!"

"Are you correct?"

Morumus winced, both at the bad Vilguran and the pain in his shoulder. "Yes, I'm *certain*. Go!"

As Oethur renewed the pursuit, Morumus got to his feet. The black flecks had vanished from his vision, and he would have an ugly bruise on his shoulder where he had landed. Yet he was unhurt otherwise. Regaining his breath, he hurried after Oethur.

At the end of the second alley, Morumus came to a wide street. Here was more market activity. Along both sides of the street were carts full of colorful wares guarded by wary vendors. Throngs of people filled the space between—shopping, shouting, and shoving. Punctuating the crowd at various points were hawkers standing on crates—fearless performers clad in garish colors. These gesticulated wildly with their arms, declaiming their wares with almost prophetic zeal. The afternoon was over halfway spent. Eagerness to finish the day's business filled every face.

Confronted by this sea of activity, it took Morumus several moments to locate any trace of Oethur or the thief. Then he noticed a ripple in the crowd off at the far right corner of his vision. Unable to see anything more from street level, he located an empty crate sitting next to a vendor's cart. He overturned it and climbed up.

Morumus had to squint to see clearly. He was looking west, and the sun shone bright that afternoon through a cloudless blue sky. But once his eyes focused, he saw that it was indeed Oethur and the thief causing the disturbance. Somehow the Norn had caught up, and the two of them were now tumbling on the ground, locked in combat. As is almost always the case, the crowds had opened a small circle around the fighting men. It was this ripple that had caught Morumus's eye.

"Help that monk!" he shouted over the heads of the people. "The other man is a thief!"

Without waiting to see whether they would comply, Morumus jumped down from the crate and pushed his way through the crowds. This was no easy task, for by now the circle around the fight had accrued several rings of spectators—and nobody likes it when somebody tries to push in front of them on such an occasion. Yet Morumus was determined.

He reached the inner edge of the ring just in time to see the thief roll away from Oethur and come back to his feet. The grubby man reached for his belt, and there was a flash of steel. When he raised his fist gain, it clutched a long knife. Unlike the rest of the thief, the knife was clean and oiled. It gleamed wickedly in the sunlight.

A hush fell over the crowd.

Rolling to his own feet several paces away, Oethur saw the knife and assumed a defensive stance. Almost without realizing it, Morumus nodded. Oethur might be a monk now, but he too had been born into a warrior house.

"What's the matter, monky?" sneered the thief as they circled one another. "Not so brave against this?" He brandished the knife.

Morumus knew that Oethur understood nothing of the thief's words, for the Norn did not speak Caeldoran. But the man's gesture and tone needed no translation. "Give it up, false grabber," Oethur commanded through gritted teeth in coarse Vilguran, "or you will lose your head instead of just your hand!"

Morumus could see that Oethur's words were equally lost on the thief. Yet as had been the case in reverse a moment earlier, the man seemed to discern the Norn's meaning. In response, he simply snarled—and lunged.

A few women in the crowd gasped, but Oethur was quick on his feet and had seen the attack coming. He easily side-stepped, and the thief, having overextended with his lunge, stumbled and fell forward. Staying well clear of the knife, Oethur kicked the man in the ribs—hard.

Several people in the crowd laughed, and Morumus nodded again—this time consciously. Apparently he and Oethur had received similar training. When fighting a single opponent hand-to-hand, detecting a lunge in advance was not all that difficult. All one had to do was to watch his opponent's waist. Hands and heads may fake, but hips cannot lie.

The thief rolled back to his feet. He paused only long enough to spit, which came out more blood than saliva. Then he lunged again.

Oethur again dodged the attack, but this time the man retained his balance and turned the missed lunge into a back-handed slash. This would have caught Oethur in the throat, had he leapt backward even a split second later than he did. But in jumping back, Oethur lost his balance and fell backwards. With practiced speed, the thief rolled the knife in his fingers to a reverse grip and plunged for the kill. The blade fell fast, aimed at the chest. Several bystanders—this time both men and women—gave alarmed shouts. Yet despite the hard tumble, Oethur managed at the last possible instant to roll sideways on the ground. The knife whisked past him and stuck fast between two stones in the cobbled pavement.

The entirety of the fight up to this point had taken less than a minute. Morumus had stood poised on the edge of the circle the entire time, watching for an opening as the men circled. Until this moment there had been none. Now, as the knife bit deep into the street and Oethur rolled clear, he saw his chance. Breaking rank with the onlookers, he rushed into the ring.

"Aaahhh!" he shouted, diving at the man. The thief, who was still trying to free his knife, looked up too late. Morumus slammed into him sideways. The thief lost his grip on the knife, and both he and Morumus tumbled.

Without his weapon, the thief was back to where he had begun with Oethur—grappling and rolling on the street, fighting hand-to-hand for advantage. He must have been tired. Nevertheless, the man fought like a cornered animal.

In truth, the thief had much more to lose. Oethur's threat had been no exaggeration. The law stated that the hand that stole would be cut off. Though the immediate loss of a hand did not prove fatal, the infection that often followed could be deadly. Those who survived fared little better. Because they were crippled, they could not do most manual work. Because they bore the obvious mark of a criminal, few would trust them with anything else.

For all the thief's ferocity, the struggle was soon ended. Though few things might match a strength born of desperation, two determined monks could. Moreover, like Oethur, Morumus himself was no weakling. He too had grown up among warriors. Together he and the Norn soon had the man pinned to the ground.

Just then there was a new sound in the street. A voice thundered over the din of the crowd, and with the voice came the sound of clopping hooves.

"Give way! Give way at once!"

The circle of onlookers parted to admit half a dozen soldiers, along with two men on horseback. The men on foot wore the imperial green and gold, and carried swords at their belts. The first horseman was similarly clad, with the addition of a red-plumed hat that marked him as an officer. His had been the voice that first boomed over the crowd—and was booming again now.

"Seize them!" He gestured at Oethur, Morumus, and the thief. The officer spoke Caeldoran, and the soldiers complied immediately. Soon all three combatants were hoisted to their feet and held tight.

"What is the meaning of this disturbance?" demanded a second voice, this time in heavily-accented Vilguran.

This was the second horseman—a figure quite unlike the others. Just as the soldiers' swords and tabards clearly marked them as such, so this man's robe indicated that he was of the clergy. Yet Morumus had never seen nor heard of a religious order like this. The usual colors for monastic regulars were black, brown or grey. Bishops wore white, and archbishops wore purple. What then was the meaning of this man's garb?

The robe worn by the second horseman was deep red, and he wore his cowl completely up over his head. His appearance had an immediate and obvious effect upon the crowd. Eyes averted. Faces became subdued. Even Oethur and Morumus, who had no idea at whom they looked, felt rather unsettled by the red horseman. In the sunlight, the shifting folds of his robe had the appearance of flowing blood. Looking upon him made Morumus feel as though he were staring at a gushing wound.

The mysteriously clad cleric feigned not to notice the effect of his arrival. He drew up his horse beside the guard officer's mount and extended one arm. A thin hand emerged from the long sleeve, and a single finger pointed down at Morumus.

"You! Explain this!" As the cleric pointed, Morumus noticed a peculiar tattoo on his hand and wrist. It looked mostly like a cross, but with its bottom split into pieces.

"Your Grace." Morumus wondered whether he was using the appropriate title. "My brother and I are monks traveling to the Court of Saint Cephan. We were buying food in the market when this thief grabbed our provisions and tried to escape." Here Morumus gestured to the somewhat soiled, but thankfully intact bag lying near the center of the circle. "We called for help and gave chase, and when we caught the man he tried to kill my brother." Morumus finished by pointing to the long knife—still planted where it had stuck.

"It is not true, Your Grace!" shouted the thief, jerking himself free of his guard and throwing himself prostrate. He may not have understood Morumus's words, but he had been watching the monk's gestures and seemed to have got the gist. "The food is mine, and the knife is theirs! Where would a simple man like me get such a fine blade? I am but a poor wretch, and came to spend the last of my money to buy bread for my wife and children. These men are not monks, but imposters! They attacked me, and tried to steal away my family's substance!"

The cleric turned toward the officer of the guard, who translated the thief's words into Vilguran. After listening the cleric asked, "What say you, Captain?"

"I say this man is lying," came the answer. "But let us make certain." He barked a quick command, and one of his regulars walked over and took up the sack from the ground. "Let each tell us the contents of the bag," said the captain. "How many loaves does it contain? The one who speaks correctly is the true owner." He pointed to the thief. "You go first."

Panic flashed in the shabby man's eyes, but he smothered it and turned his head to look at the sack in the soldier's hand.

For a long moment he appraised it, cocking his head to one side. Then he turned back to the horsemen.

"I bought four loaves, my lords."

The captain next pointed to Morumus. "And what say you?"

"There are four loaves, *and* a small round of cheese."

The captain gestured to his man, who opened the sack and ruffled through it.

"Four loaves and one cheese, sir."

"Take him." The captain gestured at the thief, and the man who had held him previously seized him again. But the thief was not finished.

"Your Grace!" He pulled away and fell to his knees again. "It is a common thief's trick to add a small trifling to a bag of stolen goods, in order to appear the lawful owner." He gestured at Morumus. "Note how he added the cheese, when my lord asked only about the loaves."

"And how do you know so much about thieves' tricks?" asked the captain after translating for the cleric. But though he addressed his question to the thief, he eyed Morumus.

"My brother"—the thief sounded doleful—"My brother lived for many years outside the law. I did not know it until he appeared on my door, short one hand. He confessed that his punishment was just, so we took him under our care. It was he who warned me of the ways of thieves." The man turned and cast a baleful look at Morumus. "Truly, Your Grace, he warned me just this morning. He warned me that with the great Council starting tomorrow, I should watch for any devilish rogues who might dare to steal under the guise of the Church."

Morumus had to admit the thief was clever, though he wished it were not so. The captain's eyes grew more suspicious, and the cleric's faceless gaze was chilling. Even some of the people in the crowd—folks who had seen the thief pull the knife but minutes ago—now eyed Morumus and Oethur.

It was at that moment that Morumus remembered Abbot Grahem's token.

Morumus had kept the disc in the pocket of his robe ever since the abbot had refused its return. But as he remembered, his heart lurched. Did he still have it, after that long chase? With his arms held behind his back, he had no free hand with which to check. Yet as he shifted in place, he could feel something thick pressed between his belt and his left hip.

Morumus praised God. He had not lost it! Then he spoke up.

"Your Grace and my lord," he said formally, "we are neither pretenders nor thieves. This I can prove, if you will but permit me the freedom of my hands."

The captain's eyes narrowed. He looked from Morumus to the knife stuck in the ground a few feet away, and then back to Morumus. The he gestured to the guard. "Release him, but be ready."

With his arms freed, Morumus reached into his robe. Withdrawing the *brer* disc, he held it up for all to see. "This token bears the name of my superior. It is true *brer*, just as we are true monks."

"Bring it to me."

Morumus obeyed. He walked across the circle and handed the disc to the cleric. As the man lifted the coin, Morumus got a better look at the tattoo on the back of his hand. It was indeed a cross at its top—of that there could be no doubt. But why then was its bottom divided? A wavy line extended from the base of the cross to each of the cleric's knuckles. What did they signify?

A moment later, the cleric handed the token back to Morumus. Then the faceless cowl turned back toward the thief.

"The disc is authentic." Despite the cleric's thick accent, there could be no mistaking the finality in his tone. He turned toward the captain. "Release the monks, and bring the thief." Then the cleric turned his head to the crowd and raised his voice. "Woe to those who attempt to deceive the Church!" he declared in an ominous tone. "They have lied not to men, but to God!" Sitting beside him, the captain translated into Caeldoran. The crowd shuddered, and many shifted uncomfortably.

The thief tried to escape, but the soldiers now held him fast. One of the guards produced cords, and they tied the man's hands behind his back. The captain and the cleric turned their horses, and the crowds parted readily before them. The soldiers on foot followed. As they led him away, the thief turned his head and gave Morumus and Oethur one last look. There was a chilling hatred in those eyes. But beneath the malice there was cold, dark fear.

Within a few minutes, they were gone. Most of the crowd had likewise dispersed or turned back to their shopping. Morumus retrieved the sack of food from the ground where the soldier had dropped it. Then he walked over to Oethur. The Norn was staring after the direction of the soldiers.

"I could not understand what the soldier leader or the false grabber spoke," he said without turning his head. "Who was that red monk?"

"I don't know." Then, out of the corner of his eye, Morumus noticed a man bent over the pavement nearby. The man was attempting to pull the thief's knife free. "You there!" he said in Caeldoran.

The man started and looked up. He began to back away, but Morumus stopped him with a raised hand.

"Do not flee, friend. You may have the knife, if you are able to dislodge it. Only please, tell me: who was the cleric in red?"

The man stopped his retreat and arched his eyebrows. "You do not know, young monk? From where exactly do you come?"

"I am from Lorudin. It is far from here, over halfway to Naud on the western sea," he added when he saw no recognition register.

"Must be far if you have no knowledge of the Red Order."

"The Red Order?" Morumus frowned. "Truly, I have never heard of them. Who are they?"

"Ah." The man stepped a bit closer, and lowered his voice. "They come from the east—from Vendenthia."

Morumus's own eyebrows arched upwards. "The barbarian territory?"

The man nodded. "'Emperor conquered it some years ago. Sometime after, the red monks began appearing."

"Amazing." The Old Imperium had never been able to tame the eastern barbarians. How had the current emperor succeeded?

The man must have thought Morumus awed by the Red Order, for he nodded. "It is said they can work miracles—though I haven't seen any myself, so I don't know." He paused. "Not that I disbelieve in miracles, you understand. I just don't like to say I know a thing unless I've seen it for myself."

Morumus held up his hand. "Peace, friend. I understand. Please go on."

"What I do know—what everybody in these parts knows—is that the Red Order are the emperor's favorites. They act in his name, and everybody who wants to keep his life obeys. If you are going to be long in this region, young monk, you would do well to remember that."

"We are going to Versaden tomorrow for the Court of Saint Cephan."

"Ah. Well, I daresay you'll see more of them there. Have a care, eh?" With this, the man stepped back and returned his attention to dislodging the knife.

"Thank you." Morumus turned back to Oethur. "Come, let us get back to the inn. Donnach and Nack will be wondering what happened to us."

"What did that man say?"

"I will tell you on the way."

Thus they started back, winding their way through the thinning crowds and the waning afternoon. Both men were dirty, scuffled, and tired. But at least they would have their supper.

part from the old imperial capital of Palatina in the far south, Versaden had no equal among the cities of Midgaddan. Bishop Anathadus had said as much when the company entered the city the day after Dericus, and Abbot Grahem—who had once traveled to Palatina—readily agreed. None of the rest of them possessed the requisite experience to argue.

The city of Versaden had ancient origins. Originally settled by the Vilgurans as a military outpost, it sat on a long island in the mist of the great Amleux River. Despite the intervening centuries, some remnants of the ancient settlement yet remained. At its southern end, a wide plateau rose above the rest of the island. This plateau was called Prasaedun Hill, and atop its summit some portions of the ancient fortress had been integrated into the Royal Palace now occupying the site. At the other end of the island, the ancient Vilgurans had constructed a large, arched bridge to connect their output with the mainland. Centuries later, this bridge—called the Archatus—still stood as the city's sole gateway. Even by ancient standards, it was a marvel. Spanning the broad channel of the river, it was high enough for ships to pass beneath unobstructed and wide enough to permit two score men to walk abreast.

In addition to its antiquity, Versaden impressed the travelers by its sheer scale. A number of streets and avenues divided the city, all of them paved and well-maintained. The greatest of these, the King's Way, cut a straight line south from the Archatus through the city center to the base of Prasaedun Hill. Halfway along its length stood the massive Cathedral of Saint Dreunos, surrounded by a sprawling public park. Overlooking all of this from atop the Prasaedun stood the Royal Palace—a city within the city. Besides the substantial residence, clusters of smaller buildings dotted the hilltop: kitchens, a smithy, stables, guest houses, servants' houses, and barracks for the imperial bodyguard. Yet for all of these, the space did not seem cluttered, for enfolding and surrounding them all were the magnificent Gardens of Caeldora.

The Gardens were like landscapes lifted from an old fairy tale—utterly unlike anything Morumus had ever seen. Colorful flowerbeds lined numerous winding walkways, hedges grew into great green mazes, and shrubs trimmed to the shape of amazing creatures dotted the lawns. Even along the main entrance to the palace, the tops of the trees had been cut to resemble rows of giant mushrooms.

Eight days had passed since the grand opening of the Court, and this morning Morumus was walking swiftly along the streets in the city below the palace. He was on special assignment. He had come to Versaden to tutor Vilguran and translate Holy Writ. Instead, he now found himself shadowing four bishops. Eight days ago, these bishops had marched in the Court's opening procession. But instead of being led by their archbishop as expected, they had marched alone. Ever since that day, Morumus's task had been to find out why—for these four bishops hailed from the country of Mersex.

Mersex was the largest country on the island of Aeld Gowan. When its king, Luca Wolfbane, succeeded to his throne as a young man, seven kingdoms blanketed southern Aeld Gowan.

Over fifty years later, there was but one. Luca Wolfbane was as capable as he was ruthless. His Mersex covered everything south of the Deasmor, and everything east of Dyfann. Even so, his ambitions had not ceased.

Since the days of Morumus's father, Luca's Mersex had been a threat to its northern neighbors. Twenty years ago, Luca's brother Deorcad—whom Luca had personally installed as Archbishop of Mereclestour and Primate of Aeld Gowan—had attempted to force the Church in both Lothair and Nornindaal to accept his claim of ecclesiastical supremacy. Under the auspices of trying to harmonize certain practices—the style of tonsure for monks, the date on which to celebrate Resurrection Day—Luca had convinced the two northern kings to call a synod. This synod had convened in the southernmost city of Nornindaal—a place called Toberstan. It was because of the outcome of this synod that Morumus was skulking through the streets of Versaden this morning.

Instead of his regular Lorudin brown, Morumus now wore the ash-grey robe of a *Nefforian*—a Caeldoran monk under a vow of silence. How Nack had obtained such a garment Morumus did not know, but the grey robe was well-known and publicly recognized. Wearing it protected Morumus from any potentially compromising conversations, and permitted him to move with almost total freedom throughout Versaden. For all practical purposes, the robe made him invisible.

The root issue at Toberstan had not been haircuts or holidays, but power. Did the Archbishop of Mereclestour have authority over the Church in Lothair and Nornindaal, or did his authority extend no further than the borders of Mersex? The Mersians saw the issue as quite simple. The Court of Saint Cephan had appointed the Archbishop of Mereclestour as Primate of Aeld Gowan; Lothair and Nornindaal were part of the island of Aeld Gowan; thus, the northern bishops were subject to the southern primate—whether they particularly liked it or not.

The northern bishops disagreed. For them, the issue had been equally clear in the opposite direction. The Church in Lothair and Nornindaal had been planted centuries before there was any organized Court of Saint Cephan—centuries before there was even a single bishopric in Mersex. Thus, neither the Mersian Archbishop nor the Court of Saint Cephan could properly seize jurisdiction over them without their consent.

The reason Morumus was stalking Mersian bishops through the imperial capital on this day was because the issue at Toberstan had never been resolved. The northern bishops and their kings had categorically refused Deorcad's demand. Deorcad—with Luca's backing—had threatened to impose it by force. Just when it seemed that war might issue, news had arrived in Toberstan that Dyfanni barbarians had invaded Mersex. Luca had left the city in a rush, and the synod had promptly dissolved. Never again had the northern kings agreed to summon a synod. For the next twenty years, the issue had stood thus unresolved. Every three years, Archbishop Deorcad would invite the bishops of Lothair and Nornindaal to attend him at the Court of Saint Cephan. Every three years, the northern bishops would refuse to even acknowledge the invitation.

Yet this year, things were different. This year—for the first time in centuries—an emperor would preside over the Court. This year, the emperor might "persuade" the Court to take action it might never otherwise take. It was for this reason that Bishop Ciolbail and Bishop Treowin had secretly journeyed to Versaden. Luca Wolfbane was the emperor's only true rival. The northern bishops hoped to convince the emperor to persuade the Court to establish an independent Primate—a separate archbishop—for Lothair and Nornindaal. They had an audience scheduled with the emperor for this very evening, before the Court concluded with its Great Session tomorrow. Until then, the bishops were keeping out of sight.

Morumus, however, had no such restrictions—*and* he spoke Mersian.

Versaden was alive with activity. Carts and wagons creaked through the streets, manned by merchants and their guards. Tradesmen and goodwives carried their bundles, and clutches of children darted in and out of alleys with the glint of mischief in their eyes. The crowds allowed Morumus to shorten the distance between himself and his quarry. Like a shade on the moors of Lothair, he stalked ever nearer to the Mersians.

Burglary is a task that always sounds more romantic in a story than it is in reality. In the stories, the burglar never has to wait in one spot for hours on end, only for his quarry never to appear. In the stories, the burglar never has an occasion where he is almost caught, jumps into an alley—and promptly stumbles over a pile of refuse to land in a puddle of tavern scraps. In the stories, the burglar never stands up from such a mess only to find himself facing down a hungry-looking dog. Yet all of these things had happened to Morumus over the past eight days.

Despite the danger and discomfort, the bishops had insisted he continue. The reason for the absence of the Archbishop of Mereclestour was a crucial piece of information. Whatever it meant, it would almost certainly have some impact on their petition to the emperor. Perhaps their position would be strengthened. If so, they should know. Or perhaps it would be weakened. If so, they needed to know. Morumus must make every effort to learn the reason behind the missing archbishop—before the bishops went for their imperial audience.

It had not been until this morning that Morumus at last obtained the opportunity. This morning he had spied the Mersian bishops leaving their quarters shortly after Rising Prayers. He had been waiting—and praying—near one of the odd mushroom-cut trees in the imperial Gardens. From that vantage he had spotted the Mersians emerging from the palace, and from first sight he could tell that something was different. Usually, he saw them by ones or twos. But this morning all four of the bishops left together. Usually, the Mersians did not seem in any particular hurry. But this morning they moved with great haste—away from the palace and down into the city. And so it was that the bishops now walked briskly towards the heart of the city, unaware that they were being followed.

It soon became obvious where the Mersians were going. Besides the imperial palace, the Cathedral of Saint Dreunos was the greatest structure in Versaden. A towering edifice, Saint Dreunos's was built in the old imperial style. A large dome topped the center of the cathedral, supported and surrounded by the half-domes of the cathedral's four wings. Below each of these sub-domes stood a tall, colonnaded entrance. The Mersian bishops were headed toward the southern entrance. Morumus did not break from the crowds until they entered. As soon as they were in, however, he peeled off and quickened his pace. He could not afford to lose them now.

Unfortunately, Morumus was looking too far ahead and paying insufficient attention to his immediate surroundings. No sooner had he stepped away from the crowd and taken three steps than he collided head-on with another man. It was a terrific crash, and both went down in a rough tumble. When Morumus regained his feet a few moments later, black spots flecked his vision. But when he turned to the man he had knocked down, he soon realized that a headache was the least of his worries.

Like an imperial regular, the man before him wore dark green. Yet rather than a soldier's tunic, this fellow wore breeches and a short coat. The golden sun of the empire was fixed on the left breast of his coat, but here it was not alone: a black crescent moon had been added within the golden circle. To match the crescent, the man carried a black-sheathed sword at his waist and wore a black hat atop his head. Sharp eyes peered out from beneath its brim. Normally, these eyes would be scanning the man's surroundings. Now, however, they were fixed on Morumus.

Morumus could not believe his ill fortune. Of all the people in Versaden, he had managed to tumble into one of the *Lumanae*! The imperial bodyguards' name, which meant "Hands of the Moon," was a fitting reminder of their reputation. Just as the moon watched over the earth in place of the sun, so the *Lumanae* ensured that the emperor's interests were not undermined by things below his notice. Moreover, like the moon, which ruled by night, the *Lumanae* did not shy from operating in the dark.

"What do you think you are doing?" The man brushed debris off his coat.

In his panic, Morumus nearly answered. This would have been fatal, for it would have destroyed his *Nefforian* disguise. But he caught himself just in time. Instead of speaking, he made an apologetic bow and gestured toward the cathedral. As he did so, he withdrew Abbot Grahem's token from his robe and held it forth to the man.

The *Lumana* did not take the token. However, as he looked from Morumus to the cathedral and back again, his anger did seem to recede a bit.

"On your master's errand, are you?"

Morumus nodded, bowing again.

"Well," he replied gruffly after a short pause, "I can appreciate that." He waved Morumus toward the cathedral. "Be about it, then—but watch where you are going!"

Relief welling up inside him, Morumus obeyed without a backward look.

The interior of the cathedral was magnificent. Arches constructed from veined marble framed the corridors in either direction. Above the arches, the walls and ceilings hung with carved wooden panels. The gold and silver overlays shimmered in the flickering light of lamps and votives. It was only with great effort that Morumus restrained his desire to stop and take it all in.

My task is too urgent. I cannot afford to be distracted.

But as he crept to the far end of the vestibule, Morumus saw that he was going to have a problem. The central sanctuary beneath the cathedral's dome was completely empty at this hour, save for the Mersian bishops standing off to one side. Even disguised as a Nefforian monk, there was no way Morumus could get close enough to eavesdrop without drawing suspicion.

His heart sank. He had to find a way to get closer, but how? Silently, he began to pray. In so doing, he instinctively lifted his eyes—and found his answer.

Along the wall of the sanctuary, just above where the bishops stood, there was a row of narrow arches.

An upper gallery!

It did not take long for Morumus to find a set of stairs leading up to the second floor. A few minutes later, he crouched unseen behind the archway directly above the Mersians.

As it turned out, he was just in time.

12

The Mersian bishops were muttering amongst themselves.

"A wretched early hour to be scurrying around like a village priest."

"My man could not believe it when I told him I wished to be up and moving this early. 'But Your Grace,' he pleaded, 'there is no Court business so early!'"

"Ha! Likely he had cherished some hopes of a late morning himself."

Well back from the brink of the upper gallery, Morumus dared not peer down too often at the bishops, for every time he did so he risked being seen. Moreover, should somebody come up beside him from either side along the upper gallery, it would not do to appear to be eavesdropping. Thus he maintained a careful, prayerful posture just shy of the arched opening. From this vantage, he might appear to be gazing either toward the altar below or the dome above.

"Hush, all of you! Somebody is coming," said the fourth Mersian bishop. Morumus could not identify the bishops by sight, yet he could distinguish each individual voice.

Sure enough, an echo of approaching footfalls could be heard as the four bishops grew quiet. In the next moment, the footfalls ceased and a fifth voice spoke.

"Your Graces"—the speaker used smooth Vilguran—"thank you for coming so early and on such short notice."

"Who are you?" replied the fourth bishop in Vilguran, "Why have you summoned us?"

"I bring tidings," said the fifth voice, "a warning for the bishops of Mersex. Your Graces' estates are in grave danger."

"What do you me—?" began the second bishop before the fourth cut him off.

"What is this warning, and how would you know it?"

"Two bishops from the northern countries of your island have come secretly to Versaden. They will appear at the Great Session tomorrow—after they have met with the emperor tonight."

"What?" Three Mersian voices spoke nearly in unison—and universally vexed. The fourth, who must have been appointed their spokesman, growled at them in Mersian before replying.

"You are sure of this? What business do the Northmen have with the emperor?"

"I am sure, Your Graces. One of my brothers saw the petition in writing. The Church of the North wishes to join the Court of Saint Cephan."

"Is that all?" sneered the first bishop. "You called us out this early to tell us the Northmen are finally ready to submit?"

"Submit?" replied the fifth voice, a quiet edge in his tone. "Oh no, Your Grace. They do not wish to submit. The petition says that they are willing to *recognize* the Court—*provided* that they are granted full representation."

"They want their own archbishop," concluded the fourth bishop.

It was the first and only time that the fifth man seemed caught off-guard. "Your Grace is most perceptive. But did you know that, at present, the emperor is inclined to grant their request?"

Now it was the fourth bishop's turn to be caught. "Grant their request? The Northmen have resisted the Court's prerogatives in Aeld Gowan at every turn. Has the emperor even *heard* of Toberstan? Does he know how their *stubbornness* distracts our king, and delays the Church's expansion into Dyfann—even to this day? He ought to put them in chains, not grant their petition!"

"The emperor has little concern for the internal affairs of your island." The fifth voice had cooled. "His concern is for the unity of his empire. As this involves the unity of the Church, he is willing to do what is necessary to unite it."

"The Northmen are not interested in unity on their own island, let alone with the emperor!" said the fourth bishop.

"Of course not," said the fifth voice. "But the emperor sees in this an opportunity. By making a push for outward unity, he elevates his own stature within—and his control over—the Court. And if in so doing he may destabilize a rival? Well, that is only so much the better. You see, Your Grace, the emperor *has* heard of Toberstan. He *knows* how the Northmen dashed the aspirations of Luca Wolfbane and his brother."

There was silence for a moment. "Why are you telling us this?" the fourth bishop asked finally. "What interest does the Red Order have in such machinations? Your society is said to be the emperor's own hand. Why are you revealing that hand to us? What is your interest in this affair?"

Morumus started. To this point he had remained perfectly still, listening from his kneeling position without risking a glance over the edge. Yet the mention of the Red Order couldn't be ignored. With great caution, he leaned forward— just far enough so that his eyes could peer down over the cusp. What he saw confirmed the bishop's words: the fifth voice emanated from a figure draped head to toe in dark red. As had been the case in Dericus, the cowl of the red monk's robe was raised—completely concealing the figure's face. Morumus jerked back.

When the red monk spoke, his words bore an unmistakable edge of fervency. "Your Graces may be assured that my order's *only* interest lies in the Saving Blood. To spread the Saving Blood we are pledged, and to this end we utilize whatever means we can. By serving the emperor we gain access to dark corners, and into these we bring the light of Saving Blood. It is only the Blood which reconciles the world and extends the Church."

"Fine words." Weariness weighed the fourth bishop's words. "But you haven't answered my question. Why do you now disclose to us the Northmen's petition, if the emperor is inclined to favor it?"

"Would Your Grace not prefer an open hand to a closed fist? You have been summoned for two reasons: first, because the emperor may be persuaded to change his position; second, because the Order of the Saving Blood is willing to help you change it."

"Why should you wish to help us?"

"Why should we not? How does it serve the Church to split your island into separate spiritual territories? Why should the Court bow to the schismatic demands of the Northmen?"

The fourth bishop snorted. "So your order sides with us, even if your emperor does not. Seems you are in a tight spot."

"My order sides only with the Saving Blood, and the great desire of the Saving Blood is for people of Dyfann. The west of your island is much like the land of Vendenthia once was: bloody, brutal, and heathen. Every effort of your king to subdue Dyfann on his own strength has failed. Now that King Luca is dead, his son is preparing a fresh invasion in an effort to shed his own reputation for weakness—an invasion doomed to failure if Mersian swords are not accompanied by the Saving Blood."

Morumus gasped. Luca of Mersex was dead?

The only thing that saved Morumus from discovery was that his gasp had four much louder echoes below.

"How did you learn of the death of King Luca?" demanded the fourth bishop.

The red monk laughed softly. "Nothing can be hidden from those who serve the Saving Blood, Your Graces. We know that Luca Wolfbane died by an assassin's hand three days before you set sail for Versaden. We know, too, that his brother died with him."

Morumus threw his hand over his mouth to prevent any more sounds from escaping. Now his task was complete. He knew why the Mersian bishops had marched without their archbishop. Archbishop Deorcad was dead. The Chair of Saint Aucantia—the highest office of the Church in Mersex—was empty.

Silence fell for a long moment among the voices below. "Your order is well-informed, however you have managed it," conceded the fourth bishop. "Yet it gives you little advantage, for all of this information will be made public at the Great Session tomorrow."

"It is not our own advantage that we seek, Your Graces—but yours. Though the emperor has noted the absence of your archbishop, he does not know the reason. He has few eyes and ears on your island, and so he does not yet know of the deaths of Luca and Deorcad. If he were to learn of them prior to his meeting with the Northmen this evening, it might change his disposition toward their petition."

"A change you claim to favor—and yet you have not told him." The Mersian did not bother to hide the accusation in his tone.

"Of course not. For without certain assurances, the information may precipitate the wrong sort of change. The death of both king and archbishop makes the situation in Mersex precarious. Luca's son cannot fill his father's shoes. If this news is not properly handled, it might actually embolden the emperor to destabilize the situation further. He might see granting the Northmen's petition as a preparatory step toward invasion—toward the conquest of your island. With the Northmen in the emperor's debt and the unpredictable Dyfanni on his west, could your new King Wodic withstand an invasion from Caeldora? Could Your Graces yourselves withstand the new power of the Northern Church that would arise in the aftermath of such a conquest?"

"How do you propose to prevent such an outcome?" From the fourth bishop's tone, he was finished sparring.

"The emperor is a practical man. If he can be assured of an outcome that will benefit him without requiring a military expedition, he will choose that which costs him least in blood and treasure. My order proposes that you provide him the necessary incentive."

"King Wodic may not have Luca's cunning," answered the fourth bishop, "but he has his father's pride. He will not consent to pay any tribute."

"Wodic is not the one who must consent or pay tribute."

"Are you suggesting *we* pay?" There was indignant muttering among all four Mersians.

"Only after a fashion, Your Graces," said the red monk smoothly. "The emperor knows there is little treasure on your island or in your sees, so he will not look for you to pay him gold. But if he can be assured that you will you pledge him your support on two proposals before the Great Session tomorrow, he may be persuaded to cancel his audience with the Northmen and stifle his ambitions on your island."

"Which proposals?"

"The first is a general visitation. The emperor is concerned about declining levels of education and piety within the Church, and wants to institute an inspection of all bishoprics in order to assess the situation and institute corrective measures. The Archbishop of Palatina has agreed to bring forward such a proposal, yet the Court has been loath to grant the necessary authority. Individual bishops and local lords tend to resent the intrusions. Yet the emperor feels quite strongly about the matter. By supporting the proposal, Your Graces will demonstrate to him that neither you nor your new king wish to stand as his rivals."

The Mersian bishops conferred. Finally the fourth bishop spoke again. "We agree to support this visitation."

"The second proposal you must support pertains to the selection of a new archbishop for the See of Mereclestour."

"*What?*" The fourth bishop all but spat his response, and several of his colleagues growled. "You would have us barter the Chair of Saint Aucantia? That is outrageous!"

"Is it? Did Your Graces protest as much when Luca gave the Chair to his brother?"

"Deorcad was many things and there is no hiding that he was ruled by his brother. But at least he was Mersian. We will not consent to subject our Church to the rule of a foreigner. Aeld Gowan will *not* be a fiefdom of Caeldora!"

"Your Grace speaks as though the whole of your island were yours." The red monk's voice had turned to ice. "In reality, you control but a portion of it—and that now tenuously. But all of that might change if you heed the advice of my order. We are not proposing that you accept the appointment of a Caeldoran archbishop."

"You said you would have us give the emperor assurances on his selection. That is a distinction without difference."

"Your Grace assumed that he would select a Caeldoran. That he will not do. The emperor is no fool. Your Graces may rest assured that the new Archbishop of Mereclestour will be a native of your own island."

"Are you saying he will nominate one of us?"

"No, nor one of the northern bishops."

"Who then?"

"There is among the bishops of Vendenthia a native of Aeld Gowan, a man trusted by the emperor. He will be the emperor's nominee for the See of Mereclestour."

"What is his name?"

"You will not have heard of him. His name is Simnor." There was a long pause among the Mersian bishops. "The emperor may trust this Simnor, but how do we know that we can trust him?" asked the fourth bishop.

"Bishop Simnor has the full confidence of my order. The Church has made her greatest gains among the Vendenthi in his bishopric. Were he a native of that land, he would no doubt be *their* Archbishop already."

"You ask us to accept a man as our archbishop based only on your word?"

The red monk's tone sharpened. "We ask Your Graces to act for your own and the Church's preservation. The Northmen have the emperor's ear. Your previous patrons are dead. Your new king is planning a reckless invasion rather than protecting his own borders. If you do not accept the emperor's selection for archbishop, it is quite likely that your land will soon face the edge of his sword and Your Graces will face the sovereignty of northern bishops."

There was muttering among the Mersians at this point, but the red monk pressed on.

"Yet if you heed our counsel, you will not only avoid imperial invasion—you will gain spiritual allies. With Bishop Simnor on the Chair of Saint Aucantia, my order will be free to bring the Saving Blood alongside the swords of Mersex in the forthcoming campaign against Dyfann. Where once loomed only certain doom, there will now be hope of miraculous success. If you accept our counsel, Your Graces will not only bring success to your king and stability to your land, you will also garner untold new souls and territory for the Church. Once this is complete, the schismatic Northmen can be dealt with at our leisure."

Silence fell. When it dragged on, Morumus leaned forward and peered down over the edge. Below him, the red-cloaked monk stood still as a statue while the Mersian bishops huddled in close conference. So low were the tones of their whispering that only the barest hints of sound escaped. Finally, after several long minutes, the bishops broke ranks and the fourth bishop turned.

"So long as this Simnor of whom you speak is truly who you say he is—a native of our island—we will agree to support him for the See of Mereclestour. Yet we have one condition of our own. In exchange for our support, the northern bishops will be arrested and placed in our custody."

"To what end?"

"A security. As you have said, the situation on our island is precarious. Once the Northmen learn of our king's death, they may send word home to *their* kings. It does us no good to prevent an invasion from Caeldora if only to face one from the north. Having the bishops as hostages will buy us both time and leverage."

"It is well said," conceded the red monk, "but the emperor will not arrest two bishops without charge."

"No? What if he were to learn that the northern bishops were responsible for the death of our king? Would that suffice?"

"It would, if it were not a false charge."

"Who is to say it is false?" pressed the fourth bishop. "In truth, even *we* do not know who murdered Luca and Deorcad. Likely it was *not* the Northmen, but what does that matter? The circumstances can be made to fit the charge. Is it mere coincidence that these bishops have come to the Court now— for the first time *ever*—just after the death of our archbishop?

Is it but happenstance that they ask him to act against his rival, knowing that his rival is dead? Surely your order might suggest it is otherwise."

"Your Graces show wisdom. You will have what you require. My order will see to it, but *after* the conclusion of the Great Session. Arresting them beforehand might draw unwanted atten—"

The red monk never had the chance to finish this sentence, for while he yet was speaking, the fourth Mersian bishop happened to glance up—directly at the arch over which Morumus still peered down! Morumus froze, and for the briefest moment thought that somehow the bishop had not noticed him. Then the man's eyes widened and his expression hardened.

"Who is that?" the Mersian growled, gesturing toward the gallery.

The red-hooded head whipped around. A dreadful cry rose from within the shadowy folds of its cowl.

"Your Graces have been followed!"

13

For several moments after being spotted, Morumus did not move. Frozen in place, he stared down at the men below him. Should give himself up and feign ignorance in his disguise, or should he flee? His adversaries had no such hesitations.

"Get to the steps!" shouted the fourth bishop to his companions. "There are only two ways up to that gallery." The other Mersian bishops sprang to action, pulling up the hems of their cassocks and running toward the vestibule at the western end of the cathedral where the staircases began.

"Make haste, Your Graces," hissed the red monk, the faceless cowl glaring up at Morumus. "The burglar must not escape!"

The sinister tone in this declamation made up Morumus's mind and freed him to action. He lifted the hem of his own long robe and ran toward the steps. His delay had cost him critical seconds, and it seemed unlikely that he could beat the bishops. Still, there was nothing for it but to try. Heavy footfalls resounded from the stones and echoed through the cathedral as the two parties raced toward the stairs. Added to these, the sound of Morumus's own heart thumped in his ears until it seemed as though there must be soldiers marching somewhere just beyond sight.

Morumus had never run so hard in his life—not even when chasing the thief in Dericus. But by the time he reached the top of the stairs in the western vestibule, he found that the bishops were waiting at the bottom.

The Mersian bishops looked up at him with malevolent curiosity.

"Who are you?" The voice was that of the fourth bishop, the Mersian spokesman.

"I'll wager he is no Nefforian," said one of the others.

"Whoever he is, he has heard too much, Your Graces." The red monk entered the vestibule behind them. His tone was as cold as death. "He must be taken."

"Agreed." The fourth bishop gave a grim nod. "You two"—he gestured from his companions to the staircase behind them—"Go up that way and don't let him pass. We'll take this set."

Morumus did not wait as the bishops and the red monk began ascending both sets of stairs. Rather, he turned and fled back down the gallery. But where exactly could he go? He had a creeping fear that the fourth bishop had been correct—that the stairs were the only way down from the gallery. There could be little mistaking the intentions of his pursuers. He must find another way down.

At the eastern end of the gallery, three closed doors faced three large archways looking down on the cathedral altar. Morumus reached the first of these while the footfalls of the bishops were still safely distant. With a hurried prayer, he grabbed the latch. Locked. He moved to the second door. It too was locked. His heart thumped in his chest and pulsed in his ears as he moved to the third door and reached for the latch. The footsteps of Mersians were much closer now. This would be his last chance.

The third door was locked.

"Give up!" The fourth bishop sounded dangerously close. "There is no escape."

Wheeling around, Morumus saw that he was surrounded. Bishops blocked the passage in both directions. The red monk stepped between the pair on Morumus's right and reached within his robe. When his hand emerged, it was clutching a knife. "Hold him, Your Graces."

The bishops hesitated, looking to their leader.

"Is that really necessary?" The fourth bishop frowned. "Perhaps we might simply bind and confine him until after the Session."

The red monk did not turn his eyes from Morumus. "No. Your Graces were followed for a reason. Even after the Great Session, what he has heard might do great damage. My order might lose the confidence of the emperor. Your Graces might risk your position with your king. It takes but one wrong report to make a sovereign see treason in place of collusion. We cannot let the burglar go."

"Agreed." The fourth bishop gestured to the two bishops at Morumus's left. "Do as he says: hold him."

Shifting his gaze between each, Morumus edged away from his attackers until he found his back to the centermost of the three doors. To his left, the appointed bishops closed in, looking uncomfortable but resolved. To his right, the grip of the red monk tightened around the hilt of the knife and he stepped forward. The hand clutching the knife bore the same, strange tattoo Morumus had seen in Dericus.

It is often said that those facing death see their lives flash before their eyes. Perhaps that is true, but in this case it did not happen. Instead, for a split second, Morumus thought of his father. And in that instant he knew one thing for certain: he *would not* die by a knife in the dark.

In the next moment, suddenly and terrifically, his awareness expanded. It felt like waking up. His gaze swept from the looming bishops to the long knife to the large archway before him. And then he knew what he must do.

He spun toward the bishops reaching for him and hissed in Mersian: "Think you that King Wodic has no ears in Versaden?" Just as quickly, he wheeled back toward the red monk and spoke Vilguran: "And think *you* that the Red Order has escaped the eyes of the *Lumanae?*"

The ruse worked. Both bishops and cleric hesitated, and in that instant Morumus leapt. It was a mere two steps to the brink of the large arch, and a moment later he slipped over its edge. Directly below him was the cathedral altar—a solid mass of stone. He caught hold of the banner that hung behind it, and for a moment his fall was delayed. Then the banner tore.

Morumus crashed atop the cathedral altar. The force of his impact broke several candles, scattered the instruments, and rolled him onto the floor. For a moment he lay stunned, his breath half-knocked from his lungs. He watched the chalice roll away across the floor of the sanctuary.

"After him!" shrieked a voice from above.

Jumping to his feet and making sure his hood still concealed his face, Morumus looked up. The red monk stood in the arch from which Morumus had leapt, jabbing with his knife as though he could pin Morumus to the floor. Through the narrower archways of the gallery on either side, Morumus could see the Mersian bishops rushing back toward the west end of the sanctuary. Yet even they had to know they could not intercept him now. He would be out the door before they reached the top of the stairs.

Perhaps it was still the rush of the moment, or perhaps there was a bit more of his father in him than he realized. Whatever it was, as Morumus turned to go he looked back up at the gesticulating monk. He knew that the cleric could not see his face any more than he could see his, yet he smiled all the same.

"Not this time," he declaimed—then dashed away.

Rather than return through the southern entrance toward the Prasaedun, Morumus exited via the east. This put maximum distance between him and the pursuing bishops—and allowed him to escape into the park facing the cathedral.

By the time Morumus emerged, traffic along the city's central avenue had thickened. He must reach the opposite side if he hoped to escape the Mersians, so he dared not pause to wade across. Instead, he tore through the midst of the wagons and horsemen and townspeople. It was a dangerous and unpopular move. He nearly got his skull kicked in by a rearing horse, and received numerous coarse appellations. Yet in the end he got across unscathed.

The Cathedral Park was a vast green oasis, set in the mist of Versaden's stone streets like an emerald amongst crude rocks. Once within it, it was easy to forget that one was in a city at all. Dense groves of large trees dotted the landscape. A spring-fed stream meandered lazily about until it emptied into a wide pond. Shady and grown, green and spacious, the park was a perfect place to lose the bustle and noise of the surrounding city. The stone wall about its perimeter not only hemmed in the park; it also kept the city out. Directly across the street from the cathedral's eastern portico, a pair of wrought-iron gates intermitted the wall and provided entrance to the park. Morumus had just rushed through these when he heard a shout behind him.

"Stop that monk!"

Glancing back, Morumus saw the fourth bishop standing on the steps of the cathedral, shaking a finger in his direction. He saw too that the Mersian's shout had attracted the attention of a pair of imperial soldiers standing nearby. Hearing the bishop's shout and following his gesture, these sprang after Morumus.

"Give way!" they shouted, and began jostling through the midst of the street.

Morumus fled into the park, holding up the hem of his robe with his hands to avoid what would almost certainly be a fatal fall. He had not got very far when he heard the soldiers shout again as they passed through the gates. Not daring to look back, he forced himself to run faster. His legs burned, but he ran on. As he did, it occurred to him that what he was feeling now—a heedless, horrible desperation—must be what had made the thief in Dericus such a dangerous and ruthless quarry. Morumus thought, too, that he now understood a bit of the fear that he had seen in the thief's eyes as the soldiers led him away. As in that case, Morumus cherished no illusions as to what would happen should the soldiers overtake him.

Unfortunately for Morumus, the men of the imperial army were better conditioned than he. As the chase wore on they no longer shouted, but he could tell they were closing the distance: over the sound of his own footfalls, he began to hear theirs drawing nearer and nearer on the turf.

"I must not be captured," he gasped through gritted teeth, and forced his feet to move faster.

Running alone would not be sufficient to escape. The soldiers were too quick. He was going to have to confront them. But how? His father's weapons master had trained him in both armed and unarmed combat as a youth, yet he had not lifted a blade or cudgel since coming to Caeldora. Meanwhile, the imperial soldiers were undoubtedly well-trained. How could he, unarmed and unpracticed, defeat two of them?

Behind Morumus, the soldiers were drawing to within a few paces. He could hear their heaving breaths interspersed between his own. Time was running out.

Ahead of him, a grove of trees loomed tall and tangled out of the grass. Seeing it, a wick of hope flickered in Morumus. If he could find a fallen branch to use as a stave, he would stand a better chance. If he could use the trees to shield himself from a twin-pronged assault, he might just prevail. It was a slim chance indeed, but it was all that he had. His heaving lungs had no air to spare, so he prayed silently: *Lord, help me!*

Strong hands grabbed his robe at the shoulders. Morumus was yanked backward in mid-step. There was a sharp pain in his ankle, then he was down.

"Got you!" said a grim voice.

Morumus resisted with all his remaining might, but to no avail. A moment later, the second soldier arrived to reinforce his fellow. There was a flailing of limbs and a flurry of motion, but in the end they forced Morumus to the ground and rolled him onto his stomach. One held him fast while the other bound his wrists behind him with a cord.

"Do you have that sack?" asked one of the soldiers in Vilguran.

"Yes," said the second.

"Put it over his head, quickly," said the first. "The bishop will not be far behind us."

A moment later, daylight and fresh air disappeared as a coarse bag was drawn down over Morumus's face. Within, he gagged with the very first breath: the interior of the sack reeked of rotten vegetables. A moment later, however, he forgot all about the foul smell—at the sound of a foul voice.

"You have caught the rogue," it said, sounding somewhat out of breath. The canvas covering Morumus's head somewhat muffled the voices, yet even so he recognized the speaker as the fourth bishop.

"We have, Your Grace," replied the first soldier. "What has he done?"

"He has desecrated the cathedral altar, and attempted to steal the holy vessels."

At this Morumus tried to respond, but no sooner had he raised his head than a strong hand forced his face back into the turf.

161

"Quiet, you!" growled the second soldier, his Vilguran rough and his tone threatening.

"Desecrated the holy altar?" The first soldier's voice was part indignant and part surprise. "Say no more, Your Grace. We will take him to the tribune immediately, although"—here his voice took on a dark, suggestive tone—"the verdict seems pretty clear."

The bishop took the hint. "As clear as the judgment of our Lord upon the wicked, and as clear as the love of our Lord for those who protect his Church."

"Say no more, Your Grace. We know what to do with these kinds."

"I am no thief!" Morumus tried to shout, a cold panic rising in his chest. "I have stolen nothing!" Yet because his face was in the grass, the best he could muster was a muffled yell.

There was a small clank of metal on metal. "The workers are worthy of their hire." The bishop lowered his voice. "Make sure nobody finds the body."

The panic that had been building in Morumus burst. He struggled and writhed on the ground, desperate to get free. But it was no use. The second soldier simply sat on him, pinning him to the ground.

"Your Grace is too kind," said the first soldier. "We will see to it."

For several minutes after that, the soldiers remained quiet as the bishop departed. For his part, Morumus spent the time in desperate prayer. He felt cold all over, yet at the same time he was sweating. Finally, after what seemed an eternity, the soldiers spoke again.

"Well, he's gone," said the first soldier.

"Best be getting on with it, eh?" said the second.

"Indeed," said the first. "Best make it quick. We haven't got all day to waste."

"Especially on a false grabber such as this," said the second in a dry voice.

Morumus's heart, which was already racing, skipped a beat entirely. *False grabber? Could it be—?*

Before he could speak, the second soldier rolled him over and yanked the sack clear of his head.

Daylight dazzled Morumus's eyes. Yet against its backdrop, there could be no mistaking the two grinning faces that peered down at him.

"Donnach! Oethur!" Then, unexpectedly, he laughed. He had never felt more relief in his entire life.

The red monk turned to the entrance when the Mersian bishop who had chased the intruder returned to the sanctuary. The three remaining Mersians stood together a short distance away.

"Where is the burglar, Your Grace?"

The bishop smiled. "He is dead. Or will be, soon enough. A pair of soldiers caught him. I persuaded them to resolve the matter away from the tribunes."

"Most excellent and most wise. We will carry on as agreed. Your Graces may rest assured, the emperor will not see the Northmen now. Only do not forget our agreement."

"We will not forget. But see to it that the Northmen are delivered to us."

"My order will see to it. Your Graces may go in peace."

The red monk waited until the Mersians were gone to open his hand and gaze at the small disc in his palm. He had found it amidst the broken bits of the altar candles, and secreted it away from the eyes of the Mersians. The burglar must have dropped it.

He recognized the wood as *brer*, though he did not recognize the name. "Not yet." He narrowed his eyes. "Not yet . . . but soon."

14

"How bad is it?"

Leaning against a tree, Morumus tested his ankle before answering Donnach.

"It's not broken." He shifted his weight from one foot to the other. "I may limp for a bit, but it should be fine."

"I'm sorry, brother, I did not intend to—"

Morumus held up his hand. "Don't be. You had to make it look convincing."

The three monks were huddled within a grove of trees in Cathedral Park—the same grove toward which Morumus had fled from the bishop and the two "soldiers." Morumus looked from Donnach to Oethur, both of whom still wore their disguises. He had already told them everything he had learned in the cathedral, so they knew his story. But what of theirs?

"Where did you get those uniforms?"

"Nack." Oethur spoke as though the mere name explained all—which it did.

"They look authentic."

"They are."

"But how? And how did you know where to find me?"

Oethur spread his hands and shrugged. "The bishop's man is very . . . what is the word?"

"Capable?" supplied Morumus.

The other two nodded.

"Nack supplied the uniforms," said Donnach, "but the whole thing was Oethur's idea."

"That you follow me today?"

"Not just today," said Donnach. "Every day."

"What?" Morumus's eyes widened. He looked at Oethur. "Is this true?"

The Norn looked away, his face reddening. "You are a difficult teacher, Morumus, but you are the only one we have."

Morumus felt a lump rising in his throat. "Thank you," he managed. But inside, he was undone. There is nothing so shame-inducing as grace returned for hate. The contrast between Oethur's behavior and his own cut him to the heart.

From the minute they first met, Morumus had cherished a special dislike for Oethur. And for what? For the fact that ten years ago, raiders from Oethur's country had crossed the border into his own. But Morumus *knew* it had not been Norns who had murdered his father!

The monstrosity of his conduct struck him like a smith's hammer. And it got worse. Despite his unsparing abuse, Oethur had taken the initiative to protect him. *Thank God he had!* What would have happened had Oethur and Donnach not been about when he fled the cathedral? Morumus knew the answer. The bishop's cry would have attracted the attention of real soldiers, and he would now be dead.

Morumus's eyes burned at the corners. All of his carefully crafted excuses against Oethur shattered. He was twice convicted and without excuse. *God forgive me.* He knew that he must ask the same of Oethur just as soon as possible. But for the moment, he dared speak no further—for fear his voice would break.

Donnach must have noticed his plight, for in that moment the Grendannathi intervened. "You will have difficulty with that turned ankle, and it is a long walk from here back to the bishops. One of us should go ahead and warn them."

"I will go," volunteered Oethur.

"No," said Donnach. "It was my idea. I will go."

Morumus looked at him. "Are you sure you can remember everything?"

"I think so. The bishop of Mereclestour—"

"*Archbishop*," corrected Morumus.

"Right." Donnach nodded. "The archbishop is dead, along with his brother."

"The king," inserted Oethur.

"Yes, yes." Donnach sounded peevish. "They are both dead, and the other bishops and the red priest have made a deal. The Mersian bishops will agree to support the emperor's choice for their new archbishop. In return, the emperor will cancel his audience with our own bishops tonight—and arrest them tomorrow. Have I got it all?"

"Almost. Don't forget the war."

"Ah, yes. The new king of Mersex is planning to invade Dyfann. The Red Order has offered to help."

"That's it," said Morumus.

"Is there anything else?"

"No."

"Good." Donnach straightened his tunic. "The two of you should wait at least an hour or two before following, just in case that bishop has set a watch."

"Good idea," said Oethur, and Morumus nodded.

Donnach started for the edge of the trees. "God willing, I will inform them within the hour," he called over his shoulder as he exited the grove.

"Pray it will be soon enough," said Oethur quietly beside Morumus.

Indeed. Morumus did not speak aloud. He was preparing to say something much more difficult.

"Oethur . . ." He used Northspeech rather than Vilguran, "There is something I need to say to you."

Oethur, who had been leaning against another tree, looked at him. "My Vilguran is so bad that you are giving up?" He gave a half-smile.

Morumus returned the smile, but shook his head. "No, it's not that. But I thought our native language might be easier."

"It is."

"Good." Morumus took a deep breath. "What I need to say, Oethur, is that I am sorry."

The Norn said nothing, but Morumus forced himself to meet his gaze and go on. "Everything you said about me before was true," he confessed. "I have been—how did you put it—an 'insufferable *scurn.*'"

"Give me my due, Morumus." Oethur spoke with grim humor. "I put it better than that. I believe my exact words were 'an insufferable, *sanctimonious scurn.*'"

Morumus winced. "Even so, you were exactly right. I admit it, and I confess it. Will you forgive me? I know I don't deserve—"

Oethur held up a hand. "I know this will be hard for you, Morumus, but try not to think too much about it."

In spite of himself, Morumus smiled at this. "Thank you, brother."

"You're welcome. And it's not your fault entirely. I *am* a stubborn student. I know it."

"That's as may be, but it's no excuse, nor even the truth behind my behavior."

"What do you mean?"

"It's a long story, and I have never shared it with anybody. But if you would like to know, I will tell you."

"We have the time, if we're going to wait for a bit as Donnach suggested." Oethur withdrew a skin flask from somewhere within his tunic. "Came with the disguise." He unstopped the cap and took a drink. "Not sure exactly what it is, but it's not bad. You want a dram?"

Morumus received the proffered flask and took a sip of its contents. The contents warmed his throat the whole way down—which was just as well, given what he was about to bring up.

"And so I was sent to Lorudin," Morumus concluded some time later, "and have spent my years since looking for some clue to the Dark Speech."

Oethur had not said a word since Morumus began. His brow, however, had drawn steadily lower, and his countenance had grown darker. Now at last, when he spoke, there was a tremor like distant thunder in his voice.

"How long ago did you say this happened?"

"About ten years ago."

"Ten years. I remember it."

"You do?"

"Oh yes," said Oethur grimly, "it was the day my eldest brother was murdered."

"What? But I thought you were the second son!"

"I am now."

"What are you saying?"

"By birth I am the third son of my father, but ten years ago, my eldest brother and the heir to my father's crown was murdered—the night before your own father's murder!"

Morumus exhaled. "I never knew—nor would I have guessed."

"Of course not. How could you have known, having left our island so soon after it happened? That's not important. What is important is that it all fits!"

"What do you mean?"

"You said it was a Nornish raiding party that had crossed into your country and burned that village?"

"That was the report my father received."

"And so they would have appeared. But what would you say, Morumus, if I told you that the raiders were not my countrymen?"

"Didn't your father agree to pay compensation to my king?"

"He did."

"Why, if his subjects were not to blame?"

"Because the peace between our countries was at stake and because, as I said, there was no other explanation until just now!"

"I still don't understand."

"Morumus, the raiders appeared as Norns because they were wearing Nornish uniforms and carrying Nornish weapons. But they were not themselves Norns. I suspect now that they were—what did you call them?—Dree?"

"Yes, the adepts of the Dark Faith are called Dree."

"It all fits. It was a small garrison that was attacked—a small tower on our westernmost border, just east of your village that was burned. Our people and yours had been at peace for so long that it was no longer manned, but my father kept it stocked with weapons and stores. My eldest brother—Alfered was his name—had taken to using it as his hunting lodge. He was there when it was attacked. That is how he died."

"And you think he was murdered by the Dree?"

Oethur nodded, his expression dark. "My other brother and I were with our father when we found them. What was done to Alfered and his companions . . . well, you know."

Morumus nodded. His head was spinning. "It fits, all of it." He looked up. "Oethur, I remember wondering how it was that the *Dree* knew just where to find us. How did they know where we would camp that night my father was murdered? At the time, I suspected it was because they were in collusion with your people." He paused, his own face flushing with shame at the thought. "But now I see it truly. The *Dree* were behind it from the beginning."

"Two sides of the border, but a common enemy."

For a short while, neither man spoke.

"I am glad we are friends now." Oethur took another drink from the flask before passing it to Morumus. "For we now share a common purpose. The *Dree* must be destroyed."

"Even so." Morumus received the flask and sipped its contents. The liquid burned as it slid down his throat, but he scarcely felt it next to the fire now burning in his bones.

"They've gone," said Nack.

Bishop Anathadus's guard looked dour as he hung his cloak on a peg by the door and came to join the others around the table. He sat down next to Abbot Grahem, who passed him the jug without being asked. Nack nodded his thanks and took a long drink. When he finished, he pushed the jug away and looked across the table.

"I'm afraid it cost rather more coin than I supposed, sir."

Bishop Anathadus, seated across the table from his man, nodded. "Think no more on it, Nack. It is in the nature of such arrangements to be expensive in proportion to their necessity."

"Even so, sir." Nack craned his neck around Abbot Grahem to look at Morumus. "How's the foot, lad?"

"Should be fine by tomorrow." Morumus wasn't even thinking about his foot now. He had a bigger problem than that. He looked at Abbot Grahem, seated between him and Nack. "Sir, I lost your token. I'm not sure when—or where—only that it was today."

Abbot Grahem put a hand on Morumus's shoulder. "Don't worry about that, Morumus. It's probably been crushed by a cart or lost in the park. And if not, anyone trying to use it will only bring trouble on themselves. I'm just thankful you're alive, son."

Morumus exhaled his relief as the abbot turned back to Nack.

"You are certain our friends will get away safely?"

"As sure as one can be in such circumstances. The men with whom they are traveling came highly recommended from several sources. The higher fee they charged seemed to reinforce this. You can usually tell a thief—or an informant—by the affordability of his services."

"Indeed." In spite of the seriousness of the circumstances, something like a small grin creased Abbot Grahem's face.

Things had begun to happen quickly once Donnach brought Morumus's news. Ciolbail, Treowin, and Nerias had been so agitated that they wanted to leave Versaden that moment. But Anathadus prevented them. If the imperial messenger found them missing when he brought the official cancellation of their audience, he warned, both the Mersians and the Order of the Saving Blood would pursue them immediately. But if they waited until after they received the notice, they would have at least a day's advantage—for, according to the report, they were not to be arrested until after the Great Session on the next day.

The Northmen saw the sense in this and had therefore agreed to wait.

While they were waiting on the messenger, it was decided that Donnach and Oethur would leave with the others and accompany them as far as Lorudin. There the princes would remain, as originally planned, while the bishops and Nerias would continue west to Naud. The ship aboard which they had sailed from Aeld Gowan had remained in port, and would be waiting for their return. If all went well, the Northmen would be gone from Caeldora before anybody could catch up to them.

The sticky point in the plan was getting everybody out of Versaden without being noticed. The only land route in or out of the city was the great Archatus bridge. But if the Red Order had eyes and ears within the imperial court, then it was certain that they would have watchmen at the bridge. Another way would have to be found. But what? And how?

It was at this point that arrangements fell upon Nack. Nobody knew how he did it, yet before the cancellation notice from the emperor came, the bishop's guard had gone out and returned with a working plan.

A ship in port at Versaden would carry the five Northmen away from the city and set them ashore downriver, where they would be met with horses and supplies sufficient to get them to Aevor. At Aevor, they would resupply from Bishop Anathadus's stores and continue to Lorudin. The princes would remain in Lorudin while the bishops and Nerias proceeded to Naud.

All agreed that it was a good plan.

Thus it had been a whirlwind of an afternoon for the entire company. Once the plan was made, preparations were hasty. Within a half hour after receiving the emperor's official cancellation, Ciolbail, Treowin, Nerias, Donnach, and Oethur departed.

"It is well that our brothers have escaped," said Anathadus. "However, we are still left with the emperor's plan to visit all the churches. What are we to make of it?"

"Morumus said the Archbishop of Palatina is involved." Abbot Grahem looked sideways at his junior monk. "There is your clue. Palatina was once the capital of the Vilguran Imperium. The archbishops of that city have been trying to make themselves head of an imperial Church ever since. The current archbishop, Ambiragust, is no different. A 'general visitation' under his supervision would be the perfect foil to further his ambitions."

"Maybe," said Anathadus. "But the Red Order's patronage comes from the emperor. Why would they wish to empower a potential rival? How would centralized authority in the Church help them?"

Abbot Grahem turned to Morumus. "Did the red monk say anything else?"

Morumus frowned. "One of the Mersian bishops asked him why the Red Order wanted to help them."

"And?"

"He said their only interest was 'to spread the Saving Blood.'"

Anathadus snorted. "More like spread their own authority. What better way to hide a naked grab for power than to wrap it in piety?"

"It would not be the first time in the history of the Church," agreed Abbot Grahem.

"No indeed," said Anathadus. "In any event, the Order of the Saving Blood is not our primary concern. What we have to deal with is this visitation. I have no intention of allowing the agents of Ambiragust to go ruffling through my bishopric."

"Do you think you can stop the motion?" Grahem asked.

"On the contrary," said Anathadus. "I think I shall introduce it myself."

"What?" exclaimed Grahem and Morumus together.

Anathadus's smile was grim. "If I introduce the motion, it will become immediately suspect. I am for the old order of the Church, and the Court knows it. By proposing it myself, I will associate this motion with my position. Nobody will vote for a general visitation after I am finished extolling the proposal."

Morumus nodded. "Poison the well."

"Precisely!" Anathadus smiled. "You see it already, my son."

Grahem's eyes narrowed. "I don't like it. It's clever and daring—but it is also a risk. What if the motion does not fail?"

176

"Then we will we be no worse off than if Ambiragust himself had proposed it, and perhaps much better. For the terms of the visitation which I will propose will keep power far away from the archbishop of Palatina!"

There was no more picturesque place to hold the Great Session of the Court of Saint Cephan than the Audience Hall of the imperial palace in Versaden. The Hall was a long, rectangular chamber with a high, vaulted ceiling. A series of glass skylights set in both sides of its roof permitted the sunlight to bathe the entire length of the room in golden rays. The light shone brightly upon the checkered, marble floor, and it cast long shadows behind the rows of columns running the length of the chamber.

A variety of abbots, monks, and priests from across the known world stood behind these columns. Each of them had come to Versaden as attendants to their superior bishops. Each of them were now riveted as the important matters of the Great Session unfolded before their eyes.

In between the columns, the bishops themselves sat in rows of chairs set up for the occasion. A few of them had dark faces, signifying that they were from lands quite distant from Caeldora. All of them wore white robes signifying their office.

Atop a dais at the front of the chamber sat Emperor Arechon himself. With barrel chest and brooding countenance, he resembled a great eagle sitting its eyrie. His coat was made of purple wool, and a shimmering green cape fastened to his shoulders. All of his buttons and fastenings were gold. His hair had been cut short and curled after the fashion of the ancient emperors, and above his locks sat the imperial crown. This was wrought of laurel and oak leaves cast in gold, and its two ends were joined above his brow by an enormous, polished emerald.

On the tier below the emperor sat five ornate chairs. Of these, four were occupied presently. At the far left sat Olleus, Archbishop of Versaden and Primate of Caeldora. Beside him sat Mervantes, Archbishop of Barchidus and Primate of Hispona. In the center sat Ambiragust, Archbishop of Palatina and Primate of Palara. On the far right sat the barbarian convert Sceaduth, Archbishop of Ubighen and Primate of Vendenthia. The fifth chair, situated between Ambiragust and Sceaduth, had belonged to Archbishop Deorcad of Mereclestour. At the moment, it was empty.

But it would not remain so much longer.

As Emperor Arechon rose to his feet, the quiet chatter among the bishops ceased. "Assembled Fathers of the Church, the time has come now to fill the empty Chair of Saint Aucantia."

The emperor surveyed the seated bishops as he spoke, his piercing gaze passing and pausing over each face. Finally, his eyes came to rest upon the Mersian delegation. "The one who will fill this Chair will face grave challenges. To the north of the land of Mersex, two nations worship God apart from the communion of this Court. To the west, a great people live in darkness, devoid of the blessings of Aesus. The one who will fill this chair must be an overseer above ordinary measure. He must be a shepherd of extraordinary skill. Yea, he must be a bishop who will not rest until good news rings from a united Church in every mountain and valley of his island.

"Assembled Fathers of the Court of Saint Cephan, few there are who would be capable of such a high calling. As Holy Writ asks, 'Who is sufficient?' Few there are indeed who might bear such a great burden. Yet there sits among you one whose worth has been proven in these very areas. Among you sits a bishop who has cared for the people of Vendenthia with all his heart, with all his mind, and with all his strength—though he himself is not of them. It is he whom we now nominate to sit upon the Chair of Saint Aucantia: Simnor, Bishop of Darunen!"

Upon the completion of his speech, the emperor sat down, and Archbishop Olleus stood. As archbishop of Versaden and host of the Court, Olleus retained the right to speak first on all questions.

"Assembled Fathers, I welcome this nomination as well-suited to the task that awaits. Yet I would ask that the bishops of Mersex speak to the question themselves. Will they have Simnor of Darunen to shepherd them?"

From his vantage point behind one the columns, Morumus watched as, one by one, the bishops of the four cities of Mersex—Marfesbury, Noppenham, Hoccaster, and Laucura—stood and registered their assent. He leaned toward Abbot Grahem, who was standing beside him.

"Do you think Bishop Anathadus will speak against the nomination, sir?"

Grahem answered in a low voice without taking his eyes from the proceedings. "Not a chance. It's not his island, and all of the Mersians have assented. Nobody will speak against this Simnor now."

The abbot's words proved prophetic. The combination of an imperial nomination and unanimous Mersian consent meant that the nomination was approved without objection. At the conclusion of the vote, the emperor again stood and smiled.

"The vote is in favor. Let the chosen of God come forth to consecration!"

A hush fell over the crowds behind the pillars. From somewhere near the middle of the seated bishops, a white-cassocked bishop stood and walked forward. At first glance, Bishop Simnor seemed unremarkable. To Morumus he appeared ordinary—even humble. His hair was brown and tonsured close. His nose was prominent and slightly bulbous at its tip, yet not dominant. Of all his features, only his eyes were remarkable. Their irises were solid black.

When Simnor reached the dais, he kneeled and the four archbishops stood. One of Olleus's attendants handed him a vial of oil, which he poured out over Simnor's head. Following this, each of the archbishops laid their hands on his head, one atop the other. When all were in position, the emperor pronounced the consecration.

"We hereby declare Simnor, hitherto Bishop of Darunen, to be separated from the said bishopric. In immediate conjunction with said separation, we declare His Grace to be hereafter styled His Eminence and Most Reverend, and upon reception of the seals of his office, to be consecrated Archbishop of Mereclestour and Primate of Aeld Gowan."

As the emperor finished, the other archbishops removed their hands. An attendant then handed Mervantes a golden mitre, which the Archbishop of Hispona placed upon Simnor's brow. Following this, an attendant handed Ambiragust a gold-overlaid shepherd's staff, which the Archbishop of Palatina pressed into Simnor's right hand. Thereupon Simnor stood, and Sceaduth—Archbishop of Ubighen—took Simnor's head in his hands and kissed him on the forehead.

Then the emperor intoned again. "Having been anointed with holy oil, crowned with the holy crown, invested with the pastoral staff, and greeted with the kiss of peace, we hereby declare His Eminence, the Most Reverend Simnor, to be seated upon the Chair of Saint Aucantia as Archbishop of Mereclestour. Moreover, we hereby welcome him as Primate of Aeld Gowan, and recognize him as seated among the princes of the Court of Saint Cephan."

Upon completion of the investiture ceremony, the archbishops seated themselves upon the five chairs. Simnor's chair was on the side of the dais closest to Morumus and Grahem, and for a split second as he seated himself, Morumus caught a glimpse of the new archbishop's left hand. What he saw made his heart skip a beat.

The red monk's words came echoing back to him: *"Bishop Simnor has the full confidence of my order."*

And no wonder! There, on the back of Simnor's wrist, was the same marking Morumus had seen on the hands of the red monks. The new Archbishop of Mereclestour was a member of the Order of the Saving Blood!

"Sir"—Morumus leaned again toward Abbot Grahem—"Sir, did you see his hand—?"

"Quiet!" Grahem wasn't even listening. "Watch!"

On the floor of the Court, Bishop Anathadus had just come to his feet. "Most Excellent President!"

The emperor, who had returned to his own seat, sat up and peered forward. "We recognize you, Father."

"Your Excellency, I would like to lay a motion before the Court."

"Proceed."

"Assembled Fathers"—Anathadus turned round to survey his fellow bishops as he spoke—"today we have witnessed a great thing. A new archbishop has been consecrated—a new chief shepherd of the Church in Aeld Gowan. We know that each of us, as shepherds of the Church of Aesus our Lord, bear a solemn responsibility to keep watch over ourselves and over our flocks.

"And yet we know, too," Anathadus's voice gathered strength as he went, "that too often the flock is put in danger by negligence—either of ourselves, or of those under us. Our bishoprics are large, and sometimes our priests succumb to the temptation to laziness in their labors. They become loose of morals and negligent in alms. They become derelict in doctrine and weak in their responsibilities. They fail to teach and preach Holy Writ. And we, brothers—we as their shepherds and overseers—we bear this responsibility.

"Assembled Fathers"—Anathadus rose to his climax—"I propose therefore that the Court of Saint Cephan institute a general visitation. Let the Court issue binding orders to this effect: that each of us be enjoined and ordered to inspect and inquire of every parish in our bishoprics. Let us further be invested with the Court's authority to require the necessary reforms. Let all of this be done according to the most ancient customs for the same, and let all decisions of this visitation be subject to the review of the next meeting of the Court of Saint Cephan. Let us purge our parishes of those things not found to have the mandate of Holy Writ! Let us empty the excess coin in our coffers for the sake of charity! Let us purge our sanctuaries of images which ensnare our people! And in all of these things, let us strive to outdo one another for the glory of God!"

When he had finished his proposal, Anathadus sat down.

Beside Morumus, Abbot Grahem exhaled. "Well, he's done it," he said under his breath. "Let us see what comes now."

Whispers raged among those standing behind the pillars, yet for a long moment there was not a single sound to be heard among the seated bishops. Then, one after another, a handful of bishops stood, each calling to be recognized first:

"Most Excellent President!"

"Most Excellent President!"

A few bishops did not even wait to be recognized before registering their protest:

"Objection, Your Excellence!"

"Point of Order, Your Excellency!"

Besides those on their feet, a majority of the bishops looked irritated.

"This is encouraging," Grahem whispered to Morumus. "Perhaps Anathadus was right after all."

According to procedure, the president of the Court, who was seated in his chair and not standing, ought to have recognized those bishops who stood before him. Yet instead of following procedure, the emperor sat mute on his throne. His expression was unreadable, and he acted as though he could neither hear nor see the protests before him. After a few minutes, the handful of standing bishops sat down awkwardly.

A moment later, the Archbishop of Palatina stood and turned to the throne. "Most Excellent President."

"We recognize you, Most Reverend Father."

"Your Excellency, I would like to second the motion—with amendment."

"Proceed."

"Your Excellency, I would like to amend the motion as follows. Let the oversight of the general visitation be removed from the local bishops, and let it be placed into the hands of a *legatorum* appointed by, and subject to, the President of the Court."

The emperor smiled. "The President asks unanimous consent to amend the motion. Any opposed?"

No sooner were the words out of the emperor's mouth than two-thirds of the bishops of the Court were on their feet. Numerous cries of "Most Excellent President!" and "Objection, Your Excellence!" and "Point of Order, Your Excellency!" rang out, filling the Audience Hall with outcry.

Morumus gasped. The term *legatorum* was Vilguran. In the days of the Old Imperium, it was to denote a body of agents called *legates*. Each legate was invested with plenipotentiary powers—that is, the power to act in the name of, and with the full authority of, the emperor himself. By substituting a *legatorum* for the oversight of local bishops, the Archbishop of Palatina was proposing that the Court of Saint Cephan cede its full authority, at least until its next meeting, to the emperor and whomever he chose to act in his name.

It was a radical proposal.

Foremost among the protesting bishops was Anathadus himself. "Your Excellency! His Eminence cannot amend my motion until it is seconded! And as it has not yet been seconded, I withdraw my motion! God help me, I withdraw it!"

Above the clamor, Arechon remained impassive. Finally he raised one hand, signaling for silence. When he had it, he spoke up. "Hearing no objection, the President rules the motion so amended."

This brought all of the bishops to their feet, roaring at the flagrant perversion of procedure. For a moment longer, the emperor sat unmoved. Then, with the suddenness of a striking serpent, he sprang to his feet.

"Order!"

In that same moment the doors at the back of the Audience Hall flew open. Through the open portals streamed two long lines of imperial soldiers. These spread out as they entered the room, flowing forward until they formed a wall on each side between the columns and the floor. Each of the soldiers carried a long, polished spear. Silence fell over the Court, and the assembled bishops quickly sat down.

"If the Court of Saint Cephan cannot maintain her own order"—the emperor's thundering tone was ominous—"we are obliged to maintain it ourselves. Now, there is a motion before the Court. We call the question. All those in favor will stand." As he spoke these words, the soldiers surrounding the floor leveled their spears at the assembled bishops.

For the bishops of the Court, the courageous thing to do would have been to remain seated. Yet as the spears aimed at them, all of the archbishops and bishops stood—save one. Anathadus alone remained seated.

"The motion carries. Be seated."

The archbishops and bishops sat down, and the emperor returned to his feet. "Inasmuch as the Court of Saint Cephan has elected to institute a general visitation for the sake of inquisition and reform, and inasmuch as it has invested our royal person with the selection of a *legatorum*, it now falls to us to appoint the same."

"Most Excellent President." The Archbishop of Palatina smiled, rising to his feet.

Arechon took no notice.

"Most Excellent President." The archbishop's smile strained, but was still in place.

Again, Arechon ignored him.

"Your Excellency." Ambiragust turned to address the emperor face to face.

The Emperor of the Vilgurans looked down on the Archbishop like an eagle considering a rabbit. "Order." He spoke in a cold tone, his eyes unblinking.

Ambiragust sat down, his expression withered. Morumus could see it plain on his face that the man had been used. *He must have thought that* he *was going to be appointed head of the* legatorum.

"The current order has carried on for too long." The emperor's voice echoed down the Hall. "For too long, this Court has been characterized by sloth and malaise. A general visitation is most needed. Yet far be it from us to entrust the oversight of such a visitation with those very persons who have sat atop the pilings as they erode. No. In order for this visitation to have effect, it must be presided over by a new order—an order that has proven its worth and usefulness in the administration of our dominion in the East." Arechon's voice rose to a shout: "A new order!"

At these words, another twin column entered the Great Hall from the open doors at its rear. Yet instead of bearing spears and wearing the imperial green, this time those who entered wore drawn hoods of dark red. Like oozing blood they came, silent and swift, until a red monk stood between every pair of spears.

Morumus could not believe what was unfolding before his eyes. The emperor had already placed a member of the Order of the Saving Blood on the Chair of Saint Aucantia.

Now he was placing the Red Order over the entire Church.

The emperor smiled. "By the power invested in us by the Court of Saint Cephan, we hereby invest our powers of inquisition and reform—the full powers of *legatorum*—to the Order of the Saving Blood."

PART III

NIGHTMARE WAKING

16

It was a glorious summer afternoon when Somnadh returned to the valley for the last time. Urien, who had been walking among the orchard outside the walls of the keep, saw him coming from afar. At the sight of his horse emerging from the woods, her heart leapt. She dashed out from among the rows of fruit trees to meet him.

"Somnadh!" She waved.

"Urien!" A minute later he had drawn up his horse along the path where she waited. Dismounting quickly, he embraced his sister.

"It is so good to see you, brother," she whispered into his shoulder.

"And you, dear one."

A few minutes later the two of them walked together in Urien's garden. A few of the servants were seeing to Somnadh's horse. A few others, on Urien's orders, were preparing a celebratory dinner posthaste.

"It smells delicious, whatever they are cooking." Somnadh inhaled as the breeze carried a waft of warm air from the kitchen across the garden wall.

"Fresh venison," replied Urien. "There is plenty of it about the forest this time of year, and we have a good supply of herbs laid back."

"Wonderful. I brought you a bottle of wine. We'll have it brought up to table."

"Will you be staying long, Somnadh? A few days?" Urien's tone grew hopeful. "A week?"

"Not long, sister." Somnadh did not make eye contact when he spoke. There was something foreboding in his tone.

Urien stopped. "What is it, brother?"

"Let us leave it until after dinner."

"Why? If you're going away again tomorrow, why not just tell me? It would not be the first time."

"It's different this time, dear one."

"What do you mean?" Urien's voice rose involuntarily. Her brother's expression was unreadable, but something in his voice alarmed her.

"Leave it for later."

"I don't want to leave it. Just tell me when you're leaving again, and how long you'll be away. I'm a grown woman, Somnadh, not a fragile little girl."

"Trust me, Urien, this is different. For your own good, just leave—"

"*Don't!*" Urien's anger curdled in her stomach. "Don't tell me to leave it again, Somnadh. I will not! You are always leaving!"

Somnadh took a step back, and his expression grew dark. Yet before either of them could speak again, they heard the sound of a throat clearing behind them. Turning, they saw one of the servants standing at the tower door.

"Dinner is ready, my lady."

With an effort, Urien regained her composure. "Come, brother." She did nothing to melt the ice in her tone. "Dinner is ready."

The main hall of the tower keep was neither ornate nor uncomfortable. On both ends stood great stone hearths—which at this time of year were almost always left cold—and a pair of doors on either side let one out into the corridors. A wheel-shaped chandelier provided light for the small table set beneath it. It was to this table that Somnadh and Urien were led.

"Thank you," said Urien after another servant had seated her. "You may bring the food to us immediately."

"And the wine," reminded Somnadh as he sat himself.

Urien called to the departing man, "My brother brought a bottle of wine. It is among his bags. Bring it to us."

As they waited for the servants to return, Somnadh attempted to engage his sister in light conversation. "The servants are all well, I trust?"

"Yes." Urien's answer was crisp.

"Did you enjoy the books I brought you last time?"

"Of course."

"And the Mother?"

"Same as always."

"And the harvest?"

"Abundant."

"Good. No Seed?"

"No seed."

"Has she spoken to you?"

"*Never.*"

"She will, in her own time. Be patient." Somnadh sounded disappointed.

The return of the servants cut short Urien's reply, which was just as well. One of the eunuchs set plates of venison and vegetables before them. The other poured wine from a clay jug into wooden cups. Then they both stepped back.

"That will be all." Urien released them with a wave. Once they left the room, she fixed Somnadh with her sharpest look. "Now. Explain yourself."

Somnadh met her hardened gaze with one of his own. His dark eyes did not blink as he spoke. "I will tell you everything before we leave the table, dear one. But first we will eat."

Urien bristled, and she would have snapped again. But then she noticed the heavy lines on her brother's face. This brought her up short. For the first time that day, for the first time in a long time, she remembered just how much older than she Somnadh was. More than this, the lines indicated to her that whatever it was Somnadh was withholding, it was going to be as hard for him as it was for her.

The anger in her subsided.

"Very well, brother. We will eat first."

By the time they had finished eating a quarter of an hour later, Urien felt much less tense. The venison had turned out as good as it had smelled, and the vegetables were indeed fresh. She had never tasted this particular wine—some sort of spiced fruit, though she was not sure which—but it had a pleasant, relaxing effect. Finishing her cup, she sat it down next to her empty plate. Somnadh had already finished.

"A most excellent meal, Urien. I see I shall not have to worry for your nourishment once I leave."

"So you are leaving again?"

"Yes."

"I knew it. How soon?"

"Tonight."

Urien sighed. "Tonight?"

Her brother nodded.

"When will you return?"

Here Somnadh paused. For a moment he looked away, and Urien sensed that he was preparing to say something awful. When he spoke again, she found that her intuition had been correct.

"I will not be returning, dear one."

It was as if a knife had been thrust into her stomach. She opened her mouth, but no words came out. All of her earlier talk turned to dust. She felt *exactly* like a fragile little girl. Tears welled at the corner of her eyes. When she managed to speak, her voice was shaking.

"Why, brother? Why will you not return?"

Somnadh's own eyes looked moist, but his voice held firm. "There is trouble back home. The king of Mersex has died. His son is preparing for war against our people. But there may be a chance for peace. So I must return home to help."

Urien's eyes were so full of tears now that vision was blurry. "Please, brother, take me with you."

Somnadh shook his head. "You know I cannot."

"Please, brother!" She couldn't stop the sob. "Please don't leave me here alone!"

"Urien, there is no man or woman in the world for whom I care more than you. But the Mother must be tended."

"Couldn't you find another?" Urien face burned with renewed anger. Tears poured down her cheeks.

"No, dear one, I cannot. You are the Mother's chosen."

"So were you!" she wailed. "You were the one who found the Seed! You were the one who carried it here! Why can you go, but not I?"

Somnadh sighed. "I was but the Hand of the Mother, Urien. I fulfilled my role when I planted the Seed. But you are the Queen's Heart. You cannot ever leave her side. It is not just an honor; it is the ancient law of our people—the sacred rule of our faith."

"There must be some way . . ."

"There is not, dear one. I am sorry. This is as hard for me as it is for you."

The moment the words left Somnadh's lips, something inside Urien broke. In the next instant, all her carefully hedged-in doubts and stored-up frustrations broke free. She leapt to her feet, ignoring the spinning sensation it produced.

"Hard for *you!*" Urien did not realize that she was screaming until after she had flung the first volley. But by then, she did not care. "Hard for *you*, brother? *Hard?* You have come and gone from this place as often as you wished! You have never had to spend endless winter months languishing in this dreary vale! You have never for a day been so alone as I have been all these years!"

Somnadh was on his feet now, and there was concern in his voice. "Please, Urien, sit back down. I know you are upset, but you must remember how great a blessing it is to serve the Mother as you do—"

Urien's wordless scream cut him off. "The Mother! The Mother! *What* Mother? She has never spoken to me, Somnadh— never! I am not her daughter, I am her prisoner! And she is no Mother! She is nothing but a jailer!" The hall was spinning furiously. Black spots were beginning to appear at the corners of her vision. Yet Urien was not finished. "I *hate* the Mother! I hate her, Somnadh! Do you hear me? *I hate her!*" No sooner were the words past her lips than the spots grew and converged . . .

Darkness enveloped her.

Somnadh's own face was flush as he rushed around the table to where his sister had collapsed. The wine had worked just in time.

"Sleep well, dear one." He knew she would until morning.

It was all he could do. Much as he wished otherwise, she could not come with him. The Mother must be tended.

A moment later, he heard footsteps in the corridor outside the hall. Soon two of the servants had appeared in the doorway. Somnadh stood.

"Take the lady to her chamber in the tower. She is not feeling well."

The servants obeyed without hesitation, and soon Somnadh was alone in the hall. He sat back down at the table. Urien's words had disturbed him—disturbed him greatly. *If only the Mother would speak to her!* If only his dear sister could hear the goddess whisper to her, she would no longer feel her duties to be so onerous. He was sure of it.

But how? The *Mordruui* were already taking more risks than was prudent.

She must be displeased. Our service must be insufficient.

Somnadh stood. There was only one thing for it. If the Mother would not speak to her own Heart, then she must not be satisfied. And the Mother *must* be satisfied. He would order the *Mordruui* . . .

More risks must be taken.

"The cycles of life are a mercy from God,
     "The seasons of earth are his servants;
     "Sun and snow, sowing and reaping,
"Hearth and harvest are hymns to our God!"

The liturgical hymn was a fitting companion to the season. Autumn was coming to Caeldora, and Donnach, Morumus, and Oethur were taking a long walk in the forest surrounding Lorudin Abbey. Two months had passed since the Court of Saint Cephan.

Many questions remained. Who were the Order of the Saving Blood? What were they after? If they cared for the Church, why had they helped the emperor overthrow the prerogatives of the Court? Why had they become the willing hands of Arechon's unholy scheme? Abbot Grahem and Bishop Anathadus had talked these matters over and over the entire journey back from Versaden to Aevor. In fact, they had talked of little else. Yet by the time Grahem and Morumus had taken their leave of the bishop, no clear answers had emerged. Nevertheless, Anathadus was not daunted.

"Take heart, brothers," the bishop encouraged them as they departed. "This is far from the first time that men have sought to wrest control of the Church from her true Sovereign. These things are difficult to bear. They may become more difficult still, for Holy Writ says that judgment begins at the house of God. Yet in the end, our Lord always brings justice to victory. He who sits in the heavens laughs, and usurpers come to a bad end. Never forget that, brothers. King Aesus is still on his throne!"

Like the harvest season, the time since the return to Lorudin had been most fruitful for Donnach, Morumus, and Oethur. Donnach and Oethur had settled in well among the brothers at the abbey, and both had begun to enjoy the threefold life of the Rule: labor with the hands, prayer with the heart, and study with the head. Moreover, both men had progressed well in Vilguran—to the point that neither needed further instruction from Morumus in the language.

With this task completed, the three men were now free to pursue more specialized interests. For Oethur, this meant learning Caeldoran so that he could minister among the farms and villages along the River Lor. For Donnach and Morumus, it meant starting work on the Grendannathi translation of Holy Writ.

Morumus was overjoyed to turn to this task at last. For one thing, he had had more than enough of burglary. If he never had to stalk another bishop, he would not mind! For another thing, translation work suited him. He delighted in learning Donnach's language—which was a near cousin to Dyfannish—and both of them enjoyed using the Herido edition of Holy Writ from Bishop Anathadus's library. Their translation would be a great, sweeping sword against the Dark Faith in Grendannath. From what Oethur had revealed to him in the Cathedral Park, the *Dree* were more organized in their homelands than Morumus ever imagined—and that was ten years ago! How much more today?

But once the light of God's Word came to the barbarians, the last shelter for the Dark Faith on Aeld Gowan would be gone.

Yet for all the joy of harvest, home, and healthy labor, Morumus continued to ruminate over Versaden. Since leaving the imperial capital, Morumus had felt . . . *shadowed*. A deep sense of unease had settled upon him, and he could not unravel it. He felt he was missing something important. *But what?* The more the question echoed in his mind, the more he suspected it was madness to continue asking. Yet he could not seem to silence the noise—except when he was absorbed in translating Holy Writ, or out walking with his friends.

On this particular afternoon Morumus, Donnach, and Oethur were taking some exercise together in the woods surrounding Lorudin Abbey. They made it a point to do so as often as their responsibilities permitted, for the forest reminded all three of the woodlands of northern Aeld Gowan. As they walked, they would often share accounts of their upbringing or other recollections of home. Because Morumus had lived longest in Lorudin, he usually led these excursions.

This day, however, Donnach had asked to take the point position. Following him, Morumus and Oethur climbed an ascending path along the south wall of the valley until they reached the ridge above. Here Donnach forsook the main path, which circled the valley along its rim, and took a more grown-over track, which plunged into the heart of the forest. Morumus could not remember having been this way before, but the Grendannathi was sure of every turn. After about an hour, they crested another ridge and dropped down the far side into a narrow gulley. At the bottom of the gulley flowed a small, swift stream. This they followed for another quarter of an hour before stopping beside a pool of modest size.

The Caeldoran woodlands did not lack for standing water, yet the place to which Donnach had led them was no mere widening of the streambed. Just prior to flowing into the pool, the stream dropped abruptly over a ledge, falling two-dozen spans to form a splendid waterfall.

"Here we are, brothers." Donnach's words held quiet satisfaction as he seated himself on the soft surface of a moss-covered rock.

"What is this place?" Oethur surveyed the water and the surrounding woods.

"A refuge." Donnach lifted one hand to point at the falling water. "You cannot see it unless you get close, but there is a cave behind that waterfall."

"Really?" Morumus followed Donnach's gesture and squinted without success.

"Yes. Some time ago, I was caught here during a storm. As I huddled against the rocks near the falls, I caught a glimpse of a space behind the water. Since I was already soaked, I figured I had little to lose. So I explored further. When I went behind the water, I found the cave. It does not go deep into the earth, but it is long enough to have a dry chamber in the back. I have used it since for overnight vigils."

Oethur half-snorted. "You might have met a bear, Donnach!"

The Grendannathi shook his head. "The opening is too narrow."

"How did you ever come this far out from the abbey?" asked Morumus.

"Soon after I arrived at the abbey, one of the brothers advised me to find a secluded place to use for extended times of fasting or vigils."

"I received the same advice," said Oethur. "This is a fine place, Donnach. Very secluded."

"This same brother told me that once I found such a place, I ought to keep it private, and for some time, I have heeded his advice. But to keep such a place to myself seems selfish. So I thought I would share it with you two brothers."

"Thank you, Donnach." Morumus smiled. Though they had been stopped but a few minutes, he already felt quite taken with the location. The sanctuary was surrounded by tall trees, thick-boled and widely-spaced. The pool itself was clear and deep, and the falling water shone like a pillar of flowing diamonds, refracting daylight from myriad facets. Crowning these visual delights, the sound of the fall was a gentle roar that soothed the ears.

The three men lingered in the place as long as they could, and dusk was fast fading as they crested the rim of Lorudin Vale on their return trip. Below them, lights were coming on at the abbey. The bell for the evening meal had finished ringing by the time they reached bottom.

"We had best make haste," said Morumus as they entered the grounds. "If the brothers are seated before we enter, there will be discipline."

"Not to mention no supper," Donnach observed pointedly.

Thankfully, the serving line was still progressing when Oethur, Donnach, and Morumus reached the refectory. A few of the brothers still waiting for their portions eyed them askance as they entered, but most paid them little heed. Only Brother Basilus—a stoutish monk who always made it a point to be last in line for meals—actually frowned at them.

"The last shall be first, eh brother?" Oethur grinned as they took their positions at the end of the line. At this, the portly monk's scowl deepened.

"I am surprised the food is still being served," said Donnach. "I did not think we would make it in time."

"Got a late start." Basilus sounded irritated. "Silgram discovered a crack in one of the chimneys this afternoon."

"How bad?" asked Morumus.

"Bad enough. Abbot says the chimney will have to be taken down and rebuilt in the spring. Until then, all the cooking will have to share one chimney."

"That will mean smaller portions through the winter." Oethur feigned concern. He slapped Basilus on the back and smiled. "Good thing you have some extra stored up, brother."

Basilus turned his head sharply toward Oethur. The expression on his face was dangerous.

Dinner itself was simple fare: a cold slab of cheese, a dense hunk of bread, and a hot bowl of vegetable stew in which to warm and soften the rest. The unornamented nature of the meals at Lorudin stemmed from the Rule itself. Except on feast days, the monks were forbidden to eat anything that they did not grow themselves. The point of this provision was not just to keep the monks of Lorudin humble and hardworking, though doubtless it did that. The point was to prevent corruption.

Despite the relative sameness of the ingredients, few of the brothers at Lorudin Abbey ever complained about the meals. Brothers Silgram and Ortto—who were twins as well as spiritual kin—were quite experienced cooks. The joy with which they approached their labors was like leaven. It mixed into the contents of their cook-pots and ovens, and the result was filling, satisfying fare. Indeed, dinner was always a most joyful occasion at Lorudin Abbey. When a day of full labor ended with a full belly, who could be anything but thankful?

On this evening, however, something was different. Morumus could sense it almost as soon as he passed from the kitchen line into the refectory hall. All of the familiar elements were present: the clatter of wooden spoons and bowls, and the chatter of the brothers across the boards. Yet just beneath the surface of this—or perhaps suspended above it—there was something else. Something foreign. A certain nervous tension seemed to tingle in the air. Scanning the room, it did not take Morumus long to locate the source.

At the far end of the hall, seated at the head table next to Abbot Grahem, was a monk Morumus had never seen. The man's hood was down, yet there was no mistaking the color of his robe. Morumus turned aside quickly and seated himself at the nearest available table. Donnach and Oethur joined him a moment later.

"The brothers seem disquieted tonight." Donnach sat down across from Morumus.

"Like soldiers promised wine, only to be given water." Oethur seated himself next to Donnach.

"Keep your voices low," said Morumus, "Did you not see?"

"See what?" Oethur started to turn in his seat until Morumus stopped him.

"Do not look!" He spoke through clenched teeth.

"Why not?" Oethur did stop turning.

"There is a red monk seated at the head table with Abbot Grahem."

Both men's eyes widened.

"Here?" asked Donnach.

Ignoring Morumus's prior injunction, Oethur made as though he were cracking his neck—pushing his chin with his knuckles first away from, and then toward, the head table. "He's right. Did you notice that he is not covering his head?"

"I did." Morumus knew annoyance rang in his voice.

Now even Donnach had to have a look. "What do you think he is doing here?"

"The visitation," said Oethur as Morumus chewed a mouthful of stew-soaked bread.

Morumus nodded as he swallowed. "That has to be it."

"You may be in danger, Morumus." Donnach took a bite out of his cheese.

Morumus shook his head. "When I fled from the one in the cathedral, I used their own trick and kept my hood up the entire time. Besides that, I'm dead. Remember?"

"If you are dead," said Oethur, "I think I will have your cheese."

The remainder of dinner passed with silence among the assembled monks. After everybody had been served and seated, one of the brothers who had finished first moved to a rough wooden lectern at the front of the hall. After offering thanks for the meal, he began reading from a large, bound copy of Holy Writ. As soon as he began, the various conversations along the boards ceased. The Rule of Lorudin Abbey was not often severe in its penalties, yet at a few points it was inflexible. The requirement for "attentive silence" during the reading of Holy Writ was one of these.

Upon the conclusion of dinner, each monk cleared his place from the table. Once the tables were bare, the four brothers assigned for the week wiped the smooth surfaces—beginning with wet rags, then with dry, and finally with oil to polish and preserve the wood. As they did this, the others made their way from the refectory to the chapel. Another of the brothers had run ahead of them, and was ringing the bell for Vespers.

The chapel was the oldest structure at Lorudin Abbey. Its design reflected its sole purpose as a place to meet for worship: a simple rectangular building with a peaked roof and a small belfry. The walls were made of grey stone, which the first brothers of Lorudin had quarried from the surrounding ridges. Likewise, the great beams and rafters of the roof—hidden by the thatch without but visible from within—had been timbered from the surrounding forest. In a very real sense, the chapel had been hewn out from the surrounding hills.

The chapel was Morumus's favorite place in all of Lorudin Abbey, for in its construction he saw a metaphor for the power of the good news: the rough refined, the old made new, creation recreated and summoned to worship.

The chapel furnishings were deliberately sparse. Unlike the Cathedral of Saint Dreunos in Versaden, there was no altar. Instead, two rows of pews divided by a center aisle faced a short wooden pulpit. On a small table in front of the pulpit sat an open copy of Holy Writ. The overall simplicity, characteristic of the Church's old order, was intended to display what the brothers at Lorudin believed to be central to religion.

The subdued pallor that had hung over dinner was even more palpable during Vespers. The brothers gathered in the chapel were clearly unsettled, and it was obvious from the direction of their glances that the reason wore a red robe and sat in the first pew. Lorudin Abbey had known for some time now about the visitation. On the very first evening after his return from Versaden, Abbot Grahem had told the community all about the Great Session and its tumultuous proceedings. Yet up until this day, none of the brothers—excepting Morumus, Oethur, and Donnach—had ever seen a monk of the Order of the Saving Blood.

Upon the conclusion of Vespers, the monks filed out of the chapel toward their rooms. As the days shortened toward winter, it was not uncommon for the men to gather for fellowship after the evening service. Silgram and Ortto usually had a fire burning on the kitchen hearth, along with something warm to drink. Yet on this night only one or two of the brothers leaving the chapel drifted back toward the refectory. Most of them walked briskly toward the dormitory and their waiting cells.

"Let's meet in my cell," suggested Donnach as he, Oethur, and Morumus exited the chapel. They had not gone more than a few steps, however, when a voice arrested their progress.

"Morumus!" Abbot Grahem spoke from behind them. "Morumus, come back here please!"

Turning, Morumus saw that the abbot still remained near the front of the chapel. The red monk stood beside him. "You two go ahead." He motioned for them to continue. "I'll be along as quickly as I can."

Dread pooled in the pit of Morumus's stomach. Each step back sent a ripple reverberating across its dark surface. He did his best to ignore the sensation, and kept his expression neutral as he approached.

"Morumus," said Abbot Grahem when he reached them, "I do not believe you have met our guest." He gestured toward the red monk. "This is Ulwilf. He is a legate of the Order of the Saving Blood. They have been charged by the Court of Saint Cephan with conducting a general visitation of the whole Church. You will remember that I mentioned such a visitation upon my return?"

Morumus could take a hint. "Yes, sir, I do remember." Pivoting toward the red monk, he bowed his head. "It is a pleasure to meet you, sir." The words were an utter lie.

"And you, Morumus," said the legate in thickly-accented Vilguran. Looking up, Morumus got his first good look at a red monk. The candlelight of the chapel interior was not very bright, yet even so Morumus could see that Ulwilf was not much older than he—perhaps ten years? He could see, too, that the monk had pale skin and very dark eyes.

"Part of Ulwilf's charge," Abbot Grahem continued, "is to investigate spiritual conditions not only among our community, but also among the community we serve. Thus he will be speaking to the people of the river villages."

"As you may have guessed, Morumus," said Ulwilf, "I am not a native of this country. I am from Vendenthia. I speak the language of the Church, but not the language of Caeldora."

Morumus nodded. He knew where this was going.

Abbot Grahem looked at the younger monk, and even in the dim light the latter could see the significance in his expression. "You will serve as Ulwilf's translator, Morumus. Be his ears and mouth when he goes among the villages. Help him in whatever ways he requires. For as long as Ulwilf is among us, this is your primary task. Do you understand?"

"Yes, sir." But inwardly he winced.

"We will begin tomorrow," said Ulwilf. "With the seasons turning, traveling will be better sooner rather than later. You will attend me at the stables immediately following breakfast. We will be gone for many weeks, so prepare accordingly."

"Yes, sir." Morumus's heart sunk. *So much for translation.*

"Good." Ulwilf turned toward the abbot. "This is all that I require at present, Abbot Grahem. I shall take my leave of you now." He inclined his head.

Abbot Grahem returned the gesture. "Sleep well, Brother Ulwilf."

"Good night, Morumus. Get plenty of rest." So saying, the red monk walked out of the chapel and disappeared into the night.

"Help me extinguish the candles, Morumus," said the abbot as Ulwilf departed.

The two men worked in silence, one on each side of the chapel. Beginning at the back, they extinguished each candle in the hanging wooden chandeliers using long snuffers. By the time they reached the front of the sanctuary and the few remaining lights, a quarter of an hour had passed. Abbot Grahem paused before extinguishing the final candle, and motioned for Morumus to draw near. In the dim light, it was difficult to tell whether the dark lines on his face were mere shadows.

"You know why I chose you, Morumus."

He nodded. "You want me to watch him."

"We know already that the Red Order is dangerous. We know, too, that they are well-connected. You saw what they did at Versaden."

"Yes, sir." Morumus would never forget.

"What we do not know—what we must find out—is what they are seeking. The sooner we know that, the better for us all."

"I understand."

"Good. Do whatever you can to gain his confidence. If this Ulwilf believes he can trust you—if he believes you are sympathetic to his work—then he may divulge something. But tell him nothing of our journey to Versaden, and nothing of those who traveled with us. He questioned me extensively today about the Court. From that conversation, I gather that the Red Order is looking for those who helped the Northmen escape. They seem to suspect Anathadus; his was the only vote against the visitation. But I don't think they have proof. Ulwilf knows that I attended Bishop Anathadus at the Court, and all the brothers here know that you left with me. So if he asks, you are to tell him that you accompanied me to Aevor in order to visit the library. Tell him that you remained there while I traveled on to Versaden with the bishop. But do not tell him of your translation, and under no circumstances are you to tell him of our connection with Ciolbail and Treowin. We don't want him to know *anything* that links us to the Northmen."

"What of Oethur and Donnach, sir? If the legate learns of them, there could be trouble."

"Indeed." Abbot Grahem's expression was grim. "The problem has not escaped my notice. I do not like it, Morumus, but I shall have to send them away for a time."

"Where will you send them, sir?"

"Oethur is learning Caeldoran, is he not?"

"He is."

"I will send him to Aevor, then. He will have plenty of opportunity to practice there."

"And Donnach, too? He would love the bishop's library."

"He would, but if the Red Order discovered them there together, it might make just the proof they are seeking against the bishop. We cannot allow that. Donnach has his translation work. I will send him on spiritual retreat somewhere, where he may pursue it without danger or interruption."

"He has a cave in the hills that he uses for private meditation."

"Excellent. That will be perfect. Will you be seeing the two of them tonight?"

"Yes, sir."

"Tell them what I have just told you, and tell them to stay away from breakfast and out of sight in the morning. Once you and the legate have departed, I will send them on their ways."

"Yes, sir." But his voice was grim.

Abbot Grahem clasped him on the shoulder. "This is a difficult business we are about, son. But our Lord is still on his throne. Never forget that."

"I won't, sir."

"Good. Have a care, Morumus. I have a sense that getting to the heart of the Red Order may endanger more than just the body. Keep watch over your soul at all times. Even as you feign friendship with Ulwilf, remember who you are. This will be your most difficult task yet."

Morumus nodded. The dread that had stirred earlier now churned in his stomach.

"I think the beasts are glad to be done."

Morumus looked up from where he was kneeling next to the fire. Ulwilf had just stepped out from the edge of the trees. They had made camp that night in a small grove just north of the Naud Road. After selecting the site and asking Morumus to build them a fire, Ulwilf went to tie the horses near the outer perimeter, where they could graze.

Morumus gestured to the fire, which he had kept intentionally low on the other man's instructions. "How is this, sir?"

"Just right." Retrieving the bag of provisions from the small mound of gear nearby, Ulwilf sat down facing Morumus across the meager hearth. "Will you?"

Morumus nodded, and they both bowed their heads briefly while Morumus returned thanks. After this, Ulwilf opened the sack and withdrew their supper: a loaf of dense brown bread, a misshapen hunk of white cheese, and a few carrots. These he divided evenly, and for the next half hour or so, both men ate and neither spoke.

Morumus stared off into the fire as he munched. The evenings had grown cooler over the past two weeks as autumn enfolded Caeldora. Since they had departed Lorudin, most of the trees had donned glorious shawls of bright orange, deep red, and sharp yellow. The air had grown crisper, too. The days remained warm enough in their full strength, yet at morning and evening the season made one like an aged grandfather—in need of a blanket to stay comfortable. Morumus found himself sitting and sleeping closer to the fire each night—and leaning toward it more and more during dinner. It was getting harder to stay warm. He wished he was back at Lorudin.

Per Abbot Grahem's instructions, Morumus had worked hard these weeks to gain Ulwilf's trust. It was very delicate business. At first, he remained neutral in translating between the Caeldoran villagers and the red monk. Yet as the days passed and he noticed Ulwilf's reactions to certain situations, he began a gradual mimicry. It was delicate work—a concurring frown here, a suspicious tone there—and it made Morumus feel slightly soiled. But it seemed to be working. To this point, Ulwilf had revealed nothing to him about the Order. Yet he had seemed increasingly more at ease around Morumus.

"I am very dissatisfied with things in these villages, Morumus."

Morumus looked up. Ulwilf had finished eating, and was now looking at him over the top of the low flames.

"Sir?" Morumus dared not venture more at this point.

"Do you know why I am dissatisfied?" Ulwilf's gaze was now fixed upon him, weighing.

Although surprised to find himself so suddenly dropped into the crucible, Morumus was not unprepared. "I suspect, sir, that it is the way these villages worship God."

"If you can call it that!"

So, he had pushed at just the right place.

"Very good, Morumus. Now," he continued, his expression less-guarded, but still measuring, "can you tell me the problem?"

Morumus thought he knew what the red monk was seeking in an answer. Yet he also knew that the risk of failure increased with each step he took. Best to answer obliquely. "Sir, I came to Lorudin at a young age. Their way of worship is the same as in the villages, and it is all that I have ever known. What you are able to see, I can only sense."

Ulwilf almost smiled, and something like sympathy sounded in his voice. "I understand, son." This was the first time he had called Morumus *son*. "Still, tell me what you sense."

"I may be wrong, sir"—Morumus kept his tone humble—"but I sense that something is missing. One senses the same thing in the worship at the abbey," he added on sudden inspiration.

For a moment Ulwilf said nothing, and Morumus's heart sank. He had failed—

Yet in the next instant, a look of quiet exultation came over the monk's pale features. "For one who has known nothing else, you are very close to the heart of things, Morumus. There is indeed something missing from the worship of the Church in these villages and—as you correctly point out—from the worship at the abbey. Behind them all is a single problem. Do you want me to tell you what it is?"

"If you will, sir."

"They have the written stories of the miraculous, yet they have no living experience of it. They have Holy Writ, but they have no Holy Mystery."

Morumus was getting close. Yet he was not sure how to get the rest of the way. After a moment, not knowing what else to say, he told the truth. "Sir, I know nothing of this 'Holy Mystery.'"

"I know, son. Before I joined the Order of the Saving Blood, I myself was in an even worse state. I knew neither Mystery nor Writ, but practiced the religion of my parents and ancestors." Ulwilf closed his eyes as he spoke.

"As a child, my parents dedicated me among the Groves of Frudheda. I grew to manhood as a warrior, and killed many enemies in the name of Lohaldir her son. I knew nothing else, and would have remained thus my entire life." Ulwilf opened his eyes, and their dark centers shown like polished onyx in the dim firelight. "But all of that changed five years ago."

"What happened?"

"A miracle. A man came to our village. We knew he was different—not only from his red robe, but from the strange things of which he spoke. He claimed to bring great tidings, and asked the elders of my people for permission to address the village. They granted it to him, and called all of us to come to the Stone of Judgment and hear what the stranger had to say. It was a beautiful spring morning: blue skies overhead, crisp air among the trees, and fresh green buds on every branch. I shall never forget that day, Morumus—the day my life changed forever."

"This man—he was a missionary? From the Order of the Saving Blood?"

"Yes, from my own order."

"What did he say?"

"He told us the truth." Here again Ulwilf closed his eyes as he spoke.

"When all of my people were assembled at the Stone, the man commended us for our zeal. He had visited other villages of our people before, and knew that we were devoted to the old gods. This earned him many cheers. He said that such sincerity could not but earn us a blessing. This earned him more cheers. Then he told us that he had been sent to bring us this blessing. What acclamations then! I myself gave a shout! But there was a twist. The man told us that, despite our sincerity, we had worshipped in ignorance. The name of the great God was not Wodu. Nor was the name of the Holy Son Lohaldir, but Aesus. The man said we were right to worship this Son and bow before his Mother. But we no longer needed to pour the blood of our children in Frudheda's sacred grove. Rather, the Holy Mother had born Aesus in her own sacred womb in order that his blood might be poured out for us—that the season of our darkness and sin might be changed forever."

Despite his wariness of Ulwilf and the Red Order, Morumus's imagination fired as he listened to this account, envisioning the scene: a lone missionary standing on a large stone, boldly declaiming to a horde of surrounding barbarians. "Then what happened? Your people believed?"

"Believed?" Ulwilf opened his eyes once again. "We nearly killed that man."

"*What?*"

"His message was believable, it was true—I myself remember feeling quite compelled by it. But to tell us that our sacrifices were unnecessary? My people had just come through a very difficult winter, one that had lasted longer than any in recent memory. More than one child's blood had been required that year before Frudheda heard our pleas and brought spring— at least, that was what we thought at the time. To imagine that so many little ones had perished in vain was a dreadful thought—too difficult to bear. The mothers of the dead, as well as the priests, began shouting for the man's blood. He was a liar, they said! He would provoke Frudheda to send an even worse winter! He would stir up the wrath of Lohaldir, who would give victory to our enemies if we believed him! Wodu himself might crush us with blasts of lightning!"

Morumus caught his breath. "What did the missionary do? How did he survive?"

"He very nearly did *not* survive. A group of our warriors had already taken up their weapons—I among them. We were about to pull the man down and drag him off when he said he could prove all that he had said. It was a clever escape."

"What do you mean?"

"Among my people, the Stone of Judgment was the place of trial—our law court. At the Stone of Judgment a man would give his defense against his accuser, and the assembled elders would render a verdict. It was no accident that this was the place where we had gathered to hear him. Our elders had chosen to call us there for this very reason. If the man's teachings were judged false, his condemnation would have the force of law. Yet in claiming to be able to prove his words, the man himself showed a thorough familiarity with our customs. You see, it was law among our people that even a condemned man could not be pulled down from the Stone if he could produce proof of what he claimed. By invoking that right, the missionary bought himself more time—but at greater risk."

"If he was already in danger of death, what greater risk was there?"

Ulwilf's tone was grave. "There is death, Morumus, and then there is dying. Among my people, a man who gave false evidence at the Stone was condemned—sometimes to pay, sometimes to die. But a man who falsely claimed the right of proof? Regardless of the original crime, he would die a painful and slow death."

Morumus shuddered. As a boy, he had heard plenty of stories about the barbarians of Dyfann and Grendannath. If the Vendenthi had been anything like them, he needed no further details. "So did he produce the proof?"

Ulwilf's voice went from grave to mysterious. "I am sitting here with you, am I not?"

"But what did he do? How could he prove all those things?"

"Are you saying you do not believe them?"

"Well—" Morumus paused.

"Well what?"

Morumus considered for a moment. "Holy Writ speaks of the testimony of God's Spirit, which enables us to know we believe. Yet it also says that we walk by faith, not by sight. 'For in hope we have been rescued; but if hope should be seen, how is it hope?' What proof, then, could the missionary produce to convince your people?"

Ulwilf's smile was wan. "You forget Holy Mystery, Morumus. I do not blame your ignorance, however. You yourself have admitted you know it not. But even so, does not Aesus himself say in Holy Writ, 'If you believe, you will see the power of God?'"

Morumus gasped. He remembered the context of that quotation. "Are you saying the missionary raised somebody from the dead?"

"No. Something even greater."

Morumus was not at all sure what to think of this. "Sir, what miracle could be greater than a resurrection?"

"Was not the act by which Aesus secured redemption greater than all his other miracles?"

"Yes."

Ulwilf leaned back from the fire so that his face was lost in shadows. "So we saw, and so we believed. The man showed us *the* Miracle. Then, as now, the Miracle removes all doubt."

Morumus was now thoroughly confused. "Sir, I do not understand."

"Not yet, Morumus. But—"

Whatever Ulwilf had been going to say next, he was interrupted by a noise in the trees.

The two monks barely had time to jump to their feet before three armed men burst into the clearing.

"Sit back down," commanded one of the three men as the other two spread to either side.

Morumus looked across the fire to Ulwilf. It took a moment before he recognized the confusion on the other monk's face. The man had spoken in Caeldoran. "He said we are to sit down."

"I think we had best obey," replied Ulwilf.

"Don't move," warned the man after they reseated themselves. Then he spoke to his companions. "Do you see any wood lying about? We'll need another log for this fire."

"Yes, sir," said the man behind Morumus, "There is a small pile beside this one." He nudged Morumus in the back with what felt like the tip of a boot.

The first man looked at Morumus. "Put more wood on the fire, but don't try anything clever."

Morumus obeyed, banking the fire from the wood he had gathered until the man told him to stop. The light from the fire increased steadily as the new fuel ignited, and through the leaping flames Morumus could see Ulwilf squinting against the waxing brightness. As the light grew, Morumus also saw who it was that had caught them. The men wore long grey traveling cloaks, but underneath these their tunics were a familiar green emblazoned with a golden sun.

"They are soldiers," he said to Ulwilf in Vilguran. Then, turning to the one he guessed to be the leader, he turned it into a question. "You are soldiers?"

"We are." The man squatted down next to the fire midway between Morumus and Ulwilf. He looked at both of them. "You two look like clerics. What are you doing hiding away in these trees?"

Morumus translated the question for Ulwilf, who was still squinting at the light and looked rather irritated. "Translate my words for him exactly, Morumus."

Morumus nodded and turned to the lead soldier. But as Ulwilf began to speak, Morumus paused and looked at him. "Sir, are you—?"

"Exactly what I say."

"Yes, sir." Hoping they would not regret it, he turned back to the lead soldier and translated as Ulwilf spoke in frosted tones.

"What we are doing is no business of yours. I am a member of the Order of the Saving Blood, and a legate of His Excellency the emperor. Who are you to harass His Excellency's servants?" As he spoke, Ulwilf extended his hands toward the fire so that the characteristic tattoos of his order were clearly visible on the back of his hands and wrists.

The tattoo was inexplicable to Morumus. The cross was no mystery, but why did its base splinter toward each finger? He had asked Ulwilf about it on one of their first days together. The legate had replied by quoting Writ: *"To those outside, all things in parables."*

Parable or not, the tattoo had the desired effect on the soldier. He was a sturdy-looking fellow, and his face did not appear to have seen a razor for at least a week. His eyes bore the experience of a man of action. Yet they lingered upon the tattoo, and when he answered there was conciliation in his words. This man knew of the Red Order.

"My apologies for the intrusion, sirs." He nodded to Ulwilf and Morumus in turn and touched his fingers to his forehead. "My name is Carruc. I am a lieutenant of the garrison at Naud. Like yourselves, I and these men are servants of His Excellency the emperor."

"Naud is several days' ride west of here," said Ulwilf through Morumus. "What are you doing so far from home, Lieutenant?" His voice was still commanding, but the soldier's apology seemed to have dulled some of its edge.

"Bad business, sir." Carruc shook his head. "And it takes a bit of telling. Are you sure you want to hear it?"

"I require it." Then, almost as an afterthought, Ulwilf gestured to two soldiers, who were still standing, and muttered something.

Carruc eyed Morumus. "What's that? What did he say?"

"He said, 'Tell your men to sit down.'"

"Oh—right." Carruc gave a quick command, and the other two men squatted down next to the fire opposite their leader. One of them pulled a flask from his pocket.

"Now," said Ulwilf once they had all settled, "tell us of your business."

"Very well. It started back in the spring, when people could be moving about again out of doors. A pair of young people from one of the outlying villages around Naud went missing. At first it was just the two of them—a lad and a young lady— and so local lord thought little of it, expecting the obvious. A few weeks later, however, it happened again. Only this time it was a different village, closer to Naud. Also different was that it was two sisters who disappeared. The lord appealed to my captain at Naud, who sent a contingent of men to search. The men found a trail and followed it southeast for two days until they lost it in the forest. After that, there was nothing more they could do. The girls were never seen again."

"Tragic," whispered Ulwilf.

"Indeed, sir," said the lieutenant. "And it gets worse. As summer came on, another child disappeared—this time from a holding just south of Naud. The boy's father was woodcutter for our garrison. Again, our captain sent men to search—but again, they found nothing. After this, the boy's father went east to search on his own. A few days later a traveling monk brought the man's belongings to our captain, reporting that he had found the man murdered along the road."

Morumus kept his voice carefully neutral as he translated this portion of Carruc's tale for Ulwilf. He remembered that night all too well. Yet he could not let on that the "traveling monk" had been he, lest it lead to questions that might betray his or the abbot's purpose in Naud.

"It has continued like this ever since," said the lieutenant. "Every few weeks, a child—or a pair of children—goes missing from one of the villages. When we find trails, they always lead south and east into the forest. But once within the trees, they run cold. Even hunting hounds are no good. Whoever is taking these children is careful, quick, and able to mask a trail."

"Might it not be Tratharan raiders," asked Ulwilf, "using the forest to escape before working back toward the coast? Or perhaps even Umaddian slavers working north from the Middle Sea?"

"We suspected as much at first, sir." Carruc nodded. "In fact, that has been our thinking for some time. Our ships never found any raiders, but we only have a few—and there are too many small coves and inlets to be certain. However, we have recently come to believe this idea is wrong."

"Why is that?"

"We found the body of one of the missing children."

"What?"

"In the most recent abduction, two girls were taken from a village just a few hours south of where we are now. As usual, the trail ran south into the woods. The servant of the local lord is an exceptional tracker, and with his help our men found one of the missing girls' bodies. From what they found, they no longer believe that we are dealing with pirates or slavers."

"Why is that?" Ulwilf leaned forward, his dark eyes fixed on the lieutenant.

"I cannot say, sir."

"What do you mean, you 'cannot say'?" Anger flashed in Ulwilf's voice. "If you know, you will tell me, lieutenant. Do not forget who I am."

"I cannot say, because I was not there, sir. I was in Naud with my captain. He received a message from the men in the village, but he did not show it to me. He told me only two things. The first of these was that he was certain that what was happening had nothing to do with pirates or slavers."

"And the second?"

"He told me we must send to Lorudin Abbey for help."

Morumus's hackles stood on end as he translated the soldier's words.

The incredulity and suspicion in Ulwilf's reply were palpable. "Lorudin Abbey? Why would your captain send to Lorudin for help?" As he spoke, his eyes fixed on Morumus. "Do you know anything of this, Morumus?"

"No, sir," Morumus replied. He was only half-lying. He remembered the haunted look in Captain Brann's eyes, and his dark words: *Grahem has come, just like before. It is like it is all happening again.* With everything that had happened since, Morumus had thought little of it.

"Translate the question, then."

"I am not certain, sir," answered Lieutenant Carruc. "My captain said only that I was to go at once to Lorudin Abbey, explain the situation to the abbot, and ask for his assistance."

"You know nothing else?"

"There is one other thing, perhaps."

"Tell me."

"As I said, sir, I am not certain," began Carruc, "but I heard from the gatemen that the monk who brought the murdered man's belongings to my captain was from Lorudin. Perhaps that explains why we are sent thither?"

Ulwilf gave Morumus another sharp look, but the younger monk only shrugged. The red monk turned his attention back to Carruc. "And how would they know that?"

"They said he carried a token from the abbot."

Morumus's breath caught in his throat. Thankfully, the noise was concealed by a loud crack in the fire as one of the logs collapsed to send up a small cloud of sparks. He felt that this conversation was moving dangerously close to a similar conflagration.

At the mention of the token, Ulwilf again looked at him. "Do you know anything about this, Morumus?"

"No." This was an outright lie, but what could Morumus do?

"No matter." The red monk then turned back to Carruc, motioning for Morumus to resume translating. "God has blessed your journey in bringing you to us, Lieutenant."

"What do you mean, sir?"

"We will help you investigate this missing child."

"We will?" Morumus turned wide eyes to Ulwilf. The older monk offered a grave nod. Morumus told Carruc what the red monk had said.

The lieutenant's expression grew uneasy, and when he spoke his tone was again cautious. "I appreciate the offer, sir. It is most generous of you. Yet my captain gave me direct orders, and without his leave I cannot deviate from them. I am sent to the abbot of Lorudin Abbey."

It was at this point that Morumus realized Carruc still had no idea that he was speaking to two men from Lorudin Abbey. He expected that Ulwilf would now reveal this fact. He was wrong.

"As an imperial legate, I outrank your captain."

Lieutenant Carruc touched his fingers to his forehead again before answering. "I understand your rank, sir, and I mean no disrespect. But this is not a Church matter."

Ulwilf's tone took on a condescending note. "You are wrong, Lieutenant. His Excellency's laws against murder merely reflect the much older injunction of God himself. Those who do murder are answerable not just to men, but to God. Your captain recognizes this. Why else would he send you to Lorudin, but to seek the help of the Church?"

Morumus translated the red monk's words, but why was Ulwilf toying with Carruc? Why did he not just tell the man they were from Lorudin?

In spite of his erstwhile caution, Carruc bristled. "That's as may be, but my captain did not ask me to peer into his reasoning. He gave me an order, and I intend to follow it."

For a few tense moments, Ulwilf made no response. He looked from Carruc to Morumus and back, then dropped his gaze and stared into the fire. By now, it had subsided to something approaching its earlier level. Morumus watched the older monk. Ulwilf appeared to be deliberating, but his expression betrayed nothing of his inner cogitation. When he looked up again at last, his response was unexpected.

"Well spoken, Lieutenant." A smile creased Ulwilf's pale face. "Well spoken, indeed. Few there are who so zealously guard the chains of command instituted by His Excellency. I can see why your captain trusts you."

"Um, thank you, sir." Carruc was as taken aback as Morumus by the red monk's sudden shift.

Morumus offered a silent prayer of thanks that things had not gotten worse. Yet a moment later, he nearly took it back.

"Having now seen your proven worth," continued Ulwilf, "let me reveal to you that which I have intentionally kept hidden to this point. We two monks hail from Lorudin Abbey itself. I myself am a trusted confidant of Abbot Grahem. I assure you, Lieutenant, your captain will not fault you for accepting our help. It will save you several days' travel, and might well make the difference in finding the murderer of these children."

"You are from Lorudin?" Carruc looked and sounded confused—and more than slightly irritated. "I do not understand. If this be so, why did you not say so from the outset?"

"'Prove all things,'" Ulwilf quoted. "'Hold fast the good.' As you no doubt know, Lieutenant, not all who claim to serve His Excellency are men of integrity."

Carruc snorted. "True enough." The men sitting across from him grunted in agreement.

"It was necessary for me to test you first, to see what sort of servant you were. You have acquitted yourself well. I will be sure to convey my assessment both to your captain and to Abbot Grahem, when next I meet them both."

"You know my captain?"

"Of course."

"How, sir?"

"Did not you yourself say that a monk from Lorudin had already visited your captain once, carrying to him the belongings of the murdered woodcutter?"

A dark fear began crawling its way up Morumus's spine as he waited to translate Ulwilf's next words. *No, it couldn't be...*

"It was you?" Carruc sounded incredulous.

"It was I." Ulwilf reached into his robe. "Trust me."

The specter of dread pierced Morumus's skull and lodged itself in the back of his head. His heart raced. He hoped he was wrong. He prayed that he was. But just in case, he braced himself. Any sort of reaction might be fatal.

"The abbot's token," said Carruc a moment later.

Indeed, there could be no mistaking it—even in the dim firelight. There, in Ulwilf's open palm, was Abbot Grahem's token. Morumus knew it at once for the one he had lost. He recognized the distinctive pattern of the *brer*. But how had Ulwilf obtained it?

When . . . where?

The realization hit Morumus suddenly, and had he not prepared himself he would have given away everything.

Saint Dreunos's.

He must have lost the token during his narrow escape from the cathedral. Ulwilf or another of the Red Order had found it there, and had tracked them back to Lorudin.

What have I done? Morumus felt cold all over as he translated Carruc's recognition for Ulwilf.

For his part, the red monk stared at Morumus. "Abbot Grahem did not tell you that he and I have known each other for a long time, did he, Morumus?"

"No, sir." Morumus knew Ulwilf was lying, but he hid it.

"I am not surprised. But you must not think ill of him for it, and you are not to question him about it. Our work is most delicate, and he was sworn to secrecy by direct order of the emperor. From this point forward, you are taken into that oath. You must speak of these things to nobody, and you must trust me absolutely. Do you understand?"

Morumus met Ulwilf's gaze without blinking. As a child, his father had instructed him in what Holy Writ commanded concerning honesty. Yet his father also had told him once that lulling a deceiver was much like keeping a secret. The best way was to forget you know the truth. Until you can expose the liar, act and speak as if you really believed the lie.

"Yes sir."

20

On an overnight in the woods, it very difficult to get back to sleep after waking. Not only is the morning air markedly colder, but the very ground on which one has slept so successfully—or fitfully, as the case may be—seems to have hardened during the night. Little choice remains but to get up, no matter how early. Such was the case on the morning after Morumus and Ulwilf met the soldiers from Naud.

It was a chill, cumbersome morning. Morumus could not tell from direct observation whether the sun had risen, for the sky was hung from horizon to horizon with sullen clouds. Yet he knew that dawn had come—or would come, soon enough—for grey light now filled the wooded grove with a pale, wan ambience.

One by one, the five men came awake and turned out of their bedrolls, rising and stretching stiffly before wandering off to find a discreet tree. After this there was a brief discussion about breakfast. Should they make a quick meal of cold provisions, or set out now in hopes of finding a fuller—and warmer—breakfast when they reached their destination? It was not a long discussion.

The mists lay low and thick in the Caeldoran valleys as they mounted their horses and turned south. According to Carruc, the village to which they were traveling lay but a few hours south of the Naud Road. The lieutenant led the group, and the two soldiers followed. After these rode Ulwilf. Per the rule of the Red Order, his hood once again covered his head. This gave him a brooding appearance that seemed to match his silent, withdrawn mood.

Last of all rode Morumus.

He was thankful for the solitude. For one thing, it afforded him the opportunity to pray—a duty in which he had been flagging of late. For another, the silence afforded him the opportunity to think about the revelations of the previous night. Just as the hooded form of Ulwilf rose and fell on the road in front of him, so the specter of the Red Order remained continually before Morumus's mind.

What was their purpose? The red monk in Versaden had spoken to the Mersians of "spreading the Saving Blood." Ulwilf had told Morumus of "Holy Mystery" and "the Miracle" only the night prior. But what did it all mean? Did any of these things have real significance to the Red Order's agenda, or had Ulwilf told him of such things just to point him in the wrong direction?

Morumus remembered one of his boyhood tutor's favorite admonishments: *"Never let the armor distract you from the man wearing it."* He had lost count of how many times his tutor had repeated this injunction, insisting that it applied just as well to books as to men. *"Make no mistake, Morumus: the man who pays careful attention is the man who really learns—and the man who really learns is the man who remains alive."*

The words echoed in Morumus's mind as he mulled over the intentions of the Red Order. In Versaden they had tried to kill him. The appearance of the missing token in Ulwilf's possession meant they knew that somebody from Lorudin had aided the Northmen. But how did it all fit together? Despite the fact that he seemed to have gained a measure of Ulwilf's trust, despite what Ulwilf had told him about miracles and mysteries, despite the fact that he knew Ulwilf was lying about the abbot's token . . . despite all this, he still felt no closer to an answer to the main question.

What was the Red Order really seeking?

It was still relatively early in the morning when the five men rode into the sleepy village of Agnorum. Most of the cottage windows were still shuttered, and most of the doors stood closed facing the narrow, winding streets. Yet dark, soot-stained chimneys poked up through the myriad thatched roofs, and from these chimneys thin smoke carried the smell of cooking food to five hungry noses. They spurred their horses forward.

Like both Naud and Versaden, Agnorum had originated from the remains of an Old Vilguran settlement. The difference between the three was scale: Naud was not a quarter of the size of the imperial capital, and Agnorum was less than a quarter of the size of Naud. In the days of the Old Imperium, Agnorum had been but a watch-post—a single stout tower situated upon the top of a low knoll along the northwestern skirt of the Tumulan Hills. From their tower, the Vilgurans had commanded a wide view of the surrounding lands. Additionally, their position had allowed them to control one of the small tributary rivers that flowed northwest out of the Tumulans to meet the River Lor.

In the days since the Imperium, little had changed about the place. The land was still wide, wooded, and wild. The meager river still flowed down from the massive hills. The only real difference was the small village that had cropped up about the base of the knoll in the intervening centuries. A small market town now sat where once had stood but a solitary tower.

Lord Arden's keep reflected both the history and slow growth of Agnorum. The ancient Vilguran tower still stood as its main and dominant structure—wide, square, and rising several stories above the ground. But the tower no longer stood alone. A sizable hall now stood beside it. This hall was obviously several centuries more recent in its construction, yet it attached to the tower at one end. Besides this, several other outbuildings dotted the hilltop and formed a sort of quad about the hall: a barracks, a stable, a smithy, and a pair of storehouses. Surrounding all of these stood a low stone wall. This wall was not a serious defensive fortification. It was too low, no taller than a man. Rather it served as a delimiter, marking the boundary of the keep.

Despite the early hour, a bustle of activity greeted the men as they rode their horses up to and through the open gates. Men-at-arms prepared to drill in the yard, and groomsmen carried fodder from the storehouses to the stable. Most significant, however, the smell of cooking fires from the kitchen attached to the main hall whispered promises of warm provision.

Lieutenant Carruc gave an order, and one of his men dismounted. The soldier vanished into the main hall while the others waited, and a few minutes later he reappeared in the company of two men. One of these was a servant. He called across the yard to summon men from the stables. The other was Lord Arden himself.

"Welcome to Agnorum, friends," he said after all of the travelers had dismounted and given their horses into the care of the waiting grooms. Lord Arden was a man whose appearance eschewed extremes. He looked neither old nor young, neither fat nor thin, and neither jovial nor grim. Yet his eye was careful, and his face bore the sort of honest composure that cannot be counterfeited. "Captain Brann sent word that help would be coming"—he eyed Ulwilf and Morumus—"yet he did not say whom I should expect."

Realizing that Ulwilf would not understand Lord Arden's Caeldoran, Morumus stepped forward and translated.

Without lowering his hood, Ulwilf nodded acknowledgement. "I am a legate of the emperor and an associate of the Abbot of Lorudin," he replied through Morumus. "I and my translator met these men on the Naud Road. They have told us of events here, and we have come to render what assistance we can."

Arden nodded, his expression grave. "The help will be most appreciated. I will take you to the body immed—"

At Lord Arden's halted words, Morumus followed his gaze, and saw that the soldiers' eyes flickered toward the hall. With the delicious smells drifting out, who could blame them?

Apparently Lord Arden sympathized. He smiled at them all. "Ah, but where are my manners? Even in circumstances such as these, we must remain civilized. Shall we have some breakfast?"

About an hour later, their bodies less chilled and their stomachs filled, the men set out from the keep. There were nine of them in the company now: the five of them who had come from the north, two of Lord Arden's men-at-arms, Lord Arden himself, and Lord Arden's servant.

The latter man was the most remarkable of the group. He was tall, powerfully built, and his skin was as dark as ebony. His name was Anbharim, and he had been captured during the previous emperor's war to drive the Umaddians out of Midgaddan. Lord Arden, who had fought in those campaigns, had taken him prisoner personally.

"But that was years ago now." Arden gave his man a firm smile. "Anbharim is now an Aesusian like the rest of us, and he has become a most trusted servant."

The men-at-arms nodded, and Morumus could see that both their lord's words and their response were honest. Lieutenant Carruc and his men appeared wary and unconvinced.

233

Ulwilf remained silent.

In fact, it was Anbharim who found the body of the missing girl. As the company moved further southeast, Morumus began to appreciate just how great a feat of tracking the servant had accomplished. They left the fields around Agnorum and passed into the forested marches of the hill country. Although neither as extensive nor as severe as the Deasmor in his homeland, the Tumulan Hills were just as thick and almost as labyrinthine. The hill country dominated a significant portion of western Caeldora south of the River Lor. Both the ridges and valleys of this territory were grown over by a dark, ancient forest. The Tumulans themselves were largely uninhabited. Most people in the region dwelt along their fringe, in places such as Agnorum and Lorudin Abbey.

The company continued southeast, plunging into the great forest. How long they rode was difficult to tell, for there was only the faintest hint of a trail, and a soupy, silver mist crept in long tendrils along the forest floor. However long it was, Morumus did not mind the ride, for the woods about him were ablaze with autumn colors. The various maples presented a panoply of fresh yellows, crisp oranges, and deep reds. Even the stately oaks, by nature the more reserved wardens of the wood, were beginning to hint at turning.

As they moved deeper into the forest, the canopy above them rose, and the trees grew further apart. Yet despite the higher ceiling and wider spacing, leaves were already beginning to blanket the breadth of the forest floor in a colorful, patchwork quilt. In short, the space through which the company rode was about as glorious a scene as one might ever hope to find this side of eternity. Even the overcast day and low-lying fog, while they might dampen and mute, could not wholly suppress the effect. Morumus had not forgotten the grim task that lay ahead. Yet while he could, he intended to enjoy the beauty about them.

After some time, he began to hear a sound amongst the trees. There was running water nearby. Yet Morumus did not see it at first, for the woodland terrain through which they rode was like an aged face: No major hills or dales, yet numerous deep wrinkles. These contours limited Morumus's visibility and obscured what lay before and behind. Lord Arden and his men, however, knew where they were going. Thus it was that, shortly after Morumus first heard the sound of water, the company crested the last small slope and found its source.

The hollow into which they descended was wide, and at its bottom a swift stream ran in and out through thick patches of mist. The trees in the hollow were tall and thick, like massive pillars upholding the canopy overhead. Through their midst the stream ran its winding course between leaf-covered banks. The contrast between the dark trunks of the trees, the brilliant covering of leaves, and the leaden water of the stream was striking. But the scene beside the stream was more striking.

An earthen mound—like a small barrow—had been raised just next to the watercourse. Several paces distant from it stood a small camp, consisting of three tents pitched around a makeshift hearth. There was a fire burning in the ring of stones, and beside it stood what seemed to be a minor reflection of the arriving company. There were two men who looked like soldiers, and a single monk. The latter was clothed all in red and wore his hood up.

Morumus blinked his eyes to make sure he was not imagining. *Another red monk?*

Ulwilf must have noticed at the same time, for his hooded head turned toward the monk. But he made no sound.

The company drew up and dismounted. Lord Arden handed his reins to one of the waiting men, and ordered one other to help in seeing to the horses. After this there followed a round of introductions. The soldiers in the camp were another pair of Lord Arden's men-at-arms. The red monk, whose name was

Bansuth, was the legate assigned to the Agnorum visitation. After everybody had been briefly acquainted, Lord Arden explained the situation to the new arrivals.

"The body of the girl is under that mound." He gestured over his should toward the stream. "Anbharim suggested that we preserve it for investigation."

When Arden's words had been translated, Ulwilf almost hissed.

"Desecration, my lord," he growled through Morumus, turning as he did to look at Bansuth. "The Church does not approve of such a reprehensible practice."

"He was told," the other red monk answered from the shadow of his cowl.

Lord Arden look unfazed, yet he raised one hand to stave off further protest. "I know, and under normal circumstances, neither do I. Yet these are not normal circumstances. Too many children have gone missing. Too many parents have been bereaved. Whoever is doing this must be found and stopped. If some clue to their identity may be found by withholding burial *temporarily*"—he laid great stress on the word—"then we must do it. When this is finished, I will take full responsibility before the archbishop and the emperor."

"As you say." But there was something foreboding in Ulwilf's tone.

"We have long used ice from a mine in the hills to chill our food stores," Arden continued. "We thought we might do the same with the body in order to prevent decay. After packing it around the girl, my men raised a mound of earth above to protect her from animals and exposure."

Bansuth nodded. "I have remained to ensure that the body is not left unburied."

"Have you done so much?" Ulwilf spoke in quiet Vilguran, and his brother monk seemed to flinch. Then Ulwilf turned back toward Lord Arden, and Morumus resumed translating. "If this must be, let us see the body and be done with it. For your sake, my lord, I hope that what we learn proves sufficiently useful to justify what has been done."

"I hope so too, for the sake of those who have died," replied Lord Arden.

At their lord's command, the men-at-arms began removing the mound.

"From the nature of the thing, this may take a while," Lieutenant Carruc observed after ordering his men to join them.

"Take your ease, Morumus," Ulwilf said as the men began, "but do not wander too far in this ill place. I must confer for a time with my brother." He motioned toward Bansuth, and the two of them moved off toward the edge of the camp away from the others.

Having no desire to watch the men exhume a body, Morumus turned away from the mound to walk along the stream. On his right, the water ran swift within its banks, following a course that wound back and forth between the arboreal pillars as it progressed northwest toward the far-off edge of the forest. Despite the fact that morning was getting on, the chill of the air and the overcast sky had caused thick patches of mist to linger, suspended above the forest floor. Morumus's thoughts felt much like this fog as he wandered beside the brink of the water—clouded, disembodied, and formless. He watched as a solitary leaf floated past him in the midst of the stream, revolving slowly as the water rushed it away. It was a beautiful, deep red. Yet in the end he knew that it would turn brown or be submerged beneath the cold water.

"'As a leaf fade we all; our crookedness carries us away like a breath,'" he quoted. He had quite lost track of just how far he had gone when he thought he heard a sound.

He pulled up short and listened. The sound came from somewhere ahead of him, and sounded almost like—was it a voice? Did he hear whispering? He strained to listen, but the voice—if it was a voice—was fleeting and indistinct. He stood very still now, his ears attenuated and his eyes fixed forward.

About a hundred yards downstream, a tendril of mist as thick as a man extended across the full width of the hollow. It coiled around the bases of the thick trees like a great serpent and hung low across the stream like a sort of grey veil beyond which nothing could be seen. The next moment, however, a gust of air rose up and stirred the veil.

Morumus's breath caught in his throat.

In the instant the mist parted, he spied a dark shape stepping behind one of the trees. The vision lasted but a moment, but he was sure he didn't imagine it. The hair on his arms and neck stood on end. The sense of unholiness was palpable. Had the thing seen him? Involuntarily, he took a step backward. In the next moment, a pair of hands grabbed him from behind.

Morumus would have yelled had one of the hands not clamped firmly across his mouth. Panicked, he struggled for a moment.

"Morumus!" Ulwilf spoke a low, urgent voice, "Morumus, it is I."

No sooner had the monk spoke than Morumus caught a glimpse of the tattoos on the hand over his mouth. He ceased struggling, and spun to face the older monk.

"Ulwilf, what are you doing here?"

"I noticed you were missing. This wood is not safe."

"Something is out there!" Morumus gestured toward where he saw the shape.

The red monk's tone turned dark. "I do not doubt it. Come." He gripped Morumus's elbow and pulled him back upstream toward the camp.

"Did you see it, too?" Morumus's heart still pounded.

"No, but those fools have left a murdered girl without a proper burial, and now they have opened her grave—all at the suggestion of an Umaddian slave! They have invited the curses of God upon themselves. They summon the minions of Belneol to pull them down!" The legate was seething.

The mention of hell made Morumus's hackles rise further. "Do you think that was a wraith?"

"I do not know. But as I said, I would not doubt it. That is why I warned you not to wander."

"Are we safe, then?" Morumus looked back over his shoulder.

"The Order of the Saving Blood fears no darkness. You are safe enough, so long as you are with me." The red monk turned his hooded face back upstream. "Come now, we must get back. They will have uncovered the girl by now. The sooner she is properly buried, the sooner we can be sure of God's protection once more. We shall speak no more of this, and you shall tell no one what you have seen. Is that clear?"

"Yes, sir."

The return to the camp did not take long, and when they reached it they found that Ulwilf's prediction had been accurate. The mound by the stream had been moved to become a pile of loose earth a few yards back from the water. Around the space where the mound had stood earlier, the whole group of men now stood in a sort of rough circle.

Less than a minute later they joined the circle. Less than a moment after that the earth seemed to drop out below Morumus. Nothing could have prepared him for what he saw.

The dead girl had raven-black hair. Her eyes were blue, like the color of summer sky. Her skin, however, was very, very pale. Morumus could see no color in it at all, and he knew even before he saw it that there was a deep gash in the soft flesh of her throat.

He had seen this girl before, in a nightmare. Some of the details had been different, to be sure, yet there was no mistaking either the girl's face or the method of her murder.

"Exsanguination." Morumus's voice shook.

His nightmare was no longer bound to the night.

The nightmare was waking.

21

"Fool!" hissed Ulwilf. "Exsanguination is a mark of ritual sacrifice. It is well-known that such things are common in the Umaddian religion."

In the minutes that followed Morumus's exclamation, things in the hollow had unraveled dramatically. As soon as he saw the body, Ulwilf ordered Lieutenant Carruc and his men to seize Anbharim. These obeyed, but now three divisions had formed of the dozen men in the hollow. To one side stood Carruc, his sword drawn and his countenance tense. Behind him stood his two men, holding Anbharim between them. The servant was not resisting, and his expression was blank. Several paces away stood Ulwilf, Morumus, and Bansuth at his side. Facing them across a space of several yards was Lord Arden, backed by his four men-at-arms.

Lord Arden's face was nearly the color of Ulwilf's robe. "It may be a ritual murder, but it could not have been Anbharim. He was with me in my keep when the report arrived that the girl had gone missing. It was only through his skill as a tracker that the trail was not lost in the forest this time, as has so often happened in the past. My men will attest as much."

Behind Lord Arden, the four men-at-arms muttered their agreement. "'Bharim helped us find the girl," said one. "Why would he do that if it had been him that'd killed her?"

Morumus looked from Lord Arden and his men back to Ulwilf. The man-at-arms had made an insightful point. He translated their words for Ulwilf.

The red monk was not impressed. "Why indeed? Perhaps to deflect attention away from his own guilt, should someone bring the connection to light!"

"Nonsense!" scoffed Lord Arden. "If Anbharim murdered the girl, he would never have led us to the body. As it is, he volunteered to help with the search."

"And just how was it he was able to succeed, where all others had failed? Do men who hail from distant lands have more skill in a forest than those who grew up in them? No. He knew where the body lay because it was he who laid it here!"

Lord Arden paused. His eyes flickered back toward the mound, where the body of the murdered girl now lay exposed. He said nothing out loud, but his expression said that he was considering. A moment later, however, he shook his head and turned back.

"If he is guilty—and I say *if*—he will be tried before me at Agnorum! Your rank as an imperial legate does not give you authority to circumvent the emperor's justice to his subjects."

Ulwilf's Vendenthi accent was coming more and more to the fore, and Morumus struggled to keep pace translating. "Slaves are not subject to the emperor's protection," he translated, trying by his own tone to interject a much-needed calm into the dispute.

Recognizing Morumus's efforts with the briefest hint of a nod, Lord Arden turned back toward Ulwilf. His face and voice shifted from the bright flame of the forge to the hardened edge of tempered steel. "Anbharim is no slave. He has been a freedman since his baptism, and now serves me as a member of my household. As such, he is entitled to the due process of the emperor's law. He is under my personal protection, and I intend to see he gets it."

Ulwilf paused, and his voice calmed. "You say he is a baptized freedman?"

Arden nodded, "That is correct."

Ulwilf's response was exultant. "Then as such, he is liable to God as well as to the emperor, and in this matter my jurisdiction takes priority over yours. The courts of the Church have precedence over the emperor's courts in matters of sorcery."

"Sorcery?" Lord Arden was shouting now. "What we have here is *murder*, man, not magic!"

But before anybody could respond further, Anbharim himself spoke.

"It was not I who took this girl." His deep voice was tinged with grief. "I am a left-handed man, and the cut is on the left side of the girl's throat. Whoever killed her was right-handed."

"You see?" said Lord Arden to Ulwilf, nodding to his man in approval. "Your accusations are all explained by common sense and observation."

Morumus translated the words, but Ulwilf was unmoved. His voice now burned. "Translate my words exactly, Morumus." He spoke sideways to Morumus without shifting his glance. "Do you understand? Exactly."

"Yes, sir." Morumus did not like the sound of this.

"You blubbering fool," Ulwilf growled, jabbing a finger at Lord Arden as if he were a child rather than a lord. "Have you not stopped for a mere moment to consider how, now that we have come to the point, your man has such a ready answer? Or have you not considered"—here he paused for dramatic effect—"that a left-handed cut is more than possible for a left-handed man, if he cuts the throat from behind while holding the neck over a basin?"

The gruesome image in Ulwilf's words had a potent effect. Lord Arden again looked toward the body before shifting his eyes to Anbharim. Behind him, his men looked uncertain. Seeing the opening, Ulwilf pressed his point home.

"How long, my lord? How long has this unrepentant Umaddian practiced his dark magic beneath your eaves without your knowledge? How long has he poured sorcery into your cup and clouded your judgment by his secret incantations? How many nights has he poured out blood to Alloch while you slept in your bed, unaware that your 'servant' was abroad, stealing away the emperor's subjects?"

At these last words, Lord Arden cast a sharp look at Anbharim. Arden's face turned ashen, and his voice shook. "Those many nights you asked my leave to keep vigil . . . those dreams . . . has it all been a ruse?"

"Oh no, my lord!" Anbharim shook his head vehemently. "Do not believe the lies of this monk! The dreams are real. The whispering shadows are abroad—I can sense them now even while I wake. I can sense them even here, in these woods! It was to pray against their rising that I asked your leave those many nights. By Aesus's blood, my lord, I speak only the truth!"

Ulwilf hissed when Morumus finished translating. "He blasphemes the Saving Blood!" He turned toward Anbharim, and his hand now shook, as though it were a knife that longed to cut out the offending tongue. Then he wheeled back toward Lord Arden.

"The lies grow bolder as he sees his spell lifting from your brow, my lord. Dare you protect this murderer even one moment longer? Deliver him to us. Let the Church purge this pox from your soul, your house, and your subjects!"

Morumus could see Lord Arden's response even before he spoke, for the man now looked at his servant with a changed countenance. "You will give him a full hearing before the bishop?"

"Circumstances hardly warrant as much, yet for your sake, it will be done."

"And you will afford him opportunity to reflect and repent, before carrying out the sentence?" There was little doubt in Lord Arden's tone as to the verdict.

"Even the most heinous criminals are offered the final confession."

"Very well." The resignation and weariness in Lord Arden's words were palpable. "Let it be done, and let this plague be lifted from our land."

"You have shown greater wisdom in these words than in all that have come before. I sense now with certainty that the shadow has lifted from your eyes."

Bansuth murmured his agreement.

Caught somewhere in the middle, Morumus translated Ulwilf's words but said nothing himself. The path of a knife was not conclusive. Meanwhile, the rest of the evidence seemed rather tilted in the opposite direction.

What happened next took the entire company by surprise. Anbharim, who until this point had stood, passive, between his two captors, heaved aside Lieutenant Carruc's men with a great shout. Lulled by the lack of prior resistance, both men were thrown sideways by the servant's strong arms. Carruc himself wheeled around at the sound, but not quickly enough. Anbharim's shoulder was in his middle before he could bring down his sword, and Morumus heard the sound of air escaping the lieutenant's lungs even as he saw the sword drop from Carruc's hand.

The garrison officer was lifted and propelled into the cluster of Lord Arden and his men. The lord, his men-at-arms, and the gasping lieutenant tumbled into a pile. Anbharim wheeled around to face the remaining three, and found Bansuth and Morumus standing alone. Ulwilf stood apart from them, having darted away to retrieve Carruc's sword.

"You can flee, but you will be found!" Ulwilf backed away and raised the weapon, wary.

Anbharim seemed to catch the sense of these words, even if he could not understand the speech. "I am no sorcerer," he growled in Caeldoran, his chest heaving. With these few words, he rushed forward.

Bansuth shot a look at Morumus. "Get behind me!"

Morumus stepped back. The red monk moved forward, a long knife clutched in one hand. Morumus could tell from the way he held the weapon that Bansuth did not share Ulwilf's warrior background.

Ulwilf could tell, too. "No, Bansuth! Let him go for now—"

But it was too late. As Anbharim closed to within a pace, Bansuth lunged with the knife. His attack was several moments too soon, and the servant easily dodged it. He grabbed the monk by the arm, and Bansuth tried to writhe free. But it was no use. Anbharim had him from behind.

"Drop the blade and I will let you go."

Instead of dropping the sword, Bansuth did a brave—and foolish—thing. Twisting his wrist, he tried to stab the knife backwards into his captor. But of course Anbharim had seen it coming, and avoided the point. Bansuth, however, was not so fortunate. As the servant shifted sideways to avoid the blade, Bansuth, whom Anbharim still held, slid straight into its path. There was a sickening gasp as the knife plunged into Bansuth's stomach.

Anbharim released the monk. Bansuth immediately crumpled to the ground, his hood falling back to expose a horrified countenance. The servant took a step back, and the monk rolled on his side to face Morumus. His hand still gripped the pommel of the knife with white knuckles, even as the telltale crimson stain began spreading over his tattooed wrist.

"*Genna ma'guad ma'muthad ma'rophed,*" he whispered, blood now oozing from the side of his mouth. He choked once, and there was a great deal more blood. For another few seconds he continued like this, spluttering his own life through his lips.

Then he was gone.

Morumus stood transfixed, the still body of Bansuth lying less than two paces away. Dull eyes stared vacantly into his own. Anbharim, however, wasted no more time. With a swift lunge forward, he pried open Bansuth's hand and pulled the long knife free. Its blade gleamed with thick, red blood. With a second swoop, he grabbed Morumus around the middle and pulled him along toward the horses. Morumus struggled, but it was no use—he was held fast. With his free arm Anbharim freed his horse from its tether. The great grey beast blew out its nostrils in anticipation. Anbharim set Morumus up first, then swung up behind him. The horse grunted once under the extra weight, but it moved with surprising spryness when Anbharim tugged the reins.

Morumus stiffened as Anbharim raised the sharp, wet, still-warm edge of the knife to his throat. He whispered in Morumus's ear as the horse stepped away from its fellows. "Do not attempt to escape or to stop me, and I will not harm you."

By now others had regained their feet, but they dared not approach. Lieutenant Carruc had recovered his sword from Ulwilf. The other soldiers had their hands on their weapons and curses in their mouths.

Lord Arden waved them all to silence. "Anbharim, release the monk, please."

"If you attempt to follow us, he will die," came the reply in a deep, dangerous voice.

Beside Arden, Ulwilf raised one arm. He extended a single, thin finger that quivered with rage. "You cannot escape the justice of God, manslayer! Surrender now, or I warn you—your dark master will find you before we do."

As before, Anbharim needed no translation. "I am *no murderer!*" Then he jerked the reins and dug his heels into the gelding's flanks. The horse sprang to action.

The whole scene had unfolded in mere minutes, and Morumus was still having trouble believing what he had seen. Despite the furious flurry of Ulwilf's accusations, Morumus had had his doubts about the evidence for Anbharim's guilt. Then the situation unraveled, leaving one man dead, one man fleeing, and one man—Morumus himself—hostage.

Now he had his doubts about his doubts.

Under Anbharim's steady hand, the horse beneath them plunged through the forest, avoiding rocks and leaping fallen brush. It is an exceedingly dangerous thing to ride so swiftly through trackless woods, yet the grey gelding was calm beneath his master's rule. It seemed to sense that Anbharim's business was dire, that his flight was desperate, and thus did not resist the urgings to go farther and faster.

As the beast carried them into the forest, Morumus wondered what would happen next. They were not returning toward Agnorum. Where, then, would Anbharim take them? Did he intend to spare Morumus, or had that been a lie? Might not a man tell a hostage anything, if it will preclude resistance and thereby facilitate his escape? He began to pray silently.

Anbharim kept moving. After the initial burst of speed to put distance between them and their pursuit, he slowed his horse to a brisk walk and pressed on. He chose their way with great care, probably trying to select paths where the soil was harder and thus less likely to imprint with clear tracks. Any time they encountered running water, Anbharim would turn their mount into it—having the horse walk either upstream or downstream for as long as he could before emerging on the far side.

The gelding was a creature possessed of great strength and endurance. It could not have been used to the extra weight of a second rider, yet it carried on as if Morumus were little more than an additional saddlebag. Anbharim seemed to have great affection for the beast. He frequently reached forward to pat its neck, whispering to it in what Morumus guessed was the language of his homeland.

As they continued riding, Morumus did his best to keep his bearings. By the direction of the sun, they were traveling due south toward the wild heart of the hill country. There were no settlements this far into the hills.

Even if he could somehow get free, to where could he flee?

Anbharim brought the horse to a halt at dusk. Dismounting, he pulled Morumus down with him and bound his hands tight behind his back with a cord from the saddlebag. Then, confident that Morumus would not be able to get far, he released him. Reaching back into the bags, he withdrew a handful of oats. He fed these to the horse, and then tied it to a tree next to a small clutch of grass.

"I am sorry, my friend," he said to the grey as he fastened its line. "It is a scant meal for one who has served so well this day. If we live until the morning, you shall have more."

Turning to Morumus, the warmth in his voice faded. "You and I will just have to fast tonight, young brother—unless you have some food tucked away in that robe?"

Morumus shook his head.

"No matter."

Morumus heard a curious note in his words, but then his tone darkened.

"Hunger is good for keeping one alert. We will have need of watchfulness tonight, if we are to live."

Under the circumstances, one might have thought that Morumus would hesitate to respond to such words. However, the combination of fatigue and frustration had shaved the edge off his fear, and made him feel bolder than he really was. He was already well aware that his situation was precarious. At that very moment, Anbharim had stooped and was wiping the blood from the blade of the knife that had killed Bansuth. Yet Morumus was in no mood for hints.

"If you are going to kill me, please spare me the suggestions and get on with it."

For the second time that day, the servant did something completely unexpected: he smiled. It was a forced, thin smile— but it was a smile. "Kill you? Not I, young brother. I have killed no man since my captivity years ago. Upon my baptism I swore to Lord Aesus never again to lift my hand except in defense of the innocent, or the life of my lord."

"Or in the case of a red monk?"

Anbharim's dark brow furrowed. "I did not kill that monk. It was his hand that wielded the knife. He meant to take my life. Instead, he took his own." He shook his head, and there was something that sounded like genuine remorse in his voice. "You were standing close by, young brother. You heard me offer him release."

"And yet you have taken me hostage." Morumus wasn't ready to absolve his captor. The heedlessness of a moment prior had passed. In its place now stood an iron resolve that he did not realize he had inherited until it appeared. *"If you are facing death,"* his father had once remarked, *"there is no need to mince words."* The words came back to him unbidden, though he had not thought of them for years. "Do you intend to offer me release?"

Anbharim's smile faded, and there was a peculiar sound in his voice. "If we survive this night, you may go free in the morning."

"That is the third time you have made such a remark. To what do you refer?"

"You would not believe me if I told you." Anbharim turned back to his horse to retrieve the blanket tied behind the saddle. "You Caeldorans do not have the dreams that we have among my people." He gave his attention to undoing the twin buckles that bound the roll. "And since you do not have them, you do not believe them."

Morumus frowned. What was it Anbharim said to Lord Arden? *"The dreams are real. The whispering shadows are abroad— I can sense them now even while I wake. I can sense them even here, in these woods!"*

Though Morumus wore a thick wool robe, he felt a sudden chill creep over his flesh. "The whispering shadows. Are they what you fear?"

Anbharim's fingers stopped working, but he did not turn. "Yes," he answered after a long pause, resuming his work at the buckles.

"What are they?"

There was another long silence. Finally Anbharim turned, blanket in hand. "I do not know."

"Yet you have seen them?"

"Only in dreams, young brother." Anbharim's voice became strained. "I have seen visions of young people playing happily, heedless of the danger they face. I have seen the shadows rise out of the ground and step from between the trees. Night after night I have seen them creep unmarked across the fields, snatching children unawares, carrying them away to their doom. Night after night I have seen the wild looks of terror in those young eyes." The big man's voice caught, and Morumus wondered if it would break.

"I saw them every time. Every time it happened, I was there. My lord would hear of it days, sometimes weeks, later. After the first few, I shared with him what I had seen. He believed me then, even if he does no longer. But there was nothing we could do. The dreams never showed the faces of the shadows, nor where the children were taken. We knew that they were vanishing into the forest, but the forest is huge and the hills are deep. It was not until a girl from our own town was taken that I saw where they took her. The night it happened, I saw in my dream the trail leading into the forest to the hollow beside the water. When news arrived in the morning that she was missing, I knew where to look."

The light was failing fast in the woods, and Morumus could now barely see the man's expression. Yet the words made him consider. He did not *want* to believe what he was hearing. There was a line across his throat where the blood of Bansuth had dripped from the blade of the knife, and he could still see the dead monk's dull, lifeless eyes. Yet he could tell from Anbharim's tone, even without a clear view of his face, that there was no trace of deceit in his words. Moreover, the man had no reason to lie to him now. He had the knife; Morumus was bound. Logic overcame emotional resistance, and Morumus could not resist the inference.

Anbharim was telling the truth.

The pure honesty in Anbharim's words did something to Morumus. Like a blast of crisp air or a splash of cold water

253

on his face, it suddenly felt as if just now—for the first time since he had seen the dead girl—Morumus was fully awake. Things had happened with such speed back in the hollow that he had not had any time to consider. But now . . .

Things began to coalesce in his mind. Certain truths began to emerge from dark corners of his memory, horrible to the mind's eye yet implacable in their advance. Morumus gasped at their appearance, and closed his eyes.

The images continued, rushing past in merciless succession to fuse together in an unforeseen combination. The vision of the murdered girl—the nightmare that he had experienced both dreaming and waking—merged with a memory from long ago.

Whispering shadows.

He saw them on the night his father was murdered.

He stood stock still as the mind did its work, almost as if he were in a trance. His mouth opened and shut, over and over—only to drop the words unformed into the swirling soup of his disquieted soul. Finally, after what seemed an eternity, the world inside his head stopped spinning.

Morumus opened his eyes. He did not understand—not yet—but he knew now the horrible truth. He had come to Caeldora years ago to be safe, to flee from those who had killed his father. Yet it takes more than relocation for a man to escape his history, and he realized now that there was a common culprit in both his father's and the girl's murder.

In that instant Morumus realized, too, that he was perhaps the only living person who knew this villain's identity.

For several long moments, Morumus was as motionless as a corpse. He wanted to weep, but he could not. He wanted to scream, yet it would not have been manful. In any event, his voice had caught in his throat. He wanted to do something—*anything!*—to release the pressure he felt building behind his eyes and churning in his gut. Yet he was helpless. A fey wind blew through his mind like barrow's breath across an empty moor. He felt cold all over, and a single word stood paramount in his mind.

Dree.

"Is something wrong, young brother?"

At Anbharim's words, Morumus felt the cords break. He could move again. The light had almost totally failed within the forest. Yet as he looked toward Anbharim, Morumus found light enough to see that the face upon which he looked was not the face of his enemy.

"You look as if you have just seen a shadow." Anbharim's concern was clear.

"You are wrong, you know."

Anbharim recoiled as if struck. "It is as I said." He snorted with a mixture of resignation and disgust. "Your people neither have nor believe the dreams." He rose to his feet, the knife now clean.

"No. That is precisely where you are wrong. I am not Caeldoran. I am Lothairin. My people are not unfamiliar with dreams such as you describe—nor am I myself."

Anbharim stopped moving. "What do you mean?"

"Among my people, these dreams are called *tidusanganim.*" Morumus remembered the conversation with his uncle as though it were yesterday. "The word is an old one in our language. It means 'time-song.' A *tidusangan* shows a glimpse—incomplete and veiled—of something that either has happened or will happen soon."

"You have had such dreams?"

"Only once," Morumus answered. He had asked Nerias the same question years ago. He remembered his uncle's reply. *"No, but others of our line have . . ."* Morumus felt the weight of the long-lost words settling down on his shoulders, *". . . the gift often runs in the blood."*

"It is not a common occurrence among us," Morumus continued, "but it passes down through the blood."

"It is the same among my people. Are you also a prince, then?"

The question caught Morumus off-guard. "My father was a nobleman, but he was not the king. Why do you ask?"

"Among my people, the dreams are a sign of nobility. Is it not also so among yours?"

"It is not." *Tidusanganim* were not common among Lothairins, but neither were they limited to the nobility. Yet something Anbharim said struck him.

"Are you a prince, Anbharim?"

"I was once counted such among my people. The land over which my father ruled had been wrested from the Hisponans by my great-grandfather. When the last emperor took them back—and when my lord took me prisoner—I lost my title." Anbharim sighed. "But that was years ago. Another life, another faith. I have no desire to go back. I gladly counted it my loss when I received baptism. What is a title among the Umaddians, compared to a title to Everlight?"

"Indeed," Morumus said quietly.

For a long minute after this, neither man spoke.

"You ought to get some rest, young brother," said Anbharim at last. "You may have a long walk tomorrow in order to reach the others. I will keep watch."

"Will you untie me?" Morumus's shoulders ached from his bonds, and it would be difficult to sleep with his hands tied behind him. "If we should have to flee this night, I will need the use of my hands."

"No. The others will be suspicious if they find you unbound, sleeping or walking free. They must believe you were my unwilling prisoner."

"I doubt they will find me sleeping. We have escaped a long distance."

"My lord has several men among his ranks who are skilled woodsmen. One was with us. They will not press on after dark, but they will be here early. I must be gone before dawn."

"Where will you go?"

"South, though I do not know where I will end. If I can reach Hispona, perhaps I may find refuge in a monastery. I have even heard it said that some of my people are priests in that land."

"It is true, even more than you know. I was in Versaden this summer for the Court of Saint Cephan. During the Great Session, I saw several dark-skinned bishops."

"Ah! Perhaps God will lead me to one of them on my way."

"I hope he will." And Morumus meant it.

After Anbharim went off to watch, Morumus settled himself in a seated position with his back against a tree. It was not a comfortable position. No matter where he sat, it seemed he managed to find himself perching on a rock or a root. As a result, it took a long time before he was able to drift off to sleep. Yet this only made things worse—for there was no rest in his sleep that night.

Morumus's dreams were filled with *Dree*. He relived the nightmare he had experienced in Lorudin. He stood again among the wooded hollow of that morning, with moving shadows in every tendril of mist and nowhere to turn where he did not see either the bloodless face of the girl or the lifeless eyes of Bansuth. After this, he relived the horrible events of the night his father was murdered. He wanted to wake up, but he could not—for he was neither fully sleep nor fully awake. Rather, he spent nearly all that night suspended halfway between the two worlds, dangling on the brink of darkness. He could not tell where reality ended and where the nightmares began. He wanted to wake, but he could not.

This went on for what seemed like hours. Even when he thought he was back in the woods, even when he was sure he could feel the rocks beneath his bottom, everything remained dark. And even then Morumus heard the hissing voices of the *Dree* all around him, and could not open his eyes. Interspersed with the hissing song of the *Dree*, he heard a wordless human scream. How long it took before he fell fully and truly asleep, he could not tell.

He was back in Lothair, riding with his uncle Nerias. Yet now he only caught bits of their conversation.

"The Dree *are in league with nobody but the devil . . . the* Dree *profess the Dark Faith . . ."*

". . . the Dree *knew right where to wait for us."*

"The old stories say that the priests of the Dark Faith . . . possessed ways of peering into distant councils."

"I could not do anything to help."

"You survived, Morumus . . . You know the truth . . . You have witnessed the Dree *firsthand, and have lived to speak of it . . . You were spared for a purpose, Morumus."*

Morumus opened his eyes.

It was before dawn. The woods all about him were filled with the familiar grey light, and he was shivering. Anbharim and the horse were gone, but he could hear voices somewhere close. He tried to stand up, but only ended up toppling sideways onto the cold, hard earth. He remembered then that he was still bound.

"Hold still, and I will cut you loose," said a familiar voice behind him. Strong hands gripped his wrists, and he heard the sound of a knife cutting twine. Once he was free, the hands helped him get to his feet. He turned around.

"Ulwilf."

"Morumus." The red monk's hood was up, of course, but Morumus could hear sincere relief in his words. "You are alive. Are you hurt?"

"No. A little sore, perhaps, but that is all."

"Thank God." Ulwilf sighed. "This was too close, Morumus. You have much potential—potential that was nearly lost. We are going back to Lorudin. You will need time to recover."

"I am—" Morumus had been about to protest that he was fine. Yet he knew this was not so. He felt . . . heavy. The things he had seen and learned were like lead clinging to his soul, and he wanted more than anything right now to talk about them with somebody he could trust. Somebody like Abbot Grahem. So he changed his sentence mid-course.

"—tired. I feel like I have been walking for days without food or drink or rest. I think you are right, Ulwilf. It is time to return."

Ulwilf nodded. "Good. Come then."

Morumus followed Ulwilf, and within a minute he saw the others. Lord Arden, Lieutenant Carruc, and the soldiers were all standing together a short distance away. Yet their backs were turned to Ulwilf and Morumus, and they seemed to be looking at something. For a moment, Morumus wondered what this might be. Then he saw a grey horse tied to a tree apart from the mounts of the others.

"Is that Anbharim's horse?" He pointed to the grey. But he already knew it was.

"It is," said Ulwilf, his voice grim. "I warned the slave—" he began, but Morumus had already stepped forward.

As he pushed his way between two of Lord Arden's men-at-arms, a mini-chorus of voices greeted him, sounding relieved. Yet he did not hear their words. His eyes were fixed on what lay beyond them.

The body of Anbharim sat unmoving before him, his back to a tree and his arms tied around its thin trunk. The sight was appalling. The flesh of Anbharim's cheeks had been split, leaving his jaw hanging unnaturally wide open and his tongue dangling limp within it. His eyes had been gouged out, but they had not been taken. Instead, they now sat—pointed up, but unseeing—atop the pile of his innards which had been placed upon his lap. The gaping hole in the front of his abdomen showed where Anbharim had been disemboweled, and there was blood everywhere.

Morumus felt his stomach lurch. Had there been anything in it, he might have wretched. As it was, he could only gag.

"Very bad business," said Lieutenant Carruc in a dark whisper.

"The hounds of Belneol found him." Ulwilf joined the group. "The slave was warned."

23

Morumus lay unmoving on his pallet, staring up at the ceiling of his cell. He was quite sure he had never been so sick in his entire life. Everything about him ached, from his feet through his thighs, up through his chest, and down his arms. It hurt to close and open his hands. He hadn't slept much the previous night—his stomach had been too busy emptying itself violently. Even now it pitched like a ship atop a high wave on the sea—warning him not to even think of food.

The illness had come upon him just the day before. He and Ulwilf had returned to Lorudin six days prior, and the red monk had hoped that they would leave again after a week—today. With the unforeseen death of Bansuth, responsibility for the visitation at Agnorum would devolve to the nearest neighboring legate. Lorudin Abbey was closer to both places than any other settlement; as a result, at least for the short term, Ulwilf's responsibilities were tripled. It was thus no surprise that the red monk should limit their time in Lorudin.

The thought of Ulwilf made Morumus's head hurt even more than it already did. He no longer had any real idea what to make of the man, or of the Red Order itself. After all the time he had spent journeying with Ulwilf, only two things were clear to him. The first was that Ulwilf was zealous. Whether discussing the perceived problems in the churches surrounding Lorudin, or retelling the history of his old life in paganism; whether threatening Lord Arden or waving a sword at Anbharim; Ulwilf never seemed to doubt the rightness of his cause. Morumus still had no idea what the Order of the Saving Blood aimed at, but this much was clear: whatever it was, Ulwilf was committed to it.

The second thing Morumus knew was that Ulwilf traded truth loosely. He had seen the man lie to both Lieutenant Carruc and himself about the abbot's token. Further, he had witnessed how the red monk ignored legitimate evidence in implicating Anbharim in the murder of the exsanguinated girl. Morumus could not figure out Ulwilf's motives in all of this. Yet whatever the reasons, Morumus knew Ulwilf had shown himself more than willing to manipulate people and mold the truth to fit his ends.

It was an unsettling combination, relentless zeal and ruthless dishonesty. It had already cost one man his life.

Yet while Ulwilf had shown so little regard for Anbharim's life, the red monk *had* demonstrated genuine concern for Morumus's own life.

"You have much potential—potential that was nearly lost . . ."

Morumus supposed he should be grateful for the compliment and thankful for the concern. It demonstrated that he was gaining Ulwilf's trust, which was what Abbot Grahem had charged him to do. Yet given what he knew, it only made Morumus more uneasy. He felt like he had made friends with a ravenous wolf.

Morumus felt even more disturbed by the memory of Anbharim. Though his actions had made him guilty in the eyes of all else, Morumus knew the servant had been innocent. Yet Anbharim's innocence had revealed a darker reality: *the Dree were moving in Caeldora.*

The *Dree* had murdered that girl. Anbharim saw them, though he did not know them by name. But Morumus did. He suspected they had murdered all of the missing children. The question he could not answer, however, was why? The *Dree* had murdered his father and Oethur's brother in the hopes of igniting a war. But what were they doing taking away children by ones or twos?

Moreover, there was the matter of the murder of Anbharim. It must have been a *Dree* Morumus had seen lurking in the mist that morning, and he was sure that the *Dree* had murdered Anbharim. But again, why? Was it just to cover their tracks? Why would they need such cover? Besides these, an even more disturbing question pressed itself upon his mind: why had the *Dree* spared him? Ulwilf had been quick to insist that Morumus's survival in the face of Anbharim's violent death was proof of latter's guilt and demonic dalliance. Yet Morumus knew better. That God had protected him he did not doubt. Yet Anbharim's guilt could not be the explanation, for Morumus was sure he was not guilty. *Why then had the Dree killed only Anbharim?*

That single word plagued Morumus: *why?* It tumbled over and over in his thoughts, splitting into a many different strands. Why had Ulwilf intruded them upon Carruc's errand in the first place? Was it to cut Abbot Grahem out of the investigation? Why had Ulwilf been so quick to blame Anbharim? Was it some deep-seated hatred toward dark skin, or some animosity toward Umaddian converts? Was it just another way to assert the growing authority of the Red Order?

The questions rolled over Morumus like the waves of nausea racking his body.

As if all of these unanswered questions were not torture enough, things had worsened upon their return to Lorudin. Ulwilf insisted that Morumus assist in his questioning of the other brothers. All but the newest novices at Lorudin spoke fluent Vilguran, so the red monk had no need of a translator among them. Rather, the only thing Morumus's participation in the interviews seemed to produce was resentment. These men were Morumus's brothers. He had known many of them for years. Having to stand passively beside Ulwilf while the red monk interrogated them about the practices at Lorudin—and the character of Abbot Grahem—was excruciating. He felt like a traitor. He was only doing what the abbot had ordered him to do, but the others did not know this. They were beginning to look at him as though he were wearing a red robe, too. Even when he was not with Ulwilf, few of them would speak to him—and those who did not avoid or ignore him outright seemed uncomfortable when he spoke to them. He took his meals in the refectory and worshipped in the chapel alone—or with Ulwilf. Nobody else would come near him now. The whole experience was just awful.

He was home, but he was more alone now than when he had been away.

Worst of all, Morumus had not had any opportunity to speak to Abbot Grahem. The abbot needed to know about the lost token, and Morumus felt he might go mad if he did not speak to *somebody* soon about everything that had happened. Yet Donnach and Oethur had been sent away, and on the few occasions when Morumus managed to disentangle himself from Ulwilf, Abbot Grahem was nowhere to be found. Morumus asked after him, but nobody seemed to know where he had gone. Or if they did know the abbot's whereabouts, they pretended to *him* that they did not. This was more frustrating to Morumus than everything else combined.

Abbot Grahem knew that he had but a few days at Lorudin before Ulwilf took them away again. Time was running out. Why then was he making himself so scarce? Morumus began to wonder: was even the abbot avoiding him?

Just the day before, Morumus had resolved to turn over the entire abbey if need be in order to find Abbot Grahem. He had been most resolved about this—no matter how long it took, no matter what excuse he had to make to get free of Ulwilf, he would not leave Lorudin until he had spoken to the abbot. Then he fell sick.

Now he lay on his pallet, staring at the ceiling. Every part of him hurt; every breath drawn felt like daggers in his chest. He felt so bad that he wondered if he might die. The next thought he knew was self-pity, but he did not care: might not death be better than going on, the way things had been going the last six days?

There was a knock at the door of his cell. The sharp raps hurt his ears.

"Come," he croaked.

The door swung open, and a single hooded figure entered the dim room.

"Hello, Morumus." Ulwilf came to stand over him, pushing back his cowl. Genuine concern etched his pale features. "You do not look well at all."

"I do not feel well at all." Morumus could only manage a near whisper. If he kept his voice low, it did not hurt as much to speak.

Ulwilf frowned. "I have been through the herbal supplies. Like most things in this Abbey, they are sorely lacking. Do you think you are well enough to travel? There may be better supplies at Agnorum."

"No." The very thought of movement made him nauseous. "Speaking to you is about as much as I can do."

Ulwilf's frown deepened. "I do not like it, but I am afraid there is nothing I can do for you here, Morumus. My duties to the Order also call at me. If you think that you might be better tomorrow, I will wait—for I would prefer not to leave you here. But if you cannot say you will be well, then I must depart today."

"I cannot." Yet even had he known he would recover the next instant, he would have said the same thing. As bad as things had become for him at Lorudin, he had no desire to leave again with Ulwilf.

Ulwilf nodded. "Very well." He stepped back from the pallet and moved toward the small table in the corner. Though most no longer trusted Morumus, one of the brothers had been compassionate enough to bring him a small pitcher of water along with a cup. Ulwilf filled the cup from the pitcher. Then he removed a small pouch from within his robe. From the pouch he sprinkled a thick pinch of a powdery substance into the fluid. He mixed the simple potion with his finger. Then he brought the cup to Morumus.

"I am afraid this is no medicine. However, it may ease your pain for a period."

"I cannot sit up."

"I will help you." The red monk knelt beside the pallet and helped lift Morumus—just enough to enable him to swallow. "Now, take this."

In taking the cup from Ulwilf, Morumus felt only a twinge of hesitation. He had not for an instant forgotten that the red monk was dangerous. Yet he also sensed in this case that Ulwilf was acting in sincerity. After all, if the man had come to his cell to kill him, he could have just as easily used a knife. Morumus was in no condition to resist. Besides, with as much pain as he was in, he was not sure death could be much worse. So he took the cup.

A pungent smell filled his nostrils. Whatever had made Morumus sick had also blanched his mouth, so he had no idea how the liquid tasted. But he knew it was strong. He could feel the effects spreading into him even before the cup was drained—a sort of dull heat radiating out from his middle into his limbs. By the time Ulwilf returned him to a lying position, the acute pain he had felt only minutes ago had been subsumed beneath the numbing warmth. The feeling was slowly moving up his neck, and he felt very drowsy.

"How do you feel now?" Ulwilf placed the cup on the table.

"Tired. Very tired, but the pain is dulled."

"Good. It is working. I have given you enough that you should be able to sleep well tonight. When you next wake, I will be gone. But I will return for you as soon as I—"

Morumus never heard the rest of what Ulwilf said, for in the next moment the effects of the potion enveloped him. He fell into a deep, dreamless sleep, and for a time forgot his troubles.

Morumus slept that whole night without dreaming. When he woke the next morning, it was again to the sharp, staccato sounds of knocking. Somebody stood outside his door, petitioning for entry. The noise made his head feel like a blacksmith's anvil.

"Enter." His voice still sounded like gravel and his throat still ached with the effort of speech.

Again the door swung open, but this time the man who entered wore no hood.

"Hello, Morumus."

"Abbot Grahem." Had he felt better, he might have exclaimed. Truly there was nobody whom he would have rather had walk through that door.

The abbot walked over to the bed. "Still feeling ill?"

"I feel horrible, sir."

Unexpectedly, Abbot Grahem smiled. "Let's see if we cannot fix that, eh?" Turning away before Morumus could react, the abbot walked over to the corner table. As Ulwilf had done, he withdrew a small pouch from within the folds of his robe. Opening this, he picked up the cup—and almost immediately put it back down. Then he bent down and sniffed at the pitcher of water. Straightening again after a moment, he turned back toward the pallet.

"Have you drunk from this cup?"

Morumus saw that he was frowning. "Yes. Ulwilf gave me something to help me sleep."

"I do not know this smell." Concern was etched in Grahem's features.

"He said it would ease the pain."

"Did it?"

"Yes."

Abbot Grahem said nothing further. Instead, he poured a bit of water into the cup and wiped it clean with the edge of his sleeve. After this he refilled the cup with water from the pitcher, added a pinch of something from his pouch, and stirred this new mix with his finger. Then he brought the finished potion to Morumus. Stooping down, he helped raise the young monk to a sitting position before proffering him the cup.

"Drink this. All of it." He held the cup to Morumus's lips. "It will help you."

Morumus drank. Though he could still taste very little, the liquid in the abbot's cup seemed almost the exact opposite of Ulwilf's. It bore no smell that he could discern, and felt very light as it rolled down his throat—almost lighter than water. The cup was empty before he knew it.

"Now lie back." The abbot eased him back down. "It will take a few minutes to work."

Morumus could feel whatever it was Abbot Grahem gave him beginning to work even before his head hit the pallet. The effect was remarkable. Whereas Ulwilf's potion had made him feel thick and warm all over, Abbot Grahem's made him feel alert and cold. In fact, he suddenly felt very cold—as though he were back home, standing atop the Deasmor in mid-winter wearing nothing but rags. For what seemed like hours, this freezing sensation continued. It bit at him from every direction in sequence, the pain increasing with each jolt. He felt that he was being thrust through with daggers forged of ice. He shivered violently. He hugged himself tight, but it was no use—he was getting colder, not warmer. The icy sensation coursed through him relentlessly, forcing him to suck air in ragged gasps. Then, just as abruptly as it had begun, it stopped. The freezing sensation pushed one last breath from his lungs. Then it was gone.

"What did you give me?" Morumus gasped, looking at the abbot wide-eyed.

"I see that you are sitting up now. How do you feel?"

The abbot was correct. The action had not registered while Morumus was in the throes of the icy potion, yet he had in fact sat up. Yet if this was bewildering, it was the next realization that baffled Morumus. He was no longer sick. When the abbot knocked, he could not even sit up. Now he no longer felt even the slightest bit ill.

"I feel . . . better." He sounded surprised, even to himself. "What happened?"

"You were poisoned."

Morumus inhaled sharply. "By Ulwilf? But why? I thought I was gaining his trust."

"Not by Ulwilf. By me."

"*What?*" Morumus could not believe his ears. If he had not been absolutely sure he was awake, he would have thought this conversation part of a mad dream.

"Couldn't be helped, son." The abbot's tone was brisk. "Ulwilf might have seen through a ruse. This particular poison is unpleasant, I realize—as is its antidote, as you have learned—

but it was necessary. It was the only way to keep him from dragging you off again."

"Oh."

"And believe you me, he was very, very loath to leave you here. Whatever you have been doing these weeks, Morumus, you seem to have gained the trust of the red monk. Well done, son."

"Thank you, sir."

Abbot Grahem smiled now, and there was fatherly concern etched in the lines on his face. "You were gone long enough that I had begun to worry. Ulwilf would tell me nothing of what transpired, but I could see that you were troubled from the moment you returned. You are a brooding man by nature, Morumus—but there has been an unusual heaviness about your countenance these past days."

"Sir, I have wanted to speak to you, but—"

Abbot Grahem held up one hand. "I know, my son. I have been unavailable. This has been intentional. I have not wanted to spoil your labors, so I have kept my distance. Ulwilf may trust you, Morumus, but he does not trust me at all. I am not sure why that it is, but nonetheless it is plain. I am sorry if it has made things more difficult, especially now that Ulwilf has turned most of the brothers against you."

"Oh sir, you have no idea. Things are far worse than you think."

24

bbot Grahem had never looked more grim.

Morumus told him everything. He began with his first encounter with the *Dree*, the murder of his father, and his rescue by Nerias. To this he added the dream of the murdered girl—the *tidusangan*—and its fulfillment. He told him everything he could remember of his conversations with Ulwilf throughout their weeks together. He warned the abbot that the red monk possessed the token. Lastly, he spoke of the shadows in the mist and Anbharim's grisly end.

"He was murdered by the *Dree*, sir. I am sure of it. I heard their voices that night while I slept. Until I woke, I thought they were but a nightmare." Morumus shuddered. "What I cannot understand is why they did not kill me as well."

"So Brann was correct," said the abbot after a long silence. He shut his eyes as if he might blot it all out. "It is happening again."

"I never understood what Captain Brann meant by that. And after everything that has happened, I still do not understand. What do you mean by 'again,' sir?"

Abbot Grahem opened his eyes. "You have kept many secrets these long years at Lorudin, Morumus."

271

Morumus was about to interject, but the abbot held up one hand.

"But not as many as you think. I knew about your father and your early encounter with the *Dree*. Nerias told me about them in the letter he sent when you first came. As for this dream of yours, I do not fault you for keeping it quiet. Why *should* you have spoken of it, to me or to anyone else? You didn't know it was anything more than a nightmare. In fact, if I recall, you *did* tell me about it—and I turned it into a jest about the Court of Saint Cephan!"

"I remember that, sir. I wish it *had* been but a jest."

"So do I. But what you must know now, Morumus—what I must tell you in order to answer your question—is that yours are not the only secrets that have lain hidden in this abbey. When Captain Brann spoke of things happening 'again,' he meant all of it: the missing children *and* the *Dree*. The same events that are happening now happened once before—when both your uncle and I were but fresh monks."

Morumus nodded. "My uncle told me it was so."

"Did he tell you we pursued them together?"

"Truly?" Morumus felt his hackles rising all over.

"Truly. It was almost twenty years ago now, and we spent two whole years tracking them. Then, as now, children had gone missing from all over this part of Caeldora. Then, as now, the authorities at Naud were charged to find the abductors. Captain Brann—he was Lieutenant Brann then—was sent here for aid."

"And you two were sent to help?"

"We four. Myself, my brother Gaebroth, your uncle Nerias, and Anathadus."

"You have a brother?" Morumus had never heard Abbot Grahem mention a brother.

"*Had* a brother," said the abbot—a little too quickly.

Morumus took the cue and changed course. "And Bishop Anathadus was involved?"

"He was but a monk in those days." Grahem gave a faint smile.

"So what did you find?"

"Very little. As I said, we spent two years with Brann tracking them across Caeldora before the trail went cold. We found one or two of the bodies—they were exsanguinated, just like your girl. We did not know what to make of such ritual killings. So—and I know this sounds macabre—we made careful notes and split up. Each of us went to a different city, to seek what we might learn from the great libraries. I went to Palatina. Nerias took ship to Mereclestour, and Gaebroth went with him. But we found nothing. Only Anathadus found anything significant."

"Where did he go?"

"Southwest—into the heart of Hispona, which at that time was ruled by the Umaddians. He journeyed all the way to the great library at Tayaturim."

A thought occurred to Morumus. "On the morning we found the murdered girl near Agnorum, Ulwilf said that exsanguination rituals are part of Umaddian religion."

Grahem shook his head. "Umaddianism is indeed a dark and false faith, and in battle its adherents can be more brutal than you might imagine. But historically, it is quite young—less than a thousand years old. Ritual exsanguinations belong to the more ancient forms of unbelief—as Anathadus discovered in Tayaturim."

"What did he find there?"

"A book. A very old and unusual book. Its spine was made of human bone, and on its cover—"

A chill traveled up Morumus's spine. "The same tree from my nightmare."

"Yes." Grahem's brows lifted. "How do you know of it?"

"I saw the book in Bishop Anathadus's library in Aevor. It is hideous."

"Indeed, but it proved invaluable."

"What did it say?"

"We could not read it. The script was Vilguran, but the language was not. We were unable to read the main text. Yet even so, there were numerous drawings. Some of these looked like charts of the seasons or the stars, and others depicted sacrificial procedures. The latter matched what we had found in the bodies of the missing children: exsanguination via a cut on the side of the throat. From that point on, we knew that what we were dealing with was a Dark Faith of old: very ancient, and very dangerous. Here in Midgaddan they belonged to a period known as the *erebanur*, which means—"

"Dark madness." In answer to another surprised—if somewhat irritated—look from the abbot, Morumus continued. "I have come across the word in my studies, and I have heard both you and Uncle Nerias use it."

"Right. Your uncle suggested the name '*Dree*.' He said it was an old name in your country for priests of the Dark Faith."

"Night-adders," Morumus said softly, remembering. "So my uncle and your brother came back from the library at Mereclestour?"

"Only your uncle came back."

"Sir?" Morumus started. "What happened to your brother?"

Grahem shook his head. "I wish I knew. When they arrived in Mereclestour, Nerias and Gaebroth determined to split up. Nerias searched the library in the city, while Gaebroth set out for Toberstan. It was said that the monastery there possessed a sizable collection, and my brother was never one to leave a stone unturned. So he went north—and vanished."

"Just like that?"

"More or less. When Gaebroth failed to return, Nerias went after him. Yet when he reached Toberstan, your uncle learned only this: that Gaebroth had made it to the monastery there, but had long since departed. None of the brothers seemed to know in which direction he had gone, and inquiries in the city turned up nothing. Without a trail, Nerias had little choice but to return to Lorudin."

"I am sorry, sir."

"So am I, but it was long ago. Whatever befell, I have no fear for him." The abbot smiled. "I think of him like Aenoch, who 'walked with God, and he vanished, for God took him.'"

Morumus nodded. Now he knew why the abbot had never mentioned his brother. "But if Nerias came back here, when did he return to Lothair?"

"Some time later." Abbot Grahem paused, then shook his head, "I cannot remember when, exactly. It was a tumultuous time. The Umaddians began a new assault, pushing north from Hispona, and more urgent priorities pressed in upon us. Lieutenant Brann was reassigned, and we monks were taken up with ministering to the wounded and the bereaved. This was in the time of Arechon's father. By the time the invasion was pushed back, the trail of the *Dree* had gone cold. After the war, Anathadus was made bishop in Aevor. Sometime after that—a year or two after the wars ended, I think—Nerias was summoned home to rule that little rock of his. Only I remained here in Lorudin. I kept my ears and eyes open, but there was no sign of the *Dree* again. That is, until that night this summer on our journey to Naud."

"The father of the missing boy from Naud. That was the night I heard you use the word *erebanur*."

"He was not simply murdered, Morumus. He was butchered. It was much like you described the body of that servant, only done with more haste. Yet this alone was not evidence in itself—a drunken tinker may be just as expressive if he is settling a grudge. But there *were* two things that pointed me to an explanation beyond bandits. The first was the full purse, which you saw. The second was something I kept to myself: a bit of broken knife blade."

"I don't understand, sir. How could a piece of a knife tell so much?"

"Because it was no ordinary knife, Morumus. The piece of the blade I recovered was made of stone. Do you understand the significance of that?"

Morumus nodded. "The knife in my nightmare. It was made of stone."

"Yes. The ritual knives of the Dark Faith are always made from stone. The book Anathadus found contained several diagrams depicting their creation—as well as the symbols with which they are to be carved."

For several moments after this, silence fell between the older and younger monk.

"Sir," said Morumus finally, "what are we going to do?"

"My son, there will be no more 'we' in this matter—at least, not for some time. Very soon you will be leaving."

"Ulwilf." Morumus groaned. "Sir, I—"

"No, Morumus. You will accompany him no farther. But he is the *reason* you must leave."

Morumus did not like the sound of this. "Sir, I do not understand."

"As you've informed me, Ulwilf now has my token. That means he knows that somebody from this abbey was in Versaden. We know from how he questioned you about it—and then lied to you when he got no answer—that he is eager to learn the identity of the token's former bearer. That puts you in a very dangerous position—too dangerous, in my judgment."

"Sir—"

The abbot held up a hand. "Furthermore, you yourself have witnessed how manipulative and ruthless this man can be. He turned the hearts of seemingly sensible men against one they had known much longer. You have done well in earning his confidence, Morumus, and in learning what you have." Here he paused, and looked directly into Morumus's eyes before continuing. "Yet from what you have told me, it seems that Ulwilf wants to recruit you—to turn you to the Red Order. And so I fear now for your own heart, Morumus. One cannot keep company with a serpent forever and expect to remain un-poisoned."

Morumus recoiled at the abbot's words. "Sir," he began, faltering and sputtering, "I would never betray you or the others. They are my countrymen, and you—sir, you are like a father to me."

"I believe you, son." Emotion was visible now at the corner of the abbot's weary eyes. "And yet"—here he turned and gestured toward the table in the corner—"you took his cup."

"But I was sick, sir, and he said it would help. I figured if he had wanted me dead, he could have used a knife more easily."

"But that's just it, son." The abbot maintained eye contact. "You *believed* him. There was no guarantee that whatever he gave you would not have killed you. In fact, death by poison makes for much fewer questions. Yet you did not even consider this. Instead, you convinced yourself to take Ulwilf at his word. What if, instead of medicine, he had given you something to loosen your mind?"

"Sir, I—" But Morumus stopped. What could he say? Abbot Grahem was correct. He considered what he had done for a long minute. How quickly he had been willing to believe the one who promised him relief from pain! The weight of the abbot's words weighed heavy upon him: if Ulwilf had given him a different potion, he might have betrayed everybody— and all for comfort. How rapidly he had justified suppressing his better sense! It was shameful, and the recognition of it was staggering to Morumus.

"I have been foolish."

"It won't be the last time in your life you'll have to admit that," said the abbot graciously. "But do you understand now why I say you must leave?"

The younger monk nodded. "Where will I go?"

"The three of you will go home."

Morumus's heart leapt. "The three of us?"

"Yes. Donnach and Oethur will be going with you. Oethur cannot remain in Aevor. He would be discovered, and my connection with Bishop Anathadus would put him at risk. The two of you might go live with Donnach in the cave in the woods, but the winter would be difficult—and to what end? It won't be safe for any of you here for a long time—especially not now that Ulwilf knows of Versaden."

"So we will return to Aeld Gowan?"

Abbot Grahem nodded. "There is important work to be done. Donnach's translation must continue. We cannot delay the work indefinitely: his people need the milk and meat of Holy Writ, and he needs your help to give it to them. Never forget this, Morumus: whatever else happens, we are still the Church." The abbot's voice gained strength as he spoke, and new light gleamed in his eyes. "The body of Aesus always has enemies within and without. In the meantime, our mission does not change. Our task is to take Holy Writ forward to all nations. Do you understand?"

"Yes, sir."

"In addition to this, I want you to take with you the book that you saw in the bishop's library—the book which speaks of the Dark Faith. When I send to Anathadus to fetch Oethur, I will include instructions for him to bring the book. Take it to your uncle at Urras. He must be warned about the reappearance of the *Dree* here in Caeldora. Moreover, many of the brothers at Urras are well-learned. With your own talent for languages, perhaps you and they together can figure out its strange language. Unless we know what the *Dree* are about, we cannot stop them."

"Do you think they can be stopped?"

"Of course they can." The abbot arched one eyebrow at Morumus and scowled at him with the other. "Whatever tricks they may have, they are not gods. At bottom they are but men, creatures of flesh and blood. A sword will do for them as well as for any of us. Their powers are counterfeit. We cannot explain it yet, but we know it. The thing, then, is to root it out—and to do that, we need to read that book."

"Yes, sir." Morumus felt again a bit foolish at his last question even while taking courage from the abbot's words. "What will you do?"

"Me?" Abbot Grahem smiled. "I'll do nothing so extraordinary. Until we learn more, there is nothing much I can do. So I will pray, work, and lead the brothers here as I always have. The Church must and will continue: we have seen the Dark Faith before—long before—and we have weathered worse than the Red Order."

A sudden, horrible thought struck Morumus. "Sir, what if they are connected?"

"The Dark Faith and the Red Order?"

"Yes."

"The thought has crossed my mind more than once, but it doesn't fit."

"It doesn't?"

"No. We were tracking *Dree* long before there was any Red Order. Further, from what you've just told me of Ulwilf's story, it sounds like the Dark Faith is the religion he forsook. Unless you think his account of the missionary was a lie?"

"I don't think he was lying. Not that time."

"Well then," said the abbot, "I don't see how the Red Order and the Dark Faith can be allied. Your uncle used to have a saying . . ."

" 'The *Dree* are in league with nobody but the devil.' "

"That's it."

"But sir, what about Ulwilf?"

"Being wicked doesn't make him a *Dree*—"

"That's not what I mean, sir."

"Eh?"

"What will he say when I suddenly disappear?"

"Very little, I suspect."

"Sir, with respect"—Morumus was a bit disturbed by the abbot's calm—"I think you may be mistaken."

"I'm not." The abbot offered a sly smile. "Because you aren't just going to go missing, Morumus."

"I'm not?"

"No. He'd never believe that. There's only one thing for it. You are going to die."

"I appreciate your coming personally to convey this news to me," said Captain Brann three days later, shaking the proffered hand of the man who stood before him. "It is a relief to me that the murderer of these children has been stopped—and I know it will be a happy report in the ears of the duke." He glanced over to where Lieutenant Carruc stood at attention near the door. "All of your men are well, Lieutenant?"

"Yes, sir."

"Good. Go see to them, then, and to yourself. Get some rest. I'll see you in the morning."

"Yes, sir." Carruc saluted smartly, then bowed out of the room. The sturdy door swung shut on well-oiled hinges and clicked in its latch.

Captain Brann turned back to the man before him. "Will you dine with me this evening?"

The red hood bowed. "That is a most gracious offer, Captain," said Ulwilf, "but I must decline. With my brother murdered, my duties are doubled. I have come to you directly from Lorudin, but I cannot return thither until I see to matters at Agnorum."

"Duty calls. It is a heavy burden at times, eh?"

"The heaviest. Yet for God and emperor, it is well-borne."

"For God and emperor. That is well said." Brann handed back to Ulwilf the small *brer* disc which the red monk had passed to him at the beginning of their interview. "When you do get back to Lorudin finally, please convey my greetings to Abbot Grahem. He and I go a ways back, as I'm sure he has told you."

"Indeed he has," lied Ulwilf. "I will convey your regards." He turned to go.

"Also, please give my greetings to his other assistant, young Morumus."

"Morumus?" The name stopped Ulwilf in his tracks. He turned back. "You know Morumus, Captain?"

"Certainly. I met him several months ago when he and Abbot Grahem came to Naud. He carried the same sort of token as you. A well-spoken young man."

"Well-spoken." Flames kindled within Ulwilf as pieces of the puzzle he had long-sought to solve began fitting together at last. "Yes. He is certainly that." He made his words sound light. "I will convey your greetings to him as well, Captain."

"Thank you." Captain Brann nodded his head in respect. "God speed you on your way."

"No, thank you, Captain," said Ulwilf before turning to exit the study. He wanted to run, but he forced himself to walk. Inside he was fuming, yet he knew that he must maintain outward control.

Control was what he needed most right now. Control was what the Order had lost in Versaden when they found the spying monk; control was what they thought they had begun to regain when the Mersian bishop reported that the monk was dispatched, and when the token had been found. Control was what Ulwilf had hoped to restore by finding and dispatching those responsible.

Morumus.

Now at last he understood. No wonder it had seemed so easy to persuade the young monk. No wonder he had seemed so eager to learn! The burglar from Versaden was not dead. The burglar had spent the last several weeks traveling with him! Now he lay unsuspecting in a sickbed in Lorudin. Ulwilf had been ready to welcome him into the Red Order. Now he saw that it had all been a ruse.

Morumus would pay.

Ulwilf swept out of the Naud garrison, the vision rising before his eyes as he went. It was a vision as red as the robe streaming out behind him—as red as the blessed Saving Blood itself.

Morumus!

The name alone boiled his blood, and his pale temples pulsed furiously within the cowl of his robe. The holy order had nearly been corrupted. The Saving Blood itself had almost been violated!

"*Genna ma'guad ma'muthad ma'rophed,*" he whispered.

There would be no forgiveness. Morumus would pay for his deception, as would Abbot Grahem his master. All of Lorudin Abbey would pay with them.

"But that would have been inevitable sooner or later."

His interviews had convinced him there was no redeeming that community. They would never embrace the Saving Blood. He had hoped to defer dealing with them until later. It would be risky to eliminate Grahem and Lorudin while leaving their protector Anathadus untouched. Yet to delay any longer was unthinkable. The rotten limb must be amputated before the disease spread. If that meant cutting higher than originally intended, so be it. He would send a pigeon to Aevor. Then he would summon his brothers, and see to Lorudin personally.

The Saving Blood was a cup of blessing to those who blessed it. But to those who defied it, it became a bowl of wrath. Ulwilf's enemies were about to drink this bowl to the dregs.

PART IV

PRINCE OF ROOTS

25

There are few joys as simple as that of walking a familiar path—especially when one has been away. Every breath is fresh, every step is known, and in the end one reaches friends or home. In this sin-soaked world, a familiar path is one of the cleanest and least corrupt pleasures given to mortal creatures.

Morumus felt something of this joy as he trod the forest trails surrounding Lorudin Abbey. He had been gone for weeks—too many weeks—and it felt wonderful to walk these woods once again. In the many years he had lived in Lorudin, he had grown quite fond of the stout old trees, the mossy rocks and the wide seas of fern. He especially loved the way the forest looked in autumn: splendid canopies above, and brilliant tapestries below.

Yet time was running out on the fall season in Caeldora. Already telltale shades of brown withered the leaves, and chill on the morning air whispered of colder days to come. Morumus could sense winter's coming in the woods surrounding him. Soon, the brilliant colors would be gone. Soon, the pleasant paths would be subsumed by white blankets. The joy of fall would be swallowed up by dreary winter cold.

Morumus felt a similar sense of bracing finality in the depth of his soul. This would be one of his final forays in this forest. He had already said secret farewells to Lorudin Abbey, and before long he would be leaving Caeldora altogether. Soon, he would be returning home to Lothair. He felt a certain joy at this—yet not a joy unmixed. A hint of melancholy tinged each of his steps as he walked. He had spent too many years in Lorudin to leave it behind unmissed.

The thin cloud of gloom seemed to evaporate as Morumus reached Donnach's sanctuary. Looming departure notwithstanding, the imminent reunion with his friend turned his thoughts in more cheerful directions. Picking his way carefully down the leaf-covered slope, Morumus dropped into the narrow gulley and came to the edge of the running water at its bottom. Turning upstream, he arrived a short time later beside the wide pool at the base of the waterfall. Everything seemed much as he remembered it from his previous visit: thick, tall trees still formed a protective screen around the small clearing—though their boughs were barer now that autumn was waning.

Likewise, the pool itself was still clear and deep, and the gentle roar of the falling water still soothed the heart—perhaps even more so, now that Morumus's heart carried heavier burdens. For a moment he simply stood and took it all in. Beyond this tiny vale, darkness stalked the land. But not here. Here knew nothing of such troubles. He stepped over to the edge of the pool and gazed into its bottom.

"Sanctuary." He gave a deep, contented sigh. "It is well named."

When he looked up, Morumus caught sight of a thin tendril of smoke wafting out from behind the waterfall. The sight made him smile.

"Donnach!" But he realized almost immediately that his shout had been wasted effort. With the water falling in front of its mouth, there was no way Donnach could have heard him from within the cave. Shutting his mouth, he walked briskly along the brink of the pool until he reached the ledge leading up to the cave. Here he stepped carefully up along a slick, narrow lip of stone to reach the cave's mouth. Then he had to remove his pack, stoop slightly, and edge sideways—for the entrance was a seam in the rock too low for a man to walk upright and too narrow for him to walk abroad. This made it difficult to traverse. But, as Donnach had observed upon Morumus's first visit, it also kept out the larger and more dangerous sorts of animals.

Morumus made slow, awkward progress. Even after he turned sideways, it was close quarters in the crack. Fortunately, the crevice was neither circuitous nor long—he could see the light of Donnach's fire within, and he would reach it in less than a minute.

"Donnach! Donnach, it's Morumus!"

"Morumus?" came a surprised reply, "Morumus, is that you?"

Morumus did not answer, for he was nearing the end of the passage. In the next moment, he was free of it. Sliding out of the crack, he found himself in a space roughly twice the size of a cell at Lorudin Abbey. He looked around. Along the wall on his right hand, Donnach had stacked a largish pile of wood for the fire. The fire itself, situated near the center of the cave, gave ample light and proved effective in warming the chamber: the air within had very little of the chill of the air without. Having absorbed quite a bit of cool mist from the spray of the waterfall on his way in, the warmth was most welcome.

"Morumus!" came a cheerful voice nearby as Morumus emerged from the passage. "Morumus, it *is* you!"

Morumus followed the voice to the far side of the fire, where his eyes found his friend. Donnach's tonsure had begun to disappear as his hair grew in again, and there were enough whiskers on his face and neck to create a patchy red beard. Yet if this bothered the Grendannathi, he gave no sign of it. His brown robe had collected a few stray bits of twigs, but seemed clean enough otherwise. In his hand he held a wooden bowl, and on his face there was a great smile.

Morumus returned the smile. "Hello brother. It is good to see you."

"And you, brother!" Donnach set down the bowl so that it would not spill, and the two friends embraced.

Stepping back, Morumus's smile turned into a grin. "For a man who has spent the last month and more living in a cave, you don't look as bad as you might!"

Donnach returned the grin with one of his own, and gestured around the chamber as though it were a palace. "Cave?" he asked with feigned indignation, "I doubt you have *ever* experienced such accommodations!"

"I relent!" Morumus held up his hands in mock surrender. "Taunt me no more with your luxury!"

At this remark, both of them fell to laughing. After this subsided, Donnach gestured for Morumus to sit down with him near the fire. Morumus did so, placing his small pack on the other side of him so that it too might dry.

"Have you eaten, brother?" Donnach picked up his bowl again and proffered it to Morumus. Its contents steamed with invitation.

"I have." Morumus declined the meal under protest from his nose.

"I was hoping you would say that. There is not much left."

For the next few minutes, the two young men sat quietly while Donnach finished his soup. Morumus was enjoying the fire, but he kept one eye on Donnach's progress—for he wanted to be the first to speak when the time came. At last, Donnach sat his empty bowl down beside him and wiped his mouth on his sleeve. Morumus saw his chance.

"So brother, tell me about your work and how you have been these past weeks." From the look on Donnach's face, Morumus could tell that his haste in speaking had not gone unnoticed. Nevertheless, when the Grendannathi spoke, the point was not pressed.

"I have been very well, thank you. Many of my people back home dwell in far humbler abodes than this cave, but until now I never have. I find that dwelling in such a place is helping me to appreciate their meager circumstances. At the least, I have learned that comfort ought to be neither over-valued nor taken for granted." He looked around for a moment at the cave, then sighed. "The isolation of this place has also taught me: there is nothing quite like unbroken solitude to teach you the value of your fellows."

Morumus nodded. After spending weeks with no one but Ulwilf, he knew in his own way what Donnach meant.

"Besides these, the time away has been a great boon for our work. I miss the daily routines of the abbey; yet being free of them, I am able to spend hours each day copying and translating. I have no other cares, Morumus. I have shelter in this cave and I have work in my hands. Even for food, Abbot Grahem has managed to keep me well-provisioned. By his instructions, I return half the distance to the abbey once a week. There, at a certain location along one of the old paths, I find a sack of food waiting for me. I am not sure whether the abbot brings it himself every week, or whether he sends others. Regardless, it has never failed."

Morumus gestured to the pack sitting next to him. "This week it has come to you by messenger—with some extra for me."

Donnach nodded. "Thank you, brother." Then, as he realized what Morumus had said, his face brightened. "Does this mean you will be staying with me for a time?"

"I'll tell you more about that soon." Morumus was not ready to douse the joy of their reunion with his grim tidings.

"Please, tell me about the work. Have you made much progress on the translation?"

"Let me show you." Donnach rose to his feet and stepped toward the back of the cave. When he returned a moment later, he was carrying a rectangular package wrapped in a leather bundle. Removing this protective cover, he handed Morumus a stout folio volume bound in chestnut boards.

Carefully undoing the leather clasp along the fore-edge, Morumus opened the volume. For several minutes after that he forgot all about the burden of events in the wider world and lost himself completely in the pages of Donnach's book. He turned page after page, reading and appreciating the fruits of his brother's labor.

The work itself was impressive in both its arrangement and quality. Each page was divided into three sections. A pair of parallel columns shared the upper two-thirds of each sheet. The left column contained the text of Holy Writ in the Vilguran language, copied in a plain, unadorned script. The right column contained the translation of the text into Grendannathi. The lines of the text in both columns were straight, and the lack of ornate embellishments upon either single letters or whole words made Donnach's script clear and readable. The only difference between the two columns was that, whereas the Vilguran column was complete throughout the volume, the Grendannathi column was much more sparingly filled.

The lower third of each page contained what looked to be notes of some sort—written in a more compact hand in a single column across the bottom of the page. Squinting in the firelight, it took Morumus a minute to realize what these were. When he did, he gasped.

"Donnach"—he looked up—"what have you done?"

The other monk, misunderstanding Morumus's tone, began to make explanation. "Is it the script?" He peered down over

Morumus's shoulder. "I realize that most manuscripts are illuminated, but a plainer style consumes less time and is more readable for—"

"You misunderstand, brother. Your script is excellent, and I am amazed that you have copied the entirety of the Vilguran so quickly. But that's not my question." He pointed with one finger toward the notes at the bottom of the page open before him. "Are these the Herido notes?"

"Oh." The flush in Donnach face receded, "Yes, those are Herido's annotations. I added some of my own where I thought they might prove useful for translating the text into my own tongue. If you look carefully, you'll see that I've distinguished between them by putting Herido's first and marking each with an *H*."

"Donnach . . . this is outstanding."

"Thank you." The other monk beamed. "Since this will be the first copy of the Holy Writ into Grendannathi, I tried to make it as useful as I could. It may be a resource for further copying or translation."

Morumus nodded. "It may indeed." He turned a few more leaves and scanned their contents. As he did, he noticed something strange. The right-hand columns were not only much less complete than the left, but their sections were much shorter and noncontiguous. For example, on the page open before Morumus, the Vilguran column contained twenty verses of text. Beside it, the Grendannathi column contained translations for ten of these twenty. Yet instead of translating ten continuous verses together, Donnach had translated five, left empty space for the next seven, translated five more, and then left the remaining three likewise un-translated.

Morumus looked up again. "Why are there spaces like this, Donnach?"

Donnach peered down at where Morumus was pointing with his finger. "You mean the gaps?"

293

"Yes. Why did you skip some of these verses?"

"Well, I realized from the beginning of this work that, even with your help, this translation is going to take a long time. So, after I finished copying the Vilguran, I decided to be very selective in my initial efforts. I used two principles. First, I translated passages which contained some central truth—particularly those that would most clearly teach my people the good news of Aesus. Second, I translated those passages that I thought might help show you something particular about my language. You are very talented with languages, Morumus. You have already made good progress in learning my people's speech. I thought that some examples might help you work out the remaining figures and twists."

"They certainly will. As to my progress," he continued, trying to fend off the compliment, "it's like I told you before. Your language is a lot like Dyfanni, which I learned as a boy. It's a small island we live on, Donnach."

"And it's a small step between true and false humility. Now, I have told you enough about me. How have things been with you? How long will you be able to stay?"

Morumus took a deep breath, then began to unfold his tale. There seemed to be no place to begin but the very beginning. He started with his father's murder, and how he had come to Lorudin. After this, he began to relate his dream—or rather, as events had demonstrated, his *tidusangan*—about the *Dree* and the exsanguinated girl. Yet he had not gotten very far when a strange thing happened.

Donnach, who had been listening quietly while staring into the fire, began to tremble.

"Donnach." Morumus dropped his narrative in mid-sentence. "What is wrong?"

"Morumus"—Donnach's voice shook and his expression paled. "Are there any monasteries in these hills and forest?"

"No." Morumus frowned. "Why do you ask?"

Donnach's trembling became even more violent.

"Donnach, what is wrong?"

Donnach turned to look at him. "Morumus, I have seen men in the forest to the south of here. I thought they were monks!"

"What do you mean?" But even as he asked, Morumus could feel his hackles rising.

"Several days ago, I was walking in the woods south of here. It was a nice day, and so I went farther than I normally go. I came to a road of some sort, which was strange. Who would expect to find a road in the forest so far into these hills? But I didn't have long to think about it, for I heard riders approaching in the distance. I got as far as I could off the road and hid myself behind a large tree. Just in time, too—there were four of them on horseback." Here both Donnach's face and voice became stricken. "They were all robed in black, and Morumus—there was a girl with them!"

"Oh no." A sickening sensation spread outward from his stomach.

"They weren't monks, were they?"

"No, Donnach. No. They were *Dree*." *And now they have another victim.*

Donnach looked aghast. "Your nightmare . . ."

". . . is all too real."

"How?"

Morumus got to his feet. "There's a lot I haven't told you yet, and we don't have time to wait. If there's even a chance that that girl might yet live, we need to act now."

Donnach stood as well. "What do you think Abbot Grahem will say?"

Morumus shook his head. "We aren't going back to Lorudin, Donnach. We're going back to this road you found."

"I am no coward." Donnach put such force in his words that, for the first time in a long time, Morumus remembered his friend was a prince. "Yet it is not wise to pursue an enemy of unknown strength with small numbers. We ought to go back for assistance."

"You're right. but I can't be seen in Lorudin. I am supposed to be dead. And if you go back without me, I won't be able to find this road."

"Dead?" Confusion filled his friend's face. "What are you talking about?"

"Like I said, there is a lot I haven't told you yet. Come on, I'll tell you the rest on the way."

26

"Drink this." Urien held out the stone cup, trying hard to keep her hand from trembling.

The girl, probably no more than ten years younger than Urien, turned away her head. It was the most resistance she could offer, for she could not push the cup away. She was bound to the sacrificial table in a cruciform position. The first rays of dawn were creeping over the roofless walls of the courtyard, and soon the *Mordruui* would return.

"I will not drink it."

Urien held it out again. "Please, it will dull the pain."

"And my wits."

"Yes. It will put you to sleep. That is how it works."

The girl shook her head, and her tone was resolute. "I cannot prepare to meet my Lord unless my mind is clear."

"Please"—Urien's voice wavered—"what they do is very painful. Spare yourself."

Now the girl turned her head to look at Urien. There was fear in her sharp blue eyes, as would be expected, but also something else. Was it . . . compassion? "Spare myself, or spare you?"

Urien recoiled as if struck. "Spare me?" she snapped too quickly, her anger flaring. "It is not I who is about to die."

The girl made no immediate reply. She only stared at Urien.

Urien could not bear the girl's silent gaze. "I should not have come." She turned to leave.

Her brother would have been enraged to know that Urien was speaking with the Mother's victims. He would have been doubly incensed to learn that she was offering them the same precious herb that their blood was intended to procure. But it was he who gave her the idea by lacing her wine the night he came to say good-bye. Now that he was gone, the *Mordruui* dared not cross her.

She was the Queen's Heart.

She could do as she pleased.

Her soul had split in two the night her brother abandoned her. For far longer than he could have imagined, it was Somnadh's presence alone that had shored up her faith. Even Urien had not realized the extent of her dependence. Despite his abandonment, Urien would never cease to love her brother. Yet something had broken in her the night he left. She realized now what had been growing within her for years.

She hated the Mother.

The Goddess Tree was indeed beautiful. The lines of her boughs were balanced and graceful. Her spotless white skin was serene and sublime. Her leaves were a deep and luxuriant red, shaped like scarlet-gloved hands at the ends of her limbs. Yet for Urien, this beauty was cold and distant. The Mother was an uncaring queen. How could she be anything more than a distant despot, when she would not speak to her most loyal servant?

The morning after Somnadh left, all the horrible questions Urien had long banished came clawing back. Her brother had taught her that the Mother is the beginning and end of all life. He had told her that the Mother has claim on all life, and thus has a right to feed upon what is hers. But if the Mother was but calling back her own, why did she not speak to her victims? And if all life returned to the Mother in the end, why should she cut it off in haste? Could not a truly benevolent and powerful goddess nourish herself without demanding sacrifice? Should she not rather be the one most zealous to protect life? What kind of Mother devours her own children?

Urien knew that she should feel ashamed to harbor such questions. But she didn't. Her brother had been gone for over three months, and her faith hung by the barest thread. She continued to serve the Mother for the simple fact that she knew no other way.

We can either dream about the gods we would like, or we can serve the ones we have.

Her father's reminder sounded empty as it echoed along the hollow corridors of her soul, yet what choice did she have?

"It is okay," said the girl behind her. "All will be well with me."

Urien stopped walking. In spite of herself, she turned back. "How can you say that? Are you not afraid to die?"

"Of course I am afraid, but I know my Lord will not abandon me."

For some reason, the girl's confidence angered Urien, and she found the heat returning to her voice. "How can you be so sure? Have you ever seen him?"

"No, but I have heard his voice."

Nothing could have so caught Urien off-guard. "Your god speaks to you?"

"Aesus speaks to all who will listen."

"How?"

"In his word."

"What do you mean?" pressed Urien, impatient for the answer.

"Whenever the priest reads Holy Writ, we hear his voice."

"Fool!" Urien felt angrier now than ever. "You hear a man speaking, and you think it is a god? How do you know the words are not just words of men? How could you ever know the words in your book are the voice of a god?" A note of dark inspiration touched her. "How do you know *I* am not the voice of your god? After all, it is *I* who hold your life in my hands."

Despite her predicament, the girl's eyes flashed. "I know my Redeemer's voice. There is power in his word—the power of his Spirit. You may mock, witch. But you have no such power."

"Today I will pour out your blood upon the roots of the Mother—a goddess I can see and touch. Where is your god's power now?"

Tears welled at the corners of the girl's eyes, but still she did not turn away. "He has promised, 'The one who trusts me, though he should die, yet he will live.'" Her voice cracked, but the girl did not break. "He also said, 'Have no fear from those who kill the body, but are not able to kill the soul.'"

"And yet you fear!"

"Only for a little while longer." Now she did turn away. "Aesus himself trembled when he faced death."

"Ha! Powerless and trembling—and dead! What good is such a god?"

The girl's head snapped back, and her eyes locked onto Urien's. There was a strange, almost dangerous gleam in those eyes now. When she spoke, the girl's words were like a dagger in Urien's heart. "He died, yes, but he was raised again to life. And as for him, so with me. Today I will be with him—alive, in Everlight. He has given me this promise. Does the demon you worship offer such comfort? You can see and touch your idol, yes. But does it speak? Has it ever promised you anything?"

Urien lashed out before she even knew what she was doing. Her free hand struck the girl hard on the cheek. "Be silent, fool!" Then she turned and stormed toward the archway in the outer wall.

The girl called after the retreating Urien. "May Aesus forgive you!" she said through sobs.

For the second time, Urien stopped—but she dared not turn back to look. She realized now why the girl made her so angry. *Confidence.*

The girl's confidence was terrifying.

"How can you speak thus to me?" she asked over her shoulder, her own voice shaking. "How can you say such things to one who will soon carry your blood in a basin?"

"Because"—the girl's voice broke and her whole frame shook within her bonds—"because I must. Even as he has forgiven me, so I forgive you. And I pray that he might yet rescue you from this darkness."

"No! No, you cannot!" Urien dropped the cup, and it struck the stones with a loud echoing sound. Its thick contents oozed onto the ground.

Urien covered her ears and fled.

Morumus and Donnach moved as quickly as they could through the forest, the latter leading the way south toward where he had seen the *Dree.*

They had been walking for several hours now, climbing into the hills as the sun climbed toward its meridian. Far from being tedious, the time spent walking seemed to have flown by; for as they walked, Morumus had repeated to Donnach everything he had related to Abbot Grahem about his journeys with Ulwilf. After this, he shared with Donnach what Abbot Grahem had told him in response—about the origins of the *Dree*, Bishop Anathadus's book, and the need for them to flee. He had concluded with the account of how Abbot Grahem faked his death in order that he might escape from Ulwilf. For his part, Donnach listened with grim fascination.

Morumus had just finished his tale as they crossed a small stream.

"We are close," said Donnach as they stepped out of the water and started up a gentle rise on the far side. Then he turned to look back at Morumus. "Is 'seven-day plague' even a real sickness?"

"Oh yes. It was brought to Midgaddan by the Umaddians. It is not very common, but it is real."

"Ah," Donnach nodded. "That makes it perfect."

"Exactly. My time as a hostage to Anbharim made it plausible, and the poison Abbot Grahem used on me mimics its symptoms. Moreover, the disease is so contagious that nobody else besides the abbot dared to come near my cell! On the seventh day after I fell ill, he pronounced me dead. They buried me yesterday."

"So the only two who know you aren't really dead are the cooks?"

"Right. Several others helped carry me wrapped to the grave, but Abbot Grahem arranged so that only Silgram and Ortto would be responsible for filling it and keeping the requisite prayer vigil."

"Nobody thought it was strange that the cooks were also serving as gravediggers?"

"Who knows?" Morumus shrugged. "After Ulwilf made me participate in his interrogations, I suspect that few of the other brothers would have been willing to volunteer."

"And the others who helped carry you—they did not see that you were still breathing?"

"I doubt it. Abbot Grahem gave me another potion which— so I was told—made the breathing very shallow. But I don't remember anything from the time I drank it until the time I woke up in the open grave. After that, Silgram and Ortto cut me free, handed me a bag of provisions for the both of us, and sent me on my way. The last glimpse I had of them, they were filling my grave."

"That must have been a strange sight." Donnach turned his attention back toward the woods in front of them. "So the original plan was that once Oethur brought the *Dree* book, we would get some horses from that village—"

"The village is called Reth. Abbot Grahem has a few extra horses stabled by a local farmer. He gave me another token to retrieve them."

"Right. Then we were to head to Naud and purchase passage to Urras. But what do you think will happen now?"

"I don't know. If we find where the *Dree* are hiding, then we will have to take the risk of returning to Lorudin. Or at least you will. Even with such tidings, my reappearance would cause Abbot Grahem considerable trouble with Ulwilf."

"Even if we brought word of a *Dree* enclave?"

"Maybe not right away, but eventually, yes. Whatever the Red Order is up to, they know that the burglar in Versaden carried a Lorudin token. That is bad enough. I also know from my time with Ulwilf that he does not like the practices of our abbey. I think he'd be more than happy to take any opportunity he could to charge the abbot with obstructing the Red Order's visitation."

"Right." Donnach sounded distracted. An instant later, he stopped walking as he reached the top of the small rise. He pointed. "There it is."

Morumus came up beside him and followed Donnach's finger with his eyes. "I see it."

About a hundred yards away, Morumus saw the road running more or less straight through the midst of the forest.

From the size of the surrounding trees through which its path had been cut—some of the largest he had seen in Cael-dora—he could tell that the road was very old. Noticing this, something stirred in his memory. He seemed to remember reading something about an ancient settlement in the Tumulan Hills . . .

"Which way did the riders go when you saw them?"

"This way." Donnach pointed to his left. "Keep your ears peeled for any sound of horses," he added as they began moving again.

For a quarter of a league, they followed the road through the forest without hearing anything larger than a squirrel rustling in the leaves. Then the ground beneath the road began to climb toward the rim of a ridge that curved away to either side as far as they could see. The two monks had almost reached the crest when Donnach stopped short and cocked his head to one side. No sooner had Morumus stopped than he heard it, too—a faint, jingling sound coming from beyond the crest of the ridge. The two men looked at each other.

"Horses," Donnach said ominously.

They scrambled to get as far away from the road as they could—Donnach going one way, and Morumus the other. The Grendannathi found shelter behind the thick bole of an oak about thirty yards off the left side of the road. Morumus did not have to go quite so far—ducking behind a cluster of large rocks to the right hand side about twenty yards distant. As it turned out, both men had reached cover just in time.

Less than a minute later, a pair of horses appeared on the road at the crest of the ridge. Behind the saddle of the first was tied a large, drooping bundle wrapped in coarse brown cloth. Of more interest, however, were the riders. Both wore long, black robes—with their hoods up. The horses were moving at a brisk walk, and their riders were talking as they made their descent toward the forest floor. Morumus remained still, listening.

"How far do we have to take this one?" asked the rider sitting in front of the bundle.

Morumus started. Were his ears playing tricks on him?

"Far enough," said the rider behind him. "But not so far as the last. You heard what happened with that, right?"

Tucked behind his rock, Morumus shook his head. *This doesn't make any sense!*

"Yes," the first rider snorted. "Quite a mess. What were they thinking?"

"They weren't. Praise the Mother they were able to cover it up. But don't think it was forgotten. They were the first called out yesterday to go north."

"Right. And if that won't be even more of a mess . . ."

The rest of their conversation was lost to Morumus as the horses carried the riders beyond earshot. He waited for several long minutes before moving. When finally he did stir, the riders were lost from sight. Glancing back across the way, he saw Donnach leave his shelter.

"That was a body strapped to that horse." The Grendannathi's tone was grim as the two men rejoined on the road. "We are too late."

Morumus nodded. "Did you hear what they said?"

"I heard them speak, but I couldn't make out the language."

"I can't explain it"—Morumus shook his head—"but those riders were speaking Dyfanni."

A few hours later it was finished. The Mordruui had done their work, and Urien had done hers. She'd offered the girl's blood to the Mother with all of the ritual prayers. Then the Mordruui carried the body away into the forest.

Now Urien sat alone in her chamber, staring at the flame of the single oil lamp on her table. It was over.

Why then did she feel so unsettled?

The girl's words stung her, it was true. It was as if they had been chosen to pour salt on all of the unhealed wounds in Urien's soul. Those wounds now blazed with the pain of fresh exposure, and she wondered if they would ever close over again. Yet she knew it was not just pain that she felt. There was something more. What was it?

The girl questioned Urien's mercy, wondering for whom had it really been intended. That was the first blow. Then she exuded such . . . *confidence* about her death. She claimed her god spoke to her in the Aesusian holy book. And then there was what the girl said at the last. Without being asked, despite all the scorn Urien had poured upon her, the girl forgave her—even offering a prayer that her god might rescue Urien, too! It was ridiculous, but it was this that rattled Urien more than all the rest. Why?

Why?

With a suddenness that overwhelmed her, Urien knew. It was not simple pain that she felt. Rather, it was the pain of yearning. Urien realized in that moment that her deepest desire was not for her brother to return. No. More than anything else in the whole world, she wished for the girl's words to be true.

The Mother demanded blood and offered nothing in return but death. The girl's god seemed to promise just the opposite.

We can either dream about the gods we would like, or we can serve the ones we have, her father's words reminded her.

But what if the gods we have and serve are themselves *the dream? What if the Mother is nothing but a tree?*

306

Urien stood. Retrieving her lamp, she strode toward the door. There was one way to find out.

"Now!" said Morumus. "None of them is looking!"

Darting from the protective cover of the forest's edge, Donnach dashed across the open space. Taking Morumus's proffered hand, he was over the short stone wall in moments.

After the riders had gone, the two men had climbed the remaining distance to the rim of the forest ridge. What they found astounded them. Beyond the ridge and hidden between the surrounding hills lay a long, narrow dale. Most of it was taken up with cultivated fields, but there was also an orchard and a vineyard. On the far end lay a stone keep. Keeping themselves within the trees along its edge, Donnach and Morumus had skirted the perimeter of the valley until they had reached the far side.

The architecture of the keep was most peculiar: a combination of two constructions. For the first, there was a main hall with a small tower that looked almost like a church. Here the stones were sharply cut and dressed, and the lines were rectangular. But all of this recent construction faced another structure that was obviously the ruin of something much older—a series of concentric rings made of rough, uncut stones. The center circle was relatively intact and almost as tall as the keep's tower. Yet unlike the tower, no roof crowned its top. If it had possessed one originally, it had long since moldered away. Surrounding this central ring were the crumbling remains of two lower circles. These looked as though they might originally have served as fortifications. Between the two structures—connecting the new with the old—was the low wall over which Donnach and Morumus had just climbed.

As it turned out, they had climbed into a garden. Stone pathways divided colorful flowerbeds, and at the center of it all was an ornate stone basin filled with water. On one end, there was an entrance leading into the keep. On the other, the garden walls joined the outer ring at another opening. Staring into this latter opening and beholding the structure into which it led, Morumus's memory flared to life.

He remembered now where he had read about the ancient settlement in the midst of the Tumulans. It had been in an ancient Vilguran text, a volume which had collected some of the earliest, and often fragmentary, histories of the Old Imperium. According to the text, the people who had occupied the Tumulans had practiced a religion so vile that it made even the oft-ruthless Vilgurans squeamish. These people refused to submit to the Imperium. There had been a bloody conflict, and in the end the Vilgurans came in force. They killed most of the people and razed their settlement—including a ringed fortress. Morumus remembered the account well, for it had been in that volume that he first came across that rare word he'd come to dread: *erebanur.*

In that moment a terrible thrill coursed through Morumus, and he realized what it was he was seeing.

"The dark madness." He didn't take his eyes off the opening in the ring wall. "The Dark Faith. You've found it, Donnach."

"What?" Donnach had been casting apprehensive looks toward the entrance to the newer keep.

"This is the place." Morumus pointed to the opening. "Those are the remains of a pre-Vilguran settlement. The

Dark Faith that the abbot and the bishop and my uncle and Captain Brann tracked—this is their stronghold."

Donnach looked hard at the entrance in the ring. "In there is where they killed that girl."

"Right, and God knows how many others."

"Should we go back now? Or should we go in?"

"There may be others in there."

"Victims or riders?"

"Yes." Morumus studied the entrance. "Either—or both."

Donnach turned to look at him. "I do not think I could leave another child to be butchered, brother. What say you?"

"I am with you." Morumus remembered all too well the body he saw near Agnorum. "We have to go in."

27

wo days before Donnach and Morumus entered the narrow valley, Oethur stood in the central square of Aevor, holding one hand over his eyes as he stared up into the sky. On an average day, his eye might have missed the small white bird flying overhead. Yet because the blue sky was so clear, the bird stood out. Oethur watched it until it flew beyond the square and disappeared from sight.

"Where have you been, little thing? Where are you going?"

Oethur wondered such things about himself, too—but found he could offer as few answers as the bird. But far from making him despair, this just made him shrug. "God knows." He had come to learn that this was enough.

Lowering his eyes, Oethur resumed his stroll through the wide square. Dozens of different sights, smells, and sounds tugged at his senses from every direction. It was market day in Aevor, and so the central square of the cathedral city was teeming with people and business. In every direction there was color and motion and sound—people haggling and peddlers lying. Sturdy booths lined all four edges of the square, forming a sort of hedge or perimeter. Moving out from this boundary toward the center, carts of varying shape and size stood in rows, leaving only enough space for foot-traffic in between. In fact, apart from the two bisecting lanes kept clear by the guards for through-traffic, the whole of the city center was a thriving hub of trade.

The lively earthiness of Aevor on market day was refreshing. Sometimes Oethur came to the bazaar to make purchases for the bishop—Anathadus insisted that the best quill pens were to be had from a certain traveling peddler. Other times he trawled the market in order to practice his Caeldoran with common people. Yet today Oethur had come just to enjoy the anonymity that comes with moving through a large mass of strangers. It was a wonderful reminder to him both of his own smallness and of the providence of God. *If God can keep and direct all these different lives at once, he is more than able to steer mine.*

By the time the sun set on this day, Oethur looked forward to returning to the cloister. At dusk he left the disbanding stalls and carts behind him, and headed south up the cathedral hill. Yet he had not gone even halfway when he saw a familiar face approaching him from that direction.

"Hello Nack."

Although not the highest-ranking officer of the cathedral guards, Nack was the man most trusted by Bishop Anathadus. It was Nack who had accompanied the bishop and the Northmen to Versaden, and it was Nack who had arranged for the latter to escape from that city in order to avoid arrest. Since coming to stay in Aevor, Oethur had often witnessed him coming and going from the bishop's study. Without ever asking, Oethur knew that Nack was for the bishop what his own father called a "third hand"—a very capable man to whom one could entrust the prosecution of discreet errands.

Yet other than brief greetings made in passing, Oethur had exchanged few words with Nack in all his time in Aevor. The guardsman was not unkind. Rather, he simply had little to say—and refused to pretend otherwise. Oethur understood this, and respected the man for it. What he did not understand was why Nack had come to meet him now.

"Bishop Anathadus sent me to find you," said Nack, resolving the question as if he had read Oethur's mind. Both his voice and expression were their typical shades of grim. "You are to come at once."

"Certainly. Where is the bishop?"

"In his study. I am to conduct you to him."

Oethur nodded. "What's this about?" They moved up the hill toward the cathedral.

"There's been a letter from Lorudin."

"Oh? When did it arrive?"

"This afternoon. Carried by a merchant from that direction."

"What does it say?"

Nack gave him a sidelong glance. "You'll have to ask the bishop about that, son."

Oethur did not bother asking anything further. He realized that his last question had pushed beyond what was permitted, and he knew that Nack was not the sort of man who would appreciate being asked to repeat himself. Besides this, it did not take them long to reach the bishop's door. Within a few minutes after meeting in the street, they stood before the study door. Nack had not even finished knocking before he received a response.

"Come!"

The guardsman swung the door inward, admitting Oethur and then himself. They found Bishop Anathadus standing near the hearth, clutching a piece of parchment and staring into the fire.

"Oethur, sir." Nack proffered a bow as he backed toward the door.

"Stay, Nack." Bishop Anathadus gestured the man inward. "But close the door fast."

"Yes sir."

The bishop waited to speak until the latch had clicked shut. Then he looked at Oethur. It was a hard look. "Abbot Grahem sends us his greetings—along with a request."

"Sir?" Oethur was not sure what to make of the bishop's expression.

"There is trouble at Lorudin, Oethur. Our friends are in danger."

Oethur drew a sharp breath. "What it is it? Has something happened to Donnach? Or to Morumus?"

"Donnach is safe, and Morumus has returned to the abbey, too. But he has brought very dark news. All three of you must flee Caeldora."

"What? Sir, what has happened?"

"I take it you know the name of *Dree*?"

A chill crept into Oethur. "I do. They are enemies from my homeland, from long ago."

"They are here, Oethur."

"Here? In Caeldora?" Oethur could not believe what he was hearing.

The bishop's expression had never appeared darker. "Yes."

"I don't understand."

"Neither do I." Every line on Anathadus's face was visible. "It has been so long."

"What are we to do?"

"This letter is a summons from Abbot Grahem." Anathadus held up the parchment to the light and summarized it. "You are to leave here as soon as possible, bringing with you the Bone Codex—that's a book from my library. You are to meet Morumus at 'Donnach's sanctuary.' Do you know the place?"

"I do." A thrill rose in him.

"Good, said Anathadus." He gestured at another door in the side wall, "The book is in my library. You will take it with you tonight. Tomorrow morning Nack will see you to a horse and on your way. Is that clear?"

"Yes, sir."

"Well then, I—" But Anathadus was interrupted by another knock at the door.

"Yes?" he called sharply, "Who is it?"

"Sir, it's Lyzigus."

"Come!"

The door swung inward again, and a face peered into the room.

"It's okay, Lyzigus," said the bishop. "What is it?"

"Sir"—the junior priest looked and sounded urgent—"it's about Bealdu. You told me to watch and inform you if I saw him coming this evening."

"The red monk never knocks," said Anathadus to the others before turning back. "I take it he is coming now?"

"Yes, with two others of his order!"

"Oh joy," said Anathadus. "How soon?"

"I saw them entering the cathedral before I came to you, sir."

"Very soon then. Thank you, Lyzigus. That will be all."

"Sir." The junior priest ducked back out of the door.

When the door clicked shut, Anathadus turned to Nack. "Go and see to any arrangements for the morning."

"Yes sir." As Nack opened the door to exit the room, the sound of footsteps could be heard echoing up the corridor.

The bishop was moving toward the second door before the first had finished closing again. "Oethur, get into the library and see if you can find the book, while I deal with whatever pressing matter Bealdu has tonight." He removed a small key from his robe and unlocked the door. "There is a lamp already lit on the table in the first room, and the book is on the top of a small shelf in the very back of the third."

"Yes, sir. What does it look like?"

Anathadus smiled wanly. "It's called the 'Bone Codex' for a reason, son. You'll know it when you find it. I'm going to lock the door behind you, just in case Bealdu's friends get curious. In you go, quickly now."

No sooner had the library door locked behind him than Oethur heard the sound of new voices in the bishop's study.

"Bealdu," Anathadus said, "your arrival is as welcome as it is unexpected . . ."

Oethur did not linger. Instead, he picked up the lamp from where it waited on the table before him and set off to find the book. He had never been inside the bishop's library before, and was surprised at the sheer number of shelves and books the bishop had managed to amass: if there was a bigger collection out there, he did not know of it.

Morumus, how you must have loved this place. Concerned as Oethur was over the bishop's tidings, it would be good to see his friends again.

Entering the third room and walking to the back, Oethur found the last shelf just as Anathadus had said: tucked sideways against the corner of the back wall, and less than half as long as the other shelves which jutted out perpendicular to it. Lifting the lamp above him, he scanned the top shelf. Again, as the bishop had said, it did not take him long to locate the book. There were half a dozen books of odd shapes and sizes on the top shelf, but only one of them had a dull white spine.

"The Bone Codex." He pulled it down with his free hand. Holding it close to the lamp, he grimaced. The spine really was bone. Was it human? Holding the book by its other edge, he turned its front toward the light. The black leather of the front cover was embossed in dark bronze with the image of—a tree? What did that signify? He did not have long to ponder, however, for in that moment he heard shouting coming from the direction of the bishop's study. Tucking the book under his arm, Oethur hurried back toward the first room. Reaching the door to the bishop's study, he knelt down and peered through the keyhole.

And gasped!

One of the red monks—a huge man whose face was hidden by a large cowl—had Bishop Anathadus pinned to his chair. The second, another hooded stranger, held a knife to his throat. The third—this one Oethur recognized from his unhooded face as Bealdu, the legate for Aevor—stood opposite Anathadus across the table. His dark eyes blazed in the light from the bishop's hearth.

"There will be no more shouting, Bishop." Bealdu was cross. "I would not want one of your toadies interrupting our business. If you raise your voice again, I will have my brother cut your throat. Is that clear?"

Anathadus made no response.

"Now, you *will* sign this bull of excommunication. Abbot Grahem has obstructed our visitation in direct contravention to the decree of the Court of Saint Cephan."

"He did no such thing." The bishop spoke as though he were *not* being held at knife point. "And you know it."

"One of his monks was caught spying on a member of our order in Versaden. The token proves it."

"The token proves the presence of a token-bearer, but it does not support your charge. Your order was not empowered until the final session of the Court. The offense you allege took place the day before. You cannot charge a man for something that was not an offense when it occurred."

"You fail to see the point," said Bealdu darkly. "The abbot deceived an imperial legate about the identity of that token-bearer."

"*Allegedly* deceived. You have but the testimony of a garrison captain—at least you claim to have it. Until my court receives sworn testimony, you have nothing. And even if you can produce it, canon law requires two or three witnesses to establish a charge."

"I am finished arguing with you." There was a stony finality in Bealdu's tone. "You were the only bishop to vote against the visitation, and you have obstructed my labors from the beginning. I should not be surprised that your pet abbot has done the same." The red monk shook his head. "I had hoped it would not come to this, but if you do not cooperate, I will be forced to make public an accusation which has come to me concerning your *own* person."

"And what charge is that, Bealdu?"

"Some of your appointments have come under scrutiny as *irregular*, Bishop. Take, for example, this abbot whom you refuse to discipline. The records show that he was not the only qualified candidate at the time of his selection. Is your reluctance to sign his excommunication *truly* motivated by principle, or by your purse? You stand accused of selling Church office."

"Simony?" Anathadus snorted. "That is the oldest trick of all. I expected more—even from you, Bealdu. The archbishop will never believe you."

"Oh, but he already has." Bealdu reached into his pocket. When he withdrew his hand, he held a *brer* token. Neither Anathadus in his chair nor Oethur behind the door needed to see the engraved 'OLLEVS' to know to whom the token belonged.

"How?" Anathadus spoke through clenched teeth. "How did you convince him of such rubbish?"

Bealdu's cruel smile broadened. "One is always ready to believe about others what one knows to be true of oneself."

Bishop Anathadus said nothing.

Bealdu leaned in over the table. When he spoke, his voice was ice. "Do you see my point *now*, bishop? If you do not sign this bull of excommunication for Abbot Grahem, I will sign one for you."

For a long moment Anathadus said nothing, only stared back at the red monk. Then, finally, a change passed over his expression. "Fine. Fine. God help me, I will sign it. Let me go."

From behind the library door, Oethur's heart clutched in his chest.

Was Bishop Anathadus really going to excommunicate Abbot Grahem?

Oethur need not have worried. No sooner had the red monks released Anathadus than the bishop sprang into action. With a quickness that caught everybody off-guard—Oethur included—he leapt up from his seat, overturned the table, and knocked Bealdu backwards. Seeing this, the monk who had held him in his chair lunged forward. Anathadus sidestepped, caught the man by the robe, and flung him full toward the fire.

Rather than smash into the stone hearth, the large monk actually fell into the fire itself. He managed to roll clear, but the force of his impact sent flaming brands and smoldering coals scattering outward in an explosion of cinders and smoke. Anathadus jumped back from the flames—and in that instant the second monk caught him—and plunged the knife deep into his abdomen. The bishop gasped.

"*No!*" The shout escaped Oethur before he could stop it.

The eyes of all four men in the study instantly turned toward the door.

"There is somebody watching!" Bealdu was already back on his feet.

"Fly!" shouted the bishop, blood spouting from his lips with the force of his words. "Fly now!"

The only thing that saved Oethur from sharing Anathadus's fate was the fact that the bishop had locked the door. The first monk was at the door a moment after Oethur leapt to his feet, but he could not wrench it open.

"It's locked!" he growled.

Oethur dashed back through the second room, but he already knew it was no good. The only door out of the library was the door to the bishop's study—and behind him, that door was shuddering under the force of a large shoulder. Reaching the third room, he stopped. The only other way out was through the windows. The bishop's rooms were on the second story of the cathedral cloister, and it would be a long drop to the courtyard below.

Setting both lamp and book down on the nearby table, he grabbed a large wood-bound volume off the nearest shelf and turned back toward the windows.

The sound of the breaking glass was drowned out by the splintering crash of the study door. Oethur paused for the briefest moment. Looking back through the open doors of the second and third rooms, he saw two red-hooded men silhouetted against the light from the bishop's fire. Though they wore the garb of churchmen, in that minute they looked for all the world to Oethur like demons.

Retrieving the unholy Bone Codex from the table, he clutched the book to his chest. The red monks were shouting and dashing toward him as he stepped up onto the ruined frame of the window. The next moment, with a silent prayer, he leapt into the dark.

"This is the place," said Morumus soberly.

He and Donnach stood in a walled courtyard between the second and inner rings of
the ancient stronghold. The space was bare, except for a long
stone table at its center. Leather thongs protruded from the
table surface in the precise places necessary to bind a person
in cruciform position: feet together and arms outstretched.
The table itself was tilted slightly upward at the feet, and
there was a recessed bowl for the head with a channel leading
from it to the edge of the table. Both bowl and channel bore
the telltale signs of recent use.

"It is hideous." Donnach pointed up to the sky—a brilliant
blue interspersed with wispy clouds—then lowered his hand
to the table. "Above, the glories of God. Below, the horrors
of man." His voice shook with smoldering anger. "How can
they be so blind, brother?"

The god of this age has blinded them.

The words of Holy Writ rose in Morumus's mind, but
when he looked at his friend's mottled face and reddened
eyes—which he knew were a mirror image of his own—he

found that he could not speak them. He shook his head, and for a minute neither of them could say another word.

Finally, Donnach pointed toward the door set in the wall of the inner ring. "Where do you suppose that leads?"

Morumus looked at the door, but he never got the chance to answer.

"It leads to the Mother," said a voice behind them.

The two monks nearly jumped out of their robes. Whirling, they saw a woman standing in the archway of the outer wall. The woman looked to be about the same age as they, and stood about the same height. She wore a green hood over a white gown, and in one hand she held a large glass lamp. With the other she held a long, stone knife. Seeing the knife, both Donnach and Morumus took an involuntary step back.

"Who are you?" said Morumus.

The woman ignored the question. "If either of you make a move toward me, I will scream—and you will be the next ones on that table. Do you understand?"

Donnach and Morumus looked at each other.

"You might intend us for the table regardless," observed Donnach.

The woman gave him a hard look. "Did you see or hear me approaching? If I had wanted you dead, you would be."

"She's right, Donnach."

The woman turned her gaze toward Morumus. "You are dressed as Aesusian monks. From where do you come?"

Morumus hesitated.

"Unless you wish me to change my mind, you will both answer my questions and do exactly what I say."

"Lorudin," he answered. "We are from Lorudin."

"Where is Lorudin?"

"North of here."

"How far north?"

"Less than a day."

"How did you find this place?"

This time it was Donnach who answered. "I saw riders in the woods carrying a . . ." He looked at the table. "Well, I'm sure you know."

The woman seemed almost to flinch. But when she spoke, her voice was firm. "You have trespassed on the Mother's sanctuary. It is only fitting that you should meet her." She pointed with the knife first to Morumus, and then to the inner door. "Open it."

Morumus walked to the door. The hairs on his arms and spine stood on end as he reached for the handle. With more than a little apprehension, he clasped it and pulled. The door swung open, and he turned back to the woman.

"Lead the way." She gestured with the knife at both of the monks, "Both of you go first. If I cannot see either one of you, I will summon my servants and you will die."

Morumus looked at Donnach.

"We have little choice, brother."

The space within the inner ring was cool and dim. High overhead, they could see a circle of the bright blue sky. Below, tall walls of windowless stone guaranteed that the roofless tower remained most hours in shadow. The diameter of the chamber seemed somehow wider from within than without, though Morumus supposed this was but an illusion. What was not illusory, however, was the raised stone circle filled with earth at the center of the chamber— nor what grew in it.

Though he had more than half-suspected it, Morumus still gasped to see the tree. Its slender white limbs seemed almost to shimmer in the dim light, and the hand-shaped leaves likewise appeared to pulse with scarlet color. From trunk to branch and from root to top, the proportions of the tree were perfect. In fact, they seemed rather too perfect, and created the impression that the white tree was more ivory sculpture than tree—more dead skeleton than living wood.

"'Under every luxuriant tree you sprawled like a...'" Morumus let his voice trail off before he reached the conclusion.

Beside him, Donnach muttered a curse in Grendannathi.

Entering behind them, the woman circled around the two monks until she stood beside the raised stone circle a quarter turn from their own position. This enabled her to face the tree without turning her back to them. Setting down both knife and lamp on the rim in front of her, she looked up at the tree. Morumus could see her lips moving, but she made no sound. A minute later, her eyes lowered again to fix on them. Eyes that glistened in the lamplight.

"I came to this place when I was but a girl," she said softly, "and here I have poured the blood of many victims upon the roots of the Mother." Her voice grew bitter and began to shake. "Yet I fear now that she is nothing. I fear she does not speak to me because *it* cannot speak. I fear that this tree is no goddess. I fear that it is just a tree, and I am just a murderer."

Neither Donnach nor Morumus said a word. Neither had expected to hear anything like this. They were transfixed.

"The last victim... like you, she was an Aesusian. She told me that your God speaks in his book to all who will listen. She told me that with him there is forgiveness—even for such a one as I." Tears streamed down the woman's face, but she pressed on. "Tell me now, you monks: is it true?"

Morumus opened his mouth, but found himself incredulous—and therefore speechless. *Was this really happening?* It was Donnach who found words.

"My own mother's father was once a priest to the old gods." He sounded somewhat hoarse but firm. "Yes, it is true. The blood of Aesus the Lord cleanses us from *all* sin."

The woman closed her eyes and looked away, and for several long moments she made neither movement nor sound. When finally she did look back at him, the tears had slowed.

"I came here to make one final attempt to hear the Mother's voice." She spoke barely above a whisper. "I was going to offer her my own blood." She looked down at the knife lying before her and shook her head. When she looked up again, there was something new in her voice. "But you say this Aesus will give me his blood instead?"

"He will," said Donnach.

"What does he require in exchange?"

"Nothing," said Donnach. "It is a free gift."

"Nothing?" The woman's eyes went wide. "What sort of god bestows such great favor without price?"

"The kind of God who paid the price himself," said Donnach, "a God of love. There is nothing you can contribute. All Aesus requires is that you trust him."

Confusion creased the woman's brow. "Truly there is nothing?"

"Nothing."

"I do not know if I can believe that. But I do know I can no longer believe *this*." She gestured toward the tree, contemptuous. Then she shifted her eyes to Morumus. "If I let you leave this valley, will you promise to take me with you?"

"We will."

"Then"—the woman's voice rose—"I renounce the Mother! No longer will I serve as Queen's Heart! If she is a goddess, let her serve herself!" In one swift, fluid motion, she picked up her lamp and hurled it at the base of the white tree. The thin glass of the reservoir shattered upon impact. Oil splashed everywhere, and a moment later it ignited. The flames spread with incredible speed, and within moments they had engulfed the tree. As the fire coursed along its blackening branches and crackled among the disintegrating leaves, the interior of the inner ring of the ancient fortress—a space that had been cold and dim upon their entry—blazed with heat and flickering orange light.

"My name is Urien." The woman turned away from the pyre of her old faith and strode toward the door. "Come. We must move quickly."

Donnach and Morumus had to hurry to keep up with Urien as she marched out through the rings of the ancient fortress, across the garden, and into the keep. "You will have to disguise yourselves," she said over her shoulder as they went. "Aesusian monks are not welcome guests in a *Muthadannach*." Retrieving a fresh lamp as they passed through the main hall, she led them along a narrow corridor to a shut wooden door.

"This is where the *Mordruui* prepare," she said.

"The riders?" asked Donnach.

"Yes, they are the only ones who may come and go from this valley." Pushing the door open, she gestured for them to enter. "Change your robes. I will go and see to the horses."

Taking the lamp, Donnach and Morumus entered the chamber and latched the door behind them. The interior of the room was significantly wider than it was deep. Along the wall facing them hung a long row of hooded robes. Facing these on the opposite wall were long knives in belted sheaths, and Morumus knew even without looking that their blades would be stone. To their right hand, a small table stood along the short wall. On its surface sat a wide stone basin. Donnach sat the lamp down next to it, and the two of them set to exchanging their monks' garb for more sinister apparel.

"Do we leave our other robes?" Donnach asked after he had made the switch.

"No," Morumus said, "we'll need to change back into them before too long."

Donnach pointed to the knife-belts on the facing wall. "What about these?"

"We didn't bring any other weapons." Morumus shuddered at the thought of strapping the ritual blade to his waist. "How's your weapons' training?"

"Out of practice. Yours?"

"The same or worse. Let's pray we don't have to find out just *how* out of practice."

"Good idea."

They had just finished cinching the belts tight when there was a knock at the door.

"Ready?" Urien asked when they opened the door. When the two monks nodded, she took the lamp from Donnach and resumed the lead. As they followed, Morumus noticed that she too had exchanged her clothing for the garb of a *Mordruui*.

Less than a quarter hour later, three black-cloaked riders struck out from the stable and trotted briskly up the road away from the keep, toward the rim of the valley. A few of the servants in the field were surprised to see them—hadn't all but two of the *Mordruui* been called out the day before, and hadn't the remaining two already gone this afternoon? Yet none presumed to stop the riders. Only a fool would dare to challenge the Hands of the Mother.

For a few brief minutes, it seemed as if Urien's plan would work. But the three riders had not got even halfway to the valley's lip when they began to hear shouts coming from the fields.

"Fire!" shouted a voice, and soon other voices took up the call so that it echoed along the road behind them.

Startled by the shouts, Morumus turned in his saddle. Back at the keep, he saw that a thick plume of smoke was rising from the roofless top of the old fortress. By now, the dark cloud was clearly visible against the blue sky. Most of the laborers looked at it in wonder. A few of them, however, had turned to look at the riders.

"We must hurry!" Urien urged her horse forward. "Do not look back!"

Morumus heeled his horse after her, but ahead of them two black-robed riders crested the valley rim.

"Look!" he called to the others.

No sooner had the riders come into view than they drew up rein and pointed. One of them appeared to be pointing toward the keep. The other, however, was gesturing toward the three riding away from it.

"Maybe they will think we are of them?" Donnach ventured.

"No," said Urien. "The others have all gone." No sooner had she said this than Morumus saw that the two riders had drawn their knives.

Morumus looked at Urien. "I don't suppose there is another way out of this valley?"

"No."

"Nothing for it, brother." Donnach drew his knife and heeled his horse to a gallop. "They're coming!"

Indeed, by now the *Mordruui* were thundering toward them, holding their weapons at the ready. Morumus followed Donnach's example, drawing the heavy stone blade from its sheath and surging forward toward the enemy. In truth, however, he had no good idea what he was going to do when they met. He was a good rider, and had received a fair amount of practice in hand-to-hand fighting as a boy from his father's weapons master. Yet what he had never learned was how to put the two together—he left Lothair before ever training in mounted combat. Looking ahead, it did not seem to Morumus that the enemy shared his disadvantage. The rider facing him seemed confident in the saddle and poised to strike. Short blades meant close quarters. There was no way Morumus could keep his distance. Moreover, these heavy robes limited his range of motion, or at least slowed it. What was he going to—?

The robe! That's it!

Passing the knife into the hand holding the reins, Morumus reached behind him. He and Donnach had both rolled up their brown monks' habits and tied them to the back of their saddles. Quickly but carefully, he loosened the cord and took firm hold of the edge of his robe. He had but seconds to pray that it would work.

At the last possible moment, Morumus sprang his attack. The rider closed to within a dozen yards and had just pulled his blade arm back sideways, preparing to slash. In that instant, clutching one end tight, Morumus whipped the robe out from behind him and swung it toward the enemy. The heavy wool unrolled just in time, and struck his opponent full on, like a heavy net. Staggered by the weight of the blow, blinded by the unfurled robe, and being somewhat off-balance already by his outstretched arm, the rider tumbled sideways off his mount.

Unfortunately for Morumus, this happened just as the two men came abreast and before Morumus could retract his own arm. Cursing in Dyfanni, the still-blinded rider flailed as he fell. His hands caught Morumus's sleeve and held on for just long enough.

For a moment, Morumus felt weightless as he was yanked from the saddle. Then he hit the ground hard and rolled, the force of the impact squeezing every last bit of air from his lungs. When he finally came to a rest, he knew he was on his back only because he could see bits of blue interspersed among the dark spots in his vision. Pain wracked his body, and for what seemed a perilous long time he could not move. All he could do was lie there and gasp.

Up! I must get to my feet! If the enemy found his own footing first, Morumus knew he would never stand again. Praying and struggling against the strong urge to close his eyes, he found a strength that he did not know he possessed—perhaps because until that moment, he had not possessed it. Morumus rose to his feet.

A dozen yards distant, the black rider lay face down and unmoving—a mass of black robe tangled with Lorudin-brown wool. Morumus staggered toward him as quickly as he could manage, hoping to press the advantage. About half the distance between them, he saw one of the stone knives lying in the dust. Was it his or the enemy's? It hardly mattered. He scooped it up without stopping and moved in for the kill. He had never taken a man's life before, but in this case there was nothing for it.

By the time he had closed the distance to a few yards, Morumus knew something wasn't right. The black-robed man had to have heard him approaching, but did not stir. Morumus slowed his pace and tightened his grip on the blade, feeling suspicious. What was his enemy playing at? But as he got to within mere feet of the man, he realized the truth. There was no movement at all, nor any sound, coming from the downed rider—no rising of the back, no gasping for breath.

The man was dead.

Still wary, Morumus nudged the man with his foot. When that failed to produce a reaction, he set down the knife and rolled the body over. It was then that he saw what had become of the second knife: it was buried lengthwise in the man's torso. From the look of it, the blade had entered the man's abdomen and been forced up toward the heart when he fell. His right hand still clutched the hilt, covered in blood.

"Morumus!"

The sound of Donnach's voice reminded Morumus that his had not been the only battle. He looked up and saw the Grendannathi rushing toward him. On his heels came Urien, still mounted and holding the reins of two others.

"Morumus," said Donnach again as he came up, "are you well?"

"Yes." Then he saw a long tear in the other monk's black robe near the ribs. "What about you?"

"A near miss. I jumped out of my saddle at him, and he almost got me." Donnach looked down at the rider near Morumus's feet. "I wish I had thought of your idea."

"We must go now." Urien glanced behind them. "The servants know there is something wrong."

"Help me get my robe free, Donnach." Morumus reached down to untangle his brown habit from around the dead rider. The robe came free from around the head with relative ease, but it seemed to have gotten wrapped around the man's left arm. With Donnach's help, Morumus quickly got it clear. Rather than try to unwind it bit by bit, the Grendannathi simply held the arm up away from the body, and Morumus pulled it down over the man's forearm and wrist. In a less than a minute, the robe was free. But what it revealed changed everything.

"Donnach!" Morumus reeled back from the dead man's hand as if it were an adder.

"What?" Donnach dropped the arm and jumped back.

"Look!" Morumus pointed at the rider's exposed hand and wrist.

"What is it, brother?" Donnach looked to where Morumus was pointing, but he didn't seem to recognize the danger.

"Donnach, those markings."

The back of the man's wrist and hand bore a terrifyingly familiar tattoo. The upper portion along the wrist was the form of a cross, and from its bottom thin tendrils extended across the back of the hand to meet the top of each knuckle. He had seen that mark several times before.

The red monk in Dericus.

The monk at Saint Dreunos's.

Archbishop Simnor.

Ulwilf.

The realization struck Morumus hard.

I have been a fool.

All along, the truth had been right there in front of him. The tattoo was not a cross with a split bottom. It was a cross with the bottom of a tree.

"My rider had them, too," said Donnach.

"It is the mark of the *Mordruui*," snapped Urien. "The sign of the Hands of the Mother." Her tone became increasingly urgent. "Come. We must go *now*!"

"No." Morumus had not felt this horrified since the night his father was murdered. "That is the mark of the Red Order."

29

All of the lines of Morumus's life converged to a single, bloody thread. At long last, he understood. And the knowledge of it was horrible.

The Order of the Saving Blood were the *Mordruui*, and the *Mordruui* were the *Dree*—the Dark Faith. Abbot Grahem had been wrong. Despite appearances, the *Dree* and the Red Order were not two separate troubles facing the Church. They were the same, and they were behind everything. The murders of all these missing children, the murder of Anbharim, the visitation of the Church . . .

It was all their doing.

The Red Order was the Dark Faith reborn. The connection staggered Morumus. Was it rage coursing through him, or fear? Or was it both?

They are behind it all.

He should have seen it sooner. When he mentioned the shadows in the forest to Ulwilf, why had the red monk barely reacted? When he and Anbharim had fled, why had the *Dree* spared him? When they had found Anbharim murdered, why had Ulwilf dismissed the whole thing as demonic retribution? Only one answer made sense.

Ulwilf was in league with the *Dree*.

The red monk *was* a *Dree*.

Now Morumus knew why Ulwilf had protected him. The *Dree* had hoped to recruit him! His conscience smote him as Morumus recalled an oft-repeated maxim of his childhood: *Never let the armor distract you from the man wearing it.*

It all seemed so clear looking back.

Morumus felt numb all over as he and Donnach and Urien made their escape north through the woods. Dusk overtook them as they fled the hidden vale, but the horses enabled them to travel quickly. Thus they reached Donnach's sanctuary just before total night descended. There they passed a cold, restless night. They dared not build a fire, not even in the cave lest some scent of smoke give away their location. They arranged things so that each of them would take a turn to sit outside and watch, while the other two slept safely inside the cave. Yet in reality, nobody slept—for without a fire, it was too cold to sleep even within the cave. Donnach and Morumus had changed back into their brown robes, so that the two sleepers in the cave might have an extra robe each for a blanket. But it did no good. Rather, all three of them shivered in shifts: one without, and two within.

They pressed north with first light, but not before Donnach took the time to bundle up his book and strap it securely behind his saddle. Morumus had been impatient at this—even the smallest delay seemed to him precarious at this stage—but Donnach insisted.

"Who can say whether we shall ever be able to return? I cannot leave it, brother."

In the end, the delay was but a short one—and once they were moving Morumus admitted to Donnach that he had been right. Abbot Grahem's admonition of a few days prior had come back to him while he watched Donnach hurrying: *whatever else happens, we are still the Church . . . our mission does not change.* Besides this, they were only about an hour's distance from abbey—and the extra few minutes had allowed a bit more grey light to filter down into the forest.

There was now no question of remaining hidden. With the *Dree's* sacred tree destroyed, who could tell how long they had to escape? Nobody in the valley had seen their faces, but Urien was sure that the *Mordruui* would leave no stone unturned once they found the Mother burned. Lorudin would be at risk, as would be Agnorum to the west. There was no time now for stealth. They would return to Lorudin at once and alert Abbot Grahem. Word must be sent to the bishop. Anathadus could then take the matter to the archbishop, who could relay it to both Saint Cephan's and the imperial court. But they had to act quickly: if the Red Order learned their identity before they could make the connection known, everything might be lost.

They saw the first signs of trouble as the path approached the rim of the last ridge. Day was still dawning in the east, yet as its red rays crept over the eastern horizon, faint smudges of smoke appeared against the light. The breeze, which had to this point been at their back—gently urging them toward home—abruptly changed direction. Suddenly their nostrils tingled with the foreboding smell of burnt wood.

Morumus looked over at Donnach riding beside him. "Do you smell that?"

"Yes." There was fear in his voice. "And there has been no bell. Morumus, it is past time for Rising Prayers."

"Is something wrong?" Urien eyed the two of them.

Morumus did not answer. "Lord, let it not be . . ." He heeled his horse to cover the last dozen yards. When he reached the valley's rim, he pulled up rein at the edge of the descent and looked down. Seconds later, the others joined him.

A half-league below them, Lorudin Abbey was a smoldering ruin. The barns and dormitories and storehouses were gone, leaving only long biers of charred timbers. The stone refectory was a blackened husk broke open to the sky: its roof, rafters, and shutters had completely vanished. Even the chapel—once an antechamber of heaven—had been reduced to an open sore upon the surface of the valley. A few small, scattered fires lapped what fuel yet lingered. Above everything hung a shroud of dark smoke.

"What has happened?" cried Donnach.

Urien gasped. "The *Mordruui* were called away to the valley two days ago, but I knew not to where . . ."

"We're too late," Morumus croaked.

Nevertheless he snapped his reins and sent his mount rushing down the path toward the abbey, hoping against all sense that he might find some signs of life amidst the rubble. He shook his head as the horse carried him down the long descent to the valley floor. "No, no, no," he protested through tears as he approached the charred timber of what had been the walls only days before. "Please, God, no!"

But God did not undo the desecration.

Reaching the valley floor at last, Morumus passed through the blackened gates and into Lorudin Abbey. He was utterly unprepared for what he found. Everywhere he looked he saw the slain. Here a crumpled limb protruded upward from a heap of wreckage. There and there and there, the broken tangles of wool and flesh marked the spot where brother monks had been cut down. No matter where he turned, he found only murder—and not merely murder, but butchery! He saw bodies of several brothers stripped bare of their robes and missing limbs—some even their heads. The farther he proceeded, the more grisly grew the scene. It had not rained in Lorudin or the surrounding forest since he returned, yet with nearly every step his feet splotched through ruddy mud.

As he approached the hollow shell of the refectory hall, the pervasive smell of smoke in the air became mingled

336

with the thick stench of opened bowels and the ferric odor of blood. He reached the threshold at the exact moment a sharp wind gusted down through the open roof and out through the gaping entry, carrying the full force of what lay within to his nostrils. Morumus was nearly overcome, and he paused in his progress.

"Lord, have mercy!" He gasped as he leaned against the outer wall, his head spinning with the penetrating reek. He knew that he should wait for the others before entering, yet strange as it may seem, he also felt a sort of duty to go forward alone. Urien had no place here, and even Donnach had only been a part of the abbey for a season. He, on the other hand, had spent nearly all his years in this place. He alone of the three had been a true part of the abbey's life. Thus he alone must face its death, however horrible. It was a bizarre line of reasoning. But at that hour, Morumus stood much closer to madness than to reason.

And so it was that he stepped alone through the grim door before him.

Nothing could have prepared Morumus for what he saw. He had seen death before. He had wandered bewildered among the bodies of the fallen. But never in Morumus's life had he witnessed the cruel fruit of bloodlust as it had been unleashed in the refectory hall of Lorudin Abbey. Well Morumus knew that death was an indignity man was not created to suffer. He understood that murder was always mistress of madness. But this . . .

What depth of depravity did it take to delight in the indignity? What cravenness of soul to consummate the madness?

The scene that greeted Morumus was like a feast in Belneol. The long tables were full of guests. At each place along the benches slouched a lifeless monk, his head lying on the board besides his plate as though he were sleeping—with

337

his throat slit open. There were no eyes in those familiar faces—not a single one!—only empty sockets from which blood had oozed down over gaping cheeks and coagulated like rivulets of dried tears. Beside each face sat a plate heaped with the man's own innards. On the other side of the plate, each man's hand had been wrapped around a wooden cup. But it was not wine that filled each man's goblet—oh no! Rather, each man clutched a cup filled to the brim with blood. And what was it that bobbed on the surface of each cup? A pair of unblinking, unthinking, unseeing human eyes.

Morumus would have screamed had he any voice at all. He would have fled, had he any ability to move. But in the face of such wanton wickedness . . . in the naked, unmasked presence of the macabre . . . he found he had neither. He did not wish to gaze upon the scene, but neither could he look away. He did not wish to gulp even one single breath of such foul air, yet his mouth gaped wide and would not shut. Though alive, he had become as one dead—unwillingly, utterly transfixed by the horror spread before him.

How long he stood paralyzed in the silent presence of that vile enormity he did not know. What was certain was that he was finally freed not by his own efforts, but rather by a sound from somewhere behind him. Somewhere outside. The moment the silence broke, Morumus felt the implacable languor that held him prisoner break.

He fled the refectory, never to return.

"Morumus," came a familiar voice from nearby.

At first, Morumus did not look up. Reason had abandoned him when he had escaped the refectory. He could not remember where he had run, only that wherever he had gone, there had been more blood and brutality. He ran the length and breadth of Lorudin Abbey, but he could not escape the slaughter. Finally he stopped running through the scenes of massacre. He had no idea where he was when this occurred—no idea where he now was. He knew only that he was sitting down somewhere with his head between his knees and his eyes shut tight. But even shut, the monstrous image of the dining hall would not leave his vision unmolested.

"Morumus," said the voice again, and he felt a hand come to rest upon his shoulder.

This time Morumus recognized the voice, and it surprised him. He lifted his head and opened his eyes, thinking he had gone mad.

But there, standing in full daylight before him amidst the ruin of the abbey, was Oethur. The Norn wore traveling clothes instead of a habit, and looked haggard—especially around the eyes. But it was truly him.

"Oethur, w-what are you doing here?"

"I arrived less than an hour after you, brother. As for the rest, there will be time to tell it soon enough. The others were concerned because they could not rouse you. Are you able to stand?"

Morumus nodded, and as Oethur helped him to his feet Morumus realized where he was. The two of them were standing in the orchard—or what was left of it, for the trees had been burned. In his madness, he had fled the abbey grounds altogether.

Oethur turned back toward the abbey walls, but Morumus hesitated. "I'm not sure I can go back in there, Oethur. Have you seen it?"

"I have."

"It doesn't make sense. Why now? Why like this?"

"I don't know." Oethur looked away for a long moment before turning back. "But do not fear, brother. We're not going back in there. We're only going to meet the others. They have the horses by the gates. We are leaving."

"Now? But what of the—?"

"Now. Donnach and I have laid stones over Abbot Grahem—there is no time for a proper burial. The rest we will have to leave. It is too dangerous to stay. We must get as far away from here as we can before they return."

"They?"

"The woman you and Donnach rescued—Urien?—says the ones who did this will come back once they realize what the three of you have done. What that is, you'll have to tell me later. But if the Red Order attacked this place yesterday, and from the look of things I think that's when they struck—"

"So you know about the Red Order?"

Oethur nodded, his face grim. "Donnach told me."

"We have to get word to Bishop Anathadus."

"We cannot."

Morumus started. "Why not? If we leave right now—"

"He's dead, Morumus." Oethur's words were flat. "They murdered him, too."

"Oh."

Morumus knew such news deserved more of a reaction. But at that moment, he was simply too drained to provide it. In a way, too, he realized that he was really not all that surprised. If the Red Order could strike dead an entire abbey, what made the assassination of a single bishop so incredulous?

"I will tell you more soon," Oethur promised, "but right now we need to leave."

A few minutes later, the four of them rode north toward the river. Oethur led, Urien and Morumus followed, and Donnach rode sweep. Morumus looked back only once. The sun was now well above the eastern horizon, and most of the morning's dark smoke had vanished. Nevertheless, not even the beautiful, late-fall morning could blot out the horrors of what lay within those ruined walls. Lorudin Abbey was no longer a close community of the saints, no longer a place of God's peace. It was now a portico of death . . .

A yawning, open grave.

30

From Lorudin the company made their way to Reth, a small village only a few leagues west from the mouth of the Lorudin Vale. Reth was one of the many minor settlements that had sprung up over the years along the banks of the River Lor, and there was nothing about the place to suggest that it might harbor fugitives. Moreover, it was from Reth that Abbot Grahem had originally instructed Morumus to draw horses. Thus it was that the four of them arrived before midday at the house of the farmer whom the abbot had mentioned.

With the abbot's token, Morumus had no difficulty in securing what they needed from the farmer. Food and shelter were provided without question. When Oethur offered to pay, the farmer cited Holy Writ.

"Abbot Grahem has sown spiritual things in me and my sons these many years, and always free of charge. Could I then accept coin to provide earthly things?"

It took Morumus a bit more effort to convince the farmer to exchange the abbot's three horses for three sets of traveling clothes. The scrupulously honest farmer felt the trade was disproportionate, and did not relent until they also agreed to accept boots, belts, and traveling provisions. The boots and clothes did not fit well, but they all felt it would be safer to travel as regular men rather than monks. Having procured all these along with their meal, the company sat down to rest and plan.

The first part of this council consisted in Morumus repeating for Oethur and Urien the full account of his portentous dream and his weeks with Ulwilf. After this he related what Abbot Grahem had told him about the roots of the *Dree* and his own—the abbot's—first experience tracking them nearly twenty years prior. Oethur listened with grim fascination. Likewise, Urien listened in silence, until Morumus spoke of the abbot and bishop and Captain Brann tracking the *Dree*.

She looked at the others. "That would have been when we first came here."

"Really?" asked Morumus. "The *Dree* have been in Caeldora all this time?"

"Yes."

"But then why has the stream of missing children not continued *all* these years?"

"There was a war five years after we arrived. The *Mordruui* took prisoners, too. For a long time, the Mother's portion was drawn from a deep well in the basement of the keep." She shuddered, her voiced fading off to a whisper. "It was so cold in that basement . . ."

"Were you a prisoner as well, lady?" asked Oethur kindly.

"I was. For a long, long time."

"But your accent—you are Dyfanni like these *Mordruui*, are you not?"

"I am." Urien shifted, uneasy.

Seated across from him at the table, Donnach gave Morumus a significant look.

"We rescued her from being a victim herself, Oethur," Morumus intervened. "She then destroyed the tree, and

344

helped us to escape—though it was a narrow thing." From here, he and Donnach related the account of the hidden valley in the hills, their battle with the *Mordruui*, and the truth about the Red Order.

After this, it was Oethur's turn to explain and the others' to listen.

"It was a hard fall from the library window," said Oethur, "but I landed in the grassy portion of the yard rather than on the stone. Once I got up, I wasn't sure where to go. Thankfully, Nack had just finished arranging things for our journey the next day and was near the courtyard. He heard the glass breaking and the shouts, and saw me jump. He got me to the stables, and then helped me escape the city. He even gave me a small purse of coins for the journey."

"A faithful man." Donnach nodded.

"What happened to him?" wondered Morumus.

"Nack? I don't know, but I doubt they'll get him. The man is very capable—more than any of us realize, I suspect." Oethur looked around the table. "The real question is, what is going to happen to us? What do we do?"

"We go to Naud," said Morumus. "That was the abbot's original plan, and Captain Brann is the only ally we have left in Caeldora. We warn him about the Red Order, and then buy passage to Urras."

"Do you think he will believe us?" Oethur sounded doubtful.

"I know that he held Abbot Grahem in the highest esteem," answered Morumus. "Whether he will believe me about the Red Order, I do not know. But I think we ought to try."

"I agree with Morumus," said Donnach.

Urien wrapped her arms about herself. "The *Mordruui* are ruthless. When they find their shrine destroyed, they will tear this country apart looking for those who did it. You all saw what they did at that abbey. They will do the same to all their enemies—and all who shelter them. If they are as influential and widespread as you say, then this country is not safe."

"For us or anybody who might help us," added Oethur. "I agree with you all. We must go to Naud."

Though they all wished it were otherwise, the company knew that they could not remain so near to Lorudin even for a night. Thus, after eating and resupplying, they bid farewell to the farmer and struck out west. Before leaving, Morumus warned the man using the abbot's token and its authority.

"Tell no one of our visit, for your good and ours, friend."

The journey to Naud was as uneventful as it was disheartening. After that first day, when it had been necessary to cover maximum distance, they dared not travel by day. Nor dared they, on days when the unbending road and the sinuous river converged, seek shelter in any of the villages along the river. The risk was too great they they would put either themselves or their helpers at risk.

Instead, they spent the daylight hours hiding in what cover they could find. Much of the country along the Naud Road was empty, so usually the best they could do was a copse of trees. Under pleasant conditions, this would not have been too bad, for it was a mere four days'—or in their case, four nights'—journey from Lorudin to Naud. Yet on the first evening of their journey, it began to rain hard. It rained all that night while they pressed on, and all the next day while they tried to rest. When the rain became even heavier toward evening on the third day, Morumus fought despair. If they road all night as they planned, they would reach Naud in the morning. But no ship without an urgent errand would put out to sea in such weather—and Nack had not given Oethur sufficient coin to create such urgency.

In the end, they need not have worried. By dusk on the fourth day, the rains were tapering off, and by midnight they had ceased altogether. As dawn approached, some clouds were still visible, but these were noticeably lighter and quickly dispersed. By daybreak, the sun ascended into a clear eastern sky. Taking heart, the four weary travelers pressed on with renewed vigor. Even the horses seemed to have found a second wind.

Thus it was that the company arrived in Naud early on the morning of the fifth day after they had left Lorudin, just as Abbot Grahem and Morumus had arrived so many months before. Morumus reflected on the similarities as they entered its streets. Just as before, many ships could be seen moored along the bone-white length of the ancient Vilguran pier. Just as before, there was a sharp tang of salt in the breezy air. And just as before, Morumus had to part company with his companions to visit the garrison. This parting, however, was not without a bit of controversy.

"You should let me come with you," Donnach insisted. "Two witnesses are more convincing than one."

"He's right." Oethur's tone was firm. "And it wouldn't hurt for you to have somebody watching your back in this place. We don't know if or how many of the Red Order may be here. Remember what happened in Versaden?"

Morumus shook his head. "This isn't Versaden. Any pursuit is a half day or more behind us. Besides, I have Abbot Grahem's token, so I'm not without a second witness. It will be quicker for me to go alone and come right back. The garrison guards gave me grief the last time when I was alone, even with the token. If I bring another with me, they might delay us longer."

Morumus finally prevailed. Though he knew it angered his friends—and even earned him a disapproving look from Urien—he set out for the garrison barracks alone. He wasn't trying to be stubborn. He just wanted to get this finished and get to sea with the minimum amount of hassle. On his own, he strode purposefully through the streets toward the center of the city and arrived at the garrison within a quarter of an hour.

As before, a pair of guards stood before the double arches of the main gate. Seeing him approach, the guards snapped to attention and stood to. Praying for a smooth process, Morumus walked up to them and presented the token.

"I am here to see Captain Brann. It is official Church business."

Looking him up and down, the head guard at first seemed a bit incredulous. But he must have thought better after scrutinizing the token. "This way, sir." He opened the gate. Morumus offered a silent prayer of thanks and followed.

Captain Brann's private study looked exactly as Morumus remembered it: compact, tidy, and arranged for efficiency rather than comfort. The man himself entered through the side door a moment later. Recognizing Morumus, the captain shook his hand warmly before sitting himself behind his desk.

"Morumus, it is good to see you."

"And you, sir."

"What brings you to Naud this morning?" he asked, smiling, "I take it you received my greetings?"

"Greetings, sir?"

"Yes." The captain's smile faltered somewhat. "Your fellow, the red monk—Ulwilf, I think? He was here just over a week ago, on business from the abbot. Like you, he carried the token, so I asked him to convey my personal greetings—both to the abbot and yourself."

Morumus gasped, shutting his eyes and drawing a sharp breath. "He found out it was I."

"What's that?"

Morumus drew a deep breath. There was no time to mince words.

"Abbot Grahem is dead, sir. He was murdered, and now I know why."

The smile vanished.

By the time Morumus finished his account, Captain Brann's face was taut. "It is my fault that Grahem is dead."

"No sir. The blame for all these murders lies solely with the Red Order. That is what you must communicate to the emperor."

"I cannot reach the emperor's ear directly." Brann's voice was grim, his eyes fierce. "But I will do what I can."

"Be discreet, sir."

"I will." Brann pulled something out of one of his desk drawers, then stood and came around the table. "Here"—he held out two items—"take these."

Morumus looked at what was in the captain's hand: a plain but sturdy knife, and a leather purse. "Are these . . . ?"

"Yes. Those belonged to Josias. As you have found and identified both his and his son's murderers, by an old Vilguran custom I may give them to you."

Morumus said nothing, but accepted both items.

"Travel safe, Morumus. Your friends have probably found passage already; there are plenty of northbound boats in port. But if that should not be true, return to me at once and I will see to making arrangements. The least I can do for Grahem is protect his last remaining sons."

Morumus bowed his head and clasped the captain's proffered hand. "Thank you, sir. Farewell!"

Morumus exited the garrison barracks and turned down the street leading toward the quay. But he was barely aware of the world around him as he walked toward the docks.

The last piece of the puzzle had fallen into place. Now he understood why the abbey was struck. He could only imagine Ulwilf's rage when the red monk had learned that the token-bearer was not only still living, but had been traveling with him for weeks.

No, I do not have to imagine it. He had seen the results at Lorudin.

But why? Why did it have to happen?

Abbot Grahem and the others at the abbey hadn't fallen in battle, or been martyred for the truth. They had been slaughtered because of a wooden token and a conversational afterthought. It just seemed so *random*, so senseless.

Morumus tried reminding himself that the providence of God bound even wicked acts to bring ultimate good, but this truth did not seem to help. He *knew* that. He *believed* that. His trouble was not with the truth, but with the experience of it.

Why could there not have been more survivors?

As if in answer, suddenly a voice called out from somewhere close by. "Morumus! Brother Morumus, is that you?"

Morumus stopped short. He recognized the voice—but he did not understand its presence. He turned.

"Brother Ortto?" he asked, trembling.

"It is I!" The man, one of the twin cooks of Lorudin Abbey, came up behind him and stopped, his smile tight. "Praise God, Morumus. It is good to see you."

"Ortto"—Morumus's his skin tingled within his robe—"What are you doing *here?* How did you—?"

"The broken chimney, brother. Silgram and I climbed up within it when we saw what was happening in the hall."

"Silgram is alive too?" Morumus's voice nearly cracked.

"Yes, though we have both been in a better way. Come, I will take you to him."

Morumus was too surprised to speak much as Ortto turned them down a side street away from the way to the docks.

Thankfully, in his excitement to see Morumus, Ortto was more than able to make up two sides of the conversation. Yet as it turned out, his tale was grim.

"You cannot imagine it, brother. It seemed just another ordinary evening. The red monk Ulwilf came back, but he'd only been gone about a week, so it didn't seem so extraordinary. He had come to see you, he said—to see if you were well enough to leave again. When he learned you were dead, he demanded to see the grave, so Silgram and I showed him the place. After that, he got very quiet, and I didn't see him again until dinner.

"Dinner itself seemed routine, too. With only one of the ovens working—I have cursed that broken chimney many times, but now I am thankful for it—Silgram and I had to spend extra time in the kitchen getting all the brothers served. It was while we were still working that the shouting began. I ran to the door to see what was going on, and—oh, brother, you cannot imagine."

"I saw it. You need not say any more."

"No, brother. You may have seen what was left, but you didn't see what happened."

"What do you mean?"

"Ulwilf was standing at the head table, chanting and hissing like some madman. At first, I thought maybe he had had too much to drink. It being harvest time, one of the vineyards from near the river had sent us up some wine. But then I saw the others. All of them, Morumus—even the abbot— seemed frozen in place. That was why they were shouting. They couldn't move!"

Morumus went cold. "Go on." Though he knew where the story was going.

"Then there were shouts outside, and everything went mad. Black-hooded figures streamed into the hall, carrying long knives that they used—well, you saw."

Morumus nodded.

"Those brothers who were still in the kitchens waiting for food fled out the side entrance—but I heard them screaming outside, too. There must have been more waiting."

"So then you and Silgram climbed into the chimney?"

Ortto nodded sadly. "What else could we do?"

"Nothing, brother." Morumus shook his head. "There was nothing you could do. How did you get to Naud?"

"After we were sure they were gone, we climbed down. They had burned the stables, but we found a pair of mules near the forest's edge. Then we headed west. When he asked us to bury you, Abbot Grahem had said he was sending you to Naud. We arrived yesterday, hoping to find you here."

"I am glad you did." Morumus marveled at how his ruminations of just a few minutes earlier had been overturned. "Praise God you are both alive."

A few minutes later, they stopped before the door of a small stable. "Here we are," said Ortto.

"This is where you are staying?"

"We dared not go to the cloister, for fear of the Red Order."

"Good idea."

"It's actually not too bad." Ortto pushed open the wide wooden door. "Reminds you of our cells back home—only bigger and bit draftier. A bit darker, too." He gestured to Morumus. "After you."

"Thank you." Morumus stepped into the barn.

A moment too late he realized his mistake. Somebody lifted a crate, revealing a lamp. Morumus blinked painfully in the sudden brightness, and it took several seconds for his eyes to adjust. When they did, it was only so that they could widen again in horror—for now he saw who it was who had lifted the crate.

"Hello Morumus." Ulwilf's dark eyes swallowed the lamplight.

Morumus took a step back—and bumped right into Ortto, who grabbed his arms and pinned them behind him.

"I am sorry, brother," said the twin, holding him tightly.

Morumus struggled for a moment, but it was no good. Ortto was not heavy, but he was strong. Giving up, he said the only thing he could think.

"*Why*, Ortto?"

"Everything I told you was true, up to the part about Silgram and me climbing into the chimney. In truth, it was only I who climbed up—there wasn't room enough for both of us. Ulwilf's men took him and would have killed him. In desperation, Silgram told them about how the abbot had faked your death—that you were not really dead, but were heading west. They did not believe him, and said they would cut out his tongue as well as his eyes. I had to do something. So I dropped down and told them that he was telling the truth. I am sorry, brother."

Morumus said nothing.

"After that, they took Silgram away—I don't know where. But Ulwilf said that if I ever hoped to see him again, I had to help him catch you. So he and I came here, and waited." Though Morumus could not see his face, he could hear Ortto's voice cracking. "Forgive me, Morumus—but he is my brother!"

"I forgive you."

"But *I* do *not* forgive *you*." Ulwilf set the lamp down on top of the crate. He stepped forward, holding up his hand. In it he clutched one of the stone knives of the *Dree*.

"Nor I you, *Mordruui*." Morumus spat the word. Despite the danger of his position, he felt only anger at finally confronting one of the *Dree* face to face.

Ulwilf did not flinch at the name, but his eyes widened. "How do you know that name?"

Morumus ignored the question. "Tell me, Ulwilf, were you involved in my father's murder?"

"Do not trifle with me, Morumus. How do you know that name?"

"You are old enough, I think. It was ten years ago, in Lothair—in the hills above the Mathway Glen. Were you there?"

"Answer me, Morumus!" Ulwilf's grip tightened on the knife until his knuckles were white.

"No! You are going to kill me regardless. You want me to answer your question? You answer mine first."

Ulwilf growled, but relented. "No, I was not there. I have never left these shores. Like your brother monk, all that I told you before was true. But my order is much older than I, and the Mother has her people in many lands."

"You have not told me the truth. You told me you embraced the missionary teachings of the Church, when in truth you are yet heathen!"

Ulwilf shook his head. "I told you no lie, Morumus. I *did* embrace the Church. Where she corrected the Old Faith, I heeded. But to embrace the refinements of the New Faith does not mean discarding the truth of the Old." He shook his head. "You still do not see it, Morumus, do you? There is one Source of *all* things—one Mother of *all* faiths. She whom all other peoples have forgotten, the Dyfanni have protected. It is she whom my people worshipped as our goddess, and it is her son whom the Church calls Aesus. They are the same."

"It is you who are wrong, *Mordruui*. You want to know how I know your name? I have been to your little shrine in the hills south of Lorudin. I have seen your white tree. It is no goddess. I watched it burn."

Ulwilf's nostril's flared. "You *lie!*"

"He speaks the truth" said a third voice from somewhere out of the surrounding gloom. The next instant Morumus heard a sickening *crack*, and Ortto's grip on him fell slack. He turned to look, and saw the cook crumpled on the floor of the stable. Standing over him, clutching a chunk of broken beam, was Donnach.

"Donnach! How—?"

"Morumus, look out!"

Ulwilf!

Morumus wheeled, but the red monk had already lunged. He could not evade the blade. But at the last second Morumus was shoved aside and sprawled sideways onto the floor.

"Oh!" Donnach gasped.

Morumus jumped back to his feet, but it was too late. In the dim lamplight he saw the horrible truth. There stood Ulwilf, his blade buried in Donnach's middle.

"*No!* Donnach!"

The name had not left his lips before the knife from Captain Brann was in his hand. In the next instant, he leapt to the attack. Ulwilf saw it coming, but was unable to pull his own blade free before Morumus was on him. The two of them tumbled to the floor and rolled a few feet, but the knife of the murdered Josias found its mark. The hardy steel plunged deep through Ulwilf's red robe—straight into his black heart.

The *Mordruui* monk barely struggled. It was over almost before Morumus realized what he had done. Rising, Morumus rushed back to Donnach, who lay on his back beside the lamp.

"Donnach!" He reached for the hilt of the knife, which still protruded from his friend's middle.

"No, brother." Donnach looked up at him. Blood-drenched fingers pushed Morumus's hands away. "It is too late for me."

"No." Tears welled in Morumus's eyes. "No, it cannot be." He reached again for the knife.

"Brother, listen to me." Donnach's voice was urgent. "I do not have much time."

Morumus stopped fumbling and met his friend's eyes. "What is it, Donnach?"

"Do you remember what you told me once about your name—what it means?"

"Yes, I told you it meant 'root mouse.'"

355

"But in my language, it means 'prince of roots.'"

"I do not understand."

Donnach winced, and for a few seconds he closed his eyes. When he opened them again, Morumus could tell that they had less than a minute.

"You must finish the work." The light in the Grendannathi's eyes was beginning to fade. "You were born of a noble house—a prince—and you are *rooted* in the two things needed—languages, and Holy Writ." He smiled. "Do you see it, brother?"

"Yes." Morumus's voice broke as he wept. "Yes, Donnach, I see it."

"Finish the translation, Morumus. Bring the good news to my people, Prince of Roots. I will wait for you in Everlight."

EPILOGUE

The taste of salt was sharp in the air as Naud receded in the distance. Urien stood at the rail of the ship, watching the land of her bondage grow fainter against the sky. Several paces away, Morumus and Oethur stood talking.

"So Ortto got away?" asked Oethur.

"No, I let him go."

"Why?"

"Why not?" Morumus's tone was pensive. "It would not have brought Donnach back."

"No, I suppose it would not. Still, it seems wrong to let him go free."

"He isn't free," said Morumus. "I am sure his brother was dead before he ever lured me to that stable. Ortto will have to live with that—as well as with Donnach's death—for the rest of his days. No, Oethur, he isn't free at all. Of all of us, only Donnach is now free."

"I will miss him."

"Me too."

"When my brother died," said Oethur, "Bishop Treowin said something to me that I'll never forget. He said, 'For those who trust the Redeemer, death is but the beginning.' I will remember those words as long as I live."

"I remember thinking something similar when my father died. He died well, and someday I will find him again. It is the same with Donnach."

"Indeed."

Silence fell between them. For a while, the only sound was the ship's gentle creak.

Finally, Oethur broke the stillness.

"You brought the book?"

"Of course. I have to finish the translation."

"You think you can do it without Donnach?"

"I don't know, but I am bound to try."

Urien drifted away down the rail until she could no longer hear them talking. She still did not understand their faith, and she had questions of her own to face.

What would Somnadh say when he learned what she had done?

Would she ever see her brother again?

Twelve *Mordruui* stood within the inner ring of the *Muthadannach*, surrounding the raised stone circle and the ruined specter within. Where once had stood the glorious Mother, all that remained was a blackened husk. Where once purest white branches spread upward in benediction, all that could be found were scattered bits of charcoal. Where once had grown the great goddess reborn, all had turned to smoldering ash.

The thirteenth *Mordruui* stood next to the circle. His tattooed hand extended from a long, red sleeve to rest upon the edge of the stone. His pale fingers shook with rage.

The desecration was unthinkable.

He knew about the treachery of the Queen's Heart. Before they died, the servants told him everything. And now he knew what he must do.

The Hand of the Mother must be informed of his sister's betrayal.

Word must be sent to Mereclestour.

GLOSSARY

Aban-Tur: the hereditary home of Raudorn Red-First

Abbot Grahem: the Abbot of Lorudin Abbey

Aeld Gowan: the name given for the great island north of Midgaddan

Aesus: the only Son of God, Savior of the World, and Head of the Church

Aevor: a city in northern Caeldora over whom Anathadus is bishop

Agnorum: a town in northwest Caeldora, built near the Tumulan Hills

Alfered: the late eldest brother of Oethur

Alloch: the deity worshipped by Umaddians

Ambiragust: the Archbishop of Palatina and Primate of Palara

Amleux: a river in northern Caeldora

Anathadus: the Bishop of Aevor

Anbharim: Aesusian convert from Umaddianism; servant of Lord Arden

Archatus: the great bridge built by the Vilgurans at Versaden

Arechon: the Emperor of Caeldora, Hispona, Palara, and Vendenthia

Banr Cluidan: a hill fort in Dyfann

Barchidus: the capital city of Hispona, seat of the Primate of Hispona

Basilus: a monk of Lorudin Abbey

Bealdu: a monk of the Order of the Saving Blood, assigned to Aevor

Belneol: the Aesusian name for hell

Bone Codex: a book bound in bone, originally found in Tayaturim

Brer: wood used to made personal tokens for Church officials

Caeldora: a nation in western Midgaddan, ruled by Emperor Arechon

Captain Brann: the commander of the imperial garrison at Naud

Carruc: a lieutenant of the garrison at Naud

Cathedral of Saint Dreunos: the great cathedral standing in the center of Versaden

Chair of Saint Aucantia: the name of the throne of the Archbishop of Mereclestour

Ciolbail: the Bishop of Dunross

Circle of the Holy Groves: the name of the council of priests for the Old Faith of Dyfann

Comnadh: a Dyfanni priest of the Old Faith, father of Somnadh

Court of Saint Cephan: the highest court of the Church; it meets triennially

Dark Faith: pre-Aesusian religion in Aeld Gowan and Midgaddan

Darunen: a city in Vendenthia over which Simnor was bishop

Deaclaid: "right hand" (Dyfanni); title of a Dyfanni priest's bodyguard

Deasmor: a range of mountains in northern Aeld Gowan

Deorcad: brother of Luca Wolfbane and Archbishop of Mereclestour

Dericus: a town less than a day's journey west of Versaden

Donnach: a prince of the Grendannathi sent to Lorudin Abbey

Dree: "night-adder"; used to describe adepts of the Dark Faith

Dunross: the capital of Lothair in northern Aeld Gowan

Dyfann: a nation in western Aeld Gowan

Eldest: title given to the most senior Dyfanni priest of the Old Faith

Emperor of the Vilgurans: the formal title of Emperor Arechon

Erebanur: a rare Vilguran word, roughly translated as "dark madness"

Everlight: the Aesusian name for heaven

Firin: a Dyfanni warrior and deaclaid to Comnadh

Frudheda: a goddess worshipped in pre-Aesusian Vendenthia

Gaebroth: brother of Abbot Grahem; vanished near Toberstan

Gardens of Caeldora: the gardens surrounding the imperial palace in Versaden

Great Session: the name of the final session of the Court of Saint Cephan

Grendannath(i): a nation and people in the far north of Aeld Gowan

Grindangled: the capital of Nornindaal in Aeld Gowan

Heclaid: the king of Lothair

Hispona: nation in southwestern Midgaddan; once ruled by Umaddians

Hoccaster: the westernmost of the five royal cities of Mersex

Holy Grove: a sacred place of worship in Dyfanni religion

Imperium: see "Vilguran Imperium"

Iron Peace: a long period of peace maintained by the Vilguran Imperium

Josias: a woodcutter from Naud

Koinos: a term applied to native Koinossa speakers

Koinossa: language prevalent in eastern provinces of the Old Imperium

Laucura: one of the five royal cities of Mersex

Legate: an official invested with imperial authority

Legatorum: a body of legates acting in the name of the Vilguran emperor

Lohaldir: god worshipped in pre-Aesusian Vendenthia; son of Frudheda

Lor: the great river of western Caeldora

Lord Arden: the Lord of Agnorum

Lorudin Abbey: monastery built between the River Lor and the Tumulan Hills

Lothair(in): a nation in northern Aeld Gowan

Luca Wolfbane: the King of Mersex

Lumana(e): Vilguran for "Hand(s) of the Moon"; the imperial bodyguards

Lyzigus: a priest-attendant to Bishop Anathadus of Aevor

Marfesbury: the northernmost of the five royal cities of Mersex

Master Lareow: weapons-master to Raudorn Red-Fist

Mathway: a river in Lothair

Mereclestour: a royal city of Mersex, seat of the Primate of Aeld Gowan

Mersex (Mersian): a nation covering most of the island of Aeld Gowan

Mervantes: the Archbishop of Barchidus and Primate of Hispona

Middle Sea: the sea which lies south of Midgadden

Midgaddan: continent between the Middle Sea and the Narrow Channel

Mordruui: "Hands of the Mother"; used as title

Morumus: a monk of Lorudin Abbey, son of Raudorn Red-Fist

The Mother: the goddess tree worshipped in Dyfanni religion

Muthadannach: Dyfanni for "Mother Glen"; sacred location of the Mother tree

Naud: a port city in western Caeldora

Neanna: a Caeldoran maidservant; formerly served Urien

Nefforian: name for a Caeldoran monk under a vow of silence

Nerias: brother of Raudorn Red-Fist, uncle of Morumus

Noppenham: one of the five royal cities of Mersex

Nornindaal (Norn): a nation in northern Aeld Gowan

Oethur: second son of Ulfered of Nornindaal, sent to Lorudin Abbey

Old Faith: the name used by the Dyfanni for their religion

Old Imperium: see "Vilguran Imperium"

Old People: a name used to describe the indigenous races of Aeld Gowan

Olleus: the Archbishop of Versaden and Primate of Caeldora

Order of the Saving Blood: a religious order alleged to have close ties with the emperor

Ortto: a monk of Lorudin Abbey; twin brother to Silgram

Palara: a peninsula nation in southern Midgaddan

Palatina: capital city of Palara and former capital of the Imperium

Prasaedun: the hill in Versaden atop of which stands the imperial palace

Primate: title given to the five provincial archbishops of the Church

Queen's Heart: the title given to the woman who tends the Mother

Raudorn Red-Fist: a thane of King Heclaid of Lothair, father of Morumus

Reth: a small town along the River Lor near Lorudin Abbey

Rising Prayers: the first prayers of the day prescribed by Rule of Lorudin

Rule of Lorudin Abbey: the rules governing monastic life at Lorudin Abbey

Saint Dreunos: pioneer missionary to the Caeldorans

Sceaduth: the Archbishop of Ubighen and Primate of Vendenthia

Semric: language and name of ancient people of God

Silgram: a monk of Lorudin Abbey; twin brother to Ortto

Simnor: a native of Aeld Gowan and Bishop of Darunen

Somnadh: a Dyfanni priest, son of Comnadh, brother of Urien

Stone of Judgment: the place of official judgments in pre-Aesusian Vendenthia

Tayaturim: the capital city of Hispona under Umaddian rule

Thane: a title given to noblemen who advise the Lothairin king

Tidusangan(im): "time-song"; a dream showing a glimpse of the past or future

Toberstan: city in southern Nornindaal; once site of an important synod

Tratharan: an island nation to the west of Aeld Gowan

Treowin: the Bishop of Grindangled

True Faith: used by Aesusians to describe the faith revealed in Holy Writ

Tuasraeth: name for the common language of Lothair and Nornindaal

Ubighen: capital city of Vendenthia, seat of the Primate of Vendenthia

Ulfered: the king of Nornindaal

Ulwilf: a legate of the Order of the Saving Blood

Umaddian(s): the name given to worshippers of Alloch

Urien: a native of Dyfann and sister to Somnadh

Urras: an island west of Lothair, home of an old monastery

Vendenthia: a nation in central Midgaddan

Versaden: the capital city of Caeldora and the new Imperium

Vilguran Imperium: name of the empire which once ruled all of Midgaddan

Warden of Upper Mathway: the official title of Raudorn Red-Fist

Wodu: the great god worshipped in pre-Aesusian Vendenthia

Jeremiah W. Montgomery is the pastor of Resurrection Presbyterian Church (OPC) in State College, Pennsylvania, and has been a pipemaker, blogger, and essayist. He and his wife have four sons, all of whom love to read.